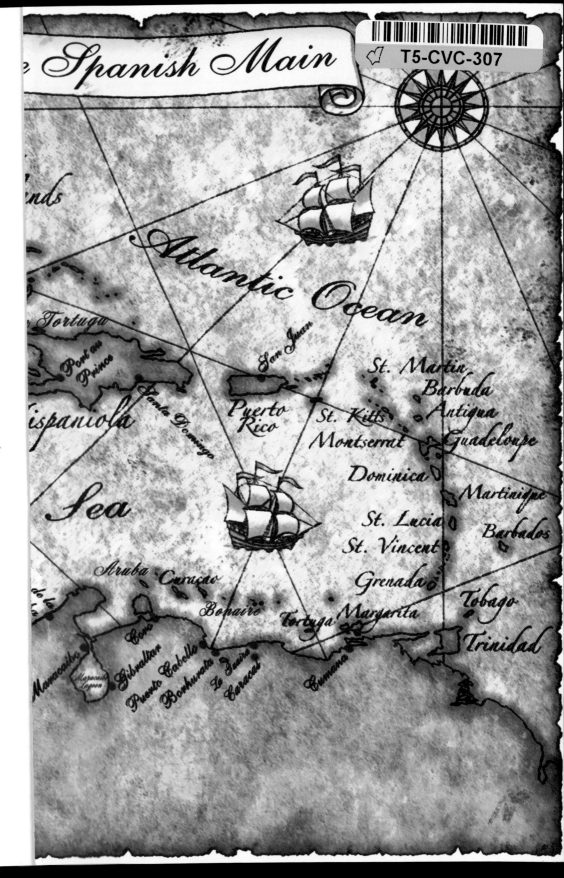

Cover and Map Designs by Vila Design
"Carácas et La Guaira" by Charles Perron, Nouvelle Géographie
. XVIII, Hachette, Paris, 1893, modified by Vila Design and Ozgur
K. Sahin, 2013
Book Design by Polgarus Studio

ISBN-13: 978-1-943274-94-9

The
Broth

Ozgur

Original map
Universelle, Vol

To Dave &
Kristen,
It was a pleasu
driving you! Tha
your interest a
in the traff

O

Acknowledgements

Special thanks to my first fan and enthusiastic friend, Amy Crowell, for all of her feedback and encouragement.

Contents

Prologue 1

Chapter 1: Port Royal 10

Chapter 2: A Constant Crew...27

Chapter 3: Player's Gauntlet...55

Chapter 4: The Lying Dutchman...74

Chapter 5: Curaçao..92

Chapter 6: A King's Ransom...117

Chapter 7: Burglar's Gambit...140

Chapter 8: Two Jailbirds with One Stone 158

Chapter 9: Windfall...179

Chapter 10: Valley of the Dispossessed 192

Chapter 11: A Fair Trade...212

Chapter 12: Window of Opportunity 229

Chapter 13: Diverse Decoys...248

Chapter 14: Under the Gun, Under the Knife 266

Chapter 15: Tales of the Three Brothers 275

Chapter 16: Work for Idle Hands..297

Chapter 17: Needs Must..319

Chapter 18: The Best Defense 347

Chapter 19: Fire Ship 367

Chapter 20: The Battle of the Harbor..................................380

Chapter 21: Rest and Restitution...394

Epilogue 409

Prologue

The Plymouth docks were even busier than normal on this fine April afternoon as Captain Roy Toppings observed from the deck of his ship, *The Pilotfish,* which was just approaching the harbor. He could see sailors boisterously hurrying about errands and duties, loading and unloading cargoes, all the while shouting to each other louder than necessary as they always did upon returning home. Apparently one of the giant East India Company merchant vessels had just arrived and her crew was eager to finish unloading her cargo so they could enjoy a mug of ale and the comforts of home. Roy's own crew was eager to make berth as well, but more because they would be paid shortly afterwards than for relief from a long voyage. They had only traveled to Calais and back, but the cargo of wool and fine ale he had sold there meant large shares for the small ship's crew of ten, and the twenty percent that was his share meant Roy could finally pay off the loan he had taken from his father to purchase the ship. Roy smiled. *Father will be proud.* The last payment was not due until the end of the year. His father had no need for the money, but he had always tried to encourage hard work and resourcefulness in his three sons. As the youngest son, Roy was unlikely to find wealth through other means. His youngest sister Constance had already managed it by marrying some Spanish lieutenant from a large and wealthy family.

Roy sighed. He had been unable to attend the wedding. He had never even met Pablo Francisco. Roy was often at sea, and had been gone each time the diplomatic vessel on which Pablo served had visited England. He had only heard of the man second-hand through Constance, who went starry-eyed at the mere mention of him, and she had mentioned him constantly. Before Roy knew it, she was engaged to be married. The last time he had seen her before the wedding, she was packing her belongings for Spain where she would live with her husband. He had not seen his sister since. She had visited twice after the move to Spain, when Pablo's ship was bound for England, but again Roy had been absent. And shortly after, they had both moved to the Caribbean along with half of the Francisco family.

As fond as he was of all his family, Roy had been closest to his little sister. He'd carried her around town on his back, taught her how to swim, how to read, how to tie a knot, and even how to punch an unwanted suitor without hurting herself. And now some Spaniard had taken her abruptly out of his life. He hoped for the hundredth time that Pablo was well worth it. Roy's mother and father seemed to think he was, and that was some small comfort.

The noise of the Plymouth docks drowned Roy's thoughts, and the looming bulk of the East Indiaman eclipsed his memories as his small sloop sailed into the harbor. "If yeh took the masts down," said Roy's first mate Russell Oliver at his side, "yeh could probably fit this whole ship in that monster's hold without even splinterin' the tiller." Oliver always marveled at any ship that could boast more than thirty cannons, as if anything less was merely for fishermen. The sight of a three-masted merchant ship of fifty guns was bound to elicit a comment.

"And it would probably be worth a lot less than what's in her hold already," Roy muttered in return. He turned to look at Oliver—never a pleasant task, considering his visage which was heavily scarred by powder burns from the muzzle of a cannon and etched with old scars from the war against the Dutch a few years ago. "Nevertheless," said Roy with a smile, "I'd rather manage this ship over that one any day. Too slow, and too much of a bother."

Oliver chuckled resignedly and shrugged. "As yeh will, sir."

"Drop sail and prepare to dock."

"Aye sir," said Oliver, and turned to the crew. "Take in sails an' prepare t' drop anchor," he shouted.

Roy turned his thoughts back to business as *The Pilotfish* moored at a dock away from the bustle around the larger trading vessels. As a balding, middle-aged man of gaunt face bearing the seal of a harbormaster approached the ship, Roy went to his cabin and returned to the deck with a small chest, ordering the men to attention.

"Good afternoon, sir," hailed the harbormaster.

Setting the chest down, Roy walked down the gangway to the dock and greeted the balding man in return. "Good afternoon, sir. Any interesting news this day, apart from that?" he said, pointing to the East Indiaman.

"Nothing very exciting, sir. A ship arrived from the West Indies yesterday, but nothing out of the ordinary. Oh, and the price of ale has gone down since rumor got out that Cromwell's brat hasn't managed to close down the few alehouses that have sprung up since his father's demise."

"Indeed!" laughed Roy, noting the eager glances his crewmen were now sharing with each other, "Well that certainly won't be a terrible blow to my business. Thanks for the news, but I needn't keep you waiting all day, as you have work to do."

"Not to worry, sir. Any cargo or goods to declare?"

"None save that deemed necessary for provisioning the ship and crew," replied Roy.

"I will of course need to verify that," said the harbormaster. Roy led him to the hold, but there was clearly nothing of value there. They came back up the ladder and made their way to Roy's cabin to continue the inspection. Finally back on deck, the harbormaster opened the small chest that Roy had retrieved and found the profits from Roy's latest venture and the crew manifest with each crewman's share marked out next to his name. "A profitable venture," said the harbormaster, sounding rather impressed.

"Aye, it was," said Roy with a smile.

"Well, everything seems to be in order," said the harbormaster. "Standard docking fee of one shilling, please."

Roy handed him two shillings and smiled. "One for the fee and one to spread our good luck."

"Thank you, sir!" the harbormaster beamed, pocketing the extra coin as he put the docking fee in his official pouch. "Good day to you and your crew. Welcome home." He made a small bow before he turned and left. Few captains were actually friendly to harbormasters unless they intended to bribe them to turn a blind eye to smuggled goods. Most were either too busy or too dishonest to welcome the prying questions that it was the duty of a harbormaster to ask.

Roy picked up the chest again and placed it on a small table that Mr. Oliver had fetched while he was busy with the harbormaster. He opened the chest and withdrew a scroll of parchment, an inkbottle and a pen. "Russell Oliver," he called. As Oliver approached the table, Roy withdrew a large handful of coins from the chest and counted out Oliver's share. "Seventy-five pounds for the first mate's share. Well done, and well earned."

"Thank yeh sir." This was probably the biggest share Oliver had ever received, and was certainly larger than any he had earned when he served with the navy. He was obviously pleased, though his wide, broken-toothed grin lent no aid to the lost cause of his face. Roy could not imagine earning so little after serving in so many battles and was glad to be able to reward the man with gentler treatment as well as gold.

"Make your mark," said Roy as he proffered the parchment. Oliver signed next to his name and withdrew with a nod. Roy called the next name, and soon all ten crewmen stood with open smiles and full purses. A couple had counted the money again openly as if disbelieving, but all were grateful. Roy stowed his documents and utensils back in the chest. "I won't keep you waiting. Enjoy your evening. You have all served me well."

The crew took their leave and walked singing into town. "They sound as if they'd already been t' one o' them alehouses that harbormaster spoke of," said Oliver. "So where will yeh be off t' now?"

"To pay back my father, and then to enjoy an evening at home. I've missed a real bed, though I imagine I'll still feel it tossing before I nod off. I acquire my sea legs more quickly than I regain my land legs lately. And you?"

"Off home t' the family. The missus will want t' be thankin' yeh, I'm sure, so I might as well do it now. Thank yeh again, sir." He clasped Roy's hand in a firm handshake. "Yeh know where t' find me when yeh've another venture in mind, cap'n." Oliver turned towards the dock.

"You old workhorse," laughed Roy. "Just get you home without getting robbed on the way."

"No worry there, sir," answered Oliver over his shoulder. "One look at me scowl an' the urchins do go scatterin' t' the wind."

Your smile *would send me packing, if I didn't know you better.* "Good luck to you," said Roy.

As Oliver waved a final farewell, Roy turned to his table to fold it up and clear up his belongings to pack them with the other items in his cabin. In the dim light of the afternoon sun through the small windows of his cabin, he packed his clothes in a bundle with his writing case and a few other important items, and buckled on his sword belt. Tucking his pistol and dagger into it as well, he at last busied himself with loading the ample assortment of coins remaining in the small wooden chest into a large worn leather purse which he tucked inside his shirt. His warning to Oliver had been no mere jest—street thieves knew a happy crew when they saw one, though all but the most desperate and the most lack-witted knew better than to accost a sailor unless he was obviously drunk. The more cunning thief would simply follow them to a nearby alehouse—especially if these were no longer only operating secretly as the harbormaster claimed—or home and wait for the inevitable celebration to end. Roy himself was not worried about thieves as long as he had a weapon on him. Few could match him when he did.

He stepped out of his cabin with his bundle in hand, closed the door and locked it, and made his way to the deck once again. Taking one last look around, he pulled up the gangway, slung his bundle over his back, and leapt onto the dock. The sun beat upon his back as he trod into town seeking a carriage, his legs still unaccustomed to land. Soon, after a brief conversation with a driver, aided by a bit of coin, Roy was enjoying the familiar swaying of the coach as it rocked almost like the deck of *The Pilotfish.*

Jostling along unconcernedly as he was borne towards his father's home in the countryside, he let his excitement over his latest venture wash over him for a while. *I finally have my own ship!* It wasn't strictly true yet, but there was no reason to stifle his sense of accomplishment at this point. Plans formed and grew in his mind; plans for how to take advantage of the burgeoning ale market and subsequent drop in prices, plans for how to gain more business in France and maybe even Holland since the war was over. Thoughts for the future swept him along as the farmland rolled slowly by outside. *Perhaps I could even make a venture or two to the Americas, if I got a larger ship.* Roy did not honestly have much professional interest in such a venture, but it would allow him to see Constance again and would probably be very profitable in spite of the risks. By the time the coach came to a halt, however, Roy was once again focused on his evening agenda, and good food followed by a real bed were quickly driving any business concerns from his mind.

Roy stepped down from the coach with his bag and thanked the driver as he walked up the narrow lane to his father's house, with the westering sun throwing long shadows in front of him. He stepped up to the door eagerly and rattled the door knocker, but it was some time before anyone answered. Roy began to wonder if perhaps everyone had gone into town, but the servants should still be about the place. Just then, old Giles opened the door. He was dressed in rather somber garb, though slightly disheveled, and looked as if he had been weeping or ill, and he seemed surprised to see Roy standing there, though Roy's return should have been expected. "Oh, master Roy!" he said, "I'm so sorry to leave you waiting. You had best come inside."

"Thank you, Giles," said Roy as he stepped inside. "Is everything all right?"

"Well…no sir. But you should speak to your mother about that. I'm afraid your father is away in town at the moment arranging for…" Giles left his remark unfinished. "You should see your mother," he repeated. "She's in the sitting room. I'll take your bag up to your room, sir, if I may."

Roy absently handed him his bag. He'd never seen Giles so obviously distraught. He had a dreadful feeling that something terrible had happened, and he remembered also that his brother Thomas, who lived in Plymouth, had been ill when Roy set out on his voyage a few days ago. Worried, he walked straightaway into the sitting room where he found his mother sitting at a table writing a letter. "Mother?" he said quietly.

She turned and he could see that she had been weeping. She set down her pen and ran to him, and he caught her in his arms as she wept anew. "Roy…"

"Mother, what has happened?" he asked now in earnest. "Why are you all in tears? Where is father?"

She calmed herself enough to speak clearly, and led him to the table at which she had been sitting. From a letterbox, she withdrew a small rolled parchment with a broken seal. "This arrived last night," she said as she handed it to him. Slowly, he unrolled the letter and began to read.

The thirtieth of March, 1659

To the esteemed Toppings family,

 It is with a heavy heart that I write to inform you of ill tidings here in the Caribbean Sea. Whilst I was captaining a diplomatic mission to the French colony of Tortuga off the coast of Hispaniola, we were attacked and boarded by a pirate vessel flying French colors. Lieutenant Pablo Francisco Delgado was aboard, along with your daughter, Constance Toppings de Francisco. I regret to inform you that your daughter was killed in the attack and was lost to the sea. Our ship was destroyed and nearly all aboard were lost. Of the original crew and passengers, only I, Lieutenant Francisco, and a woman who was with child escaped alive. Please accept my sincerest sympathies, as well as my heartfelt apologies for failing to keep your daughter safe. May her soul have rest and peace by the Lord's Will, and may you find in prayer to Him strength to aid you in this difficult parting.

My deepest respects and sympathies,
Captain Felipe Montoya Lisera

Roy did not realize he was weeping until he was already reading the letter a second time and a tear landed on the ink. A blackness entered his mind, driving out all thought, yet on the edges of it was frantic emotion, too distant to seem real, and too terrible to seek out. As his glance touched his sister's name again, the thought came into the blackness unbidden, as if from a far distance. *She is gone.* She had been taken away from him long ago, and now she was taken beyond mortal reach. *Taken.*

His gaze touched another name and the blackness vanished. His hands shook. "Roy…" began his mother consolingly. Then she stopped. Rage blazed in his eyes.

Why is he *alive?! "To love and protect," he swore, yet even if he could not do so, he should at least have died seeking vengeance!* And yet he had lived, the man who had taken her and then left her to die.

"Roy," began his mother again, touching his arm gently, "Your father is in town gathering the rest of the family and making the arrangements…"

His expression did not change. "Let me know when he arrives home," he said stonily. "I shall be in my room." He looked down at the letter, and the word "rest" was caught in tiny waves of ink where Roy's tear had fallen on the paper, wrinkling its once-smooth surface. Setting the letter back on the table, he turned sharply and strode toward the door to the hall. His eyes were already dry, and the salt stung them like seawater. He paused. "And mother…I am sorry." It took great effort to put feeling into those words while inside he was at once icy cold and burning with wrath.

She sighed miserably. "Roy, I'm—" But he was already walking into the hallway towards his room, just as he had done as a child when confronted with bad news. Yet never again would his little sister seek for him there to offer comfort.

* * *

"Nothing very exciting, sir. A ship arrived from the West Indies yesterday, but nothing out of the ordinary." So the harbormaster had said. Roy almost regretted the shilling he had given the man. "To spread our good luck," he had said. Roy's luck had turned before he had even left on his last voyage. It was now nearly May and it had taken a month for news of his sister's death to reach him. He did not know why that felt important, but it did nonetheless. His thoughts seemed random. There was rage interwoven with a sense of great loss, and his thoughts flitted from one to the other. And as the minutes passed into hours, he became aware of a growing feeling of resignation.

He looked about him at the walls of his room. There were maps and marks, decoration and mementoes from his fledgling journeys abroad, yet all now seemed shorn of any purpose or satisfaction. No thoughts of trade or accomplishments, no illusions of independence or status, nothing seemed to mean anything anymore. *Why did* he *survive?* That question seemed the only important thing left in the world and he could only think of one likely answer: cowardice. He looked out of his window, blinking at the slowly sinking sun. He felt like a rudderless ship, bereft of anchor and with only one sail, adrift on an ocean of resignation and only distant possibilities to blow him this way or that. And yet there was freedom and peacefulness in that— the only peacefulness he now had in his newfound grief. And with that, he felt a moment of acceptance for the grief.

Then his mind churned again. *Why did* he *survive?*

Quick as a snake, he drew a knife, turned and then threw it all in one smooth motion. The knife stopped, quivering in the middle of the red cross of the Spanish flag on the border of one of his maps. "It doesn't matter," he answered himself aloud, his voice strong and clear, "he won't survive long." The question fled at last from his thoughts, and with it went all doubt.

Chapter 1: Port Royal

The red and white of the Spanish navy, rippling above the docks amid a sea of English flags, seemed particularly out of place in Port Royal, or at least it did to Coya. It was an unwelcome but all too familiar sight to one such as she, who had lived long in Spanish territory, but it held little terror for her now. Indeed, the captain of that ship must have been more than a little worried that he would be fired upon as he approached, but the privateers that ceaselessly patrolled the area must have had some reason to let him pass. Spaniards were a rare sight in Port Royal ever since the English had taken most of the island a few years ago and brief efforts by the Spanish to take it back had been thwarted. The new English acting governor had since adopted a lenient policy towards privateers and pirates, and they in turn provided most of the defense for the area.

With so many ruffians and cutthroats about, few people noticed one more, especially a small woman of Incan descent like Coya who did not give anyone much of a chance to notice her in any case. She crouched by the corner of a building wearing a tattered pair of shapeless breeches and a dirt-stained shirt that was too big for her. Her black unwashed hair hung limply down her back and shoulders. She hated looking like this when she didn't need to, but she was posing as a beggar and tried to look the part. Besides, the ill-fitting clothes made it easier for her to conceal her knives, as well as the fact that she was still well-fed and strong. The sun was sinking lower in the sky, reddening beyond the trees as she kept watch on The Lion's Den, a large tavern near the west end of the docks. With three ships arriving in the same day, including the small Spanish vessel, there would be more activity at the inns and taverns tonight, and a quick-fingered and quick-witted footpad might earn enough coin to survive for a month. Begging gave her a reason to stay in that spot for a long time, though she detested it. But here she would wait until after dark, for she could see quite clearly at night and her marks were likely to be very dull-witted by that time.

Looking back to her right a little, she suddenly saw a pair of Spanish officers walk casually up the end of the next street and turn to enter The Lion's Den. *Even better.* She grinned. *Better them than the English.* Coya had learned as a child to detest the Spanish. Not only had they destroyed the great empire of the Incas, they also seemed to think it necessary to possess all lands that existed. Her people had fled the destruction of the Incas and moved far inland a hundred years ago, but still the Spanish had eventually found them. For years the Spaniards had been Coya's only exposure to Europeans, and she had thought nothing could stop them. When she had escaped to Santiago de la Vega, she was probably a thousand miles from home, and yet she was still in Spanish territory.

Then the English came. She had wondered who these people were, so similar to the Spaniards in appearance, yet speaking a language she had never heard and bearing a standard the Spanish feared. And they had won. They took most of the island and renamed the town Cagway—they had now renamed it *Port Royal* though she did not know why—and the island was ever after alive with rumor of Spanish defeat both at sea and on land, even as far as Europe. The Spaniards had fought a retreat north across Jamaica, freeing their slaves to fight the English, and though they still had a tiny presence on the island, they had clearly been outmatched by the English in spite of the lack of fresh English troops since the attack five years ago. That first battle between English and Spanish for the possession of Jamaica was the first decisive victory against Spain that Coya had ever witnessed, and though less was different under English rule than she had once hoped for, she was grateful for that one experience.

As she mused over her experiences, she noticed another pair of sailors approaching. One was a tall Negro dressed in loose breeches tucked into high boots, his open vest hung over bare shoulders in the Caribbean heat. The other was similarly dressed except for a cream-colored tunic unlaced at the neck, but he was shorter, very fair-haired and fair-skinned, and he moved with grace and confidence. Both had swords at their belts. She put on a dejected expression, cast her gaze downwards and meekly held her palm up in a wordless plea for spare coin. The two men were laughing and discussing something in English, and passed her by with only a glance, proceeding toward the tavern. *With this many privateers around, I hope those Spaniards make it far enough down the street to get robbed.* She crossed her legs in the dirt and waited.

* * *

"Wit' dis many sailors here tonight," said Ajuban in his heavy Igbo accent, "maybe we will have more luck dan we t'ought."

"I certainly hope so, my friend," replied Roy as they entered The Lion's Den. "The problem is that too many captains come through here regularly looking for new crew." Besides Ajuban, he was down to only two men after paying off his last crew, and he didn't want to end up with the dregs of the trade.

"Don't worry, captain, at least none of de big boys are in town today," Ajuban said hopefully, meaning the more famous captains in the area, "dough if dat Spaniard is here to pay a ransom, we won't have long to wait."

"Who knows? I don't even know if anyone has taken valuable prisoners lately. I suppose she could really be a diplomatic vessel, though I don't know what Spain would hope to gain by sending one here." Spanish diplomats were sometimes sent to settle a ransom, but others simply used the white flag of truce. So far nearly every Spanish vessel berthed in Port Royal during the past year had come to pay off a ransom.

"I hope for deir sake it's not anoder offer of amnesty. De last ship dey sent offering amnesty to 'de pirates of Port Royal' probably still hasn't touched bottom yet."

Roy laughed as they made their way through the throng to the bar. "Two of your finest, landlord," he called and was acknowledged with a quick nod as the busy man behind the counter handed a laden tray to a serving woman. Roy took a look around the room. The place was already busy, and more of the locals were filing in as the workday ended. Many had probably arrived early to hear what tales they could before their families expected them home. It was dark inside, and a haze of smoke was already gathering around some tables as pipes were lit. The furniture was of dark-stained oak, sturdy and simply carved, and the high ceiling was in shadow, unlit by the low windows and the setting sun. The rafters were plain and unadorned, and the walls were here and there decorated with carvings and paintings of lions and flags bearing the device of the Lion Rampant. It reminded Roy sharply of a tavern that had opened in Plymouth shortly before he sailed to the Caribbean. It had the same warm and dark atmosphere of many buildings on the damp and foggy isle of Britain, but the tropical heat of The Lion's Den was in stark contrast.

The enterprising owner of the tavern, perceiving the impending necessity of catering to a host of sailors, had constructed this establishment shortly after the English had taken the town. Cromwell's decrees against alehouses had never held sway in the colonies. Now that the restoration of the monarchy had been announced and Charles II was invited to return to England to claim the throne, several decrees and agendas of the Protectorate were being preemptively discarded. Many privateers were worried that Cromwell's agenda of Western Design—which, in the Caribbean, boiled down to a policy of fighting the Spanish and breaking their virtual monopoly on colonial expansion in the West Indies—would also suffer. Indeed, privateers and governors alike could lately be heard saying that they would support Western Design even if the king abandoned it. Some like Captain Henry Morgan even refused to call Port Royal by its new name in honor of the restoration, but rather continued to call it Cagway as it was named after the English had captured it. It was now the first of May; just over a year since Roy had received news of his sister's death, and Charles II was due to ascend to the throne in exactly one month. If Acting Governor D'Oyley or enough privateers in the area abandoned their fight with Spain after that time, Roy would find it very difficult to find new crew. *Hopefully I won't hear news like that tonight.*

As he searched for empty chairs for himself and his friend and first mate Ajuban, he spied two men in Spanish uniform sitting alone at a table speaking merrily together. Roy could not hear what was being said, but the two officers were openly speaking Spanish. Many of the other patrons eyed them darkly and everyone avoided their table. Roy, following a sudden impulse and with a word to Ajuban to stay put, unconcernedly approached their table.

"Sir." Ajuban nodded. Roy knew Ajuban disapproved, but he continued purposefully toward the Spanish officers.

"Excuse me gentlemen," Roy said amicably in Spanish as the two officers looked up at him, "As you are obviously esteemed officers in the service of Spain, I wonder if you happen to know a man named Lieutenant Pablo Francisco. He is, as are you, a renowned officer in good King Philip's navy. I have been seeking him long, and perhaps you could be of service to me in my endeavor, if I might make a request of two such men of importance as yourselves."

Both men looked surprised for a moment, but one of them—a lieutenant and the senior of the two officers—smiled mirthlessly at Roy. "We are not nannies," he replied in Spanish and sneered, "nor are we errand boys for an English fop. Seek this lieutenant of yours elsewhere. We are off duty." He laughed and turned back to his companion who, after giving Roy a quick but apologetic glance, became suddenly attentive to his drink. Many people had been watching and listening. Some had understood what had passed and a low murmur of displeasure ensued. One large young man sitting with companions at a long table near the wall stood up angrily. The man next to him put a hand on his shoulder and he sat back down again.

"As you wish," Roy answered graciously. "I am sorry to have disturbed such a busy and courteous person as yourself." He was cold with anger, but his smile was effortless as he bowed to them and turned away. He motioned to Ajuban to follow him with the drinks, and he made his way to the table of the young dark-haired fellow who had stood up. Ajuban shrugged, collected the tankards and followed.

The dark-haired man looked up as Roy approached him. "Good evening, sir," said Roy, "I'm Captain Roy Toppings. It's a pleasure to meet you."

The man stood up abruptly almost knocking over his chair, though his hand shot out reflexively and straightened it. He actually saluted. "Albert McGuinn, sir. It's an honor to meet you."

Roy laughed. "There's no need to salute, Albert, I'm not with the navy." He extended his hand and Albert, a little embarrassed, dropped his salute to shake it. Albert's grip was like iron, though given his build it was hardly surprising. "This is my first mate, Ajuban. May we join you and these other fine gentlemen?" he asked, turning his attention to the others at the table. There was general consent, and soon they were halfway through a second tankard sitting and talking merrily together.

* * *

"Why did you leave Tortuga, Albert?" asked Ajuban, delighted to find that these men treated him as an equal, even if it was only due to rank. "It sounds like you were doing well for yourself dere, and it is at least a bigger town dan dis place."

"I probably would have stayed," said Albert, "for a while at least. Although it was a depressing place, or so I felt. Every kind of human filth lived there in abundance. But I had saved up enough money to buy some land of my own, even if I decided to move away. Then I was robbed. Two Spanish sailors blindsided me in a narrow street and took everything I had."

"I'm surprised they had the nerve," said William, a newcomer to the table, "Even if there were two of them, they would have to be crazy or half-drunk or both to think of taking you on in a fight."

Albert gave him a meaningful look. "You don't have to be strong or tough if you can sneak up on someone," he said. "When I was fighting in the ring, no one could beat me. Outside in the dark streets at night, the rules change."

Roy nodded soberly, but William still looked incredulous. He had come in about an hour after Ajuban and Roy sat down, and introduced himself as "William Ward of Devonshire," but he had not said why he introduced himself in this formal way and no one had asked. Albert's expression clearly said he did not believe it was because of any battlefield exploits.

"I'm much more surprised," continued Albert, "that they had the nerve to try such a thing in Tortuga. The town is crawling with pirates who make a living from Spanish plunder." He grimaced. "It's one thing for Spaniards to attack enemy towns and ships, but to visit as a guest and indulge in petty thievery is just plain discourteous." An oddly grim and condemning tone crept into Albert's voice at this observation, and Ajuban wondered if Albert's dislike for Spaniards went deeper than the incident he had described. "If I had tracked them down," he continued in a calmer voice, "the local authorities probably wouldn't have cared if I had beaten them to death."

"But how did they manage to take everything you had if they robbed you in the street?" asked Roy. "Surely you didn't carry all of your money about with you?"

"Of course I did," laughed Albert. "Burglary was common in Tortuga, and I was fairly well known. Twice I came home to find that things were out of place or missing. I had also learned not to trust the local moneychangers, so I thought it safer to carry my savings with me so that people might think twice before trying to take it. After all, who would try to rob the best pit fighter in Tortuga?" He smiled bitterly and took another pull at his drink.

"I suppose a person didn't *have* to t'ink twice so long as two could t'ink once," observed Ajuban, to the general laughter of everyone.

"Aye, an' even thinkin' once is mighty impressive for a Spaniard," interjected an old sailor named Oscar to even more laughter.

* * *

It was getting late and Coya thought it time to abandon her act, as most beggars returned to whatever shelter they could find after full dark. Very few people had left the tavern yet, and those that had didn't look wealthy enough or drunk enough to be worth the effort. More people had gone inside than had come out, so they were probably having quite a time inside and the place must be rather crowded. *They will probably be drunker than ever after so long in there.* Hopefully they wouldn't be that much poorer for it, but it was pointless to continue begging at the corner. She gave up her place in the dirt and hid in the shadow of a woodpile leaning against a nearby wall, continuing to wait.

She heard faint laughter float from the tavern and laughed to herself. *So many people having a good time, talking and relaxing, and here I am hiding by a woodpile, waiting and working and worrying.* Coya didn't like to think about it, but every so often it struck her that she had not had that much fun or conversation, nor had she been that relaxed, for years. She supposed that was the life of a thief in some ways, but most thieves could blend into society with their victims and laugh with friends as much as anyone else. Sometimes she talked with the natives she traded with, but she wasn't much more accepted by them than she was by Europeans. Though she was not European, in the eyes of the natives she was still a woman who eked out a meager living in the wild and she was not related to their tribes at all—the Spanish called them Taíno Indians—so she couldn't even understand their native language. She wore men's clothes out of necessity; she knew she was plain to look at, and she had no marriage prospects even if she had wanted any. The natives only dealt with her for as long as her coin would buy their goods, but their interest usually ended there, and she had to hide the fact of her trade from them because there was nothing more repugnant to the Taíno than thieving. It was not so different for her people, but the Spanish had changed all that long ago for the remnant of the mighty civilization of the Incas. Coya could only speak to those of the natives who spoke Spanish, and now that the town itself was populated by the English instead of Spaniards, and though she had picked up a little bit of the language, she couldn't usually speak and be understood among the European populace.

This is useless distraction and I can't change things anyway. She sighed. These thoughts had been popping up more often lately. She supposed it was only a matter of time after the English took Port Royal that such thoughts would become more troublesome. Although she hated the Spaniards, she at least knew them. Her own people were far away, and probably almost all dead. Now the Spaniards were far away too. *Except for two of them.* She brought her thoughts and her gaze back to the tavern and continued waiting.

* * *

"Last June," said William.

"Why?" asked Roy.

"I don't know," answered William, "curiosity I suppose. This is the New World, they say, and I wanted something that was completely new. I thought maybe there would be enough raw material and untouched potential out here for me to perhaps make something bigger out of my life without a lot of civilization in the way and a lot of other people's dreams interfering with mine. I don't suppose it's so unusual a reason." He sounded almost apathetic about it all, though his face was smiling and optimistic. Roy guessed that most people didn't lightly decide to make the crossing from England, whatever William might think.

"So what have you been doing since you came here?"

"Mostly just odd jobs. I've worked for a few merchants who were hoping to build up this town a bit, but I'm not going to get anywhere being someone's shadow and checking accounts."

Roy was dubious. William seemed to be everything that the unobservant thought Roy to be: a young English fop without a care in the world. But if he could sail and fire a gun, he might be worth the effort anyway. William certainly didn't seem put off by the notions of danger or capture, and he'd said that he helped out with a little fighting on a couple of trips, but he didn't seem like an eager privateer either. *Except he seems very interested in the tales of it.* Whether or not William had an appetite for tales of adventures at sea, Roy doubted his interest would last long once he had a taste of the reality. Roy and Ajuban had recounted their last venture in the Windward Passage during a storm which had ended with the plunder of a Spanish merchantman, and the story had drawn a small crowd, but William listened more eagerly than most and even asked them for visual impressions. If Roy was going to recruit him, he wanted to see some sign that William was really cut out for life at sea. "When did you decide you wanted to join a privateer crew and fight the Spanish?" he asked.

"Yesterday," William answered, sounding perfectly serious. Everyone laughed, except for Roy who stared at him incredulously. "Well, think back to the day you decided to be a privateer," objected William, looking from face to face. "If someone had asked *you* that question the very next day, what would you have said?" This was received by another roar of laughter by everyone at the table—again with the exception of Roy, who nodded seriously and said nothing. He remembered that day all too well.

But this time the men were laughing in agreement and raising their glasses in salute to William. "Well," said Ajuban, still laughing and patting William on the shoulder, "you have to admit, captain, de man has a point." Roy did smile then, shaking off his reflective mood and raising his tankard to William with the others.

The night wore on and few people showed signs of leaving. There were many tales to hear and to tell. "Aye, soldiers be musterin' somewhere for an invasion, they say," Oscar whispered, cocking an eye at the two Spaniards who continued their private conversation several tables away.

"Hopefully they won't be coming here," said Roy. "There are plenty of privateers here to keep them away, but it is a big island and they might slip through to land troops if they were careful and fast enough." He wasn't terribly worried, especially as the Spanish ship in the harbor was bound to give rise to such speculation and patrols might even be increased, but Spanish soldiers mustering anywhere was a concern. "Why do people think they're planning an invasion?" he asked. "Spanish soldiers are frequently shuffling around the Caribbean."

"Aye," acknowledged Oscar with a nod, "but a friend o' mine 'eard 'em talkin' about bein' issued new blades an' bein' trained quickly on more modern guns."

That set many at the table to muttering darkly to each other. If it were true, an invasion would be the most *hopeful* way to interpret the news, as it would simply be an isolated case. If Spain had begun arming *all* its soldiers with anything like the new flintlock muskets, every other nation would be at a disadvantage until they could equip their men with the same, and that would take at least several months. *I'll have to keep my ears open about this.* There was little Roy could do with the news, if indeed it was more than gossip, but Spanish troop movements were worrying enough without the added concern of them being heavily armed.

There was much idle speculation about Oscar's story and other local events as well as the situation in Europe, but people were mostly concerned with events in Port Royal. Ever since the town had been taken from the Spanish, Colonel D'Oyley, the acting governor of Jamaica, had arranged several deals with privateers. He had issued letters of marque to some of the captains (with the consent of the English Parliament) condoning attacks on Spanish ships and towns in exchange for a share of the plunder. In addition to satisfying the privateer crews, the arrangement had a dual effect on the town's economy. The presence of English privateer ships operating out of Port Royal kept Spanish warships away, providing a solid outer defense for the otherwise vulnerable port and any friendly trade in the area. At the same time, the governor largely used the tribute of plunder for developing the town, and supplies taken from enemy ships compensated for the lack of trade ships arriving from England. Roads, guardhouses, businesses, plantations and residences were springing up all over the island due to this influx of wealth. "I must have worked on half a dozen building projects since January," said Albert. "It's wonderful to see this place finally prospering, and it is satisfying to see the fruits of my labors standing in front of me, but I can't help feeling that I'm wasted here." Albert seemed to resent being treated merely as a sort of pack animal due to his size and lack of trade skills.

"I know how you feel," said William. "I don't want to spend my life finding sums for merchants either. Not only do my talents atrophy, but my imagination does as well." Roy cocked an eyebrow at one of the older sailors, who shrugged. He wondered how much William thought days rocking to and fro on the deck of a becalmed ship would stimulate his imagination. He heard Ajuban say something to William and was about to turn back to the conversation, but a long overdue sight out of the corner of his eye caught his attention—the Spaniards were leaving. He turned to Ajuban and the others. "Another round?" he asked.

All assented to this, except Oscar. "No thank yeh, cap'n," he said. "I'll be needin' to make it home on me own legs shortly, an' I already feel the sea tossing in 'ere."

"I'm not surprised," said Roy and smiled, "You've already had enough ale to float a galleon." He made his way back to the bar and ordered another round, but his eyes followed the Spaniards as they made their way out the door. *Ajuban will have to take over.* Roy preferred to form his own opinions about prospective crewmembers, but there would be time enough for that in the morning when they turned up at his ship. He had been insulted, and he did not intend to let it pass.

* * *

"How long have you sailed with Captain Toppings," Albert asked, turning to Ajuban as Roy was ordering drinks.

"Only a few mont's. On his first expedition dis year, he captured a Spanish merchantman. I was a slave working aboard dat ship, and I asked to join Roy's crew. He was respectful to me de whole time, and I liked dat." Ajuban had never been more grateful and surprised than when Roy had freed him and signed him aboard, especially since he had fought against Roy's crew during the battle.

"He doesn't seem like a typical privateer," observed William. "Very polite. Noble heritage, I shouldn't wonder."

"Aye, dat's true," said Ajuban. "His fader is a noble in Plymout' or someplace like dat." He didn't know much about England.

"Really?" said William excitedly. "I'm from around there!" He looked up to see if Roy was returning to the table, apparently eager to talk more of home.

"I t'ought you said you were from *Devonsha*, or some-t'ing like dat," said Ajuban doubtfully.

"*Devonshire*," corrected William distractedly. "Plymouth is a city in Devonshire." He looked around the room. "Now where's he got to?" he muttered.

"So den is he 'Roy Toppings of Devonshire?'"

A few people at the table buried their faces in their drinks, apparently stifling giggles at William's expense, though Ajuban was perfectly serious. But William wasn't paying attention. "Where did the captain go?" he asked.

Ajuban turned around, scanning the room. A servant was carrying a tray laden with tall tankards towards their table, but Roy had disappeared. Ajuban turned back to the others and sighed. "I knew it was too much to hope for," he muttered.

* * *

Finally. Coya saw the two Spaniards saunter out of The Lion's Den. She loosened a hidden knife in its sheath and crouched low in the darkness. They were coming up the same street she had occupied earlier as a beggar, and they were both obviously drunk. She waited for them to pass by as she looked them over. If she could guess which one was more off his wits, she might not have to worry overmuch about him aiding the other, whom she would attack first. Taking her sling in hand, she gave them a good lead before following them. They turned a dark corner further up the street. She drew a small round stone from a pouch concealed in her tunic and, placing it in the sling, she rounded the corner as quietly as a cat. They had not gone far. Though most people would have had trouble seeing them in the largely unlit street, Coya's excellent night vision rendered them easy targets a mere ten paces ahead. She swung the sling a couple of times to settle the stone into its cradle for a more accurate throw, but one of the men had turned to the other in conversation and suddenly saw her. *Damn!* She stopped her hand and prepared to run. They would not be able to catch her in the condition they were in.

"Hello there, girl!" he called to her in Spanish. He leered at her and stumbled to a halt. "Are you looking for some fun? You should have said rather than waving your hands about. No need to be so shy...." He motioned her over.

She was confused for a moment, but suddenly she understood that he had not seen what was in her hand and had only dimly seen her waving in the dark. She dropped the sling and caught it behind her back, stone and all, with her other hand. She walked towards them wearing her most convincing seductive smirk, and rolled the stone down her back leg to the ground in midstride. She discreetly tucked the sling into her breeches.

"Or do you have a jealous husband you are trying not to rouse from sleep?" the man whispered as she approached. She could smell the alcohol from two paces away. "Don't worry, your secret is safe with me." He grinned at her, and she fought the desire to stab him out of sheer disgust.

Instead she hoped that he couldn't see her smirk turn to a grimace in the dark. Her voice remained even and smooth as she put her arm around his waist with her hand near his pocket and said, "The middle of the street is no place to conduct such business, my pet. Let us continue on...I know a place down the street," she whispered in his ear as her fingers discreetly explored the contents of his pocket finding several coins. She had been keeping half an eye on the other man the whole time, but he seemed to have thoroughly drowned his wits in the tavern and was content merely to leer at her suggestively and watch this little game unfold. She led them down the street to an area that still had not been fully cleared or developed.

Just as she gingerly palmed a handful of coins from her victim's pocket, she heard the sound of hurrying feet behind them and caught sight of a hand in the basket hilt of a main gauche collide savagely with the other man's temple, knocking him forward a couple of paces where he collapsed in a heap. "An 'English fop,' am I?" said a man's voice in Spanish. Grasping the coins, Coya sprang away. It was the fair-haired Englishman she had seen entering The Lion's Den earlier, but his companion was gone and he looked both angry and cheerful as he turned on the second man whom she had just robbed. She ran across the road into the trees, but he took no interest in her as he began swinging at the Spaniard. She stopped in a thicket and looked back. She soon realized that the fair-haired man was not trying to use his blade to subdue the Spaniard, but was merely using the basket hilt as a bludgeon. He moved with surprising grace and speed, though the Spaniard had quickly recovered most of his wits in the face of the ferocious assault. Coya glanced down at the handful of coins she carried: seven silver pesos— enough to last for weeks if she were careful. She sighed and looked up again, preparing to leave these two to their silly brawl in spite of the satisfaction she now felt at seeing a Spaniard felled so thoroughly. Now the remaining Spaniard had a knife in his hand.

Her eyes narrowed. As she watched for a moment, she realized that he *was* trying to stab his opponent, and still the fair-haired man fought only with his guarded fist. She was annoyed. *Typical Spanish behavior.* Why did the Englishman not change his tactics to match the Spaniard? The Spaniard began shouting for help, no doubt hoping the law would intervene, as he still could not manage to land a blow using underhanded tactics. She muttered a curse in her own language and, in sheer disgust, drew a long knife and threw it at the Spaniard.

But just then the Spaniard lunged and the knife missed him. He didn't even notice it. The fair-haired man *did* notice it however, and in a moment of apparent distraction, he failed to counter as the Spaniard reversed the thrust and scored a long gash along his side. He recoiled, using his blade to ward off more blows, and the Spaniard swept out his sword with his other hand.

Damn! I should not have interfered. The Englishman reached for his sword hilt, but Coya was afraid he would not draw it in time. She drew a smaller knife from her boot and hurled it at the Spaniard without taking time to aim. It caught him just left of where she guessed his stomach should be, and his sword fell from his grasp as he clutched at the wound.

Suddenly the sound of running feet came from around the corner. The Spaniard turned his head toward the sound and the Englishman took the opportunity to kick him in the head and snatch up his sword as he crumpled to the ground. "Psst!" Coya motioned to him from the trees, indicating he should follow her. He looked up at her curiously, then he took the first man's sword as well and followed her into the thicket holding the bloody gash in his side. They could hear the sound of many booted feet in the street now, but the soldiers had stopped following momentarily to assess the situation. Coya and the Englishman plunged silently on through the trees running alongside the road. She tried to help him along at first, but she was too short to lend him much support and he could not see the branches before he struck them. In the end, she led the way and he followed as best he could.

Soon they heard the sounds of pursuit in the trees behind them. Coya motioned for a halt and her companion stopped, breathing hard. She pointed through the trees to a narrow gap between two sheds. She could see a large washtub, and she meant to hide there. They crept slowly and silently out of the trees and scurried across the street and behind the washtub. The Englishman was still bleeding and was dripping with sweat, but he immediately ducked down behind the tub. Coya, struck by a sudden inspiration, stepped into the washtub and drew out her sling. The Englishman whispered something to her that she didn't understand, but he seemed amused. Remembering that he had spoken words in Spanish when he assailed the Spaniards, she said quietly, "I do not speak your language well, Englishman." She fitted a stone to her sling.

"I said, 'Are you going to take a bath?'" he replied in Spanish. "And my name is Roy."

She smirked. "Just wait and see." She stood in the washtub still as stone with her sling in hand. When she again heard sounds of pursuit, she wound her sling in an overhand throw and hurled the stone into the trees many yards ahead of the pursuers. She drew out another stone and did this again, now hurling the stone even farther ahead. She ducked down into the washtub and drew out a third stone as she listened. The sounds passed the place where the two of them had left the trees. She waited another moment before standing up again. This time she put one foot on either side of the tub and raised herself up so she could get a clear shot over the shed to her left. She wound the sling a third time and launched another stone yet farther ahead of the pursuers. Finally she sank down again and took cover, listening attentively. Soon she smiled and peered over the side at Roy. "That should throw them off long enough."

"That was a clever idea," said Roy.

Coya shrugged. "It is a simple hunter's trick."

"I am glad it helped the hunted instead of the hunters," Roy said, grinning.

"Let us leave this place. Can you continue?"

"Yes, the bleeding has slowed now that I've had a chance to sit still. I think I can move slowly without tearing it open again." He smiled at her as he stood up. "Thank you for helping me, though you nearly scared the life out of me at first."

"Yes," she said in embarrassed tones, "you nearly did lose your life because of me. I am sorry." She led him quietly back through the town away from the direction the pursuers had gone, creeping from shadow to shadow.

"It's all right," Roy assured her as he followed along. "I got what I came for." Roy held up the two swords he had taken from the Spaniards and grinned mischievously.

Coya was confused. "But you have a sword," she said. "What use are three of them?"

"Good Spanish blades will fetch a high price from the right merchant," he explained. "And those two fools will have a difficult time explaining to their captain how they lost the swords he issued them. I don't imagine they carry enough coin to replace the blades before they are due back aboard their ship." His smile was absolutely wicked now, and extremely comical.

Coya laughed as loudly as she dared. "I had not thought of that!" she said. "A very clever trick, Englishman. I will have to remember that."

Roy shrugged mockingly, even though it hurt his side, and imitated her voice as he nonchalantly said, "It is a simple privateer's trick."

Coya laughed again at his impression of her. "I imagine it will be more difficult for them to replace their swords than you think."

"Why is that?"

"Shall we say that I also got what I came for?" Coya dug in her pocket and held out the seven pesos she had palmed.

Now it was Roy's turn to laugh. "Ow," he said suddenly, clutching his wound.

"You should let me look at that," said Coya. "I know a place outside of the town where we will be safe and I can attend to your wound."

Roy shook his head. "My ship is closer and I have friends who will probably be awaiting me there soon." He turned to her. "You are welcome to come aboard for a while. No one will bother you there unless they want me to tie them to the anchor, and I can replace the knives you lost for your troubles." Roy looked surprised for a moment. "Speaking of which, how were you able to do that? I could hardly see a thing through those trees. I'm surprised I could see you at all, even after you signaled to me."

"I can see quite well in the dark," Coya said casually. "My whole family could, as could the other villagers. Indeed, I didn't know that others could not see as well until I fled to Spanish territory." Roy looked at her appraisingly, and she studied his face. She had been appraised by European men many times, but always in a lustful and possessive manner. She knew she was not particularly attractive, but that did not seem important to drunk or lecherous Europeans. But now, seeing Roy's expression, she saw a new kind of appraisal in his eyes—he was appraising her *abilities,* even as one warrior would judge another. She thought for a moment and said, "I will accept your invitation. I will go to your ship and tend your wound."

He smiled. "Again, I thank you. Follow me."

They set off in the direction of the docks slowly to avoid aggravating his wound, and they did not speak as they were each busy with their own thoughts. As they approached the docks, Coya broke the silence. "Roy?"

"Yes?" he answered sounding a little startled, probably at her use of his name.

"What is an 'English fop?'"

Roy sighed.

Chapter 2: A Constant Crew

"Good evening, sir," said Ajuban as Roy approached the dock where *The Constance* was berthed. He was not very surprised as he eyed Roy's torn and bloodstained shirt critically. Ajuban knew as soon as the captain had gone missing that he had gone to pick a fight with those Spaniards, so he returned to the ship shortly after Roy left. Noticing that the captain was leaning heavily on a very small native woman, he said, "I trust every-t'ing went as well as I expected?"

"You're a hard man, Ajuban," replied the captain tiredly, "but yes, I got what I came for. Those Spaniards won't find it easy to replace these." He tossed the pilfered blades to Ajuban.

"I'm glad your efforts were rewarded wit' such valuable bounty," Ajuban said sarcastically, "I would hate for de captain's blood to be spilled wit'out good reason."

"Stow it, lad. Just tell me what you can make of them and let us aboard, would you?"

Ajuban examined each blade quickly as he made way for the captain and his companion. "Dey are good Toledo steel, captain," he said, "and very new." The captain looked troubled at that, but he would have to wait to find out why. "Dey should bring a good price."

"Take them to the armory and fetch this young woman some bandages and a clean needle and thread so she can sew me up," said Roy.

Ajuban stepped aside and took another look at the woman who was now helping Roy down onto the deck. He wouldn't have called her young— probably no younger than Roy himself—but she was dressed as a man and appeared to have a sling half hanging out of her breeches. "Come wit' me," he said, addressing her in Spanish, guessing that she had grown up here and probably spoke Spanish more readily than English. "You shall show me what supplies you will need, and you can tell me what de captain did to get himself sliced up dis time." To his surprise she looked a little abashed, which didn't suit her countenance at all.

"No," she said, "it really wasn't his fault. He fought well, but I—"

"Oh, and Ajuban," interjected Roy from his place on the deck, leaning against the mast, "show her to the armory and let her pick any two knives of her choice to keep."

Ajuban raised a brow at that as he signaled his acknowledgement. "Dis is going to be a good story, isn't it?" he asked Coya.

She smiled, though a little hesitantly. If Roy was inclined to befriend the woman, Ajuban thought she must be worthy of respect, but clearly she did not expect to be treated as an equal. "That it will be," she said as he led the way.

* * *

"Him?" Roy asked as he gestured to a blanket-covered lump near the stern of the ship. "He's my navigator. Best damned navigator I ever sailed with, actually."

"But why is he sleeping here?" asked Coya. "Surely you allow your crew to sleep in town while you're docked? Sir?" she added hastily, though Roy only felt amused by the formality under the circumstances.

"Of course, but he *wants* to sleep on board. Says it helps him stay in tune with the ship." Roy rolled his eyes and shrugged. "He'll disembark if we put in anywhere for an extended stay, but for these short visits, he doesn't budge except for a storm. Who am I to argue with him? The man certainly knows his trade."

"I imagine it helps to have the navigator aboard in case you have to leave in a hurry, too."

"There is that," Roy admitted, "but thankfully the necessity hasn't arisen yet."

"So who else do you have in your crew?" asked Coya. "I don't guess that just the three of you sail against the Spaniards."

"Well, there is Martin as well, but he's the only other crewmember who chose to remain. We're in town recruiting at the moment." Roy looked down at his now clean and bandaged wound and grimaced. "Truth be told, as much as it rankles, that Spaniard wasn't far wrong. I fit his description of me much more than I resemble a privateer, at least in the eyes of most men. Brian there"—he gestured to the bundled figure of the navigator—"says that I'm a trifle too 'gentlemanly' for this trade sometimes. He doesn't mean it as a compliment either. I guess that quality tends to put some people off, and unless there's quite a bit of loot to be had, they would rather sail under someone else. Besides," he added, "I'm not much more than fair at anything beyond fighting and my general athleticism. Those are my real talents." He said it with no brag whatsoever; it was simply a statement of fact, and Coya appeared to acknowledge it as exactly that. "Even Martin stays only due to his faith in Brian's abilities, I think, rather than his faith in mine."

"But a leader must be someone that others would follow into battle," objected Coya. "The path of the warrior is straightest, and even the crooked will follow that path in the step of one who has mastered it."

Roy glanced sidelong at Coya. She certainly was not a common find among the cutpurses and tricksters in Port Royal. *Nor among any other company I could name*, he added to himself. "Well, I hope so," he replied, "or the morning turnout could be very disappointing. Anyway, Brian's cunning at the rudder and the skill of our marksmen has so far accounted for most of our success at sea. I've barely had my sword out of its scabbard in months for any reason but to clean it or practice with it."

"Sir," said Ajuban, popping his head up from the hold where he had been busy checking their supplies, "Looks like Martin took care of every-t'ing in good order. We have only to wait for de food before we sail. I hope we ordered enough…" he pondered.

"I almost hope we didn't," answered Roy. "I put in for a fair amount, but the larger the crew we get, the sooner we can find more of what we need. Very good, Ajuban. Get some rest. I'll wake Brian when it's his turn to watch."

Ajuban nodded and gathered up his blanket—no doubt he figured the night was too old for wasting money on a room—but he stopped and directed a meaningful glance at Roy. "I hope you make sure he is good and roused before you nod off, captain. If de city watch comes looking for you here, dey would be easy for sandy eyes to miss in dis dark night."

"I'm well ahead of you, my friend," he said, discreetly cocking an eye towards Coya. Obviously Ajuban was thinking along the same lines, but had left it up to Roy to say anything to Coya if he wished to. "I'll see to it shortly. Go on, off to sleep with you."

"Aye, sir." He turned to Coya who had told him the tale of the captain's fight earlier as she was patching Roy's wound. "A pleasure to meet you, miss. I hope to hear more of your stories later, if I might. Dey please de ear even if dey do flattery to some folks." He grinned mockingly at Roy, who rolled his eyes and smiled in spite of himself, as he waved his first mate away.

"Of course," responded Coya. She was obviously not practiced at these little pleasantries people often exchanged with each other, but she seemed puzzled as well. She very likely thought that she would not see either of them again, and in the morning they would sail to some unknown fortune or folly while she slept in some hidden shelter for the night. However, Roy had no intention of letting her go back to her squalid little existence without making her an offer much more appropriate to her abilities. *Now if only I can find the right way to ask.*

* * *

As Ajuban made his way down to the hold with his blanket, Coya tried to think of a similarly elegant farewell to Roy so that she could take her leave. But instead of rising to wake the sleeping navigator, he turned to her and asked her more about herself and her life on the island. He should really be resting, and her pride in her skills of healing prompted her to insist on it, but something held her back. She felt a little bit out of place on the deck of this ship with the sort of people who usually didn't say five words to her all at once, and part of her wanted to leave just for that reason, but she missed the simple pleasure of talking to people. So she stayed. She found herself telling him more than she had told anyone in a long time. She was not particularly secretive about her past, but the simple truth was that no one had asked about it in a great while.

He appeared to take great interest in her story. "You escaped from the jungle all the way to Cartagena without being captured or pressed into slavery?" he asked incredulously. "How did you manage to escape the soldiers?"

"They made such noises and fires that they could barely find *each other* through the haze and racket when it was over, let alone me. Once I had lost them, they gave up since they had already defeated us and taken our settlement. The difficulty lay in escaping the dangers of the jungle. It sees what intruders do not, and darkness is its ally rather than its enemy. It was hard living in the wilderness outside of Cartagena, but I found I could hide by day and move by night, and eventually I stowed away aboard a ship bound for here."

"They didn't find you?" ventured Roy.

"No. It was a large ship with many places to hide. There were always watchmen, and fearing they would find me eventually, I emptied a large rum barrel into a pool of stagnant water and hid in the barrel with some stolen food and the water I had brought with me. I got out to stretch in the dead of night, but I was very afraid that I would not survive the trip. Fortunately it wasn't a long voyage. I felt half dead when I managed to escape from the ship.

"It is easier living here. The wilderness is less dangerous, and more people are tolerant of the natives here." She laughed to herself, but quietly due to habit more than from lack of mirth or from any consideration for the repose of the deck-dwelling navigator. "They cannot tell me apart from the others here!" That fact amused her greatly, even years after the fact, but she quickly realized it was likely that Roy could not tell her apart from the natives here any better than the Spanish could and her mirth subsided.

"But why did you come here in the first place?" asked Roy. "Surely you couldn't know what it was like here enough to want to risk it, nor could you hope to escape an island on foot if you had to. Why put yourself in that kind of danger?"

Coya sighed. "It is true what you say. I did not know what to expect, and I was very worried that I would find it more difficult to escape any trouble here than it was in Cartagena. But I had listened to the tales of other peoples who were not friendly to the Spaniards. I hoped simply to get closer to those places so that I might find freedom and be able to sleep in some kind of real shelter for a change." She raised her head, looking Roy in the eye. "It may not show to you, but living in the wild has left its marks on me. In my family, all of the women were fortunate—we thought that we had been blessed by the gods—that age did not quickly find us. I was no exception. But now I look as old as I am, and I could feel the marks of the jungle clawing still deeper into my flesh. I had to do something." Roy did not meet her gaze, but nodded sadly. Coya knew that it was a sad story, but she was not inclined to understate it since he was so curious. Coya had spent long years feeling like a bird driven from its flock and forced to live on the ground instead of the treetops. Sometimes she felt an overwhelming need for someone to understand her situation, and these opportunities did not arise very often.

"When I arrived here," Coya continued, "it still seemed that I was in the heart of the Spanish Empire, and though life was a little easier, I began to think they would take over the whole world and I would be forever trapped outside." She laughed then. "I must say, when I watched their defeat and dreamt of what life would be like here under the English, it never occurred to me that anyone could run an entire island on the same principle I had been living from all that time: thievery." Her laugh faltered as she realized that she may have caused some offense to her host, but Roy laughed even louder.

"Well it seems to work for both of us, does it not?" he laughed. Coya nodded. "However," and at this Roy leaned towards her intently, "perhaps if that never occurred to you, then another possibility also never occurred: that if you live by the same principle as the town you are shut out of, perhaps you could find a place within that very same Brotherhood, and not be shut out anymore." Coya froze, stunned. She had caught the capitalization in his tone. He was talking about the Brethren of the Coast. She had heard the other sailors in town speak of the loose coalition of pirates and privateers that comprised the Brotherhood, though beyond targeting Spanish or other enemy ships, it was not clear to her if they had some other purpose. He laughed again. "Or Sisterhood, if you prefer in your case, though I wouldn't put it that way to the others."

A multitude of new possibilities began to assault her mind all at once, but she ignored them for the time being because she wasn't sure quite what she was hearing. "Are you…*inviting* me to be part of your crew?" she asked uncertainly.

"I believe I am," he replied. "I realize that must come as a surprise, but after what I've seen of you and what you have told me, I'd be a fool not to ask."

"But…why would you want *me* on your ship?" Coya was confused. She didn't picture herself to be particularly skilled, and certainly she didn't fit the picture of a swaggering sailor. She said as much to Roy, but even as she did so, she realized it had never occurred to her to gauge her own abilities and judge them.

Roy's laugh, while a bit incredulous, was somehow reassuring. "Coya, if you had the fortune, good or ill, to have been born an Englishman, you would have all the makings of a first-class military scout. You can see better in the dark than anyone I've heard tell of, your skills in the wild are formidable, you are cunning, clever, and much more dangerous than you appear. Since you were born as you are, I have the fortune to be in a position to extend this offer to you and possibly profit by it myself. However, I should admit," he added, "that we are privateers and not truly the outlaws that many of the Brethren of the Coast are, though that makes little difference to the Spanish."

In her culture, warriors had been judged by the others in their village. But she had been alone for many years, would not have been a warrior in her own society in any case, and she had never thought about things enough to have much of an opinion of herself beyond her ability to survive. Now, while she was often confused by the complicated use of verbal subtlety these Europeans frequently used in their dealings, Roy's appraisal of her abilities felt that much more important for being so direct and unambiguous. For the first time, Coya began to ponder all of her encounters, escapes, successes and feats with an eye for how likely it was that anyone else she had met could have survived them. She quickly realized it was not likely at all.

But she still had difficulty thinking of herself as anything but an outsider, and doubt and panic sought for mastery over the flood of new possibilities. "But…you are warriors," she said. "You are warriors and sailors. What use would I be on the deck of a ship, or in a battle?"

"Well," Roy began, "for a start, you would be a real asset on the deck of a ship at night when it is difficult for others to see approaching ships or storms or other dangers. As for battle or seamanship, obviously I'd have to see what skills you had or could be trained in, but you seem handy enough with knives and to be of some use with that sling of yours. But keep in mind, Coya, that regardless of what stories you've heard or what sailors like to boast about, most of the profit that the Brethren of the Coast makes comes from stealth, surprise and cunning, and most of it is gotten *on land,* though so far I appear to buck this trend. Those things often don't make for dramatic stories, but that's how we live, for the most part. And in that capacity, you've already shown yourself to be at least as capable as any member of my crew. Or myself, for that matter," he added.

"But you fight better than anyone I have ever seen!" Coya was genuinely surprised at his admission. Indeed, in her own culture, now long dead, such an admission on his part might have been seen as a statement of subservience. As much as she knew things to be different in this society, she felt a reflexive urge—almost a *need*—to protest.

Stunned as he looked by the spontaneity and sincerity of the compliment, Roy shook his head. "That may be so," he said, "but if you and I were hunting each other, either in the wilderness or in city streets, I would be afraid for my life."

Coya smiled. Her doubts were fading, and even if they parted ways now, she was very grateful to this strange Englishman for making her think of herself in a new light. But there was one harsh reality still nagging at her. "All right, I accept what you say, and I thank you for it, but even if you accept me into your crew, the others will not accept me. I am a woman, whatever you may think of my abilities, and many of your crew will never see beyond that, no matter what I do." She frowned slightly and sighed. This she knew to be true. English or Spaniard, native or slave, all dealt with her as "only a woman." That, apparently, was something that all peoples had in common. Only her solitude and self-reliance had even taught *her* any differently.

But Roy only laughed. "At present, 'many' is not a term that applies to my crew. Right now it's just me, Ajuban, Brian and Martin. Any crew that sign on with me have to agree to my rules, and if you join my crew, that means they would either have to accept your presence or leave my crew. As long as you earn your keep—which I have no worries about—then you have a place here."

"But what about the three others you mentioned?" Coya protested. "Ajuban was very pleasant to me, but maybe that would change if I became part of the crew."

"Well, Brian is a remarkably even-tempered man, and is very much of my own mind in matters such as this. He favors whatever gets the job done. Martin's opinion won't count for more than any other crew really, and as for Ajuban," and here Roy smiled at her, "perhaps you didn't catch the hint, but he implied that you would make a valuable member of the crew before I even had a chance to suggest it to you."

Coya was dumbfounded. She had not caught the implication, but she was feeling nearly overwhelmed at how much kindness was being directed at her in one day. She glanced toward the hold where Ajuban slept.

But Roy was not finished. "Those who wish to become new members of my crew will have to be here at this dock in five hours' time in order for us to sail with the tide. All of them will have to answer a few questions and I do like to test a few of their skills as well. It's more than most captains do, but I'm very picky about my crew. I'd like it if you were here, but if you still have any reservations, consider this: up to now, you have used your skills and talents simply to stay alive, and it has left marks on your flesh and spirit. If you come with us, you can use the same talents not only to survive, but to *prosper*—and you will no longer have to do it alone."

She looked in his eyes, and saw that he truly understood her situation. Indeed, she had never even thought about it so eloquently or clearly herself, and she began to feel an underlying sadness creep up through the gratitude and warmth she had been feeling throughout the conversation. She simply had not realized how wretched an existence she had been leading for so many years, and her emotions fought to unman her wits as she struggled to retain her composure. "I…have to think about it a little longer," she said. She turned her head towards where Brian slept so that the captain could not see her eyes. "You should wake him and get some rest soon," she said, her voice a bit more even, "you've had a difficult night."

"I will." Roy rose from where he sat and turned to look at Brian as well.

"I'd like to introduce you, if you're willing. You are welcome to sleep here on the ship for the night if you think it would be safer, but if you do decide to come with us, you should gather any belongings of yours first from wherever you normally sleep."

Coya only nodded. "Thank you," she said, turning back to Roy, "for your offer and your hospitality, captain. I will meet your navigator, and then I should go. I must sleep, and consider your offer. It is too much to take in all at once, I'm afraid."

He nodded, and she thought he would say more, but then he checked his speech as if resisting the temptation to continue trying to persuade her. She had enough to think about and not much time to consider it all, so she was grateful that he relented for the time being. Roy led her to where the navigator lay, his face shaded by his wide-brimmed hat, and gently shook him. "Wake up, you old deck-dweller," said Roy in Spanish. "It's your turn to watch, and I have someone to introduce to you."

Bleary eyed, but apparently alert, Brian adjusted his hat and looked up at the sky, just as Coya always did to assess the time upon waking. "Actually, it looks like it's well past when my watch should have started." He looked quizzically at the captain, taking in his open, bloody shirt and bandages, as well as the young dark-skinned woman at his shoulder. "I see you've seen better days. Is everything all right?"

Coya thought this man looked and sounded much more the part of captain than Roy did. In addition to his slightly tattered but well-groomed beard and mustache, there was an elegance of speech and manner that gave an air of authority more than Roy's graceful movement did. There was something else to it too. Perhaps it was the hat. "Everything is fine," Roy said, "just had a tussle with a couple of Spaniards. This young woman helped me out and patched me up." Brian raised his eyebrows. "Her name is Coya, and she apparently shares a measure of our distaste for Spaniards. Coya, this is Brian Thornton, my navigator who, in spite of endeavoring to dress more fashionably than his captain, rather spoils the effect by sleeping in his clothes on deck more than he ought to." Brian had a few creases imprinted on his arms from where they had been pressed against his shirt as he slept, and Roy inspected these in a comically frank manner as his introduction ran its course.

Brian cocked an eye at Roy with a grin, then swept off his hat and bowed low to Coya. "A pleasure, miss," he said. Lacking a dress to aid her in a curtsy (not that she was confident in her ability offer one), she bowed slightly and nodded. Yes, it was most definitely the hat.

"She is returning home at present, but she is to be allowed aboard at any time tonight if she desires. She may wish for a safe place to sleep after the commotion tonight."

Brian laughed and turned a conspiratory glance towards her. "Did this rascal get you in trouble?"

She grinned in spite of herself, and lowered her eyes. She was too emotionally wrung out to do much more.

"Ajuban is in the hold," Roy said, "Martin will be back in the morning. Hopefully some promising recruits will turn up before we sail." Coya felt the implication, but Roy said no more.

"Glad to hear it, sir. It would be a shame for a wound to be all there is to show for an evening on the town."

"Right, I'm off to sleep. Wake me at dawn or Judgment Day, whichever comes first." Roy turned to Coya and extended his hand. She shook it awkwardly. "Good night, Coya. And thank you. Sleep well, and return to our welcome."

"Thank you," she said. She nodded to both of them and stepped off onto the dock. She padded through town, keeping a casual eye open for guards or prowlers, but she could not see well. The streets were deserted and it was dark, but it was only unfamiliar tears that defeated her sight.

* * *

Coya lay in a small ditch next to the broken stump of a fallen tree. Lightning had felled it two weeks before, and no one lived close enough to bother clearing it up. With a little canvas and some branches, Coya had turned it into a crude, camouflaged shelter that she could use on calm, clear nights. There were other places she could sleep, for a fee, but it was a calm night and she needed to be alone and not cloud her mind further by dealing with any more people. She had slept in many places like this, but for the first time, it bothered her that she was so used to it.

She thought of everything that had happened, but doubt and fear still gnawed at her. As much as the strange Englishman had made sense, as much as he understood of her plight, she could not believe he knew what she could be risking. Here, there were places she could run to, places she could hide. She didn't have to rely on anyone for her survival, and she was responsible for no one else. What's more, she didn't think she could bear it if she were captured by Spaniards. She had risked much just to escape from them, but now she would have to fight them, help others against them, and depend on others to do so for her. She honestly did not know what to do. Maybe she could be more ambitious in her endeavors here on the island? Perhaps she could get ahead that way and find a permanent place to sleep? Possibilities jumbled together in her head as the minutes dragged on into what seemed like hours. She looked up at the moon and reflected upon what she had been taught as a child. The sun was as a father to her people, bringing life and prosperity, but the moon was mother. It brought reflection and understanding—and comfort. She had learned differently since then, but it occurred to her now that it was the only mother she had had for many years, and the only comfort she had known. As she lay there, the possibilities and fears eventually ran together and receded into uneasy sleep.

That night, Coya found herself running through thickets of trees, armored soldiers shouting behind. She could not see them when she turned, but she heard their angry voices cursing and threatening her in Spanish. All she could see were endless trees ahead, yet each time she turned, it seemed she had gone nowhere—the shore was just as close as before. Suddenly, as she turned again, the shore was still as close, but now there was a ship there. The cries were closer now, and she ran farther and faster, or so she thought, but still she found she had gotten nowhere. And then the cries ceased, and she found she had run deep into a jungle. She turned, but the same sight as before met her eyes. She continued on, feeling heavier and heavier, struggling now through bushes, now through mud. She fell to her knees to rest, but she continued to feel heavier and wearier. Turning again, she could see that the ship was still there, but the sails were unfurled now. She tried to stand, but she could not. Slowly, she realized that the jungle was growing over her. Vines, shrubs, trees, grasses and brambles, all were growing and growing as if years were passing—

and she felt sure that they were. She was hungry and thirsty and still she could not stand as the jungle silently crept over her, smothering her cries. She would even have welcomed sight of the soldiers now, but they were gone. She turned again and saw the ship, sailing, sailing as the leaves covered her face.

Coya awoke screaming, and seeing the twigs, branches and palm leaves next to her face, the very ones she had used to disguise her refuge, she tore at them and struck at them as she jumped to her feet. Immediately she realized where she was, and she stopped. She fell to her knees, but now she felt not heavier but lighter. She sat sobbing for a long time, but finally becoming calm again, she looked up at the clear sky, unshrouded by canopy. Mother Moon was still there, not far from where She had been. Coya nodded, and turned her gaze back to her ruined shelter and her scant belongings. She gathered her comb, her knives, her blowpipe, and her few other possessions in her blanket and stood up, turning towards the shore. She started walking back to Roy's ship, immersed in her thoughts.

As she approached the ship, Brian greeted her from the deck. "I think, perhaps, it is safer for me here," she said to him as she came aboard. He nodded. She looked around the deck. "Where would be a good spot, do you think?"

* * *

Coya awoke shortly after dawn. The captain was moving about the deck of the ship, and Ajuban was helping some other man—Ajuban referred to him as Martin—move a large crate onto the ship from the dock. She had slept soundly, in spite of the rocking and creaking of the small ship, but the motion made her feel a little disoriented now. It would definitely take some getting used to. As she rose from her spot on deck, she looked about her. She had not seen this view of the town for some time and it looked lighter somehow, and peaceful. She became aware that Martin had noticed her, but he merely shrugged and continued his task. She became immediately self-conscious, and the doubts and fears began resurfacing, but she had made up her mind to stay if she could. She silenced the worries and wandered unsteadily over to Brian. "How long will it be before new recruits are supposed to turn up?" she asked him.

"They should start arriving any time now," he replied casually, "but I daresay the captain won't start signing them on for a good hour yet. Did you have a good nap?" he added.

"I slept well, but I am hungry. Do you think I have time to find some food before the recruiting?"

"I should say so," said Brian quizzically. "Why, do you want to see the new recruits? It's not a very interesting process, I'm afraid."

Roy has not told him. Coya felt even more uncomfortable now. "Well, I will…I was told to come here to sign on if I wished."

Brian's startled expression did nothing to soothe her doubts. "Oh, I see," he stammered. "Well, yes, you should have enough time if you don't go far." He was obviously trying to recover the awkward conversation, but he stopped and pondered for a moment. Thinking he was finished speaking, she was about to thank him and head into town when he spoke again. "How about this: I'll take you for a bite to eat at a tavern near here if you like." He smiled encouragingly at her, reading her discomfort. "Then you won't have to worry about missing anything, and you won't have to go out of your way to the market for people to deal fairly with you. I don't have any duties before we sail anyway, and I wouldn't mind a good meal," he added.

He seemed almost apologetic for his initial reaction, though Coya was only dimly grasping the undertones of the conversation. Most of her experience with reading people's intentions came from her survival instincts and her fear of being cheated out of money by others, but such instincts served her little when it came to pleasant interactions. More importantly, however, she realized that Brian was already accepting her as crew after only one brief moment of surprise. Roy knew his crew well. She accepted the navigator's offer graciously and he led her to the gangway.

Martin smirked knowingly as they passed, and Coya felt the heat rise to her cheeks, but Brian had noticed it too. "Wipe that smirk off of your face, man," he said in Spanish—probably for her benefit—but with no hostility. "It will only embarrass you later. Sir," he said, turning to Roy, "we are going to get some breakfast, if there is nothing else you need."

"Very well," Roy said over his shoulder as he helped to steady the crate that Ajuban and Martin were carrying. He tossed a small silver coin to Brian.

"Pick up something for Ajuban and me as well."

"Very good, sir." They stepped onto the docks and made their way into town.

Brian did not seem very talkative, but Coya was glad for it. She had done more talking the night before than she had done in quite a while and wasn't prepared to do much more of it so soon. She did, however, feel somewhat compelled to explain Roy's invitation, but as he seemed to have already accepted the captain's decision, he appeared to be more impressed than placated. "I look forward to being relieved of the duty of night watchman," he confided. "I enjoy the night, but I don't enjoy feeling half asleep every time we reach a port."

"I know how you feel," said Coya as she relaxed a little more. "I do most of my work at night by necessity, but we were not made to be night creatures. It wears on us before long."

"Well, I hope you will forgive my relief at pushing that duty off on you, but don't worry, you won't be stuck with it all the time, especially after a long day or two of scouting around on land for the captain. Besides, I daresay I'll get stuck as night helmsman most of the time anyway, unless we've got a steady course plotted. Ah, here we are." Brian gestured to a painted wooden sign swinging above an open door. She could not read the sign, but the business had been referred to as Asilo del Marinero when the island was under Spanish rule. He led her inside. They drew a couple of disconcerting looks from others, but Brian appeared either to not notice or not care. They sat down and Brian set a peso on the table with a loud *clack*. It certainly drew the right kind of attention. However the staff felt about Coya's presence in this establishment, a peso was enough to feed a table of at least six people here without any complaints about the nationality of the silver. Pesos (or "pieces of eight," as they were often called by the English) were almost standard currency in Port Royal due to the sheer number of privateers and pirates who operated there, and those who had lived there under Spanish rule were more used to Spanish currency anyway.

They had bread and butter, eggs, fish, bacon, tea and a small round cheese, and Brian ordered the same fare (along with an orange for Ajuban) to be put in a basket "to be ready when we leave." Such orders were common enough near the docks, though it meant the owner would get to keep less of that peso as actual profit. It seemed a feast to Coya, but Brian had advised her to make the most of the extravagance. "If you join the crew," he said, "you won't have anything good to eat for some days at least. We take advantage of these simple pleasures when we can."

There were numerous other patrons, and most appeared to be sailors taking a meal before the tide. Coya kept reminding herself that she was one of them, but it was difficult to feel that it was true before she was officially part of the crew. She felt out of place, not least because they were the only patrons speaking Spanish to each other, but Brian put her at ease with his stories and bits of advice about life at sea. Most of it failed to stick in her mind simply because the life was so alien to her. At one point when talking to Brian about her only experience aboard a ship, she told him, "I was impressed with the whole business of sailing such a large thing over the sea with skill, but I never knew there could be so many different names for bits of rope, canvas and wood." Yet despite his efforts to prepare her for the experience and responsibility, she learned more about him through his talk than she learned about seafaring. She began to suspect that Brian stayed on the ship when in port not only because he felt more in tune with it when he did so, but also because he felt out of place in towns—or more specifically, in ordinary society. While his gentlemanly presence did a great deal to reassure her and direct the attention of other patrons elsewhere when desired, she realized that he was just as interested in avoiding any extra attention to himself as he was in sparing her from disapproving glances.

But while he was disenchanted with society, he felt at home on the sea. His advice about living at sea seemed as much to remind himself of what he loved about it as to instruct her. The ship was equally his freedom and his livelihood, and when he fought, he fought to protect both—though she did gather that it usually was not his job to fight. "I stay with the ship nearly all the time," he said. "Granted, most of our successful ventures so far have taken place at sea, but it isn't often the chance arises to handle both the ship and a pistol at the same time. Last time, it was all I could do to hold on to the whipstaff."

"Why, what happened?" Coya asked curiously.

"We were caught in a bad storm," Brian answered, "and in the middle of it we came upon a Spanish ship that had also been caught in it."

"And you decided to fight?" she asked incredulously. Sailing at all in a storm was a bad idea if it could be avoided, and even she knew that the maneuvering involved in naval combat could be as good as suicide under such conditions.

"Not at first," he continued. "Our mast had been damaged by the storm, and of course our mainsail was furled. We couldn't maneuver. The Spaniards must have figured that we would be easy prey, even in a storm. Even with only their topsails out, the wind was carrying them straight towards us, and they probably figured they would put a couple of shots into our rudder and board us when the wind calmed a little. Anyway, the captain ordered a few guns to the aft of the ship, along with the swivel guns and some good marksmen. The Spaniards couldn't see what we were doing because of the storm, but we could barely see them either. The captain had us load the guns with grape shot and chain shot packed with a double load of powder in oiled canvases to keep it dry. Given the distance and the fact that we were firing into the wind, it was the only way for the shot to reach their ship with any effect. The wind probably slowed it down somewhat, but the captain wanted to cover a wider area in case our aim was amiss." Brian shook his head. "I'm sure the captain dressed the tale up quite a bit while he was recruiting last night, but really we figured it was our only chance of escape short of a very bloody fight. Plunder wasn't even on our minds. I was afraid that our guns would explode with all that powder in them, but I held the rudder as firm as I could and we fired and hoped. We were very fortunate. The noise was terrible, but the guns held together and I saw their mainmast go down. At that point, I recommended that we run out the oars and head north, at an angle to the wind.

"Spanish merchant ships," Brian explained, "and especially galleons, often run heavily armed, and so are designed to keep the weight of the ship and all of its cannons close to the center line of the ship to keep it from capsizing. However, that tends to give the hull an even more rounded shape"—he cupped his hands upward and inward for illustration—"making them prone to rolling back and forth too much."

Coya groaned. "So I remember. I was stuck in the hold of one for days, and I was almost grateful that I had little to eat."

Brian grinned. "Well, in this case it helped us out," he said. "If they took their few remaining sails down, the wind wouldn't continue to blow their ship west and away from us, but their ship would roll uncontrollably in the storm. If they left them up, they would continue to drift speedily by. Large ships aren't very good at fighting against the wind, but small ships like ours do well under such conditions, at least with sails out. Anyway, they decided to keep their topsails out and pass on by. We didn't even hear any answering shots, which surprised us as the time, though we were using long oars in the storm and our men were rowing their arms off to get away. It certainly wasn't easy to keep the ship heading north in that wind.

"However, once the storm had subsided, the captain was curious to find out what had become of the ship, and we needed to head back south anyway to get out of the Windward Passage. I had lashed together some temporary repairs for the mast, so we cautiously made our way south after daybreak. We found the ship, but it appeared to be abandoned and sinking. As it turned out, our volley had done more damage than we had originally thought. In addition to the mainmast, the bowsprit was torn to pieces, probably along with whoever had been manning the guns right behind it, and some of the grape shot had blown clean through the hull in a number of places. It must have been the extra gunpowder that did it, because normally grape shot doesn't do that much damage to a ship's hull and the chain shot was aimed at the mast. Yet in this case, the hull damage was enough to start the ship sinking. I guess they couldn't repair the damage for some reason because we found that all of the cockboats were gone along with the crew. They probably took some of the more valuable or portable cargo with them, of course, but it wouldn't have been possible for them to take all of it on cockboats. There was plenty left for us to salvage before the ship sank."

Coya had been listening intently, though she couldn't grasp the mechanics of it all. However, the tale intrigued her greatly, the more so because it was of something completely outside of her experience. Brian merely shrugged it off as good fortune. Coya shook her head. "It takes talent and skill to turn a bad situation into good fortune."

Brian conceded the point with a nod. "The captain certainly has a knack for that," he said, looking at her thoughtfully. "I imagine that recruiting you as a result of his mishap last night will serve as another such example." Coya did not know how to respond to that. Brian seemed equally casual with his compliments and his disdain, as if both were merely observations about a society peripheral to him. But he continued, "Speaking of which, we should probably get back to the ship."

They finished their tea and rose to go, leaving the peso on the table. The owner snatched it up before they were halfway across the floor. A serving woman handed Brian a large basket with the provender he had requested. He thanked her and motioned to Coya to follow him out. As they passed back out into the street, Coya had a brief but sharp pang of gratitude. It was the first time anyone had ever paid for her to eat. She was surprised how much emotion she felt at the realization. "Thank you for breakfast," she managed to say matter-of-factly.

"Hmm? Oh. You're welcome."

He's so oblivious. But Coya was glad for his casual reaction amid so many new and overwhelming experiences.

They made their way back to the docks as the streets became increasingly busy. There was already a fair crowd of sailors loading goods and provisions aboard ships, as well as men unloading goods from a couple of new arrivals in the harbor. Roy's ship had a small and varied gathering near it, and Roy appeared to be standing next to a small portable table with Ajuban at his side. Coya surveyed the men, noting that no two of them seemed to share more characteristics with each other beyond unshaven stubble or the signs of uninhibited drinking the previous night. She pointed to one man and said, "That one is a warrior. The captain will surely take that one."

Brian looked as she pointed to a large, dark-haired man. He was tall, but not exceptionally so, though he was broad and obviously well muscled. But the same could be said for any number of laborers in town. "What makes you think he is a warrior?" he asked curiously.

"He moves well and stands like a predator."

Brian took a second look, but he obviously had not the eye for such things. He ventured to say to her that the man had good posture and a confident look about him, but that was all he could tell. He shrugged. "Well, as long as he can shoot straight and hoist a sail."

Coya frowned. "I'm not experienced with either," she said. "Will that be a problem, do you think?" She was worried, though perhaps without cause. Roy had not asked about such skills, but she had made her way of life clear to him when they had talked.

"Don't worry, the captain wouldn't have asked you here and risked offending other potential crewmembers if he didn't feel it was worth it." He smiled slightly. "I have to get back aboard and prepare for departure. You should join the line if you want to be recruited. Just do what the captain says and everything should be fine. Good luck." He waved and made his way past the recruits to the ship.

Fighting down a sudden attack of nerves, she made her way slowly to the back of the line of recruits. She was trying to be unobtrusive and no one heeded her for some time. She wondered how the captain decided who would be recruited and who would not. He appeared to have some weapons by the little table. Some were made of wood, but others were not. She hoped she would not have to fight anyone with those in order to be allowed aboard. She certainly didn't want to fight the strong warrior. Or Roy. She also noted a number of pistols on the little table. She had used a pistol a few times before, but only for hunting small game. The weapon was ill-suited to hunting, as it tended to scare off any animals in the area when it was fired. She had found it to be much more useful as a trade item than a tool, but she did not live as a warrior. Sailors certainly had good reason to carry them, and she remembered how effective they had been in the hands of the Spaniards who had attacked her village. Many of the sailors around her carried them, including Roy. She noticed with some surprise, however, that while Ajuban had one tucked into his belt, he also carried a crossbow on his back. It was an odd weapon for a sailor, but it seemed to suit him. Ajuban appeared to be doing nothing more than looming impressively next to the captain. Coya heard a few people passing by mutter something uncomplimentary about such a choice for a first mate, but no one in line seemed to mind. *These people probably all met him last night.* She didn't know why the thought hadn't occurred sooner, but she suddenly realized that she had seen a number of these people enter the same tavern last night as she waited in the street.

Her looking from face to face apparently caught the attention of the man in front of her, because he turned towards her in surprise. He immediately realized that she was waiting in line and laughed. He said something in English and laughed again. While she realized he had probably made some sort of joke at her expense, a new concern dawned on her. She wondered if any of these new recruits spoke Spanish at all. She was sure that no one within a thousand miles spoke her own language. She frowned, but Roy appeared to be setting up a mock duel and everyone was turning to watch. The man in front of her shrugged and did the same.

Roy himself squared off against the dark-haired warrior, but the fencing swords they held had corks and pads on the ends. It was still dangerous, as a good thrust could shove the point through the corks and into flesh, and the captain was still wounded, but Coya soon found that there was no need to worry. The warrior was nearly as fast as he was strong, but he obviously had not trained with such a weapon before. Roy, in spite of his wound, moved like a dancer. She watched in fascination. This was the first time she had seen anyone actually fencing, though she often saw people carrying such swords and had heard how they were used, in spite of her initial assumption that the thin blade would snap as soon as it hit anything. Once she realized that this was not so, the idea made much sense to Coya. Such a weapon made it unnecessary for a warrior to be strong, and it made fast opponents much deadlier. But that had been her reaction to the *idea* of it. Her first actual sight of it left her with only one thought: it was beautiful. It seemed odd to her how such a beautiful dance could end in death at any moment. She longed to see what it would look like if the large warrior were as well-trained as Roy, and if they did not have corks on their weapons—they made the weapons look clumsier. She had no desire to see anyone hurt, but the gracefulness of their movement was breathtaking.

Martin had been carrying a couple racks of small cannon shot aboard, but he stopped to watch the duel along with a growing crowd of others who had noticed the impressive spectacle. Coya noted that the warrior was good at dodging Roy's thrusts (though Roy was obviously holding back). He ducked and bobbed his head back and sideways continuously in a way that reminded her of a chicken, but this was obviously part of some form of fighting he *was* familiar with. His footwork was also very good, and his slashes were well-aimed, but Roy could deflect anything with the flick of a wrist—no, a flick of his *fingers*. She became aware that his wrists were barely moving. *I wonder if I might learn how to do that.* But she remembered the man who had laughed at her only moments before.

Roy ended the mock duel with an approving nod, and began speaking to the warrior in English. He gestured to a row of naval pistols and then out towards an empty dock next to the one Roy's ship was berthed at. Coya followed his gesture and realized that a row of empty bottles had been arranged on a rail, with two more set up on the narrow posts at either end of the rail. The warrior picked up a pistol and made his way through as the crowd parted for him. He aimed and fired, but no bottles broke. Coya was surprised that someone had the nerve to chuckle. The warrior looked surprised as well. He turned an irritated stare at the offender who abruptly ceased his mirth. The warrior turned and, walking back to Martin (who appeared to jump slightly at the attention), plucked one of the small cannonballs from his load. He made his way back through the crowd and threw the shot with great force out towards the bottles—more specifically, towards one of the posts. The ball struck it, and the post snapped and fell into the water along with the bottle atop it and several others from the attached rail. He turned back to glare at the man who had chuckled, and walked back to the captain. Whether or not he had aimed at the bottles, it was an impressive display. Coya grinned, though she had little reason to feel proud. Perhaps she was proud that her judgment had been correct: the captain would be a fool not to sign him aboard. The captain appeared to agree with that sentiment, and the warrior was signed on.

There were several more such tests as the others in line took their turn, though Roy did not seem interested in testing everyone. Of those that did run through the exercises, most had to spar with Ajuban. The good-humored first mate appeared to be quite competent himself, and Coya continued to angle for a better view. Her height was against her, and the line had become more of a semi-circle as they all shifted to watch the displays. At one point, the man ahead of her turned to her again as she poked her head around him to see. He seemed angrier this time and was making dismissive gestures, but she could understand little of what he said.

She was considering what to do when Roy himself intervened. He came striding down the line and pointed to both of them, gesturing for them to follow him. Coya obediently followed. The other man looked confused as Roy picked up two wooden practice weapons from the table. One was the length of a knife, and the other was sword length, though both had rounded edges and flat tips. Roy proceeded to dip both tips in the inkbottle on the table and then blot them with a rag until they were almost dry. Coya noticed that the ink stains on the rag were red. Roy handed the sword to the man and said something to him in English. But he handed the knife to Coya and said in Spanish, "Mark him when I give the signal to fight." She nodded. The crowd was already laughing, thinking that he had obviously and deliberately given the advantage to the man as a way of teaching her a lesson, but Coya knew better. She seemed to be the only one who noticed that Roy and Ajuban were not smiling with the crowd. She was surprised to feel a little nervous. Even though no one would likely get hurt, a lot depended on this fight and she was not used to such direct confrontations. But she had practiced her skill often, and she let her instincts flow through her. Roy had them stand five paces apart. She set her feet and stood ready, as did her opponent. He didn't seem nervous at all, but that simply made her more confident. Roy raised his sword in the air, and then swept it down signaling them to begin. Coya took one step and threw the knife, knowing full well that if she missed, she would be unarmed. But surprised, her opponent failed to move in time, and the knife struck him square in the chest leaving a small red mark on his white tunic.

No one had expected this except perhaps Roy and Ajuban. Some people immediately began laughing while others jostled to see if he was marked or if he had been struck by the handle. Others appeared to have been in the process of handing money to other onlookers, betting on who would win, but the money had not even left their hands before the fight was over. As soon as everyone realized what had happened, they all began laughing except for those few who had already placed bets beforehand and lost. As for her opponent, he looked a little bit angry, very embarrassed and not at all amused, but he did lower his weapon and concede gracefully. Coya felt some sympathy for the man. After all, he had seen what they all had: a small Indian woman who had warranted no serious consideration. Now they all ridiculed him for thinking just as they had. But that was how people behaved. Even her own people had done so.

She became aware that several of the onlookers were shouting things at her and laughing, but she sensed that they were laughing at her opponent. "Very well done," Roy congratulated her in Spanish, speaking loudly enough so that most could hear that he wasn't speaking English. Most of the onlookers seemed confused, and a few seemed indignant. He ignored them and asked her if she had ever used a pistol before. When she indicated that she had used one a few times, he asked her to try to hit one of the bottles. She picked up a pistol and nervously walked past the now silently staring crowd. She had never shot at anything so far away, and did not think she would hit one, but she aimed, held her breath and fired. No bottles broke, but she did see some wood splinter. That was good enough for her. Apparently it was good enough for the crowd as well, since no one shouted or laughed. There was some muttering, and some of it sounded approving, but it was dawning on most of them that the captain was seriously considering signing a woman aboard as part of the crew. Worse, she was being tested for the same skills that they were. Many people shook their heads and muttered to each other. Many of those who had already signed aboard looked concerned. She abruptly realized that since they had already signed aboard, they could not decide to back out of their agreement if she joined the crew unless the captain permitted them to. *I hope they won't be angry with me for it.*

But in spite of these misgivings and the general feeling of disapproval, she was allowed to sign aboard. She marked an *X* on the paper, even as several people stepped out of line and walked away, but she did not feel any remorse or foreboding. She was confident that the captain would deal with any problems that came of allowing her to sign aboard, and she almost pitied any crew that would decide to mutiny against him and Ajuban. As she thought this, it occurred to her to look for the large warrior who had dueled with Roy. She wanted to know his reaction. It mattered more to her, somehow. She had been proud of his success in combat, and in some strange way she wanted some measure of similar recognition. But his reaction held neither a hint of what he thought of her success nor of any prejudice or disdain. He looked...*pained*. She could not find any other word for it. He did not seem annoyed, angry, insulted, or even lustful—just pained, somehow.

A smaller man at his shoulder said something to him and clapped him on the shoulder. Coya was surprised when the smaller man then walked directly over to her and introduced himself in Spanish. "Greetings miss," he said as he extended his hand. She proffered hers and, to her surprise, he bowed and kissed it. "I'm William Ward of Devonshire."

"My name is Coya," she replied awkwardly. "Are you a nobleman?" He certainly was acting like one, except he was also treating her as if she were a noblewoman, and she felt more embarrassed by that than by any of the attention she had gotten from the crowd earlier. He was even wearing fine gloves, though he had removed one before taking her hand. Someone nearby laughed as he passed, though she was not sure if it was because of her question or William's behavior.

"No," he answered her, ignoring the passer-by, "but manners are not lost on all others." At least it meant he would not leer at her, whatever else he might do. "This is my friend Albert McGuinn." He gestured to the warrior who had now followed him over to her.

"How d'you do, miss?" said Albert in broken Spanish, bowing a little bit with nervous and downcast eyes. She sensed immediately that while Albert was a confident warrior, he was very uncomfortable in social situations. She thought she understood his pained reaction a little bit more. Such things had been virtually unknown in her society. Warriors were proud and dominant in all situations. They might know their limits well enough, but any warrior who displayed such meek behavior was simply not tolerated or respected. Her time among Europeans showed her that such behavior was often accepted among them, and was even considered a virtue. She had learned to adapt, but for anyone to display such nervousness or deference in regard to *her* was a new experience.

"You fight well," she said. "I knew you would be signed aboard. I had said that the captain would be a fool not to take you, and he is not a fool." Was the man actually *blushing?*

"You told the captain that?" asked William incredulously. Albert looked mortified.

"No, I told Brian—that's the navigator—before he went back aboard."

"Oh…when was that?" William looked confused.

"When the captain was setting up at the table."

Albert must not have been following since William had to translate for him, but then he seemed surprised and asked, "How did you know before you saw me fight?"

William laughed. "It sort of shows in the dark, you know." Albert looked confused and Coya looked at the cloudless sky curiously. "Just an expression," William added. "Come on, I think the captain is just about done recruiting." He said something to Albert and motioned for them to follow him up to the table with the other new recruits. The number of new crew was much smaller than the line had been. Apparently a couple of men had asked to be dismissed once Coya signed on, and the captain had granted their request. He was explaining things to some of the crew—now with Brian nearby, translating to Spanish and French for her and a Frenchman who had signed on—when she, Albert and William approached. He apparently refused to justify his decision, but he explained what some specialized duties would be for certain individuals. For her, this included night watch duties, scouting on land, and any hunting or tracking that would be necessary. She also learned that William was to be considered the ship's cook for rare occasions when cooking was possible. The single masted ship did not have much in the way for cooking facilities, and most sailors' rations were in the form of biscuits, salted meats, and a limited supply of fruit, none of which would benefit from cooking. Coya shrugged. He hadn't proven to be more than an average combatant when he was put to it, and Coya felt sure that *she* could arm-wrestle him. He seemed out of place, but the captain no doubt had some reason to sign him on. William was also her backup for night watch duties, which would doubly relieve Brian. Martin and Albert were in charge of the cannons, as well as being the obvious choices for duties of the "fetch and carry" variety.

In addition to mentioning these duties, the captain also made it clear that he expected his crew to adhere to rules of conduct spelled out in their contract. These included a number of rules (and punishments for their infractions) that were apparently fairly common among the Brethren of the Coast, addressing such things as respecting property of the ship and crew, following orders, terms of compensation, drunkenness on duty and general shipboard conduct and tasks. However, Roy added a few of his own rules in addition to these, owing (he said) to the fact that privateers were not outlaws like many of the Brethren, and privateer captains expected them to behave accordingly. No slaves were to be bought, sold, degraded or held captive without good reason, no crewmember should mistreat or degrade a female in any way, and surrendering opponents should be given full quarter unless otherwise specified by the captain. "In particular, I wish to emphasize the issue of the treatment of women," said Roy. "In addition to any other women we may encounter, we have a female crew member. She is here under my protection, and any crewmember who mistreats her will be deemed a mutineer and shall be treated accordingly." Roy's earlier descriptions of such treatment had not been pleasant.

Coya felt a curious mixture of relief, embarrassment, fear and delight upon hearing this pronouncement. She had never been singled out so pointedly, and while she was hopeful that it would prevent any incidents between her and the crew, to have someone in a position of great authority in her life taking such overtly protective measures on her behalf was nearly as disconcerting as William's etiquette. *Hopefully it will not breed any resentment.* She turned to see if Albert still had that pained look on his face, and also to avoid the gaze of the crew. But Albert appeared to be doing his best to loom over her and stare challengingly back at the crew. She simply could not figure him out, but she supposed she would have plenty of time to try.

Roy ended his speech about shipboard responsibilities and smiled at the small group. "We are a small crew," he said, "but I feel confident that this is one of the most skilled and clever crews in the Caribbean." Coya counted fourteen of them, including the captain and his original crew. Even by her own limited knowledge of privateering she knew without being told that it was a small crew. "Besides," Roy continued with a wink, "a smaller crew means bigger shares." They laughed as the captain led them aboard, though Coya still didn't understand the details of payment. Nevertheless, she trotted onto the deck unconcerned and strangely light of heart. She had only been aboard a ship once before, and that was as a stowaway. However small the crew was, they were the biggest group that Coya had been an equal part of since her home was invaded. For the moment, it troubled her little that she still had not met most of them and could not speak their language.

Once all were aboard and everyone's belongings had been stowed below, the captain gave some orders, and men promptly leapt into action to hoist anchor and set the mainsail, leaving Coya to find a place on deck where she wasn't in anyone's way. It didn't take long to get the small ship underway and headed due east. When everyone was relatively still again, the captain summoned the crew amidships and began speaking. Coya looked questioningly over at William who was next to her, and he whispered a translation back to her, "He says we are headed for the south coast of the island of Hispaniola and that an unusual number of Spanish ships have been in that area lately."

"How does he know?" Coya was curious rather than disbelieving.

"I have no idea," William replied as the captain continued speaking. "I expect he hears rumors, but that's just a guess. This life is nearly as new to me as it is to you." Coya was surprised by the revelation. She had not considered the possibility that others on board had about as little experience with these matters as she did. Again she wondered why Roy had hired this man. William was certainly intelligent and he had seemed to know what he was doing with the variety of ropes involved in getting the ship moving, but beyond that he had no obvious talents she could discern so far. "The captain also says that those who do not already speak English will need to learn the basics of the language," William continued, "and that it will be their responsibility to learn from those aboard who can help them. Training in other skills, he says, will follow as time allows."

Roy dismissed the crew one by one so they could attend to their duties, then turned to her and William, addressing them again in Spanish. "Coya, you should stick with William for now and learn what you need to learn. William, teach her all the English you can, and when you help her learn her way around the ship, teach her that in English too." He smiled briefly at Coya and clapped her on the shoulder. "Welcome aboard *The Constance*," he said.

Chapter 3: Player's Gauntlet

As Coya was shaken awake, she heard the sounds of hurried activity on deck. Justin, the crewman she had dueled on the docks, waited for her eyes to focus before pointing to the powder magazine. "Carry," he said in English, gesturing up towards the deck. She nodded and hopped out of her hammock, headed for the magazine. She had not had time to feel daunted by the prospect of being solely responsible for learning English before Roy had (thankfully) ordered William to help her. He was a good teacher and understood the difficulties of the English language. He was also able to capitalize on the fact that she had picked up bits and pieces of the language since the English had come to Jamaica, though he and some of the others had laughed with her as they attempted to explain the difference between *port guns* and *gun ports*.

Justin began grabbing shot and slow match to hand to Albert who was waiting at the hatch, and as Coya handed the powder kegs up, she asked, "Ship?" Albert nodded. "Nation?" she asked. She had learned mainly words that related to seamanship and battle so far.

"No flag," said Albert. Apparently Roy wasn't taking any chances and was preparing for a fight.

When she had finished, Justin said, "Up and wait," motioning her up the ladder. He would be remaining in the hold with his carpenter's gear to conduct any necessary battle repairs and she would remain above, ready to shuffle goods between the hold and the deck.

"Did you sleep well?" asked Roy in Spanish as Coya clambered onto the deck blinking in the sunlight.

"Yes. What is our situation?"

"Large sloop," he said without taking his eyes from his glass, "nearly as maneuverable as us, but riding low in the water without her colors flying. She's trying to lure us onto some reefs, but the shallows just even the odds."

"What odds?" she wasn't sure she liked the sound of that.

"They outgun us," he said.

"I'll wager she's Spanish, Ajuban," called Brian from the whipstaff. "What do you say?"

"A peso says she's not," Ajuban called back.

"I'll take that bet too," Roy said to Ajuban.

"I'll wager the captain *decides* she's French," William said to one of the other crewmen nearby as others began to place small bets with each other to cure the boredom of waiting. Everyone was at their post now, the guns were loaded, and they had but to wait.

Coya contented herself with observing how the men managed to sail the ship and how they responded to the captain's occasional orders. Her people had used boats, of course, but only simpler paddle boats. Push one direction; the boat goes the other. Simple. Her first sight of sailboats and ships had left her feeling puzzled that her own people had not used them since the principle of sails immediately struck her as being obviously useful. However, it was long before she realized that ships used the wind in ways she could not fathom. A skilled crew could use a ship's sails to virtually steer *against* the very wind that filled them. With a system of ropes and rudders and sails, a crew could maneuver a ship in nearly any way they chose regardless of what the wind was doing. Indeed, several of the conversations Coya had overheard in Port Royal made it clear that battles often hinged on that ability to maneuver. Now that she was learning how it all worked, it seemed at once less magical and more miraculous. It struck her that seamanship was just as complicated, elegant, and deadly in its practicality as what she had seen of Roy's fencing at the docks.

After what seemed like an hour, Roy squinted and peered through his glass again. "What is it, captain?" asked Ajuban.

"She's run out her starboard guns, but she's also raised the French flag."

"Do you t'ink she's trying a bluff?" Ajuban asked.

"I think she's laying her cards on the table," Roy answered momentarily. He closed his telescope again. "There are a lot of French ships in these waters, though they usually sail more openly. She may be a smuggler or pirate, but it seems clear she's not looking for a fight."

"Could dey be Spanish?"

"It's possible they are duping us with that flag, but I think they wouldn't show their guns just yet if that were so—we're too far away. No, I think they're telling us they are French and are daring us to take issue with that."

"Salute?"

"Salute," confirmed Roy. "I'd rather not attack a French ship without need. These waters are dangerous enough."

Coya had no idea what that meant, in spite of Ajuban and Roy feeding her occasional translations about what was going on, but when Ajuban barked "Salute!" Martin bobbed their own flag—Roy's privateer flag, the usual union jack with a white crest in the center (which Roy had decorated with a skull and two outward-facing cannons)—down and then up again twice. The French flag on the other ship bobbed once in acknowledgement.

"Brian," shouted Roy, "let's give our French dainty some breathing room. Get us out of these shallows and we'll try our luck further out."

"Aye, sir," answered Brian from the whipstaff.

* * *

"What do you t'ink dat French ship was so afraid of, captain?" Ajuban asked Roy in a lower voice as Coya went to help the others return shot and arms to the hold.

"I don't know," Roy answered, feeling slightly troubled. Sometimes he felt he was troubled too much by these little misgivings, though Ajuban was much the same. "As far as I know, the French have decent relations with everyone in these waters. I had even considered flying French colors, but somehow I dislike doing that sort of thing unnecessarily. The French ought to be even safer here than the Spanish, even though these are Spanish waters. Besides, English pirates would think twice about attacking French ships anywhere near Tortuga." Tortuga was one of few places where English pirates could regularly recruit crewmen.

"Maybe dere's some trouble we don't know about yet, sir. Perhaps one of de captains has been preying on French ships lately."

"Maybe. I should think we'd have heard something by now if that were true though."

"Where are we to make for now, sir?" asked Ajuban, returning to practical concerns. "We'll soon get into bad waters wit' no-t'ing wort' looting if we keep going."

"Maybe south," Roy said casually. "There are quite as many warships near New Granada as there are here, but there are more small ships to prey on as well. We'll have to chance it if we don't find a cargo soon."

"Let's discuss it over some-t'ing to eat," said Ajuban. "All de suspense gave me an appetite."

"All right, I feel starved as well. Let's see what's in the biscuit barrel."

"Wit' luck, biscuits and no-t'ing else."

After fetching biscuits from the hold, Roy led the way to his quarters where they could have half a pint of ale with their hard tack and discuss their next move.

"Captain?" Ajuban said as he sat down.

"Yes?"

"I told you dat ship was not Spanish. You owe me a piece of eight."

"Bugger."

In the end, they did agree to turn their attention to the coast of New Granada, and steered south-southeast to put themselves between Dutch and Spanish waters along the route from Curaçao. However, the days spent on the open sea yielded no sight of sail and Roy noticed that the crew was beginning to get bored. Coya appeared to be in good spirits, spending a great deal of time talking with William and Albert, and of course Brian who often shared her night shift. She was picking up the language as quickly as could be expected, and appeared also to be a sure hand before the mast. She still had a bit of trouble fitting in with the rest of the crew, but that couldn't be helped. The other crewmembers seemed to be getting on rather well, despite the lull in activity. William clearly had a head for numbers as he had claimed in Port Royal, and Brian was teaching him some of the basics of navigation, while Roy himself spent hours teaching Albert how to use a sword. Those more used to the life simply whiled the time away with dice and cards, as well as their regular duties, but they were spoiling for action and the food would soon begin to spoil as well (except for the biscuits).

However, as they sailed closer to Paraguaná, Roy began formulating a plan. When the lookout cried "Land ho!" late one afternoon, Roy took the precaution of flying a Spanish merchant flag.

"Ajuban!" he called, and the first mate approached. "Start teaching the crew some of the basic commands in Spanish. They should know them anyway for when we get into a fight, and they may as well learn them now." Understanding enemy commands could be the difference between death and survival in the heat of battle.

"Aye sir," said Ajuban.

"And find someone to rename our ship in Spanish," Roy said in a hushed voice.

"Sir?" It was a very unusual order.

"I have an idea, but I'm still thinking it over," replied Roy. "We may have to play at being Spaniards for a bit. I don't want to give details just yet though."

No sail was sighted that day, but the crew began reciting each of the commands they were instructed in Spanish as they worked, doing their best to mimic a proper accent. Roy instructed that emphasis should be put on those tasks necessary for being boarded and for making way, in case they were stopped by a Spanish warship, but the longer they went without sighting another ship, the more he began to favor his plan.

William had repainted the name *La Constanza*—apparently he was somewhat of a skilled artist as well—and he had even made it look a little dirty and worn so that it would be less obvious to observers that the name had been recently repainted. But he and Ajuban, as well as others among the crew, began to look askance at the captain as they practiced telling each other to weigh anchor or trim the sails in Spanish.

Finally Roy called Ajuban and Brian into his quarters for dinner, leaving William at the helm. "I've resolved that we will sail for the Maracaibo Lagoon," he began, as they waited on his explanation, "We may find a cargo before we reach it, and be able to beat a hasty retreat to Curaçao, but if not, we will sail straight into the lagoon posing as a Spanish merchantman." Brian simply nodded. Ajuban looked worried.

"But captain," he said, "you realize dat if dey find out who we really are, we will never get out of de straits past deir patrols."

"I know it's a gamble, but once we get into the lagoon, we can probably outgun or outmaneuver any other ships there, and there are always small cargo ships transporting goods from Gibraltar and the other towns at the south end to Maracaibo to circumvent the long overland route." Any ships sailing to or from the settlements on the lagoon would have to pass through the straits of Maracaibo, but they were all smaller or flat-bottomed craft that could navigate the shallow waters. The patrol ships that often guarded the approach were another matter.

"I agree that getting out again might be a problem," put in Brian, "but they almost never send patrols far into the lagoon. As long as we don't dawdle afterwards, we should be able to get out again before word reaches any of the warships."

"With luck," said Roy, "no one close enough will hear or see anything until we're long gone, but we'll have to stay closer to the middle or south end of the lagoon. The marsh lightnings at the south end should make navigation easy at night, and should make it much more difficult for other small ships to slip past us in the dark."

"On de oder hand," cut in Ajuban, "if we come away empty-handed, de patrol at Maracaibo will certainly want to know why a merchant ship dat arrived empty is also leaving empty. And Coya and I will have to pose as slaves."

Roy thought for a moment. "That will only be a problem if we are stopped both entering and leaving the lagoon," he said slowly. "Either way, I would rather see if I can hide Coya. Even as a slave, her presence aboard would seem unusual. And I don't want her to think we might sell her to the Spaniards," he added with a chuckle. "Well, what do you think? And how do you think the crew will take it?"

"It is certainly risky," Brian began, "but I think we can manage it without too much trouble as long as everyone is convincing and the Spaniards aren't already on their guard over anything."

"I agree," Ajuban commented, "but I'd rader not be trying dis wit' such a green crew. I t'ink dey will follow your lead dough, especially if Brian and I don't seem too nervous."

"May fortune be with us then," said Roy, raising his glass.

"Good fortune," they echoed, raising their own in a toast.

* * *

Coya climbed periodically down from the tiny crow's nest to stretch her legs and massage the calluses on her hands from clinging to the rigging all night. She had never imagined that such tedious tasks would be so taxing on the limbs, but she hoped it was only a matter of time before something worthwhile happened. As good as it was to belong with a group of people and have real conversations with them, she could only get so excited about hanging about in the rigging, performing menial tasks, learning English, and waiting.

But she enjoyed the night watches. As uncomfortable as it was up in the rigging, it was the only time where she could be both awake and alone if she wanted. Having been on her own for so long, she had not expected to grow weary of the company of others, but she had become accustomed to having time to think and listen and to be free of all responsibilities. Interaction with the crew wore at her sometimes. She supposed it made sense that a sudden change from a solitary life to being crammed into a small space with a dozen other people would have that effect, with or without the language difference. At night she was alone, except for Brian, with whom she spoke sometimes when she wished for company. Being up in the rigging alone with the sea provided her only relief from interaction, and the only thing she had to be wary of was her duty.

She glanced at the coast to the left, but the land appeared to be little more than a barren wasteland with wide beaches. *Still no sight of a sail.* "Brian?" she asked, "What do you know of that land?"

Brian, who had grown accustomed to her sudden questions and attempts at conversation, answered, "That is called Paraguaná," he said, "and it is almost an island, but at lowest tide it is connected to the mainland on the south by a long, narrow sand flat. On almost the opposite side of that large mass are the tidal straits between two great spurs of land that thrust towards each other on either side of the channel. It will take us some hours to round this island on the west. When morning comes, we will perhaps be close enough for you to see the channel."

Coya nodded, though she couldn't quite imagine what he meant by "sand flat." "Do ships ever come that way? Through the channel, I mean?"

"Only the smallest ships and longboats, and only at high tide. Smugglers sometimes use it in the dead of night, on their way eastward. There is a watchtower overlooking the channel on the other side, but by the time they can signal any warships to the area, the smugglers are usually long gone." He smiled.

Brian enjoyed this life, as she had noted before. When he was at the helm, he looked more like a captain than the captain did simply because he so obviously *belonged* with the sea. He also wore his ornate hat nearly all the time. As a matter of fact, strangers had mistaken him for the captain on several occasions, and Roy had even made use of it a couple of times, though Coya had heard only infrequent allusions to this. She had no doubt that Brian was living exactly the life he wanted to lead, though certainly he wouldn't mind being richer. In any case, he had been living this life for many years before he met Roy, and his knowledge of the sea was extensive. He seemed to know every reef, shoal, inlet and bay for a thousand miles, and he never got turned around on the open sea. Of course Coya had no basis for comparison, but if the captain and Ajuban were to be believed, Brian was about as skilled a navigator as anyone outside of the Royal Navy could ever hope for. He knew these waters even in the dark just from memory, which was precisely why he was generally on duty at night.

She remained silent for some time, staring out into the ocean and back to the coast. "I heard the others say that we were near a major trade route for the Spaniards," she said presently. "Are there ports further south from here?"

"Aye, more than half a day's journey south and west lies the town of Maracaibo, guarding the Maracaibo Lagoon. Ships are always coming and going there."

"Don't they have patrols?" Coya asked. It seemed only common sense.

"Aye," agreed Brian, "they have patrols most times, but we hope to get lucky before then. But if not, the captain has some ideas in his head." Again Brian smiled, but he would not tell what the captain intended, and Coya asked no more.

Slowly the land slid by, and Coya returned to the rigging from time to time, alone again with her thoughts, but she spotted no sails before light began to grow in the mist-enshrouded east. She could not see the channel that Brian had spoken of, but she was too tired to care as she made her way to the hold to wake Ajuban. "Your watch," she said as he stirred. "No sign of sail, though it is a hazy morning."

"All right," Ajuban muttered drowsily. "Get some sleep, we may run into a patrol before you wake, if no-t'ing else. I'll go wake de captain." He climbed up the ladder to the deck, as Coya curled up in the now empty hammock and fell fast asleep.

She awoke barely an hour later to the commotion of hurried feet and Ajuban gently shaking her. Brian was already shaking off sleep and climbing up to the deck. She tried unsuccessfully to mutter, "What is it?" in Spanish, but Ajuban needed no prompting.

"It's a Spanish war galleon. Dey are not yet headed dis way, but de captain wants de two of us out of sight anyway, so dey don't get too suspicious."

That thought had not occurred to Coya before. Now that she was openly part of a crew of privateers, she had not thought that she might have to hide her presence aboard for any reason, even when Roy had ordered that the Spanish colors be flown. Her presence aboard would at least arouse the curiosity of any patrols. It appeared that surviving by deception was not so much in her past as she had unconsciously believed, though she supposed that she had been signed on, in part, because she was adept at that very thing. *Oh well, at least I don't have to* do *anything. I'm so tired…*

"If dey decide to stop us," Ajuban continued, "You may need to find a place down here to hide."

I may *not have to do anything*, she amended to herself.

Ajuban crouched in the hold for what seemed an eternity to Coya as she lay anxiously in her hammock trying to stay both calm and alert, neither of which was very easy in her weary state. Eventually Roy came by the hatch and said without bending down, "She is heading west with the wind, away from us." Coya and Ajuban heaved a sigh of relief. "They shadowed us for a while, but the captain must have decided he wasn't curious enough to fight against this wind. Still, we had better make good time," he added, peering down at them slightly, "they will eventually head back to port, and we can't count on fighting any battles with them in the area if they can cut off our escape to the north."

"What now, captain?" asked Ajuban, squinting up through the hatch. "Shall we continue as planned?" Coya caught something in his bearing and glance as he said this. *They've already discussed this very situation.* Brian had said the captain had an idea, and no doubt Ajuban was wondering whether or not it would be used.

"Yes, as planned. Coya," the captain fixed his attention on her now, "I don't wish to keep you awake longer than you need to be, so I may as well tell you now: we are headed into the Maracaibo Lagoon, if we can manage it."

"Sir?" she replied quizzically.

"The waters leading into the lagoon are closely guarded. We will be pretending to be Spaniards so that we may enter, but this means you must hide when the time comes. Your presence here would draw attention."

Coya nodded confidently. "I will hide in an empty powder barrel," she said matter-of-factly. She had already given thought to it as soon as Ajuban had brought up the possibility. "What about Ajuban?" she said concernedly. He was rather larger than she was. Ajuban winked at her.

"Don't worry," said Roy smiling, "it is fairly common for strong slaves to be aboard cargo vessels, isn't it Ajuban?"

"Aye sir, I hear dat it be so…" He sounded amused.

"Nevertheless, you had better stay down there for another half hour or so until that galleon is out of telescope range. Catch a few winks or something."

"Aye, captain." Ajuban smiled and stretched out in the hammock opposite from Coya.

At first he said little so that Coya could sleep, but she instead plied him with questions about the plan he and the captain had made and the place they were going to. She and Ajuban were seldom on duty together, and he seemed to stay close to the captain most of the rest of the time, so Coya had not spoken with him at length since that first night when she had met Roy. At that time, Ajuban had been tired and mostly just listened to her tale. Now he was awake and quite talkative, and she found that he was the most pleasant company she had enjoyed since they set out from Port Royal a week before.

As he spoke a little of himself and his travels, he also explained Roy's remark to him earlier. "I used to be a slave aboard a merchant vessel. De Spaniards bought me from raiders for a bolt of silk, and dey brought me over from my own land when I was about t'irteen years old. I was sold to a plantation to help tend de groves and pick oranges. Never was I allowed to eat one of dem 'til dey were starting to rot, but I had to pick oranges every day and be careful not to bruise any or to snap de branches." His eyes, unfocused by the act of remembering, did not look unhappy. "Most of his slaves were boys because dey were less likely to hurt de branches at de top, and he did not have much more use for me when I got much bigger since he had many sons. So he sold me to a merchant captain for a good price. De captain he sold me to dough, he needed someone strong to lift and carry and help aboard his ship. Four years I worked for him before Captain Roy attacked de ship. He did not like dat I was a slave, so he set me free, even dough I had fought for my master. I asked to join him. He seemed like a good man." Ajuban grinned. "Never did t'ink I'd be an officer dough."

Coya began to see that when Ajuban signed on, he must have felt much as she had felt when Roy extended her the same offer. He had not been living off the wild all his life, and he could talk to other slaves, but he had not known real freedom and fair treatment since he was thirteen years old, until Roy had freed him. "How did the rest of the crew react when you signed on?" she asked curiously.

"Some did not like it," he shrugged. "One of dem tried to get me into trouble by stealing a pistol and saying I did it, but de captain believed me."

"What did he do to the man?" Coya asked. She remembered Roy's rules about stealing and acting against other crewmembers.

"He knew dat dese t'ings happen wit' such sudden changes, so he went easy on de man." Ajuban grinned. "He let me beat de man, and we dropped him off at de next port."

Eventually the Spanish vessel had moved far enough away that the captain called Ajuban back to his duties, and after a few more moments musing over her amiable conversation with him, Coya dropped off to sleep. It was early in the afternoon and nearly time for her to rise anyway when she was again awakened, this time by William. "It looks like you'll get your chance to play stowaway, miss," he said. They had reached the entrance to the Maracaibo Lagoon, and a Spanish warship—one of the flat-bottomed barques that was equally capable of patrolling in the shallower waters of the lagoon—was patrolling the surrounding waters.

Coya wasted no time in idle banter as she made her way to the powder magazine and the barrel she had earlier decided to hide in. She could already hear orders on deck being barked in Spanish. "They are close?" she asked William as she pulled the lid off her barrel.

"Yes, but the captain didn't see any reason to wake you until it was necessary. I am to help you with your little hiding place if necessary."

"I could use help with the lid," she replied as she climbed in and folded her legs up to her chest in the small space, "but otherwise I will need no assistance."

"So I see," he observed with some admiration. "You look like you've done this before."

"I have," she said.

He cocked an eyebrow and tossed her some colorful folded cloths. "The captain thought these should hide with you," he said. "I'm sure you won't mind the padding."

Coya quickly realized that the cloths were actually flags—probably every flag of non-Spanish origin aboard the ship. "Very wise," she said and motioned for him to replace the lid.

He waved cheerily and did so, before moving two other barrels back to their places in front of her and tying them all together.

Perhaps I will see a real battle soon. She shifted in the cramped darkness thinking that battle might involve Spanish soldiers rather than the merchant sailors she had expected to fight. *Good.*

* * *

As the Spanish soldiers finished boarding and stood at attention with their muskets, the captain looked over the crew briefly and turned his attention to

Roy, who also stood at attention. "At ease," he said in Spanish. Roy had thankfully taught his crew enough for them to know what that meant. "You were in the navy?" he asked Roy.

"Yes sir, three years behind the mast."

The captain nodded. "I am Captain Emilio Torres of the warship *El Sabueso*," he declared. The Spanish ship, *El Sabueso,* was idly sailing against the wind to keep it moving slowly without requiring time to raise the sails in the event of battle, so that whatever chance might befall, it could be steered in any direction for quick speed and maneuvering capability. Captain Torres was obviously no fool and was not taking his duties lightly.

"Captain Ricardo Francisco of *La Constanza,* at your service," said Roy and saluted.

Captain Torres returned the salute. "You are a trader?" he asked.

"Yes, making my way for Gibraltar."

"I see," said Torres. "What cargo do you carry?"

"None at the moment, sir."

Torres frowned slightly. "No cargo?"

"No sir," he said, "there were merchant ships from Spain in port, so we hoped to beat them here while goods are still to be had." Roy smiled a conspiratory smile.

"I assume you'd have no objection if I were to inspect your ship then?" Torres enquired, cocking an eyebrow expectantly.

"By all means, sir," Roy nodded. Every pistol and cannon aboard was loaded in case Torres should decide to impound his ship, though only a close inspection would reveal it. It was perhaps dangerous to risk the discovery, but Roy felt it was far less dangerous than being at the mercy of a Spanish warship.

Torres barked some orders at a couple of soldiers who went to search Roy's cabin. He wasn't worried about that—he'd concealed the few items that could point to his nationality, and his letter of marque was currently folded in a cloth inside Ajuban's breeches. But as he climbed down to the hold ahead of Captain Torres, Roy began to sense that this probing went beyond ordinary duties. Normally a captain would send his men to inspect the hold, and even then only when given some reason. Perhaps there was a problem with smuggling in the area. *This vigilance will make it harder to get out of the lagoon again with any loot.* Roy's heart sank.

Captain Torres looked carefully around the hold, but the shot, oars rope, and other goods were all laid out as they should be, so he made his way to the powder magazine. This was in a separate area behind a wet felt curtain and tied together as powder barrels should be, but the Spaniard approached the barrels and popped the lid off of one of them anyway. Fortunately it was one of those in front and he found only powder. Roy had little trouble putting on a look of indignation, but remained quiet. Torres kept glancing at him, probably for a reaction. He pried the lid off the next barrel with the same result. Roy made no outward reaction, but hoped very hard that the man did not reach for the next barrel. Coya could be explained as a stowaway if necessary, though Roy would have a hard time convincing Torres to let him handle the matter. However, the flags she was sitting on could not be so easily explained. Roy knew he was much faster at drawing a weapon than most people, but a fight in this situation would by no means be welcome, particularly by the magazine.

Fortunately Captain Torres was tiring of this little game and merely kicked the third barrel. Seeming satisfied that there was nothing liquid inside like rum or wine, he turned back to the decidedly honest Captain Ricardo Francisco. "Everything seems to be in order here, so I won't detain you any further, captain."

"Thank you sir," said Roy. "If I may ask, is there a problem in the area?"

"What port did you say you were from?" asked Torres, again with a note of suspicion that was not lost on Roy.

"Cumana."

Torres shrugged. "Governor Alfonso Diego of Maracaibo has recently offered amnesty to pirates and privateers in this area," he said matter-of-factly. "We're trying to make sure that we catch any pirates carrying goods before they sell the goods in Maracaibo and then pay the amnesty with their ill-gotten gains. And of course smuggling is always a problem, though we're more concerned about piracy at the moment. It is also our duty to escort to Maracaibo, without incident, any privateers who ask for the amnesty."

This sounded like an absurd level of precaution to Roy, particularly as

Maracaibo was quite well defended normally, and Roy began to wonder again about the tale of Spanish soldiers mustering for invasion, however sincere Captain Torres sounded. If they were mustering in Maracaibo, the added security would be quite sensible. "What area does this amnesty cover and what are the terms?" asked Roy. "As long as I'm trading in this area, it would be good to know the particulars."

"The amnesty requires that privateer captains sign an accord not to attack Spanish vessels within the area bounded by this coast and the fourteenth parallel, from the port of La Guaira to Santa Marta. In return, their ships will not be seized or attacked without cause, though may be searched for proper documentation of cargoes. Any captains who are known to have committed crimes against the crown must pay a portion of the damages they have caused before they can sign the amnesty."

"I see," said Roy. "That seems like a very large area for one amnesty to cover. It seems quite generous to the other governors in the area for Governor Diego to take pains to enact such a protection in their waters as well."

Torres chuckled and lowered his voice. "Between you and me, I think he just wants to secure his own trade routes from start to endpoint, but that's his affair if he can manage it. Either way, an amnesty is not a guarantee of safety. I should keep an eye out all the same, if I were you."

"Captain," said Roy, "with all this talk of piracy, I wondered if you might know the whereabouts of my brother, Lieutenant Pablo Francisco. He is a naval officer in the Caribbean. When last I heard from him, his ship was berthed in Santo Domingo on Hispaniola, but when I arrived there last, he had gone. I saw another large warship earlier this morning as we approached, and I wondered if he might be stationed here."

The captain had stopped and listened to this story with some interest, but said, "I do not know the name, and as he is a lieutenant I should certainly have heard it if he were on duty here. Why should talk of pirates make you think of him?"

"Well, you see," said Roy, "he is a widower. He and his wife were aboard a ship that was attacked by pirates and she was killed. It was a terrible tragedy, and I thought he might have asked to be involved in such an endeavor as these patrols if he is aware of them."

"I am sorry," answered Captain Torres, sounding sincere. "If he comes here, however, I will inform him of your inquiries and of our endeavors."

"Thank you, sir."

"Now," said Torres with a sigh of completion, "if there is nothing else, I will let you be on your way."

They climbed out into the sunlight again. Captain Torres gave orders to his soldiers and with a salute they were soon rowing back to their ship.

* * *

Though it was but a short time before Roy sent someone to let Coya out of her cramped quarters, he did not give the all clear until *El Sabueso* was out of telescope range, and he ordered that the same standards should be maintained as they passed within sight of Maracaibo, which should be at dusk if the wind held. Coya stood stretching her arms and legs as Ajuban came down to the hold. "Sounds like dat was a bit of a close call," he said.

"I know," she answered at length as she stretched, "I might have been able to pose as a stowaway if it hadn't been for these," she said holding up one of the flags for emphasis. "Thankfully it was not necessary. Next time we should hide them somewhere else."

"Hopefully dere won't be a next time," he said.

"From what I heard of the conversation with that Captain Torres, we may be searched on our way back out of the lagoon too. It would be wise to plan for it in any case."

At this, a worried look crossed Ajuban's face. "I don't know how we can get cargo out if dat be de case," he said. "And dat we can't plan for until we know what de cargo will be. If we find one," he added. "We might have to sneak past de patrols on our way out, or just outrun dem."

"Nevertheless, the disguise was well done. Clearly the captain put much thought into it...though I don't understand why he felt the need to make up that bit about his enquiring after his brother and that story about pirates."

Coya had expected this comment to puzzle Ajuban, but to her surprise he looked incredulous and a bit annoyed, groaning, "Oh no, tell me he didn't!" and Coya was the one who was suddenly puzzled.

"He has done this before?" she asked. "Does the story have some significance?"

Ajuban swept up the folded flags from one of the powder barrels and sat down on it with a sigh. "What was it dat you heard him say?" he asked. After Coya told him the story Roy had told, he said, "De story is almost entirely true, you might say." Coya looked surprised, but he continued, "Dere really is a Lieutenant Pablo Francisco in de Spanish navy, he is supposedly somewhere in de Caribbean, and his wife really was killed by pirates. But de lieutenant is not de captain's broder...he is de captain's broder-in-law."

Coya thought for a moment. Her Spanish was excellent, but there were some social and familial terms that she was only vaguely familiar with. Then it dawned on her, and she began to feel sad for Roy, for the first time. "You mean...she..."

"She was de captain's sister," he nodded sadly.

"So," she began uncertainly, "he means to find this lieutenant to, what, convey personal belongings? Find out more details?"

Ajuban looked embarrassed. "Ah. No. De captain wants to kill him."

"Why?" Coya asked incredulously. She carried no love for Spaniards, but what she had just heard seemed to go against all sense.

"He blames de man Francisco for his sister's deat'," he answered, half staring at the floor. "Some-t'ing about how he should have protected her or how he failed her. De captain is obsessed wit' it. In fact, I don't t'ink he would be in de Caribbean living dis life if he was not seeking dis man."

Ajuban was very serious now, and Coya found herself being surprised by the sharp contrast between the picture this story painted and Roy's usual friendly and cool manner. "Well, does he have any reason to think that? Some details about the tragedy?" She felt a need to make some sense of it if for no other reason than to eliminate the apparent dualism in her image of the captain.

"I do not t'ink so," shrugged Ajuban. "I don't ask him about it much, and he does not go out of his way to say more, but he does not seem to care who knows, or I would not be telling you any of dis. I t'ink he was very close to his sister. You probably did not know dat her name was Constance?" Ajuban gazed at her meaningfully.

"The ship?"

"Aye."

Coya sat silently thinking for a moment, and Ajuban was busy with his own thoughts, but presently she said slowly, "I have seen people who have lost loved ones become hysterical and violent towards the wrong people, but Roy does not seem like a violent man." She did not think that anyone that graceful and precise could stay as such and yet be possessed of such seemingly unwarranted rage. It occurred to her that if he really could contain such duality, it made him infinitely deadlier. She felt at once a thrill of awe and of fear, and noticing it, she felt just a little depressed.

Ajuban laughed grimly. "Not a violent man?" he mused. "No, not like most men are. But I do not t'ink dat he had any special dislike for Spaniards before his sister's deat'. Remember dose two Spaniards he attacked when you met him?" Coya nodded. "He asked dem about dis Francisco in de public house dat night, and dey were very rude to him. Even den, he responded politely to dem, left dem alone and had a good time drinking, telling tales and talking to de new crew, as if all was forgotten."

"Den I turned around and de Spaniards were gone, and so was de captain." Ajuban sighed. "You know what happened next: he stalked dem like a cat so even you did not hear, and attacked dem." He leaned closer, glancing back towards the ladder to the deck and lowering his voice. "You told me yourself how ferocious his assault on dem was."

The memory of that fight was clear to Coya, but she began to see the whole incident in a different light. She had imagined that he was taking revenge for some vile insult immediately preceding the incident, or that he simply hated all Spaniards as she did for some reason akin to her own, though afterwards it had seemed almost like a game to him. "But why then did he not try to kill them?" she asked suddenly. "It was very clear that he was avoiding doing so, even at his own peril."

Ajuban shrugged again. "I don't know. Who can say? I don't understand it very well. Perhaps it wouldn't be an obsession if it made sense. One t'ing is for sure dough," he added conspirationally, "I do not envy dis Pablo Francisco."

Coya didn't know what to feel about it. Pity for any Spaniard was somewhat alien to her experience, but her motives had always been as simple as her society. She wondered if her motives would become as complicated as her new "society" was becoming.

Chapter 4: The Lying Dutchman

The Constance passed Maracaibo after dusk, but without incident. The wind had slackened a little, but the weather was still fair during Coya's watch. The crew had turned in readily as soon as they had choked down their less-than-appetizing dinner (which only differed from breakfast by including some cured fish). Apparently the tension of being boarded by Spanish soldiers while pretending to be Spanish themselves had taxed the crew's nerves somewhat, though they all chuckled and agreed that it was very neatly done. Fooling one's opponents made for nearly as good a tale as battling them, but the crew's lust for loot would be fresher for a little rest.

Since they were sailing in dangerous waters far from a friendly port, Roy had ordered an extra watchman during the night, so Coya was joined on deck by William. Coya was in a quiet mood, so William mostly enjoyed the night air when he wasn't taking instruction from Brian. He seemed in some ways to be the oddest of all the crewmembers—including Coya herself. He unabashedly enjoyed every new experience and never seemed concerned, afraid, or even bored with anything that had happened or might happen. It seemed more like a grand experiment to him; he was rather like an infant that has just learned to walk, exploring everything it can, and he treated the voyage as though it carried no more danger than that.

For the moment, Coya was content merely to observe what to her were oddities of character in the people she now shared space with, and it was much easier for her to observe them when there weren't so many around at once, particularly in the dark when they couldn't really tell that she was watching them. She privately wished that a different crewmember would share her watch each night just for this purpose.

Brian kept the ship toward the eastern shore of the lagoon to take advantage of the east wind and to keep an eye on the main trade routes, but the night dragged quietly on except for one small ship riding high in the water—"We'll not wake the captain for such a small and empty boat," Brian had said—and a few lights in the small settlements scattered along the coast. He had spoken in some detail about where they were now, though the eastern sky began to cloud over in places obscuring the view, and Coya realized that she was probably closer to her own homeland than she had been since she had left it years before. The realization seemed like an abstraction in the rhythm as the waves and her thoughts slid quietly by.

She awoke the following afternoon to the sound of light rain on the deck—a curious sound, not quite like rain on a rooftop—followed by the sound of someone pumping the bilge. Upon taking her daymeal, she learned that the day had so far been very uneventful. "This rain will keep a lot of traders in port until it passes," said Albert ruefully. "There has been no sound of thunder, but it would be foolish for them to venture out onto the high seas to encounter it."

"It could be good luck or bad that it will be harder for ships to spot each other at great distances in this," suggested Martin, meaning that they might at least remain concealed until their prey was close.

"Aye, dough it may cut de odds a bit to stay closer to de shore," suggested Ajuban. "Dere are usually enough ships making short journeys just to cross de lagoon and save de long trip around it by road."

The officers had discussed whether to stay closer to the middle of the lagoon to have as much visibility of traffic as possible or to stay close to the shore, but in the end Roy chose the coastal route, though not too close. "In addition to keeping an eye on the ports," he'd said, "we may need to find a sheltered bay quickly if the storm worsens," so they sailed just within sight of the shore.

Albert's prediction held true, and they encountered no ships while the storm held, though it showed definite signs of slackening just a couple of hours before dusk. As the rains turned to mists and a few rays of sun cast long shadows to the east, the crew began to get restless. They were sailing near the southern end of the lagoon now and were probably only hours from the trade town of Gibraltar. The colorful flashes of the marsh lightnings were a new sight to Coya. Though muffled by the low clouds as the light faded, the constant flashes would improve visibility on the water at night. Even so, they would soon have to either turn back or skirt around to the western shore of the lagoon in search of prey. The officers had already begun discussing just this dilemma when Albert shouted, "Sail ho!" from the rigging. He was pointing slightly east of due south, and eager for some worthy target, all eyes followed his gaze.

Roy immediately snatched up his telescope and gazed curiously at the ship for several moments, shading the lens from the drizzle with his hand. Ajuban waited at his shoulder expectantly. "A cargo fluyt," Roy muttered for Ajuban's benefit, "Dutch, by the look of it."

"Dutch!" said Ajuban, surprised. "I'm surprised he got into de lagoon at all, wit' all dose patrols we encountered. Do you t'ink he's a smuggler or some-t'ing?" Few other merchants traded with the Spanish colonies as Spanish law prohibited its colonies from trading with any nation but Spain.

"I don't see how they could expect to get back out again as such, but I have no qualms about pursuing such a plunder." Roy grinned at his companion. "Load all guns. I want full sails in this weather until we've caught up to them."

"Load de guns," shouted Ajuban to the crew, "Full ahead!" A few cheers followed by excited remarks and much bustling around the deck answered him. The wind was due east and the captain was already discussing tactics with Brian as Ajuban put Martin in charge of the cannons and ordered Coya and Albert to load the ship's small arms.

When things had calmed down a little, Coya learned the full details of the situation as she sat with Albert and a small array of new flintlock pistols. Although she had little knowledge of and no dislike for the Dutch, she was excited. She had expected to be more afraid than she was, but she was caught up in the collective release the crew felt to be finally doing something after days of waiting. Besides, from what she had heard, the crew of the Dutch ship looked no larger than Roy's crew, and their ship was built for carrying large cargoes through shallow waters rather than for maneuverability.

"Unfortunately," said Albert as they shared their thoughts on the matter, "the cargo fluyt design does pose one problem for us: it can carry more and heavier cannons than *The Constance*. However, if the captain is right and their crew is as small as ours, they would be hard pressed to operate so many cannons at once. And I daresay the captain looks like he has a few tricks up his sleeve." He gestured towards Roy who stood in the stern smiling and speaking in a low voice with Ajuban and Brian.

The Dutch ship had been relatively close when they spotted it due to the poor visibility, so it was not long before they intercepted it. Roy had run up his English privateer flag and did not in the least attempt to disguise his intentions towards the Dutch ship. The captain of the cargo fluyt had evidently decided therefore that he had better make a run for it by sailing west with the wind—a much better point of sail for a cargo fluyt than for a small sloop like *The Constance*. But Roy had anticipated this and was quickly cutting off their escape as his southerly course took full advantage of the wind as well. Suddenly the Dutch ship—*Peddler van de Golf*, Coya was told— trimmed its sails and slowed, and as it did so, its starboard gun ports opened. "Man the port guns and prepare to fire!" shouted Roy. "Thirty degrees to starboard," he shouted to the helm, and then pointed to Albert and Coya, "You two: two pistols each and come with me." The rest of the crew had armed themselves already, so the two of them each took an extra pistol and followed Roy—and Ajuban with his crossbow—to the starboard rail, just before the bow. As they got there, they heard a low *boom* immediately followed by Roy's command, "Fire!"

Coya had been puzzled by the first *boom* for just a moment before she realized that the other ship had fired on them. Then suddenly Coya realized that the battle had already begun. She had only a moment to ponder the strangeness of battle without seeing the faces of one's enemies before she heard the sounds of impact from the enemy volley. Fortunately most of the incoming shots whistled by and into the water behind them, except for one that snapped a rail at the stern. The Dutch gunners had been foiled by the speed of *The Constance*. Coya glanced at the cargo fluyt as Roy's own volley arced towards it. The cargo fluyt had turned slightly to fire its guns, but appeared to be turning back again. Coya was satisfied to see that the ship appeared to take more damage from the exchange than *The Constance* had, but Roy was already barking commands again to the rest of the crew as she gripped a pistol in her hand and waited with Albert and Ajuban for orders. "Due south, full ahead!" he cried. He appeared to be trying to close the distance as quickly as possible, but the Dutch vessel began to slowly and ominously turn towards them to expose its port guns to them.

"Trim sails," shouted Roy, "hard to port, man the starboard guns!" He peered out at the other ship as Ajuban repeated the commands, then finally he turned to the three of them again brandishing a pistol. "Shoot at anyone you see manning a cannon on deck," he said earnestly. "We need to delay their next volley as much as we can and clear the way for boarding." Brian was doing an admirable job of turning the ship quickly as the gun crews hurried from one side of the ship to the other to man the starboard guns. William and Justin trimmed the sails to reduce speed and turn even faster, and the cargo fluyt simply could not match them. Try as it might, the square-rigged ship would not turn fast enough into the eye of the wind to bring its guns to bear on *The Constance*. However, there was one cannon near the bow of the ship manned by four men that looked as if it posed a problem. *Peddler van de Golf* was quite close now, so Roy, Ajuban, Coya and Albert all crouched by the rail aiming at the four men and fired on Roy's command just as the quartet prepared to fire. Three of the men fell—one with Ajuban's crossbow bolt in his chest—and Roy gave a satisfied grunt as the fourth prudently decided to take cover.

Then Roy appeared to realize that his own ship had finally come about before the Dutch ship and promptly ordered the starboard cannons to fire. The volley tore through the cargo fluyt. It was not aimed low enough to sink the ship (or damage any cargo), but it greatly disrupted those on deck. Two more men fell, and most of the rest scattered as *The Constance* closed the distance. It appeared to Coya that at least two of the enemy gun ports were substantially wider than they had been before, so hopefully the heavier guns were damaged and would be unable to fire a point blank volley in return. "Ready your grapnels," shouted Roy, "Prepare to board!" Coya noticed the gun crews loosening pistols in their belts and picking up coiled ropes with grappling hooks that they had prepared while she and Albert had been busy loading the pistols. "Albert, man the swivel gun until we board. Ajuban, you shoot anyone who pops his head up." Ajuban had already reloaded his crossbow and continued to peer over the rail at the other ship. Roy followed suit, crouching with his telescope resting idle in his left hand. After a moment he sighed. He seemed annoyed. "Coya, you'll have to go run up the black flag."

"Aye sir," she said. Now she understood why he was upset. She had been told that the privateer flag, or any other battle flag, indicated that enemies who ran up a white flag of surrender would be given quarter and treated fairly. It ensured less work and fewer casualties for both sides, but required the victim to admit defeat and to lose their cargo, as well as possibly their livelihoods. The black flag, however, meant that the enemy could expect no quarter, and was often reserved for those enemies who fought on after it was obvious that they were outmatched. The cargo fluyt still flew Dutch colors rather than the white flag, and no doubt Roy was loathe to cause unnecessary injury to the Dutch crew, but the Dutch captain continued to prolong the fight and to force Roy to risk the lives of his men. Roy had given the order grudgingly, but Coya ran to comply, keeping low in case anyone decided she made a good target.

The ships were only yards apart now, and Coya heard Roy shout, "Grapnels away!" as she lowered the privateer flag. However, it was at that moment that several of the crew pointed at the other ship and she heard Ajuban cry, "Look sir, she's surrendering!" It was true, the Dutch crew seemed to be surrendering and a bloodied sailor was frantically tugging on the line to raise the white flag. The crew cheered as they threw their lines over, and Roy shook his head as Coya glanced at him questioningly. She let the line drop and joined the boarding party. The crew of *The Constance* had won its first cargo.

* * *

"Who is in command here?" asked Roy as both crews assembled on the deck of the cargo fluyt. He looked with some sympathy on the somewhat informal gathering as two of the Dutch sailors lay dead and half a dozen others were wounded. In all, there had been fifteen men crewing the merchant vessel and barely half of them were still fit to stand. As Roy enquired about the captain, he looked questioningly at a smaller, wiry-looking fellow who was plainly the most well-dressed of the lot, but as Brian was often mistaken for the captain of *The Constance* due to his fashionable dress, Roy preferred to simply ask. As expected though, the man stepped forward and tried not to glower too obviously at his captor. "Your name, sir?" asked Roy expectantly.

"Marius Gilbertsen," he answered with a Dutch accent.

"I'm Captain Roy Toppings. You have my word that you and your crew will be treated fairly as long as you deal straight with me and hide nothing." Gilbertsen nodded with a hint of a scowl. "Now then," he continued, "what is your cargo?"

Gilbertsen sighed resignedly. "Four tons of sugar, three barrels of rum, and half a ton of coffee." There were murmurs of approval from the crew of *The Constance*. It was a smaller cargo than such a vessel could hold, but it was valuable. It was especially so when split between so few crewmen as *The Constance* carried.

"Nothing else?" asked Roy.

"No cargo," replied Gilbertsen with some heat. "Just my own few possessions of little value that I have aboard, and those of my crew."

"And where were you bound?" asked Roy with a slight note of suspicion. "What is your business? You are not in Dutch waters." He was anxious to know how this Dutch trader expected to get past the Spanish patrols without being seized.

"I know it, sir," Gilbertsen's scowl was ever deepening, "but a man has to earn a living. I am registered with the Spanish government as a Spanish vessel as well as Dutch, for which I pay a fee. As long as I don't trade Spanish goods with the Dutch, or Dutch goods with the Spanish, I am allowed to function for either nation."

Roy had heard of arrangements like this before. It was often the case with Spanish governors that they would create such dispensations knowing full well that they would be used for smuggling goods between nations. Their colonies would benefit from business with foreign traders, and they themselves would collect the "fees" for maintaining such licenses. However, Roy noted that Gilbertsen kept half an eye on his crewmen while he explained the situation.

"Why were you flying the Dutch colors if you were transporting Spanish goods?" he asked archly.

"When one encounters an English ship in Spanish waters, it's generally safer to fly the flag of Holland. Or at least it is in the Caribbean," he added. England and Holland had already had one war over the Navigation Act that Oliver Cromwell had imposed, but the two nations were usually on much friendlier terms in the Caribbean than in European waters.

"And where were you bound?"

"Cuba," replied the Dutchman. "To the port of Santiago."

"I shall, of course, expect the paperwork from you as well," said Roy. He hoped it would get him past the patrols, if they bothered stopping him again, though he might just make a run for it if he got the chance. "Anything else I should know? Any slaves aboard, either as cargo or deckhands?" he asked. If there were any more like Ajuban, Roy would certainly be foolish not to at least ask.

"None."

"Very well. Ajuban, take some men below with Captain Gilbertsen here to inspect the cargo and begin loading it if everything is in order."

"Aye sir," said Ajuban with a curious glance at him. It was unusual to send the captain of the captured vessel down to the hold with the boarding party, but Roy wanted Gilbertsen out of the way for a moment.

When they had gone below with Albert and five others of Roy's crew, he addressed the Dutch crew quietly. "Is he telling me the truth?" They glanced at each other nervously, though some were merely confused—they didn't all speak English, it seemed. "Any fit and able man here is welcome to sign aboard my crew, so you need not fear reprisals, but I want an answer either way. I do have an English letter of marque," he added for those not interested in taking part in unsanctioned piracy, "but it won't do much for you in the eyes of the Dutch authorities."

One of them quietly translated for the others, and in the end four of them stepped forward wishing to join. The one who had done the translating was one of them, and it was he who answered Roy's question. "No sir," he said, sounding slightly relieved. "We were bound for Curaçao, and we have never transported goods of any kind from one Spanish settlement to another since I joined the crew four months ago."

The others indicated the same, even one who had been with the crew for seven months, and another added that he believed Gilbertsen was wealthier than he let on. "He's none too free with our wages, and at our last stop he brought aboard some other item that he put in his quarters." The sailor didn't know what it was, but it had been brought aboard in a thin crate and the captain was very particular about how it was handled.

"You have my thanks," Roy told them sincerely. "All of you. But tell me, what kind of captain is he?" Such a question usually dug up more about his opponents than his own quick assessments, but it also told somewhat about those answering it. He was almost surprised when the three of them who spoke English, as well as a couple of the crewmembers who had neglected to answer his other questions, all answered more or less at once.

"He has a cold heart."

"He's a weasel."

"He's a hard man," said a more tactful sailor.

"He's only interested in his own profit."

They all but tripped over each other's variations on these answers, half with grins and half with indignant scowls. Roy laughed. "All right, all right," he said. Then he turned to the four men who had stepped forward wishing to join his crew. "When my first mate comes back, I'll have him sign the four of you on. In the meantime, you'd better move out of the way." He moved aside as Albert appeared from the stairs to the hold with Justin and Ajuban and began forming a human chain to load the cargo aboard *The Constance*.

However, Ajuban approached him and muttered, "Every-t'ing is in order captain, but I t'ought you should know dat dis ship is fitted below as a slaver." He seemed disgusted, though such things were common in the Caribbean, especially among Dutch vessels.

"Thank you, Ajuban," he said, "But we appear to have already confirmed the nature of our host's character. Is he still in the hold?"

"Aye sir, I left him dere under guard."

"Good man. Anyway, it seems that the good captain has not sold slaves to the Spanish for at least several months. It appears he has only been selling Spanish goods in foreign markets."

Ajuban's eyebrows shot up. "Dat's interesting," he said, "dough it fits wit' some-t'ing else I noticed: dere's only enough food on board for about t'ree days. Dat's not enough to get to Santiago unless maybe de wind was wit' dem de whole way. Was he going to Curaçao? And if he was, why lie about it to privateers? De cargo is branded too, but from what I hear, dey wouldn't shy away from buying branded goods in Curaçao, and it's de only Dutch colony closer dan Sint Maarten."

"Yes, that's where they said he was headed," Roy gestured to his four future crewmembers who were now keeping together and away from the rest of the Dutch crew. "We will have to go there ourselves if we can get by the patrols. Load any of their food that we need—we're taking on those four sailors. When you're done loading, I'll need you to sign them on. In the meantime, have them help load the cargo."

Ajuban grinned broadly. "Aye sir," he said. He was obviously looking forward to seeing their faces once it dawned on them that he was their superior officer, though Roy suspected that others of the crew would have joined if they hadn't picked up on that already. The crew must have realized that their ship was fitted as a slave ship, and one or two of them glanced very uncomfortably at Ajuban when he came up from the hold.

"Oh, and see about loading a couple of extra cannons aboard if any are still serviceable, and are small and light enough to get aboard with so few men. I've quite made up my mind about that at least." As a rule, Roy only took cargoes from honest, upright enemy captains, leaving supplies and personal effects behind. He'd had little reason to treat Gilbertsen any differently at first, but it was fast becoming clear that the man was neither honest nor very upright—especially to his crew.

With a wave, he ventured down into the hold to have a look around for himself and to fetch the Dutch captain. Gilbertsen was sulking by the bulkhead glowering at the men hauling his cargo up to the greedy hands of the other privateers on deck.

As Roy stepped into the hold, he noticed a wide, thin crate leaning open and empty against the bulkhead, but he made no sign. Instead he stood with arms folded, openly considering the Dutchman, who glowered back. "Is this all the cargo of value on board?" Roy asked at length.

"Yes, yes," Gilbertsen snapped, "just this and my meager personal possessions which would be of little value to you, as I have said."

"Meager, eh?" drawled Roy. "Well, we'll have a look all the same while you dig out the cargo papers, shall we?" Roy smiled, gesturing with his hand for Gilbertsen to lead the way. They made their way past the stream of men spiriting away the Dutch cargo, Gilbertsen's face like a thundercloud. On deck, Roy beckoned to William, Coya, and Ajuban who ordered Albert to take over the loading process. As much as he had groaned in Port Royal about always getting stuck with menial labor, Albert was acquainted enough with such work to keep it well-organized, and he was whistling as he worked.

"Key," chirped Roy, holding his palm out to Gilbertsen as they reached the door to his quarters. The Dutchman lifted a silver chain from his neck and passed it to Roy. It contained two small keys—one undoubtedly to the sturdy weapons locker belowdecks. The other fit neatly into the lock of the captain's cabin, but Roy put a restraining hand on Gilbertsen's shoulder as the Dutchman started into the room. "Not so fast, captain, there is a lady present." Coya looked perplexed for a moment as he motioned her in first, but then shrugged and led the way. She was, after all, his official scout, and Roy didn't want Gilbertsen to be the first one into his cabin where any number of weapons (or even crew) could be waiting ready to hand.

As it happened, there were actually a few weapons lying around, but they seemed more ornamental in purpose. There were a couple of very nice-looking rapiers crossed above the small desk nailed to the floor, and laying over some papers was a wheellock pistol with a carved handle inlaid with mother of pearl. It appeared not to be loaded. The furnishings were somewhat restrained beyond that, except for the oddity of a rather fine portrait of a lady hanging on one wall. "Unusual to have that decorating your cabin, isn't it?" asked Roy, pointing at the mahogany-framed portrait. "Wouldn't it suit one of the walls of your home better?"

"It is of no real value, I simply happen to like it," answered Gilbertsen. "I don't spend enough time at home to appreciate it there."

"Ah, I rather thought that you might have only just acquired it, as it looks like it might very well fit that narrow opened crate in the hold. Please excuse the assumption." The Dutchman's face darkened at that, but he offered no argument. Roy liked the man less and less with every passing exchange, but lying seemed so natural to Gilbertsen that it was fun to needle him a bit. In any case, Roy couldn't see much value in transporting a portrait around in the hope of selling it. The frame was probably worth as much by itself. "Papers?" he enquired. Gilbertsen pointed to a desk drawer and took up a seat on the bed. Coya was keeping an eye on him, but Roy leaned in to his companions briefly and whispered, "Keep an eye out for anything unusual," barely loud enough for them to hear. William merely nodded. He seemed to be absorbed in the painting, but Roy turned back to the desk.

Eventually he found the documents he was looking for, though his heart sank. He found that the cargo had all been approved for export specifically to Santiago, signed for and stamped by a customs official in Gibraltar named Ciro Hernandez, but they were very specific about who was shipping them. It seemed that perhaps one of the only things Marius Gilbertsen had not lied about was his name. *I should have realized these might not get me out of trouble.* If anyone else showed those papers, it would be obvious that something was wrong—particularly if they were shown at any port other than Santiago.

There was also no mention of the painting in the document. Even if it had been claimed as a personal item, it should still be listed as such. He pocketed the documents and looked up at the portrait again in puzzlement, only to discover that William was still staring at it. Ajuban was casting a glance over the rest of the room, though mostly keeping an eye on Gilbertsen, but William seemed to have forgotten that anyone else was present.

Roy stepped closer to ask him what he was doing, but just then William spoke up. "Sir, this is a Diego Velasquez." Roy noticed Gilbertsen's exasperated expression—he looked anything but pleased at the observation.

"A who?" asked Roy nonplussed.

"Diego Velasquez," William repeated. "Oh, he's sort of the official portrait painter for King Philip of Spain. The woman in the portrait is one of the king's cousins."

It was definitely not something one would expect to find hanging in the captain's cabin of a Dutch cargo fluyt. "Worth much?" Roy asked.

"I'm sure that King Philip would pay a high price for it. Someone looking to curry favor with him might pay more." Roy made a mental note to ask

William sometime how he knew so much about art. "It will probably be worth much more once the artist dies, if the public are as kind to him as King Philip is," William added. "If they are not, it will be worth less at that point."

Roy turned to Gilbertsen who was looking downright sulky now. "A curiosity, would you say?" The man said nothing. "How much did you pay for it, or are you merely transporting it for someone?"

"It's mine," snapped the Dutchman. "It cost nearly everything I had, as well." Roy doubted that. Only a complete fool would spend his last doubloon on a portrait of some foreign king's cousin, whatever the reason. The only truly foolish thing about Gilbertsen that Roy had seen so far was his propensity for telling highly transparent lies. "Anyway, you lot don't seem as if you're likely to be doing business with anyone looking to curry favor with the king of Spain," Gilbertsen snickered.

"So how did you come by it?" Roy persisted. "It wasn't listed on your cargo manifest."

"Mind your own business." Clearly the Dutchman was tiring of this little game. "Just take what you're going to take, and get off of my ship."

"Right. William, see if you can get that pretty painting over to my cabin without damaging it. I expect you know more about how to store it than anyone else here does. Put it in my cabin."

William grinned broadly as Roy tossed him the key. "With pleasure, sir," he said, making his way out the door.

Ajuban was keeping a close eye on Gilbertsen now, as the latter was looking absolutely livid, though he still simply sat on the bed. Coya was handling one of the rapiers she had taken from the wall. Roy had quite tired of Gilbertsen's lies and his attitude, and had privately already decided to strip the man's ship of gear and of his possessions as much as was practical. He scooped up the merchant's coinpurse from his desk and was about to tell him his decision when Ajuban suddenly spoke to their host. "So, Captain Gilbertsen, shall we discuss why your bed is not nailed to de deck?"

Good man, Ajuban! Roy certainly hadn't noticed it himself. "Yes, a capital notion, I'd say," he said. *No wonder he keeps just sitting there on his bed like a hen on an egg.*

Roy motioned for him to stand up as he helped Ajuban move the bed as far as they could in the small room while Coya kept watch on the Dutchman, brandishing one of his own rapiers at him. William came back in with another sailor carrying the narrow crate from the hold—apparently he had not been quite as absorbed in staring at the painting as Roy had thought, if he had remembered talk of the thin crate—as well as some spare canvas and oilcloth, but they both stopped to watch as the captain stooped to examine a small closed latch in the deck, fitted with a lock. "Key," Roy demanded once again. This time Gilbertsen merely stared daggers back at him and didn't budge. "I can get in there with or without your help," he warned.

"Then it will have to be without," Gilbertsen said flatly.

Roy shrugged and turned his gaze to Coya. "I believe you told me that you're handy with locks," he said in Spanish. He had picked that much up from her stories of living on the fringes of society in Cartagena and what was now Port Royal. He expected that she might somehow force or pick the lock, so he laughed in surprise when she merely tugged the pommel clean off of the rapier she was holding and handed it to him. There was a key attached to it that had been buried in the hilt. "How on Earth did you notice that?" he asked her incredulously.

"It was weighted differently than the other one," she said matter-of-factly.

Of course. Anyone skilled at throwing knives would be used to judging the weight distribution of blades in their hands. Roy was used to it himself. He stooped to the floor and, fitting the key in the lock, opened the hatch and withdrew a small chest. The hatch compartment was really only big enough to hold the chest, and there was nothing else underneath it. Roy at once popped open the latch on the chest and dug inside. Apart from shattering Gilbertsen's claims of pennilessness by containing many gold and silver coins (mostly Spanish doubloons and pesos, Roy noted), the chest also contained a document that turned out to be a coffee contract from a plantation owned by someone named Ramón Chavez. "Interesting," he said as he read, "according to this, the same customs official who signed your export papers is also the point of contact between you and this Ramón Chavez." He arched an eyebrow at Gilbertsen. "A definite conflict of interest for a customs officer, getting mixed up in supply contracts. So who is this Ciro Hernandez, anyway?" It didn't matter that he received only a glare for answer. Clearly this

Hernandez was a go-between for all kinds of smuggled goods. It was certainly disturbing that the contract should make a specific mention of his name, as if whoever might read or enforce the contract might see some special significance in the name of a customs officer. On the surface it seemed more of a liability than an asset to this Ciro Hernandez to have his name on the contract, but something about it nagged at Roy. *Well, I suppose it's academic anyway. For the moment.* Nevertheless, the contract could potentially help get *The Constance* past those patrols outside the Maracaibo Lagoon, though he couldn't quite see how.

Tucking the document away with the others, he turned to Gilbertsen, his mind made up. "Captain, if you spent half as much effort on being a good and honest merchant—or even a good and semi-honest smuggler—as you spend on all your lies and secrets, you might be really good at it."

"So that I could work harder and still end up being looted by every freeloader with a gun on the high seas?" retorted Gilbertsen.

"You would at least have been wealthier at the end of *this* day than you will be now." He drew his pistol and addressed his crew once again. "Put Gilbertsen and his remaining crew in a longboat. Strip the ship as much as possible and sink it. Get to work, we make way by dusk."

Before long, as Roy had ordered, *The Constance* was underway to escape the Maracaibo Lagoon. He was pleased to be able to notice in the evening twilight how much lower in the water the ship was due to all of the plundered cargo and supplies. Two more eight-pounders crowded the deck; one on either side, and a new swivel gun adorned the stern of the small ship. It was virtually all the firepower such a tiny craft could possibly boast, and Roy hadn't had the time or manpower to load any of the other guns into his hold. He wanted to be long gone before any other ships came to investigate. Barely a mile away, he could see the twilit silhouette of *Peddler van de Golf* tilting awkwardly where it was anchored, gun deck already completely submerged. Not much further away, he could still make out the tiny dark shape of the boat that rowed its way slowly through the drizzle towards the shore carrying Gilbertsen and his eight remaining crewmembers, only two of which were probably fit to row at all. He had made more of an enemy of Gilbertsen than was strictly necessary by sinking his ship and sending him off with food, dry bandages and supplies for only one day adrift, but neither he nor those men had been forthcoming with him. *If they decide to stand by such a man, then they must expect to share in the price of his decisions.* Roy still felt a little pang of sympathy for them, wishing he'd been able to patch those wounded men up better than he had, but he'd done what he could. He sighed and turned his back to them, focusing on what must be done now.

Most of the crewmen were heading down to the newly stocked hold for sleep, having worn themselves out with hauling and securing cargo, but others wished to dice together and discuss their plans for their share of the loot. Even Albert was wakeful, though he had done more than his share of the hauling. Ajuban manned the helm while Brian and Justin, who both had some skill at carpentry, worked a few yards away from him at repairing the rail that had been the only obvious damage from the battle. Roy wanted it to look as natural as possible before any patrols found them, so they had cut away pieces of the cargo fluyt's rails as it would be much quicker to adapt these than to make any convincing repairs from new timbers. Brian and Justin did their best to take the modified piece and fit it in such a way as to appear natural, but William helped to hide any signs of damage. Coya was just beginning her watch, but Roy waved her over and approached Brian, Justin, William and Ajuban. "With luck we should reach open waters after sunset tomorrow," he said once they were all attentive. "I intend to try to slip by the patrols in the dark if possible, but we should be prepared for the worst." He explained about the papers and why they would not be sufficient to fool the patrol ships. "And they don't mention the painting at all," he added. "Speaking of which, William, how on Earth did you know about that painting?"

William smiled, apparently pleased that he had proved useful as more than a deckhand. "I've dabbled a bit in many things, but art is something I have pursued with more diligence."

It dawned on Roy that this must be the reason William almost constantly wore gloves. He probably wanted to keep his hands as free of calluses and sores as possible. William certainly was turning out to be an interesting fellow, however he might do as a privateer. As he mused about how William might be able to help in selling the painting, Roy was struck with another idea. "Would you come with me a moment William?" he asked abruptly. "I have an idea, but I will have to discuss it with you somewhere drier." The others looked at him quizzically, but William seemed pleased as he shrugged and followed, leaving Brian and Justin to continue work on the rail themselves. *Now if only his talents can stretch to duplicate a particularly problematic customs document...*

* * *

In the end, William's forged document was not put to the test. Brian managed to sneak by the patrols in the dead of night with no lanterns lit, relying on his knowledge and Coya's keen eyes. However, Roy was impressed enough with William's effort that he decided to retain the document for possible future use. William had been able to duplicate the writing well enough, but the seal had presented a problem. After a few attempts to etch the symbol in slightly softened wax had failed, William said, "I might have more luck simply separating the seal from the original and fixing it to the forgery with a little melted wax." It had worked perfectly, as far as Roy was concerned. The only ways in which the forgery appeared to differ from the original were that *Marius Gilbertsen* was replaced with *Ricardo Francisco*, the dates were current, and the painting was included on the manifest as a personal item. This more than anything else sealed William's usefulness to the crew in Roy's eyes, and he was glad indeed that he had taken the risk of signing him on without having had any clear notion of why he should do so.

It had already been a full day since Roy had run up the Spanish flag again to pass Maracaibo and then slipped by the patrols at night. Now he and his crew were once again in open waters and should pass Aruba during the night. He expected to reach the Dutch port of Curaçao by noon and sell his cargo as soon as possible. *With luck I'll be able to sign on some more crew.* He wanted to go after bigger cargoes or possibly raid a settlement or two. Bigger cargoes and more men would mean a cramped hold and crew sleeping on deck, but none would resent the larger payout that would result from a full load. Roy had been very fortunate not to lose any men against the Dutch ship, and that would be something that would impress potential recruits, but without new crewmen, it was only a matter of time before an unlucky volley would kill half his men. He hoped the Dutchmen who had signed on could help him in

Curaçao, but although Roy was convinced that they would not simply desert him once there, they still had to earn their keep. *I could certainly use more crew who know one end of a sword from the other.* He would just have to see what was available. In the meantime, he contented himself with chewing on his inadequate evening biscuit and looking forward to a room in Curaçao with a mug of ale, a soft bed and a proper meal as he dragged himself to his cabin for the night.

Chapter 5: Curaçao

The tide was low as *The Constance* sailed into the harbor of Curaçao. The docks were bustling with activity, and though Ajuban had never been to Curaçao before, he was surprised by the array of ships there. In addition to all of the smaller merchant and fishing craft, there were a pair of Dutch warships guarding the harbor—the larger of which looked to be an antiquated Spanish galleon that must have been captured—as well as a small French sloop and a Spanish barque with a name painted in large flowing black letters on the stern. Ajuban wished for probably the hundredth time that he could read better. Roy had been teaching him, but he was still a beginner. He felt reasonably sure that he had not seen this ship before. Nevertheless... "Captain," he muttered, nodding his head in the direction of the vessel.

Roy gazed at it briefly. "*La Fortuna?*" he said in answer. "Never heard of her. Hopefully her crew won't cause us any trouble here."

Ajuban attempted to hide a smirk. *Hopefully* you *won't cause* dem *any trouble*. It was flying a diplomatic flag (as was the French sloop), but Spaniards frequently used barques as warships and pirate hunters.

"Drop anchor," said the captain.

"Drop anchor!" shouted Ajuban to the crew. He had once thought it was a wonderful novelty to shout orders and have others carry them out, but sooner than he would have expected, the novelty wore off and it just seemed silly on a ship as small as *The Constance* when Roy could just shout them out himself. He had always adapted to things quickly, but some parts of this life he would never really understand.

Ajuban enjoyed his first sight of Curaçao. It seemed to be a thriving town and conveyed a welcoming feeling in spite of the way the buildings were crowded together. Shops lined the streets near the docks on the left, and the low fortress walls stood solidly on the right, hiding the governor's house from view according to the Dutchmen. The town was very flat, and though he could see a couple of churches poking out from the mass of rooftops, the rest was obscured behind the waterfront buildings. The one thing he liked best about privateering, apart from the good food and comfortable beds when in port, was the freedom to explore new places. Of course most of the time this freedom required that someone else accompany him or that he appear to be running an errand. Still, it was as much freedom as he could really hope for without being rich or living in the wild like an escaped slave.

Roy already had the men hauling cargo up to the deck. He had not been to Curaçao before either, but he had been told that the best way to run afoul of customs agents in Curaçao was not by transporting illegal goods, but by *hiding* the activity and thus depriving them of their bribe. It was well known that illegal goods were freely traded in Curaçao, largely due to the colony's position in the Caribbean: close to many Spanish colonies and far removed from the Dutch trade authorities in Sint Maarten. Anything could be had in Curaçao, and probably at a quarter less than its usual market price. They would probably take exception to goods plundered from Dutch ships, but then it was fortunate that Gilbertsen's goods all carried Spanish brands. No one would need to know what ship had actually carried those goods. Being raised in a tribal culture had not prepared him at all for the intricacies of business, but he found it all fascinating. He had learned more about mercantile business aboard the ship that Roy had freed him from, but when he signed aboard *The Constance,* he found that his knowledge of business had not prepared him for the subtleties of illegal trade and the black market.

He attempted to explain more about illegal trade practices to Coya as she finished with her own duties on deck, but she had lived on the fringes of society for many years and was somewhat accustomed to such dealings already. "Most people wish to keep as much of their hard-earned coin as possible," she said, "and many of them have such dealings to compensate for the other ways in which they feel they were cheated out of their earnings." Of course not everyone had a very responsible notion of what they had actually earned or deserved, and Ajuban supposed that all smuggling and piracy had its basis in that reality at some level. He figured that one could either contemplate the morality involved in it at each step of every transaction and every encounter, or one could simply look out for oneself and trust that the rest of the world was doing the same.

With all the cargo brought up from the hold, the crew quickly assembled on deck and Roy waved the customs officer aboard—a sandy-haired middle-aged man carrying a ledger and sweating in his uniform. "Is this your vessel, sir?" the man inquired in English, as *The Constance* had sailed into port flying English colors.

"It is," Roy responded, "Captain Roy Toppings, at your service," he added with a bow.

"Everything accounted for here?" the man asked sounding somewhat bored.

"I believe you'll find everything in order," Roy answered, handing him a document.

Ajuban studied the man's reaction as he skimmed over the document—Roy's letter of marque, not the cargo manifest. The man appeared just as bored reading it, but it seemed a little more exaggerated as he began speaking again. "Right, docking fee of one ducat please," he said, folding the document and handing it back to Roy, who handed him six pesos instead. It was roughly three times the docking fee. "Welcome to Curaçao," he intoned, sounding just as bored as before, "enjoy your stay." He barely looked up as he nodded at Roy, scribbled something in his ledger and stepped off the ship. He had gotten what he wanted. Indeed, he hadn't even bothered to open the cargo to keep up appearances.

"Right," Roy began, turning to face his now eagerly muttering crew, "Brian, William, Albert, take two of the Dutch sailors with you and see if you can find any buyers for our goods. The other two will come with me, Ajuban, and Coya to do the same. All of us going on these business trips need to bathe first." No buyer would appreciate the smell of three or four unwashed sailors lingering in their places of business. "Justin, Martin, you guard the ship. The rest of you, enjoy yourselves. We meet back here after the church bells toll five o'clock." The crew dispersed as they nodded at Roy and made their way enthusiastically into town, though Justin and Martin sighed resignedly as they took up their posts on deck. Earlier that morning, Roy had paid out the coins that had been in Gilbertsen's money chest (minus a few that he had decided would go to the customs officer, as well as the twenty percent that Roy kept aside for the crown) and the crew was eager to sit down to a good meal and spend some of their earnings. Five hours left plenty of time for that, even for those who still had to locate buyers, and hopefully by then the crew would be back at the ship to move the goods to whoever would buy them.

"Captain," Ajuban began, as they made their way to an inn near the docks, "should we get some-t'ing to eat too, before we try to find a buyer? I know I could certainly do wit' a change from biscuits and dried meat."

Roy turned to ponder the two Dutchmen. Ajuban couldn't remember their names. "What do you think, you two?" Roy asked them, "can you tell me where I might find buyers for our cargo? Who was Gilbertsen going to sell it to?"

The one who didn't speak English—Ajuban thought his name was Bert— looked to his companion to translate and they conferred briefly in Dutch. "He often sells to different people," said the other man. "He has sold rum and wine, and even some sugar, to a tavern keeper and brewer named Willem van Kemper a few times, and he often sells a wide variety of goods and supplies to Mrs. Rutger, an outfitter near the docks. She trades with nearly all sorts." He added the last in an undertone.

"Excellent," chirped Roy. "Where is this tavern of Mr. Van Kemper's?"

"It is not far into town." The Dutchman pointed northeast. "About half a mile."

"Well, since it appears we are closer to Mrs. Rutger's, we will try her first when we're done here." Roy gestured to the inn they had just reached. Ajuban didn't intend to hire a room—he was actually quite comfortable sleeping on the ship, and it didn't seem worth hiring a room if they weren't going to be there long—but the use of their baths would be most welcome. He could smell the reek of his companions all too distinctly. "If either lead shows promise, I think you two have earned a meal at this tavern you spoke of."

The Dutchman translated for his friend and they looked pleased. They had no coin and could expect no wages from the plunder as they had fought on the other side. "Thank you, sir," he said, and his companion uttered the same haltingly with a bow. "She is that way." He pointed to a long, low building further east up the docks.

Roy nodded, and they continued on inside the inn. The innkeeper was pleased to accept two stuivers for all of them to use the baths. Once they had washed, they followed the Dutchmen north along the dock and found a sign in Dutch outside the outfitter's warehouse with the name "Melanie Rutger" underneath. Inside it looked very much like most of Mrs. Rutger's business consisted of trading in ship supplies. However, shops of this sort often traded in cargoes as well since they saw a lot of trade with privateers, smugglers, pirates, or anyone else who captained ships. Such businesses were able to capitalize on the impatience of plundering crews wanting to move their cargo as fast as possible, or those who simply didn't have the wit or inclination to negotiate deals with several different merchants. If Mrs. Rutger had the right contacts in town—and Ajuban had no doubt that she did—she could resell any goods quickly and at a markup. In a town with a thriving black market like what Curaçao boasted, it was hardly surprising to find such a business operating nearly in plain sight, but a great many such businesses were run by women and Ajuban still could not figure out why.

"Hello," Roy said approaching the counter. There was a plumply pretty woman there who smiled as she noticed them enter. "Are you Mrs. Rutger?" he asked in English. Dutch merchants in the Caribbean often spoke English, especially those who bought and sold questionable cargoes.

"Yes, at your service," she answered with barely any accent. "And you are?"

"Captain Roy Toppings, at your service."

"And what may I do for you today, captain?" she asked.

"I understand that you run an outfitting business and I perceive from glancing at your wares"—he gestured around at the shelves, crates and piles around her warehouse—"that you are undersupplied in some goods that I could perhaps furnish you with."

"It is sadly all too likely, sir," she responded gravely, glancing at her surroundings which plainly displayed a more than adequate quantity of any supplies that one might need aboard a ship, with the exception of cannons. However, Ajuban knew that Roy was suggesting she could do with certain trade goods rather than actual shipboard supplies. "With this amnesty the Spaniards are offering—you have heard about that, have you?—fewer clients are in need of…certain supplies and I am forced, alas, not to stock as much." She shook her head as if in comment of the times. Ajuban didn't understand why both of them were speaking so covertly since such illicit deals were common in Curaçao, but perhaps it was best to keep up the pretense in case some local authority decided to start paying attention to Dutch trade laws. "However," continued Mrs. Rutger, "there are perhaps some goods that I might be convinced to unburden you of, at a discount. If you and your associates will step into my office?"

Her office contained a few other items that might not be said to be standard naval provisions, such as a barrel of ale, a crate of tobacco, and three bolts of red silk. Ajuban also noticed the tobacco carried a Spanish brand he had seen before, though he could not read it. Fortunately the presence of these particular goods would not drive down whatever price she might offer for their cargo through claims of a surplus. In the end, she offered to buy all of their goods, though as expected, she offered reseller prices: five ducats per ton of sugar, seventeen per barrel of rum, fifteen for the half ton of coffee, and a pittance for the wheellock and matchlock pistols plundered from the cargo fluyt. "Most of my clients won't buy them anymore," she explained. "There are so many flintlocks that come through here now that even wheellocks are fast becoming antiques, and only the most ornamental ones sell for much."

Roy's crew had already been able to switch to flintlocks due to the thriving black market in Port Royal. On nearly every ship they plundered, they had found wheellock pistols and muskets, mixed in with the older and cheaper matchlock designs. When Ajuban had wondered at this, Roy explained that these old firearms were still the standard issue for most soldiers simply because no government had yet confirmed the general superiority of the flintlock or passed on an order to start using them, though he said the Roundheads had used an early version against the Cavaliers during the English Civil War. Ajuban later understood when he asked about these strange terms that Roy was referring to the Parliamentarian forces and the King's forces respectively. But privateers, smugglers, pirates, mercenaries, and anyone else with a practical mind, no military ties, and a little extra money had already begun snatching up the new flintlocks at every opportunity. They were simpler with fewer moving parts than wheellocks, easier to maintain, lighter weight, less prone to misfires, more accurate, and most importantly, loading them was so much faster that a flintlock could fire three shots for every one that a wheellock could fire. Roy attributed much of his success to them.

Ajuban certainly didn't miss the old wheellocks, and the matchlocks were far worse. These used a slow fuse that made use in damp conditions inefficient at best, and at worst posed any number of dangers ranging from the ability to see and smell the slow fuse at a distance or in the dark, to the inability to load and then store them for long periods of time rendering them useless against surprise attacks. On top of that, holding the slow fuse made loading and firing more difficult. Roy had of course trained him to use all kinds of firearms, but half of the time when he missed his mark with the matchlocks, he was sure it had been because one of his hands and part of his vision had to be occupied with touching the slow fuse to the powder in the flashpan. They were still faster to use than wheellocks, but the flintlock outperformed both of them in every respect. Of course he preferred his crossbow to any of them, but sometimes it simply was not suitable for the situation.

So Roy, after long experience trading the wheellocks for practically nothing on the black market however much it might have cost to make them, made no attempt to negotiate on that point. The way Ajuban saw it, the price they got for those would pay for ordinary food and supplies for their next voyage. They could probably just buy those from Mrs. Rutger as well. "I will return later this evening with any goods that I can sell you," Roy told her. "Is eight o'clock all right?"

"That would be perfect," she answered. She smiled as Roy kissed her outstretched hand and they stepped out into the street in search of a good meal at Mr. Van Kemper's tavern.

"So," Ajuban said turning to the Dutchman (he had heard Roy introduce him to Mrs. Rutger as "Tiede"), "how is de food at dis Van Kemper's tavern?"

"I don't know," replied Tiede, sounding excited. "I've heard it's very good, but I have never been able to afford to eat there."

"Ah," Roy answered, looking slightly crestfallen. Ajuban laughed. Now he understood part of why the two Dutchmen were so pleased that Roy had offered them that meal.

His laughter ceased, however, as an uncomfortable thought struck him. "Will dey even serve us dere?" he asked, gesturing to himself and Coya.

"Don't worry," said Tiede with a dismissive gesture, "I've seen all sorts going in there. I believe Mr. Van Kemper knows where most of his business comes from."

"Wit' luck, we will have even more business wit' dis Van Kemper fellow dan just eating dere. Aldough I'm afraid dat eating dere is all I'm looking forward to right now."

* * *

Glancing around at the other patrons and at the place itself, Coya could see why Tiede had never been able to afford Mr. Van Kemper's establishment. Simply named "Van Kemper's," the place was clean and pleasing to the eye, with highly polished and intricately carved dark woodwork throughout. A few simple but graceful chandeliers banished any shadows from the high ceiling, though the large south-facing windows provided plenty of light during the middle of the day. The walls held a few simple paintings, and were themselves painted with floral and vine patterns along the higher reaches near the ceiling. An inviting smell hinting at some sort of beef stew mixed with that of fresh bread wafted over as serving women carried wide wooden trays out from the kitchens. Fine-looking polished pewter dishes laden with all manner of fare made their way onto a couple of far tables, reminding Coya that she had not eaten a hot, well-prepared meal in a week.

The room was huge, but Tiede had explained that Van Kemper's was a popular spot to play at cards and dice as well, though there was only one table with a dice game going on at that hour. Coya had seen from outside that the building had two floors, though she supposed the upper floor was for housing Van Kemper and the formidable number of servants bustling through the place. According to Tiede, the brewery was located behind the kitchens and let out alongside the outbuildings into an alley. Roy led them all to a table near the bar, set out a gold doubloon on the table—Spanish currency was generally accepted in Curaçao—and made his way over to talk to the barman. Tiede and Bert ordered for the table, and soon they were all deep into mugs of good ale while Roy stood talking to Mr. Van Kemper himself. Willem van Kemper appeared to be a husky, middle-aged man, slightly shorter than Roy. His blond hair was beginning to go white, and he had a proud cast to his jaw, but he wore a pinched, guarded sort of expression while talking business.

Coya could not hear the conversation, but Roy soon came and sat down with them, snatching up his own mug. "It seems that our host is willing to offer a reasonable sum for the rum," he told them. "He is familiar with the brand, and I think I can get twenty one ducats for each barrel. He appears to be interested in the sugar as well, but he couldn't take more than half of it. We haven't settled on a price range, but it sounds like he will pay more than Mrs. Rutger will in any event."

"Dat was easy," said Ajuban with mild surprise, "assuming he sticks to it. I hope dat de oders have as much luck as we are having."

"Hardly luck. These two had some very good advice for us," said Roy, gesturing to Tiede and Bert and raising his glass for a toast. "To new shipmates."

"New shipmates," said the others with raised glasses. The two Dutchmen looked very pleased.

Coya was as enthusiastic as Roy. She couldn't believe her ears. Once she understood the basic exchange rate to gold ducats (which turned out to be somewhat smaller than Spanish doubloons or English pounds), she had thought the Rutger woman's prices sounded fantastic, and Van Kemper was offering more! Considering the comparatively small cargo and the ease with which they had defeated the Dutch crew, it seemed a windfall. Certainly enough to compensate for several days of boredom at sea, though her legs still felt as if they were on the ship. "How much of that would each of us receive?" she asked, a little in awe.

Roy laughed, perceiving the shock in her tone. "Well, although it's never a good idea to count one's chickens before they are hatched, I will try to explain." He leaned back in his chair, apparently contemplating an answer she assumed would be simple. Then he began explaining, and she realized that it wasn't simple at all. "First of all, let us assume that one ton of sugar sells for sixty shillings." Here Roy took sixty small silver cobs—Spanish reales—from his purse to represent shillings. "Twenty percent of them, or twelve shillings"—he removed these from the table—"go to Colonel D'Oyley, the acting governor of Port Royal so that he won't hang us for piracy." Coya started at that. *Hang us?* "I get ten percent as captain (and not a widely known one)." Here he removed another six coins. "Getting a flat percentage keeps me from appearing to deliberately get most of my crew killed just to get a bigger share. Then Brian and I figure out how many shares there are in the entire crew. Each full member of the crew gets three shares; Ajuban and Brian get five shares as officers. With two officers and eleven full crew, not counting our new Dutch crewmembers who unfortunately fought against us, that makes forty-three shares. Since there are only forty-two coins left out of the original sixty, and each crewmember gets three shares, you would get roughly three shillings, and the officers would get five." He slid three coins across the table toward Coya for emphasis and five towards Ajuban.

Coya thought for a moment. Perhaps it wasn't as much as she had thought. "I am confused," she said. "I get three shillings as my portion of the spoils?"

"You get three shillings for your share *of one ton of sugar*," corrected Roy. Coya nodded with relief. Much of it sounded familiar, as Roy had explained it to the entire crew before they boarded in Port Royal, but she had no head for abstract figures. The example helped, but she might just ask William or Brian to explain it in more detail later. They seemed to understand such things well. "The rest of the cargo will sell for considerably more," Roy continued, "and they will pay in ducats, but we won't figure out how much each share is worth until we have sold everything that we can." He collected all of the oddly shaped Spanish cobs and stuffed them back into his purse.

"Captain," she said, "what do you mean about the acting governor? Would he really hang us if we did not pay him this bribe?" An expensive bribe, no doubt, but it began to sound worthwhile.

Roy and Ajuban both laughed loudly. "I had never thought of it that way," said Roy. "Not as a bribe, anyway. But you are right, in a way. It is a business contract, of a sort. That contract is the document you have probably heard me refer to as a 'letter of marque.' It is a legal document that authorizes me to attack ships of enemy nations in exchange for paying twenty percent of the spoils to the Crown—the representative of which is Colonel Edward

D'Oyley, in Port Royal. He is somewhat…flexible with his definition of "enemy nations," but if we were to attack a friendly vessel, he might just hang us all for piracy. Governors of other colonies—even one or two English ones—might do so regardless of who we attack." *Then why are we in a Dutch town after attacking a Dutch ship?!* Coya suddenly understood a larger part of why Roy had been careful not to mention what ship was carrying the cargo he was trying to sell. She felt her stomach a bit unsettled. Politics was beyond her, but she might just need to start learning enough of it to keep from hanging. Fortunately discretion and secrecy were second nature to her after more than a decade of living as an outlaw in all but name, but that made it even more difficult to understand the casual way in which the others spoke of such things. Curaçao must indeed be every bit as much a haven for outlaws as Roy and Ajuban had indicated for them to be able to speak so freely now.

Coya could not help but glance around to see if anyone was listening to them. "What does this Edward D'Oyley do with his share?" she asked curiously, in an attempt to change the subject.

"Well, officially the money is used to help govern the colony of Port Royal, pay the soldiers, build and repair the roads, maintain the ports and naval vessels, and run the courts. Unofficially, Colonel D'Oyley can use it for whatever he wants. However, since England can neither afford to send ships and soldiers to defend the colony, nor much money to maintain it, Colonel D'Oyley does use most of 'his share' for those purposes. He is no fool."

Tiede had been conversing with his friend Bert during most of the discussion, but he had been paying attention to what Roy said of Port Royal and its governor. "Governor Frans Diedrik is of the same sort," he said with a measure of respect. "Living so close to many Spanish colonies and trade routes as we do, and so far from other Dutch colonies, Curaçao has to maintain itself for the most part. The Spanish still have not forgotten how we captured it from them. The old galleon in the harbor is reminder enough for any who sail near. We captured it from them along with the island."

Roy and Ajuban continued asking him about the colony and its neighboring islands of Aruba and Bonaire, but a serving woman arrived with platters laden with broiled meats, warm bread, cheeses, fruits, and a dozen boiled eggs, as well as bowls filled with the same beef stew that the other patrons were enjoying and Coya was content to attend to her meal only sparing half an ear for the discussion. She had been more than a week without much in the way of fresh fruit except for a rather soft orange she had been given after a few days at sea, and she only became aware of her craving for it as a platter arrived bearing finely sliced bananas, cactus fruit and papaya artistically arranged around three small bowls filled with berries and sections of citrus fruits. It was difficult to keep up with their speech in any case—she still was not very conversant with English, especially with anything beyond things she might hear on the deck of a ship or in her dealings on the outskirts of Port Royal. Roy had continued to weave Spanish throughout his conversations with her, and generally attempted to help her understand, but neither Tiede nor Bert spoke much Spanish.

However, she remained attentive and occasionally someone would translate a part of the conversation for her, so she gathered that the Dutch colonies were primarily trading ports flung far apart and producing few things themselves beyond what was needed to sustain their existence. The Dutch had neither the numbers nor the soldiers to maintain more and larger colonies in the Caribbean. Aruba was barely habitable and was mainly only good for fishing, while Bonaire was populated almost entirely by slaves and workers on the corn plantations, or those made to harvest the island's dyewoods and salt. Curaçao itself thrived mainly on trade (legal or otherwise) but also sported a significant amount of usable farmland. Anything the island could not produce could be acquired through trade, and indeed there were so many ships coming through selling illegal or foreign goods that legitimate Dutch merchant vessels rarely bothered to go there unless they could sell nowhere else, due to the inevitably lower prices their goods would fetch. The Dutch colonial merchants would trade with anyone, and that went double for merchants in Curaçao. They simply couldn't afford *not* to.

There were few nobles in Curaçao. Most preferred either to stay in Holland or had only ventured as far as Sint Maarten and Sint Eustatius in the Lesser Antilles. Many who made their way to Curaçao were also shrewd merchants themselves and made a fortune trading in smuggled or plundered Spanish goods. While they commanded more respect and knew more privileges than everyone else, they had little more authority than the other merchants. Indeed, Frans Diedrik was no more than a particularly successful businessman and shrewd administrator who had been clever enough to secure and maintain his position as governor.

Much of what Coya understood of these conversations made her feel somewhat less worried about being caught and hanged for piracy. It appeared that few in Curaçao cared what nation any particular ship was from as long as it carried valuable cargo. If possible, officially sanctioned merchants from the Dutch trade fleet (if Tiede were to be believed) were scorned more than any others simply because of their attitude that they were the only ones who had a right to trade there. However, they were also possibly the only ships that one could attack and expect to hang from the docks of Curaçao for it later.

They had sat for a good three hours eating and talking when church bells nearby tolled four o'clock. Roy and Ajuban had gone with Mr. Van Kemper to his brewery in the back where he kept his office, leaving Coya feeling somewhat awkward in her attempts to converse with Tiede in her broken English, but they soon returned smiling. "We had better get going back to the ship," said Roy. He pressed a peso into the serving woman's palm as she continued clearing away platters and bowls—all surprisingly empty, considering how much they had contained—and muttered something to her about being delightfully attentive, which made her smile. Roy seemed to be very good at making people smile when he wanted to, though Coya herself didn't often smile. As they stepped out into the street under shadows lengthened by the close buildings, Roy told them, "Mr. Van Kemper has offered fourteen ducats for two tons of our sugar, and we did settle on the price I predicted for the rum." He seemed well pleased with himself. Coya certainly thought it sounded good, though she still could not figure it out herself. It sounded as if she would be receiving many times three shillings. "Even if the others don't have any luck, we will still do very well, except for that painting. Hopefully William can find someone to sell it to. I don't fancy keeping it on my cabin wall on the ship. If it would even fit," Roy mused.

"I suppose we'll find out soon enough," said Ajuban. Coya was not so hopeful. She couldn't imagine anyone spending as much on a mere *picture* as William had implied it was worth, though nobles did have strange tastes. Even so, Tiede had said there were few nobles in Curaçao.

They picked their way through the streets and back to the ship. There were many more people in the streets now, mostly women going to the markets to purchase fresh bread and meats for their evening meal, though there were also many sailors and cargo handlers who made their way into town after a hard day's labor. As they came within sight of the docks, Coya observed that both the Spanish and French vessels were still in port and wondered again what they were doing in Curaçao. "I'm sure we'll find out tonight," said Roy when she asked him about it. "Once we have made all the arrangements for our cargo, we will head back into town to hear what there is to hear. We may even find a few new recruits to sign on."

"How many more can the ship carry?" she asked in surprise. *Many more and we'll have no room for cargo.*

"We could probably house another ten or twenty before the ship would get too crowded for much cargo," he answered, apparently divining her thought. "Usually privateer and pirate ships run with very large crews in cramped quarters," he said. "Don't worry though, I'll make sure that you at least have your own hammock. Men often have to sleep on deck for a while after a ship with such a large crew takes on cargo, but you won't have to. Besides, since you normally sleep during the day, it would be awkward for you to sleep on deck with everyone else trying not to trip over you." She sighed with relief and nodded gratefully. She was sure that she would have nightmares of getting pitched off the deck by a sudden wave or gust of wind if she had to sleep on deck unless the ship was in port. *That can't be pleasant in the rain.*

They made their way to where *The Constance* was berthed and it seemed that Brian, William and Albert had just returned with the other two Dutchmen in tow. Brian and William were talking together but spotted them as they approached and stepped onto the dock to greet them. "Captain," William began somewhat excitedly, "we've had a good deal of luck this afternoon."

"Go on," said Roy.

"Luuk here," said Brian before William could continue, as he gestured to one of the Dutch sailors, "said that he knew of a baker in town named Lisanne Hebert who might buy a portion of our cargo of sugar. She not only agreed to buy two tons of it for fifteen ducats, but she also passed on some other useful information. Apparently there is a minor noble here named Andries van Friedrich and Mrs. Hebert has heard that he is interested in starting a coffee house here in town, so we paid him a little visit."

"Captain," William cut in excitedly, leaning closer, "he wants to buy some of the coffee, and is willing to pay a good price for at least a couple hundred pounds of it, but he's also interested in the painting." This was definitely good news. "We set up an appointment for six o'clock. However, he does wish to discuss the matter with you personally, if possible." Suddenly he looked at Brian and the captain questioningly, apparently hoping that he had not overstepped his authority by interrupting Brian. Even Coya had learned enough not to interrupt Brian or Ajuban when they were making a report to the captain.

Brian looked exasperated, but also a little bit amused. "The lad made a good job of talking up that painting to Van Friedrich," he said, and William appeared to relax a bit.

"Good work, William," Roy grinned. "As it happens, I am available. I assume you have eaten?"

"Yes sir," William replied, relieved.

"In that case, I'd appreciate it if you came with me. Since you did so well dealing with Mr. Van Friedrich, I may need you to help me bargain for a good price on that painting."

"He lives just outside of town on his plantation, so we will need to leave soon, sir."

"Right. Ajuban, Albert, you come with us. Tiede, Bert, hire a wagon and help the others to get the coffee and that pretty canvas loaded onto it," Roy ordered. "Luuk, you hire a wagon or two to close that deal with Mrs. Hebert—it is Mrs., is it?—and take Martin and Justin with you. Then take the rum and the rest of the sugar to Van Kemper's tavern. We agreed on twenty one ducats per barrel of rum and fourteen for the sugar, so don't let him pull any last minute bargaining. We will meet back here when we're done." Martin and Justin stirred, happy to finally get to leave the ship. Roy gave them some coin for the wagons. "Oh, and Tiede," Roy continued, "when you've loaded the cargo, check in with Brian to see if he needs you to do anything else, would you?"

"Yes sir."

"Brian, you and Coya guard the ship while we're gone." They nodded, as everyone began bustling about. Justin and Martin handed Coya their loaded pistols for guard duty before joining the others and seeing to their new duties. She wasn't sure whether it was the meal or the hours on land that had helped her to regain her land-legs, and she sighed inwardly about having to go back to standing around on deck as the ship rocked beneath her, but she was much more content after the meal. *That was the best meal I've had in years.* That had not occurred to her until now. She supposed she would enjoy getting used to it.

* * *

As the wagon trundled slowly towards the pleasant looking villa atop a low hill in the distance, Roy listened to William recount his earlier visit to Andries van Friedrich in greater detail. According to William, the reason Mr. Van Friedrich could not decide how much of the coffee he wanted was that he could not open a coffee house without a guaranteed means of buying coffee. "What he really wants is a shipping contract," William explained. "The Spanish have got such a stranglehold on the coffee trade that even in Curaçao it is expensive. Most of what gets smuggled in is snapped up for personal use by those who can afford the exorbitant prices it fetches, and that's when there is any to be had at all. He is willing to pay those prices to buy coffee for his own personal use, but he can't afford to pay the same prices simply to keep his business stocked." William seemed to understand a great deal about the problem, and Roy was quite familiar with it as well. Sometimes smugglers even deliberately refrained from signing any such contracts simply because it would be more profitable to them to keep something that was considered an expensive delicacy by one nation from becoming a widely available commodity there. Marius Gilbertsen, for example, had apparently agreed to a contract with Ramón Chavez through the Gibraltar customs officer named Ciro Hernandez, but whether he would have offered as much to any of his buyers was questionable. From what Roy had seen of the man, Gilbertsen was just the sort of fellow to try to maximize his profits at anyone else's expense.

"He asked if you could provide him with such a contract," William continued, "but I had to admit that I wasn't sure. I don't know how often you run across such cargoes, or how much effort you want to put into that sort of commitment, if you even intend to come back here often."

"You did well not to encourage him," answered Roy after some thought. "It is certainly a tempting notion, but I'm not sure how much time I want to spend here either. Besides, although I have run across several such cargoes before, a contract would be very difficult to maintain without simply becoming another smuggler. Now that we don't have Captain Gilbertsen to pick on, finding such cargoes more often than the local smugglers do could be nearly impossible." Ajuban chuckled at the remark about Gilbertsen. Roy knew he had no love for any slave trader, and he was convinced that if Gilbertsen had never traded slaves and did not intend to ever do so, he would have removed the iron pins, chains and manacles from his hold. Oddly, Ajuban had no problem with the practice of slavery. He had told Roy that his own people had practiced slavery, as had all the neighboring nations, but such slaves were usually those who had committed crimes or could not pay their debts, and they were treated fairly well. The notion of treating slaves as a commodity to be collected, bred, bought and sold just for profit was not only *alien* to Ajuban, it was despicable.

Roy was brought out of his musings by the sight of Van Friedrich's elegant house with its organized gardens and hedges as the driver turned the wagon down the lane towards it. A stable hand appeared to have been told to watch out for them and he directed the driver along the path to the left of the house after Roy, William and Ajuban stepped from the wagon at the main entrance. Albert stayed with the goods. He was the obvious choice since his size would make him appear simply to be waiting for orders to unload the goods, but his main function was really to guard them. William had given Roy no reason to distrust their host, but he was not about to take chances. It did happen from time to time that a prospective buyer would attempt to steal the goods they were being offered since the seller usually could not alert the authorities without it being revealed how the goods were initially obtained, though such an occurrence would be odd indeed in a town like Curaçao where few authorities cared where goods came from.

They were not kept waiting as Van Friedrich's butler swept the door open before they had quite reached it and showed them inside. The house had an open feeling to it, rather like Mr. Van Kemper's tavern, except that the chairs and shelves, stands and all other woodwork were stained in much lighter tones, giving the rooms a slightly washed out appearance in the failing daylight. Roy noticed that there was not much gilding on the decorative pieces lining the hall, but every strip of wood was intricately carved or painted and there was an abundance of excellent glassware. There were also a number of paintings ornamenting the walls, though these were generally landscapes. "These are all of excellent quality," William said quietly, indicating the paintings. "A couple of them appear to be from Florence, or at least the content is definitely Florentine, though I do not recognize the artists."

"That knowledge could be useful if Van Friedrich tries to undervalue the painting," Roy considered. "He obviously doesn't spend his money on anything but the best quality, and the fact that he's interested seems to me to speak volumes." Roy hoped that he would feel the same after seeing the painting.

"I think we need have no fear that he will undervalue it, sir," answered William, sounding somewhat deliberately tactful. "Those interested in the arts generally deplore showing any ignorance of such matters more than they deplore missing a bargain. Even if he decides that it is not quite to his taste, he knows that he could sell it elsewhere for a tidy sum. No, the main thing he will argue in negotiation is the *condition* of the painting—which is excellent, by the way—and he may hope to rely on our ignorance of such matters."

William had very carefully refrained from saying "*your* ignorance of such matters," but Roy didn't care either way. He was very much out of his depth with most academic pursuits, and he was more relieved than embarrassed that William could compensate for it. "If you have anything to interject during our negotiations, do so," said Roy decisively. "This is obviously more your area than mine, and I don't feel the need to put my rank before profit."

"Yes sir," said William seriously. Roy couldn't see any hint of satisfaction on William's face, though he imagined that he saw William stride somewhat more purposefully, as if there was nothing more in his head than determination to carry out his duty. Roy was pleased and a little bit surprised at that. Start heaping too much praise and responsibility on your crew and often you would soon find that they became more and more insubordinate. But for all his airs of noblesse and scholarship, William so far seemed genuinely not to have an arrogant bone in his body.

They were shown to a room on the ground floor furnished like a study, though rather the size of a parlor. The evening sunlight poured through the large west-facing window as the sun sank towards the horizon illuminating a large desk cluttered with ledgers, a couple of maps (one of which appeared to be a map of Curaçao), and a gilt glass tray ornamented with birds and bearing a matching wine pitcher and six wine cups. Candles had already been lit in anticipation of sunset. A young man, though a bit older-looking than Roy, rose from his seat behind the desk as the butler announced them in English, "Captain Roy Toppings and his men to see you, sir."

"Good evening gentlemen," said the man. "I am Andries van Friedrich." He was a slender, sandy haired man of a height with Roy and with a neatly trimmed beard and moustache. His green eyes had a merry glint, but his manner was somewhat reserved. He wore a red silk vest embroidered with gold over his white, gold-trimmed tunic after the manner of a merchant, but he had little other ornamentation about him.

"Captain Roy Toppings," answered Roy as they shook hands. "This is my first mate, Ajuban." Roy gestured to his dark-skinned friend and was pleased to see Van Friedrich shake hands with him with no evident distaste. "You've already met William." Roy was grateful for being spared introducing the man as "William Ward of Devonshire" himself, though he was respectful of William's desire to be introduced that way, silly as he thought it.

"Please, sit down," said their host as he sat back behind his desk.

They made themselves comfortable in the cheerfully painted chairs, which were also intricately carved like all of the other woodwork, and proceeded to make small talk as a servant came in to serve wine before leaving them alone again. "You are new to Curaçao?" asked Van Friedrich.

"Yes, we only arrived this morning," answered Roy.

"Aboard what ship?"

"*The Constance*. She's a small trade craft, but she's fast."

"I will have to keep an eye out for her in the future," said Van Friedrich.

"Being so far from the harbor usually means I am the last to know of any goods coming in, unless I keep an eye out for such things."

"In this case," said Roy easing into a business manner, "we were happily referred to you specifically for your refined tastes and eye for quality."

He hoped that he would not have to go into great detail about the source of the referral and be forced to reveal that he had attacked a Dutch ship and taken on some of her crew, but Van Friedrich did not ask. "Yes, quality goods can be difficult to come by in the Caribbean sometimes, especially with any sort of regularity."

"Certainly that is the case, though ports such as this do their part to break the Spanish monopoly on some of those goods."

Van Friedrich chuckled somewhat bitterly. "Not enough for a man to count on," he said. "I had a mind to start a coffee business with my wife, but we don't get enough of it coming through this port to make the venture profitable."

"So I understand," replied Roy. "Unfortunately there aren't enough profitable bargains for Spanish coffee in this area. The Spanish growers in the area know the export value of their crop all too well, and so do the merchant captains. I imagine they wish to keep it as high as it is. For my part, I don't plan to be in the area long enough to maintain such a trade." Having implied that he could not maintain a contract for a regular supply of coffee, Roy watched as Van Friedrich shrugged and opened the ledger in front of him.

"I quite understand," he said. "Well, I can purchase as much as two hundred pounds of your cargo of coffee, though I should of course like to inspect it first. If it is fresh and of the brand that I was told, I will pay five ducats for so much, as William and I had agreed."

"Shall I have my men bring it here?" asked Roy, "Or would you prefer to come out to the wagon?"

"Have them bring it here," answered their host. "And have the Diego Velasquez brought in as well. I am quite excited to see it." He sounded sincere on that point, and his eyes gleamed with anticipation and curiosity.

Roy sent William out to instruct Albert. Many people that Roy had dealt with had expected to see Ajuban do some of the fetching and carrying merely because he was usually viewed as not much different than a slave, but he did not consider it appropriate for an officer aboard his ship to carry out such functions except when necessary, no matter what others thought. Andries van Friedrich showed no confusion, however, and Roy had already begun to like the man. He was straightforward (or at least as much as anyone who traded in illegal goods could be), amiable, obviously sensible, and he did not so far seem to have a habit of looking down his nose at people.

As they waited for Albert and William to come back, Van Friedrich spoke more of his business plans. "I had originally meant to open a café adjoined to Mrs. Lisanne Hebert's bakery, but my business partner was lost in a hurricane late last year, I believe. At least I haven't heard from him since, and he would have been in that area at the time. Fortunately, I had not yet bought the land, though Mrs. Hebert certainly could have used the added business."

"That was in November, was it not?" asked Roy. "I was lucky to sail to the Caribbean some months earlier, but I heard that the storm devastated much of the area near Saint Kitts."

"Yes, including some of Sint Maarten, as it turns out," replied Van Friedrich. "I have since had a couple of dealings indirectly with a plantation owned by a Spaniard named Ramón Chavez, but there has been nothing regular enough on which I can rely. So I wait and watch."

Roy's ears had perked up at mention of Ramón Chavez. *That was the name on Gilbertsen's contract.* "Is this Chavez slow to agree to a contract?" Roy asked as casually as possible.

"I am not sure, but his shipping partner certainly is," he answered with disgust. "He's a local man here, and I think that he knows it is difficult for Spaniards to find foreign shippers in that area. He has no doubt heard a story circulating in some of the Spanish colonies that Chavez was paid a good deal of money by the president of New Granada for part of his land that contained a number of valuable artifacts which had originally been carried off by refugees from the Incan Empire. Anyway, Chavez reportedly wasn't given much choice about it since it was disputed whether or not the land was actually covered by his grant and he had never explored that part of it, but I think that his shipper is demanding even more money for his services since Chavez received payment for that portion of his land."

Marius bloody Gilbertsen, I'd wager my ship on it. "Intriguing," Roy remarked quietly. "You wouldn't happen to have heard the native name for that place, would you? It chances that I have a learned associate who has made some small study of the old Incas and other mainland tribes."

Van Friedrich looked quite surprised. It was rare for anyone to study the Incas (particularly as doing so in Spanish territory was considered inappropriate by the representatives of the Catholic Church there) and doubly rare for anyone beyond Spanish territories to know such a person. "Ch'umpi Jallp'a," he replied baldly. "I have no idea what it means, but if you find out anything about the place, I would be quite interested in hearing it. Who can say?" he mused, "It may give me an advantage over this troublesome shipper."

"Of course," said Roy, "It is the least I could do since I owe you for the knowledge." He fought the urge to smile at Gilbertsen's expense. Or at least he would fight it until after he left Van Friedrich's house.

William soon came back bearing the thin rectangular crate that housed the Velasquez painting, followed by Albert with one of the hundred-pound sacks of coffee perched between his shoulders. An aroma of coffee began to steal through the room as he set it down on Van Friedrich's sturdy desk where a space had been cleared.

Van Friedrich was quickly convinced by the smell that the coffee was fresh and of good quality, and the sack had obviously not been opened or tampered with in any way. "And now for the painting," he said after his inspection.

William opened the crate and displayed the portrait with, Roy noticed, a certain degree of artistic flair. He had stopped in a part of the room that had an excellent quality of light for such an inspection, and Roy doubted that it was by accident. As William had suggested, Mr. Van Friedrich did not attempt to undervalue the painting itself, but rather remarked on several indentations and a scuff on the frame. He did not attempt to argue the condition of the painting itself at all.

"You can always have it reframed if you like," said Roy, "but the value of the frame alone is rather high."

"Besides," William cut in, "any such item would have the same wear—probably more—after a voyage across the Atlantic, and this has made at least one trip in addition to that. One of the woodcarvers you doubtless consult regularly"—William gestured to the intricate woodwork ornamenting the room—"would certainly not balk at such terms."

Mr. Van Friedrich smiled at William with grudging respect. "You are a rare find among sailors, my friend," he said.

In the end, he agreed to pay two hundred twenty ducats for it. It was worth more, by a fair margin, but William seemed to think that was as much as anyone was likely to buy it for outside of Spanish territory, and Roy really had no other use for the thing. It was certainly a worthy capture, either way. Mr. Van Friedrich asked his butler to bring him his strongbox, and to have someone show Albert to the pantry where the coffee would be stored. He counted out the equivalent coinage of two hundred twenty-five ducats (some of which he paid in a similar weight of Spanish doubloons and English broads, laurels and unites), which Roy stored in a wooden coffer he had brought for the purpose. After being assured that the coffee was safe in storage, Van Friedrich rose and personally escorted them outside where he bid them farewell. "Well, gentlemen, it has been a pleasure doing business with you, and I hope to have more such fruitful dealings with you in the future. Enjoy your stay in Curaçao."

They lit lanterns, turned and mounted the empty wagon, and departed for the town once more. "Well, we just have time to get back to the ship and make our eight o'clock delivery to Mrs. Rutger. Then I suggest we all have dinner and a bit of leisure at Mr. Van Kemper's tavern."

"We can certainly afford it now, captain," said Ajuban.

"Indeed. I will be even happier once all of the deals are complete and I have some new crewmembers aboard. Keep a sharp ear for any local news you hear tonight," he added. "I've a mind to see if there is anything worth pursuing down here since I don't spend much time in the area."

"Aye, sir," said the three crewmen together.

* * *

"Send in the ambassador, please," Andries van Friedrich said to his butler. The negotiations with the Englishmen had gone well and smoothly, obviously leaving both sides feeling that they had received a bargain. Such transactions made for good future business relations between all concerned, and Andries could not have been more pleased with the timing of this particular transaction. A good part of why he felt he had gained the upper hand was because of the French ambassador's visit to Curaçao, and he was very sure that it would not take much negotiating to convince the ambassador to help his plan along.

The butler shortly returned, followed by a tall, ornately dressed man with shoulder-length blond hair framing a gaunt-cheeked face. His pointed blond beard and thin moustache simply made his face seem longer, but his gaze was sharp and present. "Marquis Jean-Baptiste Augustin of France, sir," said the butler as the other man entered and made a slight bow.

"Andries van Friedrich," said Andries bowing deeply. "Please, have a seat." They sank into their chairs across the desk from each other, and were left alone as the butler closed the door.

Presently, the marquis asked jovially, "So what is this business proposition of yours? You said something about a gift for young King Louis that he might use to show his power and reach. I must admit that I can't imagine such a thing coming from the Caribbean, but I suppose this is exactly what you mean by 'reach?'" His manner was unusual in a diplomat, although of course this was not a diplomatic visit. He seemed to be on the edge of amusement as soon as he began speaking, and the characteristic remained in his features throughout the entire interview. His sharp gaze carried somewhat of the wit of the rascal, but it was known that he was a personal friend of the young King Louis. He himself looked to be little older than thirty years of age.

Andries grinned in turn both at the Frenchman's manner and at the reminder of his own idea. As Andries spoke, the marquis leaned in, interest mingling with the amusement on his face. "I have just acquired a genuine Diego Velasquez painting of one of King Philip's distinguished Austrian cousins"—he gestured to the wall behind the marquis where the work was already hanging—"and I was at once struck by the notion that King Louis might have more use for it than I. If, for example, he were to have it mounted in a room in his noble palace where he has a habit of entertaining visiting Spanish dignitaries, the effect could be quite satisfactory."

There was no doubt about the amusement on the ambassador's face now. "A most tantalizing inspiration, I must admit," he said, shifting his gaze from the painting back to his host. "What would you seek in exchange for such an opportunity as this, Monsieur Van Friedrich?"

"Simply this: I will sell you the painting for half the price of two hundred twenty ducats that I paid for it, if you will have a reasonable supply contract for coffee beans drawn up for me from any of the more reputable plantation owners in your Hispaniola colonies." He had been obliged to come to the point more quickly than he had dared hope, but the marquis appeared to value frankness as much as he did. The marquis seemed to be considering the notion, and from his expression, Andries soon became confident that his proposal would be more or less accepted.

Chapter 6: A King's Ransom

Merely an hour later, having concluded all business transactions and paid the wagon drivers extra for their time, the crew of *The Constance* met back at the ship expectantly. Mrs. Rutger had offered thirteen ducats for the remaining coffee, but Roy felt it wise not to inform her of who had purchased the rest of the coffee since she might have hoped to sell to Van Friedrich herself. Brian very quickly tallied each man's share based on the same system Roy had explained earlier at Van Kemper's tavern—leaving aside a few expenses and a one ducat bonus for each of the Dutch sailors, as Roy felt they had at least earned that much and that they must have expenses needing to be paid in Curaçao—and everyone was quite pleased that the smallest shares topped fifteen ducats. That was roughly equivalent to six English pounds—more than most of them would have been likely to earn in several months on honest wages. Roy thought Coya looked surprised, and she took great care to conceal the coins on her person to thwart cutpurses and street toughs. Some of the men were already making their ways into town with respectful and amicable nods to him. Martin even clapped him on the back. The Dutchmen seemed doubly grateful that they had been allowed to join the crew—one ducat was at least as much as their wage from Captain Gilbertsen would have amounted to, and Luuk and Bert both had families to support. The other of their number, Jacob, made it clear that he was going to have a good evening at a local tavern and sauntered off with a salute to Roy and a wave at his friend Tiede.

There was no longer much need to guard the ship as all the cargo had been sold, but Brian, as well as a few others who spoke no Dutch, had no desire to lodge in town for the night. All except Brian wished to venture out on the town though, but Roy let it be known that he hoped to leave the following morning on a new venture. "So I expect you all back at dawn tomorrow," he told them as they parted. "Not even coming out for a bite to eat?" he enquired turning to Brian again hopefully.

"Maybe next time," said the rumpled-looking navigator. "Though I might pop into town to pick up some tobacco or other personal effects," he added.

"I suppose you could have one of the dock runners fetch you a meal." *An hour off the ship wouldn't kill him.*

Brian laughed. "Don't worry about me, sir, you just have a pleasant evening," he waved to Roy, Ajuban, Coya and the others still standing there.

Roy shrugged and gestured for the rest of the group to follow him. They had already bathed that day (though most had arranged for rooms for the night as well) before meeting back at *The Constance*, and now they all decided to go back to Van Kemper's. Not only was the food there good, it was also a large place and the gambling would attract more sailors than other men as so many sailors eventually took up the pastime to alleviate boredom at sea. It was an opportunity to show off how well their last venture had paid, though Roy had made sure to tell those of his crew going to other, cheaper establishments to make sure it was generally known that the captain was dining at Van Kemper's should any potential new crew wish to see him. The mention of the expensive venue would hopefully impress them. Privately though, he hoped that the quality seamen patronizing Van Kemper's would throw him a few welcome surprises like those he'd found on his last recruiting mission. Coya, Albert and William had certainly earned their places, and even Justin—in spite of his initial condescension towards Coya—had not really grumbled since he signed on, and proved to be a competent and willing crewman who wasted no time completing any task he was assigned.

Some in their group had not been to Van Kemper's, though the Dutchmen had all gone for the evening except for Tiede. They did not have as much to spend as the rest of the crew, and they had homes to go to, but Tiede came with Roy and his group. He would be useful since none of the rest of Roy's party spoke any Dutch—an even bigger handicap when dealing with Dutch sailors than it was when dealing with Dutch merchants. William and Albert both seemed excited, and William fancied a bit of gambling, but

Albert seemed to want to rebuild the small fortune he had raised as a pit fighter in Tortuga and had so disappointingly lost there. From the way the man moved and fought, Roy could well believe his savings had been a good deal more substantial than today's share. He had been training Albert how to fence, and in return, Albert had begun teaching him the style of bare-fisted fighting that he knew (though they trained with pads and gloves). For the last week, they had paired off in one such lesson or another, and each had a very high respect for the other as a fighting man. Indeed, Roy felt a certain kinship with Albert, as if they shared somewhat of the same nature even if they found it difficult to maintain much conversation with each other. He would also be glad to have the burly Englishman by his side in case anyone let it slip that they had attacked a Dutch ship while their group was surrounded by Dutch sailors in Van Kemper's tavern. The local government might not take too much notice, but most of the local sailors would. Roy had told everyone to say that the battle had been with a smuggler out of Gibraltar, and by no means to call the ship a "Dutch cargo fluyt" if they could possibly avoid it, but drink had a way of loosening men's tongues. No one was likely to experience anything worse than a beating over the issue, but it wasn't worth the risk, and he could not think of a better way to put off new recruits.

Eventually they reached the corner where Van Kemper's tavern sprawled halfway down to the next street, and Roy could hear the hubbub from within well before they pushed open the door. As welcoming as the place had been during the day, it was better suited to nighttime. The chandeliers were complemented by candles now standing on every table, and the interplay between the flickering candlelight and the high raftered ceiling made the shadows dance, disappear, and reappear, emphasizing the darkness outside rather than dispelling all trace of it. It produced a subtle effect that Roy could only describe to himself as that of making someone wish to stay put inside for a long time in the comfortable hum of good cheer and laughter. Willem van Kemper greeted them warmly, or at least as warmly as his pace would allow. He did not serve tables himself or handle drink orders as he apparently had a large enough number of servants even for the crowd that packed the room to bursting, but he had enough to do just with organizing the staff, shouting to the kitchens, and dealing with those patrons who wished to speak with him personally.

Tiede helped them order as he had before, but now there were roasts and fish, ham, heaped portions of seasoned potatoes and vegetables, steaming breads, chilled wines, some sort of dish involving cheese and thinly-sliced lamb (very unusual for the climate), two whole roasted chickens, and (surprisingly) a fresh apple tart. It seemed a feast, and their table received many glances from the other patrons, probably for the sheer extravagance and variety of it, but that would simply make people more inquisitive about Roy and his crew, which was all to the good. Albert alone asked for ale, seeming somewhat disappointed at the prospect of wine after a hard day's labor, however fine it may be. But a tall tankard was brought to him, and his spirits brightened visibly as he remarked with some surprise on the quality of what he tasted.

They talked and laughed together spiritedly—even Coya seemed much more relaxed than usual—but each of them was eager to hear news and acquaint themselves with the others filling the place. They had all seemed to get along wonderfully as a crew, but after spending a week at sea with the same small group of people, *anyone* would welcome a change in company, Roy not least. William dashed down the last of his wine and excused himself, making his way to a far table where men played cards. Roy was not surprised. Anyone who introduced himself as "William Ward of Devonshire" would be much more likely to play a gentlemanly game of cards rather than engaging in a plebian activity like dicing. He grinned at the thought. He could see another man at that table who looked like he belonged there even more: a young but dignified looking man with a thin face and a blond beard. His thin moustache was not ample enough to hide his amused expression, but Roy could not tell if that was the man's usual expression or if he wore it for the sake of the game. He appeared to be engaged in some version of three card brag, and a few large stacks of coins sat in front of him, so it was unlikely that his amused expression betrayed any particular reaction to what was in his hand. His hair hung to his shoulders, but it was flattened where his hat must normally sit when it was not hanging from one of the posts of his chair as it was now. He was well-dressed, and Roy stamped out a thought that he must be a captain or somesuch. *Fool!* He was beginning to think like a witless deckhand. *If clothes make a captain, then I'll find myself asking Brian for orders before long.*

He glanced over to another table where men were dicing. None of them had stacks of coins half as large as any of the card players in front of him, and none of those coins were gold, but they appeared to be in their element all the same. Tiede and Albert headed in that direction, but Albert only watched as Tiede sat down at the table, placing a small pile of silver in front of him. Soon only Roy, Ajuban and Coya remained. Their table was cleared but for their goblets of wine, and the empty chairs beckoned to newcomers. This was how Roy liked to recruit. He often felt that it was appropriate for the captain and first mate to sit together when men came to ask them questions. It gave an added air of authority to anything the captain said that was absent if he was alone. In some ways it seemed foolish that it should be so, but captains were usually only impressive aboard their ships. In a tavern, they were just other men, and anything they said could be suspect. A captain with no subordinates at his side was not very inspiring. One man sitting self-importantly in a tavern seemed comical at best, lonely at worst. Two men together sitting self-importantly in a tavern suggested organization and comradeship, regardless of what sense would dictate. Coya sitting there with them was an odd touch though. Her presence might add intrigue, or it might inspire doubt. If people thought she was an officer and that they might have to obey her at some point, they might think twice about joining his crew. "Don't feel like mingling or gambling?" he asked her in Spanish.

She started a little. "I'm not sure I would be welcome," she said apprehensively. "And I don't speak English well enough yet to do either, let alone Dutch."

"It's of no matter," he assured her. He *hoped* it was of no matter. "Keep an eye open though for anything unusual."

"Do you expect trouble?" she asked with idle curiosity. Her tone suggested that she kept an eye out for trouble no matter what she was doing, but really he had just wanted to give her some feeling of purposefulness in case she was feeling isolated or otherwise ill at ease.

"No, but establishments like this can be interesting, especially in such a town as this and with this much money circulating in one room." He didn't think it likely that anything more interesting than unusual new faces with strange stories or news to share would trouble them tonight, but she nodded and kept an eye on things. *At least she looks more imposing and mysterious now.* He hoped that added to the atmosphere that he and Ajuban were trying to create. The peculiar quality of light in the room that reminded one of darkness certainly helped.

Before long, others began to fill the empty seats and, perceiving Roy as an Englishman, they asked where he was from and what brought him to Curaçao. He told them what little news he could, but he had to apologize since he had been at sea for a while and was new to the area. "Really?" they asked. "Where have you been?"

"Well," Roy began, leaning forward, "We set out from Port Royal a week ago. We needed to pick up a cargo, and we thought the Spaniards might be able to furnish us with one, so we set out for the coast of Hispaniola…" The men he was talking to seemed to take his meaning and to have no especial love for Spaniards, and they looked wonderingly from him to Ajuban, and sometimes at Coya, as he told his tale.

* * *

Coya was most aware of how much she stood out in the social atmosphere surrounding her. When she had been to the tavern earlier, most people were simply having lunch, and she had not particularly stood out, but now everyone seemed to want to speak and laugh and carouse with nearly everyone else. She had no idea what the captain had meant by "interesting" when he told her to keep an eye open. It seemed like a normal enough tavern from the little she had glimpsed of such places before, though she had admittedly been peering in through windows on most of those occasions. Either way, she wasn't likely to overhear anything interesting since she could barely make out anything that was said except for a few snatches of English here and there.

She did pay quite a bit of attention to her companions though, especially to Roy and Ajuban as they held their odd little interviews with other strangers. It was not long before she got the distinct impression that they were putting forward some sort of grand image, in a way. It reminded her somewhat of a warrior recounting his exploits to the elders when asked to prove himself worthy to command. They made their last little adventure sound much more interesting and daring than she remembered it though, and it seemed to make a good impression on several patrons.

Between these conversations, they kept her up to date on some of the news they had gathered. Some of the men there had been approached by a Scottish captain named Sir Sebastian McLaughlin who was looking for crew to raid the nearby Spanish town of Coro. In fact it seemed that many of them were interested in taking him up on the offer, as Coro was generally known as a small town with few defenses and no real fleet, and McLaughlin had a local reputation for his cunning raids. Roy seemed disappointed by that, as it would cut into the number of recruits he would be able to take on, but he was still hopeful of getting some new additions. Roy still did not have a solid notion for a next venture beyond picking off stray Spanish vessels, but news that there had been several recent raids on the town of Caracas by natives living in the surrounding hills seemed to interest him. When she asked him about it, he explained, "Raids by natives could very well mean that Caracas has fewer soldiers at the moment, so they might be particularly susceptible to a more organized endeavor."

"But wouldn't they be more on their guard as well?" she asked.

"Possibly, but they will be on their guard for the same kind of raids," he answered. "Most such raids are made in a disorganized fashion by people who have only a few gleaned weapons in need of repair. Beyond that, they usually use rocks, clubs, knives, or other simple weapons, and they only tend to take supplies and weapons since they have no use for gold and silver in the wilderness. If there had been attacks by pirates or bandits in the area, it would not likely be worth it for us to raid the town ourselves. They would have less of value to plunder and they would be wary of well-armed men in the area."

Coya nodded. It made good sense as he had stated it, but she had simply never thought of such differences before. Not only had she always been among the knife-wielding, supply-stealing variety of raiders when she lived in the wilderness, but she had also always worked alone.

"Speaking of natives," Roy continued, "have you ever heard of a place called Ch'umpi Jallp'a?"

She snapped her mouth shut when she realized that she had been gaping. She had never thought she would hear that name from anyone else's lips again, and certainly not this far away from the place. "It was my home!" she said, stammering slightly. "Where did you hear that name?"

Roy certainly appeared surprised by the revelation, but not half as surprised as she felt. "I heard it from Andries van Friedrich," he said. "It appears I have some news which might interest you very much," he said with a look of concern in his eyes. She hung on his every word. "He told us that he had received shipments of coffee before from the plantation of Ramón Chavez, the same man named in the contract we took from Captain Gilbertsen. Apparently, part of Chavez' land was bought by the president of New Granada who, under the viceroy of Peru, rules New Granada and most of the colonies in the north and west of South America. I asked the native name for Chavez' land, and Van Friedrich said it was Ch'umpi Jallp'a. I'm afraid that the tract of land that was purchased by the president contained a number of valuable artifacts that Van Friedrich said had been brought there by 'refugees from the Incan Empire,' as he called them." Roy's tone softened even more. "It seems likely that the artifacts are to be taken back to Spain, if I know anything about how these sorts of treasures are handled."

"In that case, they might end up at Cartagena to await the treasure fleet," said Coya. Her heart sank. All of the treasure that made its way to Cartagena was kept in the newly-finished fort of San Felipe, and the fort was well-known to be perfectly built and beyond any thief or plunderer as long as enough men stood to defend it. She remembered the imposing sight of San Felipe from every time she had visited the Cartagena marketplace. Any treasure brought there was released only when the treasure fleet arrived with many trade galleons and warships to collect goods on their way back to Spain, and raids on the treasure fleet were rarely successful. Usually pirates and privateers could only hope to pick off the stragglers, and the chances of recovering the relics from her home in such a fashion were virtually non-existent. "They must have found the temple and plundered it," she said angrily. "That was the only place where any artifacts of value were kept. I thought they would have plundered it long ago." *I shouldn't be this upset. I accepted all of this long ago.* But hearing about it as a recent event made the loss seem fresh.

"Mr. Van Friedrich said that Chavez had not yet explored that part of the land. If it was a temple and has only recently been discovered," Roy added, "maybe the priests—is that what they are called?—escaped."

"They did not live there," she told him. "It would have been sacrilege to do so. The temple was only where rituals were performed. Besides, I think they would take any relics they could carry away if they had escaped from there."

"Mr. Van Friedrich told us only that much," Roy said apologetically, "but I don't know how old the news is. He made it sound recent, but if the relics would be taken to Cartagena, they may already be there by now. I will try to find out more, if I can."

She nodded gratefully. After having told him her story back in Port Royal, she was glad that he had not been as casual with this news as others might have been. She certainly was glad not to hear it in passing from one of Roy's buyers. In any case, it seemed that there was not much she could do about it, so she tried to settle back into her chair and keep up with the other doings in Van Kemper's. William's pile of coins appeared to have dwindled while he played cards, and the gaunt, amused-looking blond man's pile appeared to have grown. Tiede was apparently holding his own at dice, and Albert was talking animatedly with a few of the sailors that Coya had understood to be part of this Sebastian McLaughlin's crew. She also noticed a respectable-looking man sitting on a stool by himself who appeared to look periodically at her table as well as that of Sir Sebastian. He seemed to be debating something in his mind, and he looked just a little dejected. She felt a strange surge of sympathy for him. Certainly he was not the only person sitting alone, but he seemed the only person who wasn't content with that. She studied him when he was not looking in her direction and noted that he was well-dressed and wore a fine gold ring with a sizeable diamond set in it on his wedding finger. Coya knew that it was unusual for a man to wear a wedding ring at all, much less one with ornamentation. He looked middle aged, but his eyes made him seem older somehow. He bore some resemblance to the blond card player whose winnings were even larger now, except this man's pointed beard and moustache were mostly gray and he had a kindly expression, though his gaze was no less piercing.

She mentioned all of this to Roy when the man's attention was once again diverted to McLaughlin's table. Roy studied the man briefly. "He doesn't appear to be the carousing type," Roy said thoughtfully. "I wonder why he is so interested in us. Hopefully he isn't Gilbertsen's brother or something," he laughed. The complete lack of resemblance between this man and Gilbertsen brought a grin to Coya's lips. "Anyway, he doesn't look like someone who is easily impressed," Roy said with a note of decision in his voice. Coya soon became aware that Roy's and Ajuban's postures had changed—their expressions were no longer so intimidating or, well, boastful. When the gray-haired man looked to their table again, Roy waved him over good-naturedly, and to Coya's surprise, the man only hesitated for a moment before smiling and making his way across the floor to sit down with them.

Roy greeted him cordially and introduced them. "This is my first mate, Ajuban," he said. "This is Coya, another member of my crew. I am Captain Roy Toppings, but I am guessing that you already knew that."

The gray-haired man looked surprised. "My name is Jan Huisman. A pleasure to meet you all," he said and shook hands with all of them. It was a Dutch name, but he spoke perfect English, right down to the accent from what she could tell. "How did you guess that I knew who you were?" he asked.

"My friend here is very observant," Roy said gesturing to Coya.

Jan again looked surprised, but he looked her in the eye and she could see no hint of prejudice as he asked her with some wonder, "You are from the continent, are you not?" He had asked her in Spanish, which he also spoke perfectly.

"I am." Now it was her turn to be surprised. "You are *also* very observant."

"I have some experience with the natives that help out some of the local, ah, merchants," he said. From what she had understood, "local merchants" in Curaçao often meant smugglers.

"Indeed?" said Roy with interest. Coya was glad that the conversation seemed to be going forward in a language she knew well. She was already deciding she liked this kindly gentleman. "It must serve you well to place you in such a position in life." He gestured to Jan's large diamond ring.

Jan chuckled under his breath. "Well, yes, after a fashion. But my experience is more with their wounds than their business."

"You are a doctor?" said Ajuban in very impressed tones.

"And a surgeon," Jan elaborated, "I trained at the university in Montpellier." Roy whistled and Ajuban bowed low in his seat. Coya was astounded. She little knew the differences between a doctor and a surgeon except for one very important one: while European doctors were much like medicine men in that they could heal the sick with mixtures and salves, as well as sound advice, a surgeon had the knowledge and skill to actually *cut people open* to heal some illnesses or injuries that mixtures and salves alone could not cure. She had come to realize that her people knew generally less of medicine than the Europeans (though she thought they knew more in some specific areas), but surgery was very rare and limited among them whereas the Europeans had expanded the practice greatly. Even so, surgeons were so rare that there were not usually more than a handful in even large towns. She had heard of only half a dozen in Cartagena, and that was the only real city she had ever seen.

Roy, however, recovered quickly—possibly because, as a European, the reality of surgeons was less remarkable, though his words did have a slightly deferential tone when he spoke now. "This explains much about your appearance, except for why you seemed to be debating whether to approach me or Sir Sebastian over there. What can I do for you?"

Surgeon or no, Coya could sense that Jan was not quite in his element here. "I have noticed that you are recruiting and I was curious about what your intentions are," he said. "I can give you some potentially useful information about recent events in the Caribbean that you may not have heard, as I have different sources of information than most sailors. But I may be interested in joining your crew. I have heard what Sir Sebastian intends, but I have yet to speak to him personally."

"Why would you want to join *any* crew?" asked Roy incredulously. "Your position is surely advantageous enough to you to make such a risky trade hardly worthwhile. Even as a navy doctor you could not hope to do so well. Besides," added Roy, gesturing to Jan's wedding ring, "a family would seem to make the risk even less appealing, I should think."

"It is true that my position makes other situations less tempting," replied Jan casually, "but though I intend to keep my reasons to myself, it should suffice to say that I am in need of large sums of money that are quickly attainable (though I do have some standards about how this is accomplished), and that I am in no one's debt or disfavor. As for this," here he gestured to his ring, "I am a widower, but I wish still to honor my wife's memory in this way."

"A strange explanation, to be sure," said Roy after some puzzled thought. "I will enquire no more as to your motives out of respect for your privacy, sir, but what you ask is easy enough." He began to tell the surgeon about their encounter with the merchant vessel in the storm before Coya had signed on, as well as the recent encounter with "a shallow draft merchant vessel with a touch less maneuverability than *The Constance*," (presumably working his way up to discussing his next venture). To everyone's surprise, Jan's questions were so shrewd and his grasp so quick that he deduced that they were speaking of attacking a Dutch cargo fluyt. But Jan seemed not to mind, and soon Roy was telling him everything.

"Marius Gilbertsen," Jan explained, "would sell his own mother to hungry cannibals if he thought they would cough up a gold doubloon, or if his inheritance from her amounted to as much. He once brought me a crewman who had been hooked by a boarding grapple. Not only did the man have to pay for his treatment, he also had to pay for the carriage to transport him to my infirmary, pay for the duties that other crewmen had had to take on in his absence, and he was given no consideration for the fact that he had participated in the fight. The only reason Gilbertsen gets any crew at all is because his trips are nearly always without incident and so the pay is reliable. If it ever got out that this was not the case, he might find himself either out of business or forced to pay his crews more."

Roy's expression became flatter and flatter throughout the surgeon's narrative. "I don't suppose such a rumor could be circulated without incriminating us? Or perhaps once we're gone from here? At any rate, I will make it a special point to attack his ship if I ever spot him at sea again, or even if I hear about him making a trip that is convenient for me to intrude upon." He sounded quite serious.

Jan began speaking approvingly about the idea, but Coya's attention was distracted by a man who had just entered Van Kemper's tavern. He was dark-haired and tightly built, and openly wore a Spanish uniform and officer's rank (as well as the typical beard and moustache that most Spanish officers seemed to prefer), but it was not that which captivated Coya's attention. The man moved like a cat, and he radiated physical danger. The only men in the room she could compare him to in that sense were Albert and Roy himself. She tugged discreetly at Roy's sleeve. "Be wary of him," she said in an undertone, "he carries himself like a born warrior."

Roy nodded ever so slightly and glanced at Ajuban. Ajuban seemed to register a flicker of understanding, though Coya could not tell why, and suddenly stood up. "Anoder round of drinks, sir?" he asked jovially and somewhat loudly in English.

"Please," said Roy to be heard over the hubbub. Ajuban rose and went to the bar to speak to the bartender that the Spaniard had approached. Coya could hear no more, but she noted that both Jan and Roy viewed the scene askance whenever they could not be observed by either bartender or Spaniard. *Perhaps this is what he meant by "interesting."*

* * *

Ajuban approached the bar and ordered three more ales for his companions. His intent was to order an inconspicuous yet significant amount so that he would have as much time at the bar as possible to wait without lingering long enough to attract attention. He was naturally very curious, which was in part how he had been made a slave in the first place, but even that had not stopped him from being curious. His curiosity was frustrated where reading was involved, but that simply made opportunities to overhear things more tempting. He was respectful of the privacy of his friends, but strange Spaniards were another matter.

"I wish to speak to Mr. Van Kemper about a mutual associate of ours," the Spaniard said cryptically to the bartender in Spanish. He had a rich, musical voice, though he spoke somewhat too lowly for many ears to hear.

Ajuban had not realized that the bartender spoke Spanish, but the bartender only nodded and replied, "One moment," before motioning for Ajuban to wait and disappearing through a door at the end of the bar.

He had ordered in English so as not to put the Spaniard on his guard and he pretended ignorance of anything of interest going on nearby, but he did

129

not risk a glance at the man to see his reaction. It appeared there wouldn't be anything of interest going on until Willem van Kemper came out anyway, but Ajuban was very curious about who this "mutual associate" was and why the Spaniard had been so cryptic. He did not have long to wait though, as Van Kemper stepped briefly out of the door following the bartender and motioned for the man to follow him as he popped back inside. *Great, now I have to wait for t'ree ales to be poured before I can follow dem wit'out drawing attention.* He fully intended to do so, despite the danger, but it was the simple truth that the thought of danger barely entered his head. Still, he had learned some caution as a slave, and the captain wouldn't want a first mate that was completely reckless. He waited as the bartender poured out three agonizingly tall tankards of ale, and he didn't hurry as he paid and brought them back. Then, as the bartender was busy with other customers who had been waiting, he made his way over towards William's card game and diverted towards the door Van Kemper had gone through. He made as if he were trying to get the attention of one of the other patrons, and as soon as another servant came out of the door he bustled inside.

Van Kemper had some Negroes in his establishment for cleaning and serving and running errands, so Ajuban imitated their purposeful and subservient stride as well as he could. Considering that he had been a slave once himself, and the fact that he was dressed much the same as the servants in the tavern (neat, but plain and functional), it wasn't difficult. He had been worried that there might be someone who spotted him and made a fuss about his presence once he slipped in the door, but he had not expected the door to lead to a stairwell to the second floor. The kitchens were accessed through another door, but he had counted on this door leading to some other part of the main floor. *Dis is a bad idea...* But he kept going. If he were caught on the second floor, it might be harder to escape a beating, but all he could do was to go back or to make his way up the stairs as quickly as possible.

Once he was up, he was relieved to realize that there seemed to be fewer people on the second floor and none of them seemed to be in the hallways at the moment. He tried a few doors after making sure he heard no one inside any of them, and found two rooms that he could perhaps hide in should he hear anyone approach. Soon, however, he made his way around a corner and heard voices behind another door. He crept cautiously towards the sound, trying to keep an eye on both the corner and the end of the passageway. He was pleased to find that he could hear Willem van Kemper and the Spaniard behind the door, and he was even more pleased to find that they were speaking Spanish.

"How much has the king authorized?" asked Van Kemper.

"Ten thousand pesos," replied the Spaniard. Ajuban thought he spoke a little bit stiffly or grudgingly, but that amount of money would make anyone twitch.

"Ten thousand?" said Van Kemper suspiciously. "He must want Colonel Valdez very badly to offer that much."

"The amount was authorized to forestall any possible negotiation," answered the Spaniard irritably, sounding as if he did not intend to tolerate any. "His Majesty needs Colonel Baron Valdez conveyed to Spain quickly to aid him in his extensive European campaigns, not that it's any business of yours."

"Major Benito, it *is* my business to enquire after anything that might make one of my charges more valuable to his captor. However, I believe that the sum you are offering for Valdez does, as you say, eliminate the need for much inquiry."

"Good, good. Then we can go ahead with the exchange?" asked Benito.

"Yes, but we had better wait until very early in the morning. I don't want to draw too much attention, and that much silver would draw anyone's attention. I suggest four o'clock. I will keep an eye out for you at that time."

"Very well, I will—"

At that moment, Ajuban heard running footsteps coming from around the far corner at the end of the hall. He ducked around his corner trying to look as if he was on some sort of errand until he could find cover. One of the unlocked doors he had found was near and he stepped inside, closing the door just before he heard raised voices in the next room. He heard only snatches, but it seemed that someone had been caught trying to break in at the back entrance to the alley. He heard hurried footsteps leave the next room and head down the hall—away from the front stairs. He waited for a moment so that any other staff rushing in that direction could do so without spotting him. He listened closely, and apparently someone was still waiting in the next room. Probably Major Benito.

Ajuban took a quick look around the room he was in while he waited. It explained much of the conversation he had overheard. The room was simply furnished with a table, a couple of chairs, a bed, a chamber pot, and a small window with bars on the inside. The door was very solid and appeared to have a sturdy lock and no way to bar the door from inside. It was obviously for keeping people inside, and Ajuban had guessed from the conversation that in addition to his tavern and brewery business, Van Kemper also ran a hostage brokering operation. There were usually a few in any large town that dealt with pirates or privateers, but Van Kemper's was nicer than most. Some consisted of no more than a few thugs guarding a cellar with their captives in chains. Van Kemper obviously treated the prisoners in his charge fairly well, which was wise. The taking of hostages at sea was generally considered a simple means of extracting more plunder from the situation, and plunderers did not usually harbor any personal grudge against their captives, nor did they wish to make enemies of powerful or influential people. It was a business transaction, nothing more. Hostage brokers often viewed the situation similarly, as they received a percentage of the ransom (sometimes as much as twenty percent), though those with fewer resources or who had to operate more secretly generally had little choice but to shut the captives in a secure cell of some kind and guard them diligently.

But Ajuban didn't stop long to ponder all of this. Once he had waited for the sounds of hurrying footsteps on the upper floor to draw further away, he quietly crept out of his room and shut the door just as quietly. He did not look around, but instantly adopted the manner of someone who belonged there as he had done before, and set off back towards the stairs. If anyone spoke to him, it was likely to be in Dutch, but hopefully anyone who saw him wouldn't even suspect him until he was close enough to the door to make a break for it. Van Kemper kept some very tough looking men about to ensure that nothing got out of hand downstairs, but none of them looked to be very quick on their feet.

He was down the stairs and almost to the door when another servant opened it and stepped onto the stairs, but the small man appeared not to pay any mind to Ajuban and hurried on past him. With his heart in his throat, Ajuban seized the opportunity of the open door to slip out into the tavern without drawing attention. Thankfully the bartender was looking away, and Ajuban stepped casually over to watch the card game briefly—the blonde man had a slightly larger pile of coins before him now, but appeared to be watching the dice game as well—before making his way back to Roy's table. He heaved a sigh of relief as he sat down.

"How did your little adventure go?" Roy asked. "You're still in one piece and unbruised, so I assume you were at least successful in not being noticed?"

"I had a little help getting back out," he answered. "Dey caught someone trying to break into de back way, by de alley. I overheard someone tell Van Kemper, and all de servants went dat way long enough for me to come out. Except for dat last fellow," he added with a frown.

"What fellow?"

"A small balding servant of Van Kemper's," said Coya. "He went through the door Ajuban came out of, and only seconds before Ajuban appeared."

"You were paying attention," Ajuban laughed under his breath. "You have sharp eyes." *He* was impressed at any rate. There would have been no telling when he would come out, and she surely had not been staring at the door the whole time.

Coya grinned. "I was the only one here who saw you go in the door, so I glanced up every time I saw it open. But then someone *did* tell me to keep my eyes open," she said with amusement in an aside to Roy.

"I admit," Roy said to Ajuban, "that I was very engrossed in my discussion with Jan. To me it seemed that you were there and suddenly when I looked up, you were gone."

"Any interesting news?" Ajuban asked of Roy and Jan.

"Oh yes, very interesting," Roy answered with a smile, and Ajuban realized that his own curiosity was getting the better of him once again and that Roy had also noticed. *He knows me all too well.* "But come, first let's hear your tale. What of the Spaniard?"

They all leaned in to speak more quietly together in the din of the room's merriment. "It seems dat our friendly brewer is also a hostage broker," said Ajuban to the surprise of the two men and the puzzlement of Coya. "He has some hostage dat de Spanish king wants, by de name of Colonel Valdez. Dis Spaniard—Major Benito is his name—said dat de king is willing to pay ten t'ousand pesos for his immediate release! Dey want him for wars in Europe, so he said, and dey don't want to waste time in haggling."

"Colonel *Javier* Valdez?" asked Jan in a tone of awe.

"Could be," Ajuban shrugged, "Benito called him 'Colonel Baron Valdez.'"

"He would be quite a capture," said the surgeon, "but I can't see him fetching that much. Still, it has to be him. Besides, he's the only one by the name of Valdez who is well-known enough in the Caribbean to *possibly* warrant such a ransom from King Philip."

Roy appeared to be considering, but presently he said (more to Jan than anyone else), "There is one thing that troubles me about this though. Colonel Javier Valdez *is* well-known, but he is known for his campaigns in the *Caribbean.* He is said to know almost every island and a very sizeable amount of every larger landmass that has been explored in the New World. His military exploits on land are largely thought to be due to this, but he has never been to Europe in his life, from what I hear." Roy seemed to have an unusual amount of information about Spaniards in these lands, but Ajuban supposed he had heard much because of his obsession with Lieutenant Francisco. "Valdez would lose that advantage in Europe, and I can't think Spain is so desperate for good officers that they would pay so much for a Caribbean colonel just to ship him to Spain."

"Perhaps dey really mean to use him for a campaign in de Caribbean den, but dey obviously wouldn't want anyone to know about it."

"They could mean to try retaking Port Royal again," suggested Jan.

"They would be foolish to approach the island," said Roy. "Acting Governor D'Oyley is on his guard after the last attempt failed, if indeed he was ever *off* his guard, but Valdez certainly has enough talent to do it, if he can land his troops first." Ajuban thought back to Port Royal and the story of a Spanish troop muster, but he had no doubt that Roy was thinking along the same lines.

"Could this have something to do with the Spanish fleet that was destroyed in a hurricane?" asked Coya.

A Spanish fleet? Obviously Ajuban had missed something.

"It's possible," answered Roy. "That fleet could have been going anywhere in the Caribbean." He turned to Ajuban, "Jan was telling us that there is an old tale being circulated of a Spanish fleet that was destroyed by a hurricane late last year just east of the Caribbean. Apparently there were a few survivors, but who knows how much more there is to the story?"

"I would t'ink dat a Spanish invasion force, if dat's what it was, would have its own officers," said Ajuban, "but I don't suppose dey would pass up de opportunity to involve Valdez in deir plans if dey could. But *ten t'ousand...*" He shook his head. Even as an African among Europeans, he could retire comfortably on ten thousand pesos.

"But why should Willem van Kemper get involved in this at all?" asked Coya. "I mean, what does he get out of holding the hostages?" No one had told her exactly what a hostage broker was.

"He gets a percentage of the ransom when it is paid," explained Jan, whose sympathetic manner seemed to indicate that he had been taking on the task of keeping her in the conversation.

"Usually ten to twenty percent," put in Roy. "I've never heard of a broker's take being more than twenty."

"Van Kemper could be one of dose who earns dat much," added Ajuban. "From what I saw of de rooms upstairs, it seems likely enough."

"Did you find out who captured Valdez?" Coya asked him.

"No, dey didn't discuss it. Sometimes brokers aren't even allowed to mention de captor's name, dough usually in de case of privateering, de captors *want* de word to spread. It helps dem to hire more crew." He grinned. That was, after all, what they were doing at Van Kemper's in the first place.

"Well, until we have more information," said Roy cocking an eye at Ajuban, "there's nothing to be done about it. Paying the ransom and finding a use for Valdez may be nothing more than some fanciful notion of King Philip's that made it past his advisors. Hopefully I shall one day have the good fortune to capture such a valuable prisoner, though he'd likely be more trouble than he was worth. But we must all keep our ears open for any other information on this matter. Colonel Valdez is not a man to have running loose under your nose and I'm sure Colonel D'Oyley would appreciate knowing what he was up to. Well done, Ajuban! Now that you've indulged me (and yourself, I'm sure) on this little matter, perhaps Jan can continue what he was saying about the shipping lanes near Hispaniola."

Ajuban had evidently missed quite a bit of talk while he had been snooping upstairs, but a cautionary look from the captain signaled to him that he remembered the rumor in Port Royal very clearly and that they would discuss it privately.

"Well, as I was saying," began Jan after a little thought to remember where the conversation had previously gone, "there have been a high number of attacks on French merchant vessels, so of course they are willing to give a good price to anyone who has been known to beat back such attackers. It is said that these pirates are primarily of English origins, and several Spanish warships have been known to engage them in exchange for French compensation in the form of supplies from the French colonies there."

"That's odd," said Roy. "The captains that I have spoken to out of Port Royal—pirate and privateer alike—do not typically target French ships, nor do they bear any special grudge against the French. Many of them would also find themselves very unwelcome in Tortuga should they do so, and Tortuga is still one of the places where an English captain can find ready crewmembers."

"Nevertheless," said Jan and shrugged, "it appears that English ships are plundering their ships with abandon, and there appears to be some sort of agreement between some French merchants and governors and the Spanish navy, though of course there could be nothing official without breaking Spanish trade laws. As long as the supplies are 'given' to the Spanish, there is nothing illegal about it. Of course, this is only what I've been hearing from others."

"That might explain what you were saying earlier about Santo Domingo's trade flourishing lately," said Roy. "Especially if some of these 'supplies' are valuable trade goods."

"Maybe, though that was a very vague impression I've gotten rather than any solid information," Jan said noncommittally. "There are always fools with rumors of gold mines every time trade makes an upswing in any given area too. It's hard to get a clear picture of the situation second-hand, but Santo Domingo might make a good target if you can muster the force to go after it."

I wonder if he has any idea how small de crew is, Ajuban thought. He didn't think it stood much chance of turning into a hundred men in Curaçao, even if by some miracle *The Constance* could hold so many. Roy was clearly thinking along similar lines, as he asked, "Is there any other news of interest that you have heard?"

"I don't know how much use it will be, but Thomas Pritchard, the governor of Barbados, appears to have lost his daughter. She was last seen leaving the Barbados docks after arriving back from England. Her two escorts were found dead."

"She was probably kidnapped," said Roy unconcerned. "I'm sure her father will receive a ransom note soon, but I don't intend to get involved. I doubt we'd find her anyway, and Barbados is far from here."

At about that time, William came back to their table carrying a full tankard and was seemingly in good spirits. "How did you do?" Roy asked, looking up.

"I believe I broke even," said William cheerfully. Clearly he did not expect to do even that well. He sat down, and without preamble declared, "The grinning man with the large pile of winnings is a French diplomat." He took a long pull at his ale, and smiled as though he were talking about prospects for fair weather.

"Really?" said Roy with interest. "He certainly has a good face for cards. I don't think I've seen that smile crack yet."

"Considering how well he plays, he doesn't appear to have any reason for it to crack," replied William, "but you're right, he is very composed."

"This is Jan Huisman," Roy said as William glanced around at him and nodded. "He is a surgeon who is apparently interested in joining a crew. Jan, this is William Ward of Devonshire, an able member of my crew."

William seemed more surprised at Jan's vocation than by Roy's use of his self-applied title. "Looking to give up the stationary life?" William joked, but continued more seriously when Jan seemed about to explain. "That's all right, your reasons are your own, and they can't possibly be worse than mine. I'm pleased to meet you."

"And you," said Jan awkwardly. "So what is the diplomat's name?"

"Oh him? He introduced himself as Marquis Jean-Baptiste Augustin. He's a very agreeable fellow, but very sharp-witted. I wonder why he is here."

"He was paying a great deal of attention to de dice game earlier," put in Ajuban.

"I hadn't noticed," said William, "but I was concentrating on cards for the most part, and seeing if anyone was interested in joining the crew. I sent one or two over your way."

"Yes, we've had a few visitors," said the captain.

At that moment, Ajuban noticed a fairly dark-skinned man, dressed very much as he was himself, walk into Van Kemper's and look around for a moment before heading quickly for the marquis. Ajuban pointed this out to the captain, who watched intently. The two of them appeared to speak quietly and briefly to each other before the man bowed and walked out again. The marquis appeared in no hurry to quit his game though.

"Probably just his serving man," Roy said and shrugged, but Jan's eyes shifted back to the marquis frequently as they resumed their conversation.

A few more sailors—two Dutchmen and an Englishman whose friendliness seemed rather more put on than genuine and who eyed Coya discreetly a few times—visited their table as they sat on into the evening, and Ajuban noted that Jan now remained with them instead of paying a visit to Captain McLaughlin as he had originally considered. It was not long before they saw Major Benito emerge again and make his way from the establishment. "What do you t'ink, captain?" asked Ajuban.

"No, my friend," answered Roy, "He is probably returning to his ship and I wouldn't want him to see you shadowing him."

"Aye, sir."

But to Ajuban's surprise, Jan abruptly stood up and extended a hand to Coya. "Shall we?" he asked. She looked as puzzled as everyone else.

"What did you have in mind, Mr. Huisman?" Roy asked with the barest hint of suspicion in his voice.

Jan leaned in to whisper to them, "Since his servant left, the marquis has played exactly three more hands of cards and has withdrawn without bidding each time. Now that Benito has left, the marquis speaks with the bartender, and I doubt it is to order more wine."

"What is so strange about that?" asked Roy puzzled.

It was William who answered, with a sudden expression of understanding on his face. "The marquis has not withdrawn without bidding for even two hands in a row since he started playing, as far as I can tell."

"I think our mysterious marquis is about to go somewhere," said Jan, "and I thought your friend Coya might accompany me to find out what it is about, but I'd like to leave before he does if possible." Roy nodded at Coya, who promptly took Jan's hand and rose to depart. "If I see you no sooner," said Jan to the rest of them, "I shall doubtless see you at dawn tomorrow."

Ajuban glanced casually in the direction of the bar after they left. The bartender had gone upstairs again, and the marquis was back at the gaming table saying his farewells to the other players as Jan had predicted. "So what do you t'ink of our new crewmember, captain?"

"Assuming he agrees to our terms," answered Roy, "I think he may prove his usefulness with far more than our wounds."

Chapter 7: Burglar's Gambit

"Who are you?" asked Willem van Kemper in a stony voice, though he was more curious than he was angry.

"Benoit Fiennes, monsieur," the pale man answered meekly in English with a heavy French accent. He already had a bruise coloring his pale cheek from when he had been caught, and that was apparently enough to convince him to cooperate to some degree.

"And why did you attempt to break into my establishment?"

"Pardon, monsieur, but I only wished to beg for a meal—"

Willem nodded to his hired tough, who slapped the Frenchman hard on his bruised cheek, sending him sprawling to the floor with his hands still tied together behind him. "No lies!" said Van Kemper. "Beggars do not try to pick locks, nor do they look as well-fed and well-dressed as you do. And they do not beg near my doors, if they have any sense at all. What are you doing here?"

Fiennes hesitated a moment, then answered flatly with downcast eyes, "Monsieur...I was hired...to enter your brewery and discover what details were in your ledger."

The man must think I have gravel in my head. "What, during our busiest hour?"

"I thought your ledger would be locked up after hours, but that the brewery would be less active at the moment," Fiennes pleaded.

"If a locked door didn't bother you," Willem shot back, "why would a locked cabinet?"

"I didn't expect the door to be locked! And you might have taken the ledger upstairs with you at night. When I found the door was locked, I only tried to open the lock in desperation, which was apparently noticed." It was unusual for any outer doors to be locked at such a busy hour, that was true, but Willem van Kemper had greater need for security than was apparent to the general populace.

Not that he felt the need to address such an assertion. "If opening locks was a matter of desperation for you, you would not carry tools specifically for that task," he said gesturing to the set of curiously shaped, delicate iron tools on the table behind him.

"I have only accomplished it once before," Fiennes muttered, seemingly embarrassed.

"And who do you claim hired you?" Willem was fast losing patience, but he didn't want to use any more force until he was absolutely certain he was hearing more lies. However, Willem's assistant and bartender chose that moment to open the inner door and call him over. Annoyed at the interruption but endeavoring not to show it, he patiently stepped close enough to whisper and asked, "What is it?"

"The Marquis Jean-Baptiste Augustin wishes to speak with you immediately, sir."

Willem was definitely intrigued. He currently housed no French hostages, or else the request would seem quite commonplace. Perhaps the man was concerned with one of his other hostages or simply wanted information on Major Benito, but Willem detested entertaining too many speculations when he could just as quickly find out the truth. "Very well," he answered at length. "Show him to my office. I will be there momentarily."

"Very well, sir."

After his assistant left, Willem turned to his "interrogator." "Keep him here," he ordered. The man merely nodded as he clutched the club in his left hand just a bit more tightly. Fiennes didn't appear to be interested in going anywhere.

Satisfied, Willem made his way back to his office where he could dimly hear the hubbub from the tavern once again, and found the marquis already seated and the bartender waiting anxiously by the door. He doubtless had many customers to attend to and no one to cover for him at such a busy hour, but he was first and foremost Willem's assistant, and he knew that *no one* was allowed in his patron's office outside of the company of either him or Willem. "What can I do for you, my lord?" asked Willem, not waiting on introductions as he waved his aide away.

Only when the door had closed again did the marquis turn his gaze from it to look at him directly. "I have traced a wanted fugitive to this establishment. A French renegade named Benoit Fiennes. I am informed that you have him in custody. I wish to confirm that this is so. Will you take me to him, monsieur?"

Willem van Kemper became aware that his usual spontaneity as a facilitator and businessman had temporarily deserted him. He was only thankful that his mouth wasn't hanging open. "Of course," he replied simply. It was really the only thing he *could* say to the request of such a high-ranking diplomat. *Fugitive?* If he were lucky, there would be a reward. He felt he should at least have considered that the two Frenchmen plaguing him right now were somehow concerned with each other. "Please, follow me."

The marquis rose and followed him out the door, which he made sure to lock before proceeding toward the back room where Fiennes was held. Fiennes appeared perplexed and a little worried when he saw the well-dressed marquis, but his expression changed to one of horror once he heard what the man had to say.

"Benoit Fiennes, I arrest you in the name of King Louis of France as the convicted murderer of Admiral Castanega, Captain Ortiz, and Colonel Santana of Spain." The marquis smiled as always, but his smile held no amusement now.

Mr. Fiennes began trembling and stammering in French, but the marquis only made some sharp, chastising-sounding remark and turned back to Willem. "Monsieur," he began, "I must ask that you remand this man to my custody under diplomatic privilege. I am informed that he did not successfully inflict any damages on you or your property, but you will be rewarded for his capture. As for his penalty," here he glanced again at the shriveling Fiennes, "there can be no stiffer penalty under French law than the one he has already been sentenced to."

"How did you find out that he was here at all, not to mention what he did here?" asked Willem, trying not to sound as suspicious as he felt. It seemed clear that Fiennes had been lying about his reason for being there, but Willem was not one to take such situations at face value.

"I knew he was in Curaçao, and I knew that your establishment was a reputable place for hostage brokering, so I reasoned that he would likely come here at some point, if any valuable Spanish hostages were here." The marquis leveled a knowing look at Willem that made him feel far from pleased. He didn't like anyone knowing too much about his business, and certainly not about whom in particular he kept upstairs, but he said nothing and the marquis continued. "I spotted him playing at dice and signaled to my man who followed him when he left. My man was coming to let me know what was going on at your back door when he witnessed your capture of Monsieur Fiennes, and he let me know at once what had happened." The marquis sighed. "I meant to have him followed to where he was staying and to apprehend him while he slept, but you have saved me a great deal of trouble, Monsieur Van Kemper, and I thank you for it."

"You are welcome," said Willem feeling rather bored with the situation. Things appeared to be just as the marquis explained them, and if so, Willem had saved himself a great deal of trouble as well. Castanega, Ortiz, and Santana had each been captured, held for ransom, and killed by an intruder before the ransom could be paid. Willem had not heard that all of the deaths had been by the same man's hand—this was especially surprising since Castanega was murdered in a cell in France, not in the Caribbean—or that the murderer had been caught and put on trial, but the killings were part of the reason for Willem's tight security. If he had supposed the man for a mere burglar, he might have let him go with only a beating after confiscating his belongings, and then no doubt Fiennes would come back a bit more cautiously. It was likely that he had only come during a busy hour because there were fewer lookouts and it would be easier to blend in once he was inside. But now he was caught and Willem had other things to attend to. "I appreciate your thanks, and I am glad to have aided the king of France in this matter…but you spoke of a reward?" To Willem van Kemper, money was the only relevant interest remaining in the matter.

"I regret to say," the marquis replied apologetically (but with little hesitation, Willem noted), "that the reward is currently only one hundred French Louis d'or due to the fact that we already knew his whereabouts, but I can compensate you a further thirty ducats of my own for saving me the bother of apprehending him myself. I have had rather a good turn at cards tonight."

"Indeed," Willem replied dryly. No doubt he could get more from the Spanish government just to hand him over to the Inquisition, and the marquis knew it, but the smiling diplomat had only to pay a visit to Governor Diedrik to have Fiennes remanded to his custody, and then Willem would be lucky to receive any reward at all. The marquis doubtless knew that as well. "I would be happy to render him to you for…such a sum." He felt sure that his expression told exactly what he thought of that sum, and he felt no compunction to rein it in. He glanced back at Fiennes, who was positively quaking by now and looking for ways to escape, but Willem's club-wielding brute had picked up on the direction things were going (though he spoke only Dutch) and wisely kept an eye on his captive.

"I will need his personal effects as well," said the marquis, eyeing the odds and ends sorted on the table.

"Of course," said Willem, hurrying to be done with the whole affair. But then a new thought struck him. "Just a moment, if what you say is true, surely he was trying to break in to kill one of my…guests?"

"What of it?"

"We found no weapon on him," Van Kemper pointed out, his suspicions creeping back.

"Then you didn't look hard enough," the marquis said simply. "I assure you he has one. Do you know the manner in which his victims were killed?"

Van Kemper gulped, though much more from embarrassment than horror. "They were garroted."

The marquis knelt down by the cowering prisoner and unfastened the clasp of his necklace. It had appeared to be an ordinary silver chain, but as the marquis held it up, Willem noticed it was more like a twisted wire than a chain, and the clasp formed two small bars that could be easily grasped with the wire protruding between the fingers of either hand. "This one is a bit plainer than the one he used before he was caught, but no doubt the effect is much the same." Van Kemper said nothing, but gathered up Fiennes' personal effects and handed them to the marquis who put them in a small pouch with the garrote.

The marquis counted out a hundred pistoles and thirty ducats onto the table and—none too soon for Willem van Kemper—Fiennes was handed over, his wrists still bound behind his back. "Are you sure you don't need any help in escorting him back to your ship?" Willem asked purely out of courtesy.

"My man is waiting outside," said the marquis, "but I thank you nonetheless." There was the amused smile again. "Oh, Monsieur Van Kemper, I would appreciate it if you kept this matter confidential, under the circumstances. Certain parties might wish to take revenge on this man, and King Louis would be most displeased were he robbed of the privilege of witnessing the execution."

No doubt "certain parties" was a reference to the Spaniards in the harbor. Major Benito's ship as well as his appearance in the tavern must have caused a good deal of speculation already. "Of course. Good evening, my lord. My man will escort you out the back way."

When they had all gone and Willem had gathered up all the coins into a now bulging purse, he heaved a sigh of relief. It really wasn't a bad conclusion to the whole business, especially as Willem himself had done very little to bring it about. He had not long to enjoy it though before there came a familiar knock on his door. "Mrs. Lisanne Hebert wishes to speak with you, sir."

Sooner or later I will have to delegate some of these business meetings to him. He rubbed his eyes tiredly. "Send her in, please," he said.

* * *

Marquis Jean-Baptiste Augustin strode briskly through the streets of Curaçao under a fine, clear evening sky with bright stars, his prisoner and his man, Kalam, in tow, though he heeded little but his inner curiosity as he focused on maintaining his own outward expression. *Who does that parasite have locked up in his cells?* He was still vaguely amused by the whole business, though it rankled to hand over so much coin unnecessarily. He had truly only guessed that Van Kemper had any Spanish hostages, though it seemed reasonable enough considering the Spaniard's presence and the actions of the man he was currently escorting to his own ship. Van Kemper had all but confirmed it by his chagrined reaction, but he was an astute businessman and had said nothing more about it.

"It appears, Kalam, that Monsieur Van Kemper's associates didn't see you when they captured him," he said, his thoughts momentarily returning to his present company. He shook the prisoner's arm for emphasis.

"You had no trouble having him transferred to your custody, my lord?" asked Kalam in an accent usually unexpected in one as dark-skinned as he was. Most people figured Kalam for a slave, but he was a well educated Egyptian who had learned French at a university rather than under the tutelage of a master's whip.

"Not much trouble. Monsieur Van Kemper is naturally a suspicious man, as any man who engages in his trade is, but he was out of his depth and he knew it." Jean-Baptiste was only sorry to have ended his evening so early, considering his winnings at the card table.

They said nothing more as they proceeded towards their ship anchored in the harbor. They held their prisoner by either arm, but endeavored not to be obvious as prisoner and escort. The prisoner himself merely walked steadily with downcast eyes, also silent. He seemed particularly dejected whenever they chanced by a watchman, but none commented as the trio made their way aboard. A few of the crew glanced around at them as they escorted their companion to the hold, but they were trained well to keep quiet. Finally they were away from prying eyes.

The prisoner raised his head to look Jean-Baptiste in the eye, but he looked no less dejected. "I'm sorry, my lord," he said.

"It's all right Damien," said Jean-Baptiste clapping him on the shoulder. "Who knew they would have guards at the back door at such a busy hour? But what did you find out?" he asked eagerly.

"Nothing for certain," said the would-be Benoit Fiennes. "When the Spaniard entered though, the other sailors got to talking. One of McLaughlin's men thought that Javier Valdez had been imprisoned here. I thought it was worth looking into."

"Quite right, lad, quite right." *Valdez? Now that* would *be worth looking into.* "If he is there, I wonder how much that man was offering for him and who wants him." Colonel Valdez was certainly a man to keep under one's scrutiny.

"After that fiasco, my lord," said Damien in disgust, "I'm sorry to say we may never find out. Even so," he said with a smile, "that was smart work guessing that Monsieur Van Kemper had a hostage at all and to put him off guard quickly enough to read his reaction. I would not want to play cards with you, my lord."

Jean-Baptiste laughed. Damien thought so highly of him, for whatever reason, and that was a far more reliable form of loyalty than anything money could buy. "Perhaps, but neither would I relish the idea of playing *dice* with *you*. I can't believe how lucky you were that they didn't find your dagger." He removed the hidden dagger from Damien's sash and cut the man's bonds with it.

Kalam looked stunned. "They didn't find *that?*" he said pointing at the dagger. It was at least as long as his hand. "They must not have been very sharp at all."

"That brute with the club knew what he was doing though," said Damien probing his tender cheek. "This will be hard to paint over, my lord. Perhaps I should lay low for a few days until this heals a bit."

"Very probably," said Jean-Baptiste, "but don't wash out your hair or remove any other aspect of your disguise. Should anyone in authority wish to be assured of your presence, it may be necessary to clap you in irons at a moment's notice, and you had better look the same if that happens." He was sure it was no pleasant news to hear that even a bath would likely be forbidden for days, but Damien appeared to accept it as due course under the circumstances. "Anyway," he continued, "there may be another way for us to find out what we want to know."

Damien and Kalam both looked perplexed. "Do you wish me to see what I can find out, my lord?" asked Kalam quizzically.

"No, you have served your master well enough already, Kalam. The trade deals you have helped me to arrange on behalf of Captain LaSalle will no doubt please him greatly when you return to Tortuga. There is no need for you to get mixed up in our business any more than you already have, I'm sure. But, Damien, shortly after you left Van Kemper's, that Negro first mate at the far table succeeded in sneaking upstairs. Perhaps we can find out what we wish from him or from his captain."

"My lord," said Damien in earnest, "I must warn you. The little native woman with that same crew followed us all the way here. I am certain, though, that she doesn't speak a word of French," he added in response to the marquis' look of alarm. "I would have told you at the time, but I was supposed to remain silent, and it might have endangered our secrecy for no purpose."

"Well," said Jean-Baptiste after a protracted hesitation, "She likely saw no more than we wished anyone to see then. Nevertheless, we must be wary." He couldn't see any other way around it, and he was beginning to feel the hour heavy on his eyelids. "I will go to my room in town for the night, and perhaps she will follow me. I will take Kalam with me, in case her intentions are in line with her profession," he said anticipating Damien's objection. "I did leave Van Kemper's with quite a sum of money on me, as far as anyone else is aware, after all."

"I'm sorry about that as well, sir," said Damien, referring to the "reward" Jean-Baptiste had paid for his release. "I know how much you enjoy a good night of cards."

"Think nothing of it," he said. Sometimes Damien's subservience to him seemed downright unmanly. "Kalam, fetch the key to the manacles and give it to Damien." It would be much easier that way if Damien had to chain himself up. "I will be back in the morning. Come, Kalam." With a wave, he and his companion made their way back onto the deck and looked around the dock surreptitiously, but the native woman was nowhere in sight. *No matter.* Jean-Baptiste was rather skilled with a weapon himself anyway, and he was too preoccupied to worry about it much. He was more worried about this news that Valdez might be held at Van Kemper's, and still more about the possibility of him being released. *If he really is here, it's a shame that "Benoit Fiennes" won't be able to pay him a visit now.*

* * *

148

"It's a pity that I didn't hear any more than that," Jan told Roy later at Van Kemper's tavern.

"It's all right," assured Roy, "it doesn't appear to have much interest for us in any case." Roy was having a long evening, and was decidedly worn out. He did not feel that he had much more concentration to spare for the speculation his companions seemed to be enjoying.

"Begging your pardon captain," said Jan excitedly, "but two things we can definitely infer from what I heard are that the marquis and his servant know Van Kemper is a hostage broker, and that this prisoner of theirs tried to break into the place."

Roy tried to clear his mind a little more and sat up straight. The wine was beginning to affect him too much for this, but Jan had made a very good point. "But perhaps this prisoner didn't know anything about Van Kemper?"

It was William who chimed in at this point. "If he was remanded to the custody of the marquis, it's very unlikely that he's just a petty criminal."

"And the prisoner didn't look surprised at all at the conversation," added Jan.

"He was probably still dejected about his predicament," replied Roy tiredly. He felt a little bit impatient about the whole issue, and couldn't see any reason why he should be concerned or get involved in any way. "Even if he did know about Van Kemper's trade or about Valdez being held here, it doesn't appear to affect anything for us. Every other government in the Caribbean has reason not to wish for Valdez to be released, and Valdez has undoubtedly made some enemies on a personal level as well. Anyway, both of them are currently out of our reach and we set sail tomorrow." Roy was not looking forward to being up so early. Mercifully, the tide would not rise until late morning, but he still had (he hoped) some new crew to sign aboard prior to that.

His statement appeared to convey some sense to the others, and Jan subsided to simply speculating about it with the others in a more subdued fashion. Coya was still hanging on every word, partially because she had been unable to get close enough to the marquis without risking being seen, and she didn't exactly blend into the evening crowd in such an affluent district. Jan had gotten downright *lost* in the crowd and happened to round a corner to stumble upon the marquis and his unexpected prisoner in time to overhear a small part of the marquis' conversation with his servant. Despite the accidental nature of the situation, Jan had obviously risen in Coya's esteem over the matter. Roy listened to their talk for a while longer with half an ear. Albert soon joined the group again, and Roy turned to talk to him instead, glad for a distraction from the speculations about everyone they had seen during the evening.

"I think you must have already spoken to anyone interested in joining a crew," said Albert. "I sent as many your way as I could, but I'm no good at telling tales and whatnot. Mostly I just had a good time, and if anyone was impressed with how much silver I had, I simply let it be known that it was due to being part of your crew." He grinned. He *had* seemed like he was having a good time, and nearly every time Roy had glanced his way, Albert was pulling from a tall tankard of Van Kemper's excellent brew. For all that, the man seemed as sober as ever, apart from having a rather rosier complexion.

"Wealth does speak for itself," agreed Roy. "Simply having a good time is mostly why we're here after all, though I'd certainly not mind a larger crew. I've talked to some interesting newcomers," here he nodded at Jan, "even if there haven't been very many visitors to our table."

"I suppose we'll find out how things will be in the morning," Albert answered with an appraising glance in Jan's direction and seeming none too inspired. *No doubt sizing Jan up as a combatant.*

For some reason it mattered to Roy that Albert not be puzzled about his decisions—probably because the two were so much alike at heart. "He's a surgeon," he whispered briefly to Albert, who nodded his understanding. Roy looked around the room, muttering the question that formed in his mind as he scanned the dwindling crowd, "Where's Tiede?"

"Oh, he did quite well at dice on his last few tosses," Albert replied grinning. "He left for home shortly before I joined you. *That* one will be as loyal as any of your crew, sir. Apart from you providing the stake for his dice winnings, I heard him telling a few other people—discreetly, of course, but I think they all shared the same grievances—about our encounter with Gilbertsen. They were greatly pleased by the turn of events. No doubt they had served under him as well."

"Jan here has been telling me more about Gilbertsen as well," Roy put in, "and if you hear any news of him in the future, I'd be more than happy to heed it and go after him again if it's at all convenient. The man sounds every bit as bad as he seemed, or worse." Albert nodded, reflecting Roy's own smirk. "In the meantime, I think I'll head back to my cabin. I'm about done in."

"I'll see you in the morning then, sir."

Roy wished everyone a good night, and he and a few others left the table to head for their respective lodgings. Coya and Ajuban remained talking quietly while others held conversations around them, but he paid them no mind. He felt a general sense of contentment, and would have plenty of time for other concerns in the morning.

* * *

"T'ink about it," Ajuban said in hushed tones, "right now, all dat silver is in Spanish hands and belongs to no one else. If we could somehow get to it ourselves before it leaves de ship, we'd all be a lot richer and dis Valdez fellow would stay where he is!"

Coya had to admit to herself that Ajuban's idea certainly had merit. She still had several reservations, but if they succeeded, everyone but the Spanish (and Willem van Kemper) would benefit. *Except for...* "Just a moment," she said, "wouldn't that also take money away from whoever captured Valdez?" She didn't want to make enemies with other crews who were no less her fellow Brethren of the Coast, whether they were actual pirates or simply other privateers.

"It's true," admitted Ajuban, "but de captain can always pay dem deir share of it if he t'inks it appropriate and dey might even get a second ransom if Spain is desperate enough to free Valdez. Besides," Ajuban persisted, "we don't even know who it was dat captured him."

"But the local governor, this Frans Diedrik, wouldn't he be upset? I mean, aren't there stiff punishments for crimes against diplomats or something?" Coya's knowledge of the laws of any of these European nations was very limited, but she was reasonably confident that wronging a visiting diplomat was akin to wronging a local lord, even if the "diplomat" was really only there to pay a ransom.

But Ajuban had an answer for that as well. "Dat is true, if de diplomat is in de city, but de captain told me once dat diplomatic vessels are considered de territory of whoever dey belong to, and deir own laws and enforcement of dem take precedence dere." Coya couldn't begin to imagine why this had come up in conversation between Roy and Ajuban, but she made it a point to remember to ask sometime. "What dat means," Ajuban continued with a wicked grin," is dat it is de responsibility of de Spanish captain—Major Benito, in dis case—to guard what is aboard his own ship and de crime is not in Governor Diedrik's jurisdiction and *is not his problem* as long as it takes place on de Spanish ship."

Coya was very impressed with this logic. For a moment she was at a loss for other objections to raise, beyond the sheer danger of what Ajuban was suggesting. He pressed his advantage and continued.

"If dis Benito fellow is only here to pay de ransom, Diedrik is even less likely to care since no diplomatic relations will be impacted by it. And if he found out Valdez was being ransomed, he would probably be glad not to see de man freed wit'out having to get involved himself." Ajuban lowered his voice still further and leaned closer. "Of course, it would be better for de governor if no one was killed in his port or on de ship. Murder could cause more problems for him even under de circumstances. If it could be done wit'out dat complication, and no one found out who did it, we could all be dat much better off as we sail away tomorrow." Ajuban looked very self-satisfied as he sat back with a grin. He was, however, not the one who would be risking his neck. Still, she could not deny that his idea was very solid. She still had one reservation though.

"Won't the captain be upset about us doing this to a business partner like Van Kemper?"

Ajuban looked a little uncomfortable at that. "I don't t'ink so," he said. "I hope not. But Van Kemper can barely be counted as a business partner after one transaction and a night at his tavern. And Van Kemper will probably only t'ink dat de French had some-t'ing to do wit' it, after dat problem wit' de marquis' prisoner. But de captain could probably come to an arrangement wit' Van Kemper if need be." He nodded as if he had only approved of what he had said after he said it.

Coya sighed. *Well, that leaves just the issue of the danger. Is it too much to risk?* She thought about what she would have to do. Somehow she (possibly with Ajuban's help) would have to subdue a watchman or two aboard *La Fortuna* without being seen or making much noise. Then she would have to creep to the captain's cabin and probably pick the lock. If Benito had any sense at all, he would be in the cabin and not staying at a local inn, so assuming she would be able to get in without waking him up, she'd also have to creep right by him—right by this man who radiated danger from his very footsteps—and pick up what was probably a chest full of loose coins, sneak out again without letting the coins clink and clatter in the chest too much, and make it back to the dock carrying the thing. But for a share of *ten thousand* silver pesos, and the opportunity to make complete fools of the Spanish… She thought for what seemed like a long time. There were many dangers to consider, but she had realized for the first time when she met Roy that she tended to undervalue her skills. *I can see in the dark, and they can't. And I can probably escape if anything goes wrong.* She always had, she realized. Slowly she mustered up her courage and her confidence, and nodded assent. "I will try," she said.

Ajuban grinned broadly. "Well den," he said conspirationally, "let's get out of here and go see what we're up against."

Soon after, having said goodnight to Albert and William who had been having a conversation by themselves, they returned to her room in town where she left her boots. She outfitted herself with a set of crude lockpicks that would work on most doors, a couple of knives, her sling and a few stones, then they made their way towards the docks. It was very late, but there were still some people wandering about the area. However, there were plenty of spots where they could linger unseen in the shadows and watch. They watched for quite some time as the docks emptied of anyone but the city watchman (who seemed to be half dozing) and they whispered together about the best way to subdue the ship's guard and how to creep close enough. Thankfully there was only one watchman who stood on the low deck, but Coya wanted to make sure he was not due to be relieved soon. She had just noticed a pile of crates shielded from the view of both the city guard and the

Spaniard when another guard came on deck to relieve the first. Coya immediately made her plan.

"Ajuban, you wait here." She pointed to the city guardsman and said, "If he wakes up or notices anything, you subdue him. Signal to me if anything goes wrong. I'm going to try to make it to those crates and knock out the watchman on deck with a stone." She was in her element now, and her confidence was growing as she gave "orders." Ajuban nodded at each point, content to follow her lead. This was her area of expertise, after all. "I'll wait a few minutes for the first guard to fall asleep belowdecks, and this one will probably be on duty for at least an hour so I won't likely be disturbed. If I fail, we run for it. If I fell him, you signal if I'm noticed or if I can go. I'll run to the waterside and wait for you to see if anyone appears on deck due to the disturbance. If not, you signal for me to go and I'll climb aboard."

Ajuban merely nodded once more and made sure he could see the harbor watchman and the Spaniard without being seen himself. They waited in silence for ten or fifteen minutes. "Ready?" whispered Coya. Ajuban nodded, and Coya quickly and quietly made her way to the crates near *La Fortuna* when the Spaniard routinely scanned in other directions. From here she could see Brian sitting on the deck of *The Constance* keeping watch, but he was little more attentive than the port watchman (who must still be fast asleep, as Ajuban signaled the all-clear to her) and he was farther away. She peered over the crates, her sling in hand already fitted with a small, smooth stone. When the guard began scanning the farther docks again, she whirled the sling slowly to settle the stone into its cradle and then let loose the stone with an overhand throw, hoping the gods smiled on her this night.

The stone caught him hard in the temple and he collapsed in a heap without uttering more than a barely audible groan. The stone bounced into the water with a faint splash. If she had missed, she would almost certainly have had to flee and the whole plan would have been in vain. And she still might have to flee. She ducked down and looked to Ajuban, who soon signaled for her to go.

Making it to the water, she hid herself in the shadows between the ship and the dock, trying to remain invisible without falling into the water. She did not want the added difficulty of dripping and squelching while trying to sneak into Benito's cabin. She waited, straining her ears for sound of movement aboard, and staring at Ajuban almost unblinkingly waiting for his signal. His gaze was fixed on the deck for a minute or two, but she heard nothing. Finally, he signaled for her to go. So far it had worked! The rest was a matter of stealth, but this was the most dangerous part of the whole plan.

She climbed quickly up to the deck sparing a glance around before hauling herself over the rail. She hoped the guard would be unconscious for long enough and that she hadn't actually killed him, but she could not afford to waste time checking on him beyond noting that he was still sprawled unmoving where he fell. She crept back towards the captain's cabin, keeping to the shadows as much as possible so as not to be observed by anyone else on the docks. She listened at the cabin door for what seemed like far too long, but she had to make sure that Benito was actually asleep before she would dare try opening the lock. She was quite sure she could escape should he wake up during the process, but to have a man like him alert and on his feet while she attempted any of this was enough to make flight seem very dangerous. After a few moments, having seen no light from under the door, and unable to detect any sound within, she fished out a thin metal tool and busied herself with the lock. *I hope he is a deep sleeper.*

She heard the lock click and winced at the sound, pausing to listen for any sound from within. Then slowly and carefully, she opened the door a crack, just enough to peer into the room. The door creaked slightly, but she kept her hand steady and her gaze focused on the interior of the room. It was a small room, and that helped to dampen sounds, but the bed was only a few paces away from the door. Coya could clearly see Benito in the little light that came through the windows. He appeared fast asleep. She gazed around the rest of the room to get the general layout and to see if she could spot where the ransom money might be kept, but she did not need to look for long. Not six feet away stood a desk with a small chest sitting on top of it, and if that wasn't where the ransom money was, then it would almost have to be in some compartment like the one Marius Gilbertsen had under his cabin bed.

She opened the door further, doing so quickly enough to minimize the creaking, and when Benito showed no sign of waking, she crept to the desk to inspect the chest. She found that it was locked, but that it was also very heavy.

She hefted it briefly, trying not to shift the weight of it and rattle the coins that she hoped were inside, but it seemed to be about the right weight. Coya was an old hand at gauging how much silver was in a purse by its weight, but this was probably in gold and was the most coin she had ever held before. She wished she could open it to find out if that was indeed what was inside, but she didn't want to risk opening the lock right there. However, she was presented with a new problem that she had not thought of: how to carry this heavy, bulky chest off the ship. She certainly couldn't climb down with the thing under her arm, and if she jumped, she would probably make a lot of noise. Either way, she decided that she would deal with that problem when she had to, and focused on creeping quietly out of the room with the chest in her arms. Now that she had it, she was determined that nothing should stop her from spiriting it away.

Coya crept out of the small room, and put the chest down outside as she shut the door on a blissfully unaware Major Benito who would no doubt be in a fury when he awoke. She did not risk locking the door again, but instead hurried to the side of the ship holding her prize. She did venture a little shake at that point, and was pleased to hear the sound of coins rattling inside. She peered over the side, now having to deal with the problem of getting off the ship. It was only about a seven foot drop to the dock, but she couldn't really land properly with this box in her arms. Quickly making a decision, she crept back a little distance along the side of the ship, swung her feet over the rail, and jumped into the water. She was aware that the splash might alert someone, and swimming farther away with such a heavy weight was an impossibility, so she braced against the underwater support beams of the dock and quickly heaved the chest up onto the dock and herself after it, not worrying overmuch about the noise. An idea was forming in her head, and the fact that she was soaking wet might actually help. *If I can just get to Ajuban without being seen...*

She ran quickly to the pile of crates she had hidden behind earlier, and peeked out to signal to Ajuban. He looked very worried—clearly he had heard the noise—but she motioned for him to follow her and he nodded. She then ran out towards the nearest street, ducked around a corner, and waited for him to catch up. "Quickly," she said, once he caught up to her and they were out of sight, "take this back to the ship. Try to make sure it doesn't drip too much, and keep out of sight. I will set a false trail through town and I'll be back at the ship later." Ajuban nodded and looked a bit bemused, but she hurried off leaving drip trails from her clothes and wet footprints in her wake. *I did it!* She felt elated as she ran, and knew that when the thrill and danger wore off, she could enjoy a good sleep after her long labors. But as she pounded barefoot through the streets, she amended the thought. *After I retrieve my boots from the inn, that is.*

Chapter 8: Two Jailbirds with One Stone

Roy was at first inclined to be annoyed after hearing what Ajuban and Coya had been up to, not least because his sleep had been interrupted. He unknowingly brought up many of the same arguments that Coya had posed before, but Ajuban had answered them all reasonably well and Roy was now more thoughtful about the whole business. Evidently the whole thing was Ajuban's idea, though whatever he thought about the idea, he was greatly impressed with Coya's part in it. "She actually stole aboard the ship, crept into Benito's cabin, and made off with the ransom money right under his nose?" he asked incredulously. They had yet to hear Coya's own account in detail, but Ajuban indicated that's what the plan had consisted of. *I certainly hope she performs this well in the wilderness.*

Roy needed to think quickly. It was just possible that soldiers would search the ships over the matter once it was reported, and Roy had better not have any evidence on board. "Let's pry this thing open," he suggested to Ajuban. "Then we can take the contents and burn the chest. No one will fault a privateer for having more than ten thousand pesos, and no one could prove where it came from. Oh, and put another man on watch. I want someone keeping an eye on that Spanish ship, as long as they aren't too obvious about it."

"Aye sir," said Ajuban with a grin, no doubt perceiving that his arguments were accepted for the present. He left Roy's tiny cabin and came back a minute later and handed Roy a prybar.

"Right," said Roy standing up and wedging the bar under the chest lid, "let's see what we have." The wood and lock gave a sharp *crack* as he forced the chest open, but the first thing he saw in the dim candle light when he opened the lid was a signed document with a broken seal. He set it aside for the moment, for beneath it was a large mass of mostly gold coins, with some silver mixed in as well. He had no doubt that the sum totaled ten thousand pesos. Both men gave a low, appreciative whistle. After sifting to make sure there was nothing else mixed in (and just to savor the moment a little), Roy turned his attention to the document. He soon realized that this document was for Benito himself and would not have been handed over to Van Kemper with the ransom. It read in Spanish:

The seventh of May, 1660

To Major Manuel Benito Tubon,

Please pay the enclosed monies for the ransom of Colonel Baron Javier Valdez Endoso to Mr. Willem van Kemper of Van Kemper's tavern, Curaçao. I trust you will use all discretion and good judgment in handling the matter as the ransom amount is considerable and we would not wish to draw attention to the transaction in such a place.

Once freed, please conduct Baron Valdez safely to Coro, to the house of Captain Adán San Ramón Peña. He will there be briefed on the situation. Godspeed and good luck.

Admiral Sergio Cadiz Juarros

Roy read the orders out to Ajuban. When he was finished, Ajuban said, "Admiral Cadiz is about to be very upset, I t'ink."

Roy grinned, but he was still pondering the letter. "It's dated the seventh of May, but that was only two days ago. The admiral must be in Coro himself, or somewhere close like Puerto Cabello...or Maracaibo. Coro would take the least time to reach with Valdez in hand, but what his ultimate destination might be is uncertain. I wonder what they're up to. There must have been something to that rumor about a troop muster. Major Benito must have some idea what's going on."

"Do you t'ink Valdez knows?" asked Ajuban.

"No, it says he will be briefed once he arrives in Coro, and I think they probably hadn't even approached him yet. Who can say?"

Roy committed the letter to memory, and then held it in the candle flame. "It wouldn't do for anyone to find this here either," he said as he watched the letter disintegrate.

"What now, sir?" asked Ajuban once it had turned to ash and they were left pondering the message and the chest full of coins.

Roy thought for a moment, then said, "Get Brian down here to count out these coins and log the total, and to find a place to burn the chest." Starting a fire on board would draw too much attention, and the small ship had no galley for cooking. "I think you and I should relieve the watchmen on duty. I want to see what this Major Benito does next."

They left his cabin with the candle still burning next to their newfound riches, the chest still wet along with Ajuban's tunic. Coya had done well to advise Ajuban on that point, Roy thought—his first mate had evidently used his shirt to shroud the chest and keep it from dripping a trail along the docks to *The Constance*. Ajuban went below to wake Brian, but Roy stood gazing at the ship berthed next to his, *La Fortuna*. He was glad that the place where the guard lay was not very visible from his own deck, which was lower than that of the Spanish barque. All he could see was the man's boot, and only after a careful inspection. It would be easy to believe that his men had neither heard nor seen anything amiss in the night—indeed he would have to tell Brian to be more attentive in the future, as he had apparently dozed off during watch. But suddenly he heard a door bang open and a man utter a few loud curses in Spanish. He shifted his position to appear as though he was on watch, and discreetly motioned for Ajuban and Brian, who were just stepping up to the deck, to stay out of sight. With a curious expression on his face, he turned an obvious glance over to the deck of *La Fortuna*—any watchman worth his salt would want to know the cause of the noise, so he stood and watched. He was happy to see that his own watchman, who had relieved Brian, was also attentive.

It was Benito. He had left his cabin and was moving purposefully toward where his watchman lay on deck. He must have noticed that the chest was gone and had come out to check on the situation. He spared a glance at the two men on the deck of *The Constance*, but hurried to his watchman. Roy looked on with (he hoped) a look of mild disinterest. Once Benito was out of sight, Roy did his best to look away, so as to indicate that he had no idea that there was an unconscious guard sprawled on the man's deck, but listen as he might for any snatches of conversation, he could only hear the frantic tone as Benito revived his man. *At least he is alive then.* For Coya to have killed someone aboard a diplomatic vessel could have made Roy unwelcome at the port of Curaçao for as long as Frans Diedrik was governor there, if his crew's part in it were ever discovered.

As he mused over such thankfully irrelevant possibilities and listened for all he was worth, he became aware that Benito was now hurrying back to his cabin, and soon after he appeared again dressed and armed, and wearing a cloak in spite of the heat. He muttered some orders to another of his men who came on deck, then he leapt down onto the dock, heading off into the town. Slow suspicion dawned in Roy's mind as he realized that Benito had not attempted to alert anyone at the docks about what had happened. Quickly he ducked down to speak to Ajuban and Brian, still poised to exit the hold. "Ajuban," he said, "arm yourself and come with me. Brian, take care of that chest, and tell Coya when she returns that we've gone to follow Benito and that she must keep watch for a little while though she is doubtless very tired." Both Brian and Ajuban looked surprised, but Brian nodded and followed Roy as the latter ran to his cabin and rushed back out while still buckling his sword belt and tucking an extra pistol into it. Ajuban was already waiting, holding a tall staff and no doubt other weaponry was responsible for some of the bulk under the spare shirt he had donned. "Come, Ajuban!" said Roy, but suddenly paused and turned to Brian. "Oh, and Brian, also tell Coya, 'well done.'"

* * *

Manuel Benito was furious. He had slept fitfully, ill at ease about the idea of transporting such a huge ransom to Van Kemper's tavern in the dead of night as had been agreed. Conducting *any* business in the dead of night was ill advised, but in a town such as Curaçao, conducting such business during the day could be even more foolish. Besides, he had been ordered to be as discreet as possible. Having awoken for what seemed the tenth time and finding yet again that the meeting was still nearly two hours away had done little enough to calm his nerves, but when he had noticed the great blank space on his desk where the ransom money should have been, he had nearly shrieked.

His first thought was that one of his crew had taken it. But he had personally made sure that none of them could even have seen the chest apart from the first mate, and he trusted the man with his life. He trusted his crew as well, but ten thousand pesos would test nearly any common man's loyalties. However, it was then that he had discovered the unconscious guard and other likelihoods became much clearer to him.

He was at least glad that his guard was alive and had apparently been attentive and not shirking his duties. The knot on the man's head supported his story somewhat, as did the blood on the deck, though he seemed disoriented. Manuel made sure that all of the men who served under him were well trained and loyal, and he prided himself that he was one of few men who did not have to resort to bullying and violence to achieve that. No, to overcome one of his men, particularly one of this crew that he had hand-picked due to the mission's importance, and then to pick the lock on Manuel's very cabin and make off with the ransom without anyone noticing, that must have required a professional burglar. And who in this town had the connections to know a professional burglar well enough to summon him on such short notice? And who in this town even knew about the ransom at all? Willem van Kemper.

Manuel quickly made his way through the winding streets past several reputable businesses, which were soon followed by less and less reputable ones as the streets became even narrower. He had himself—rather wisely, he thought now—become acquainted with a professional burglar in Curaçao: a last resort, should the deal with Van Kemper fall through. But he had told the man nothing except that he might be needed at a moment's notice and in the middle of the night. He had not told him why or where he might be needed, but had advanced the man gold rather than answers as either one or the other had been required.

Of course it was always possible that someone other than Willem van Kemper was responsible for this outrage. Any typical resident or indeed any typical visitor in Curaçao would have had the motive, and Van Kemper could very well have been indiscreet about the transaction. He might even be acting under Governor Diedrik's orders. And there was that aborted break-in attempt that had interrupted his interview with Van Kemper in the first place—that might have had something to do with it. But Manuel was not nearly as interested in assigning blame as he had been when he had first discovered the theft. With or without the burglary, the ransom money would be gone. And with or without the ransom money, he was leaving Curaçao with Baron Valdez. The mission was far too important, and if anyone too clever had hold of that chest and the orders inside, the mission may already have been compromised. He could waste no more time on the ransom or on Van Kemper. If he didn't get Valdez out before the scheduled meeting with Van Kemper, he could forget about ever getting Valdez out by any means other than military force. And the military too could not wait much longer.

* * *

Roy and Ajuban followed as quickly as they could, but Benito was moving fast. Roy was anxious that Benito should not hear them, and any sounds in the street at this hour could alert him. *Especially as he is no doubt already on his guard.* There were times when they fell behind and Ajuban would scout ahead to find him again, but finally they tailed the man to a small house near the west end of town. It appeared somewhat run-down on the outside, as did most of the houses in this district, but it was larger than most and displayed a couple of glass windows that seemed out of place amongst the neighboring houses. Benito was only just slipping inside the open door into the darkness within when they caught sight of him. The door closed and Ajuban hurried up to the door quickly and quietly, motioning for Roy to stay back in the shadows down the street. Roy crouched eagerly waiting as he watched his friend cock his head towards the door and then slip around the corner to the left. It occurred to Roy as he stood there expectantly awaiting some clue as to Benito's peculiar actions that he might have been wise to bring Tiede or one of the other Dutchmen with him, but aside from the fact that they had all gone to their homes in town, they might well have proved less stealthy than he and Ajuban. Ajuban would be just as likely to understand any conversation he overheard as Benito apparently conversed with the locals in Spanish, but Tiede might have some idea to whom the major might be speaking.

Roy did not have long to wait, however. He soon saw Benito emerge again, this time in the company of another hooded and cloaked figure, thinner than himself. It was not cold enough for such garb by any stretch of the imagination, but Roy could not see the face under that hood as the two approached. Roy sank back around the corner and waited for them to pass. The two were not speaking, but moving furtively and quickly through the shadows back the way Benito had come. Ajuban appeared in the street nearby after they had gone and Roy stepped out to join him. "Did you hear anything?" he asked.

"Very little," replied Ajuban, "but dey are going to Van Kemper's tavern, and de man in de cloak was not pleased about de risk dey are taking. T'ankfully, he was upset enough about it to raise his voice."

Roy thought quickly. They must be planning to break into Van Kemper's tavern, and this man only just found out. *He must be a burglar!* Benito had planned things very well, it seemed. The fact that he had a contingency plan for something as routine as a ransom was very disquieting though. *He must want Valdez very badly indeed.* As Roy had observed earlier, Colonel Javier Valdez was not a man to have wandering around loose, especially if a heavily armed Spanish invasion force was being assembled. If Roy could act now and keep Valdez from freedom, it would be very much better for England. Acting Governor D'Oyley would no doubt agree, especially as Roy could think of no one more capable of helping the small Spanish force left in the northern region of Jamaica to recapture the whole island for Spain than Valdez was. Roy had followed his misgivings by following Benito, and it had paid off. Now he made up his mind to act. "Ajuban," he said earnestly, "follow me!"

He strode off down the street as gracefully as possible with Ajuban in tow, stopping at every corner to make sure Benito and his companion were out of sight before flitting to the next corner. "We must go as quickly as we can to Van Kemper's," he whispered as they paused at one corner after nearly catching up to the two men. "When we get there, we must wait for them to break in if they have not already done so. Then you go around to the opposite entrance and warn those inside that they have burglars inside and where they entered. I will wait outside the door that they use to enter and catch them if they should emerge." Ajuban nodded his understanding, and they continued on after the trailing shadows of their silent quarry.

When they arrived, they saw the two men huddled around the back door—the very same door that the marquis' prisoner had tried to force earlier that evening. Roy could not see what they were doing, but he could guess. No more than half a minute had passed before the door swung open and the two figures made their way quickly inside, shutting the door behind them. At a nod to Roy, Ajuban hurried off toward the front of the establishment as he had been ordered. Roy crept closer to the rear door, still keeping to the shadows and away from the windows. He drew a pistol, and took up a close watch on the door. With any luck, Valdez would remain a hostage, and Benito would end up a prisoner as well, if he survived the night. And Roy and his crew would set sail ten thousand pesos wealthier.

After only a few minutes, he heard a sudden commotion from inside. It sounded muffled as if it were coming from elsewhere in the building, but he stiffened as he heard raised voices and hurried footsteps. Without warning, the thin cloaked man came hurtling out the door at a full run, but Roy sprang from the shadows. "Stop right there!" he shouted, leveling his pistol at the hooded man, stopping him in his tracks. The man's hand darted inside his cloak faster than Roy would have expected of someone taken at unawares like that, but Roy was faster and he was taking no chances. His pistol was pointed directly at the man's hooded head, and he fired without hesitation. Blood spattered from beneath the hood, but Roy started as he heard another pistol shot. He quickly realized that the man must have actually reached a pistol concealed in his cloak before Roy had fired, and his grip on the trigger had tightened as he was hit. *Well, there won't be any question of whether or not I used unnecessary force.*

The cloaked figure fell slowly backwards on the cobblestones as guards and other staff of Van Kemper's spilled out of the doorway. Roy called out to them in placating tones, pointing his pistol upwards in a gesture of supplication and explained his presence. Satisfied with his story, the guards moved to inspect the fallen cloaked figure, and Roy joined them. The man's face, if it had ever been a pleasant sight, was not so now. A fair portion of it appeared to be broken or gone, and the rest of it was covered in blood from a horrible wound approximately where his nose should have been. One of the younger guards retched as he turned away and none wished to continue gazing at the sight of the burglar's ruined face.

Roy was far more concerned about his friend though, as well as the whereabouts of the major, but finally Ajuban emerged with a bound and unconscious Benito in his arms, a notable lump on his forehead nearly matching the one on Benito's, and a very flustered-looking Willem van Kemper in tow. "Would someone explain what is going on?" said Van Kemper in irritated tones. He glanced at the fallen man with clear disinterest as a guard covered the disfigured face. If the sight sickened him at all, not a trace of it showed.

"Perhaps we should wait for the city guard," said Roy lightly as they heard the sound of a whistle near at hand. "I imagine they will wish to know as well, and I may as well save myself the trouble of repeating it all." If anything had shaken Van Kemper's composure, it was the notion of the city guard asking too many questions. As far as Roy was concerned though, he had merely thwarted a burglary. If there was any hint that Roy knew of Van Kemper's unofficial trade in hostages, suspicion might fall on him for the theft of the ransom. With any luck, Van Kemper would not find out about that until Roy was long gone. Until then, he intended to feign ignorance about it as much as possible. *I hope Brian carried out my instructions already…*

* * *

The guards had questioned Ajuban and the captain for nearly three hours until dawn was at hand. At first Ajuban thought such treatment was rather excessive. Then he learned that they had also questioned Willem van Kemper and Major Benito, and the situation began to make more sense. Apparently Benito had only remained unconscious a short while after they had all been taken to the fort and separated from each other (though Ajuban and Roy had been interviewed together), and Benito had mentioned that ten thousand pesos had been stolen from his ship. Ajuban and Roy had been given little more detail of Benito's words than that fact, but it was clear that Willem van Kemper was suspected of arranging the crime, as were Roy and his crew. While it seemed a simple enough matter for the two of them to shrug off suspicion on the grounds that they would have no way of knowing of the presence of such a treasure aboard *La Fortuna*—and Ajuban supposed it was even easier for Willem van Kemper to deflect accusations of the theft, if he was honest about what the money was for—the matter had certainly required quite a bit of time answering questions and waiting for the guards to return from questioning the others. "I wonder what de major told dem de money was for," Ajuban whispered to the captain after they had been released.

"I don't know," said Roy, "but while Benito could easily expose Van Kemper as a hostage broker without fearing any retribution himself, it is unlikely he would wish to disclose any particulars about Valdez or why the Spanish crown is so ready to part with ten thousand pesos to secure him."

"I imagine dat he wouldn't want to risk Valdez being taken into custody by de governor eider," said Ajuban thoughtfully. "Not if he t'ought dat dere was still any hope of getting him back."

They wound their way back along the road from the fort in the morning light on their way to the ship where they expected to see Brian talking to potential recruits as Roy should be doing at the moment. There was much traffic near the fort as soldiers and messengers passed to and fro with fair regularity, so that the two did not dare to speak more openly. Ajuban could tell that the captain was slightly nervous about the night's exploits, and Ajuban felt similarly, but they both shared a growing exhilaration at the prospect that they would actually get away with it all. And of course it was amusing to ponder the predicaments of Major Benito and Mr. Van Kemper and to speculate about what tall tales they might be coming up with to explain their business with each other.

The captain's story had been simple, and therefore very difficult to gainsay. He merely claimed that he was alerted to shouting and curses on the deck of *La Fortuna*, and had found Benito's furtive movement away from the docks to be somewhat suspicious. Having little love or trust for Spaniards, he had summoned his first mate and followed Benito, thus witnessing his visit to the mysterious cloaked man and the forced entry into Van Kemper's tavern.

He had then decided to alert the proprietor and help to catch the burglars, and possibly even earn some sort of monetary reward for his aid. He had not hesitated to add that he still harbored the hope that a reward may be forthcoming once Van Kemper was released, though he was incensed by the notion that he might have robbed the Spaniard. "I find it far more likely," the captain had suggested, "that this Spaniard never had any such sum in his possession and merely sought to acquire for free what he could not achieve through honest trade." He had been able to offer no explanation for the shouts that had been heard from *La Fortuna,* but both he and Ajuban noted (with considerable amusement) that their interrogators took quite some time to return after the suggestion of fraud was planted. With luck, Benito and Van Kemper would still be sorting the whole thing out with the guards when *The Constance* set sail.

Ajuban felt how tired he was as they approached the ship and found Brian speaking with a number of men who had turned up to sign aboard. He had not slept at all and as each new wave of nervous tension dissipated, he was reminded again and again of that fact. "You may go belowdecks for a few hours, if you wish," said Roy as Ajuban yawned widely. "You look about done in. I can handle this." Roy gestured to the short queue that had formed by his ship.

"T'ank you, captain," Ajuban replied gratefully.

"Oh, and tell Coya she can stop playing lookout since there are plenty of people on deck now. I want to hear the details of her night's work." Coya looked like she wouldn't be of much more use as a lookout anyway without some sleep. She was nodding where she stood. "I will wake you when we weigh anchor," added the captain.

"Aye, sir." *If de guards don't come and wake me first.*

* * *

"Anything?"

"Nothing, sergeant," answered the dust-covered corporal. "Everything seems to fit the Spaniard's story."

"Go on," said Sergeant Josef Pylman, motioning his subordinate into the room and closing the door behind him.

"The soldier that Major Benito mentioned does indeed have quite an impressive welt on the side of his head," began the corporal. "He has been cleaned up, but I thought it better not to move him. His account is clear enough, but he has difficulty standing. A deckhand was still washing blood off the deck."

Josef was disappointed but quite unsurprised. Far from trusting that Benito was telling the whole truth, Josef Pylman was simply a pessimist. If a complicated incident with no easy or obvious resolution presented itself to him one week before he was due to retire from service, he viewed it as a matter of course. He also knew that his men were thorough, and if they told him that they had found nothing, he could trust that they had done their best. "What of the marquis?" he asked, with an air of faint resignation.

"The marquis vouched for the fact that his prisoner had remained chained in the hold all night. By the state of the man's appearance when I descended to the hold to look at him, I hardly doubt it. His clothes and boots also showed no sign of dampness beyond that found in the ship's hold."

Josef sighed. "I don't suppose you found anything else that needs looking into on this matter?"

The corporal looked a little self-satisfied as he said, "I did pay a visit to Captain Toppings' vessel, *The Constance*, and the officer on duty allowed me to search the ship, but I found no chest matching the major's description. I was told I'd have to get an order from the governor to conduct an inventory of the captain's private funds, since the captain was not present. They claimed to have noticed no robbery in the night, but the officer on duty acknowledged that he was less attentive than he should have been."

Josef nodded. "Thank you, corporal, well done. That will be all," he said. The corporal clicked his heels, nodded and left, but Josef remained a moment to think. It seemed obvious to him what was going on, but that didn't make the situation easier to handle. It was generally known among the authorities that Willem van Kemper was a hostage broker, and the governor did not object to such trades being practiced in Curaçao, with certain restrictions. He supposed that Benito really had been robbed, and the money that was stolen was for a ransom. However, Benito had not directly stated this, knowing full well that if any official statement was made to that effect, and the hostage named, he would have to be remanded to the governor's custody and no offer of ransom could be made to the governor, nor would the governor officially accept one. He was a man who held as much to the letter of the law and to official Dutch policy as he could while unofficially encouraging the opposite approach in any way that would benefit the colony and the Dutch presence in the Caribbean.

What was truly strange was that Benito had not invoked any claims of diplomatic immunity. If he had, and if his paperwork was in order—which the port authority had doubtless made sure of as they were rather more scrupulous on that particular point than they were about their other duties— then he would be set free, provided he left town immediately. For him to endure all of the questions and hassle, he must have some strong reason to wish to stay in town, and that reason undoubtedly had something to do with something—or someone—that he wanted from Van Kemper's tavern. Such determination over a hostage made Josef uneasy, in spite of the unusual circumstances brought about by the apparent theft of the ransom payment. He greatly desired to retain Major Benito, but Major Benito could claim immunity at any time and the governor was not fool enough to ignore it. Since the major might make such a claim at any moment, Josef needed to act quickly. Too quickly to explain all of these half-formed notions to his superiors and have them relay the details through the usual channels. Making up his mind, he quickly made his way to his captain's office. It was he that was awaiting a report, and he had given Josef the task of investigating the incident at Van Kemper's tavern.

As Josef was admitted into the office, he saluted and gave his account of the affair as briefly as possible. His captain looked impressed, but also confused and worried. "He still has not claimed diplomatic privilege?" he asked incredulously.

"He has not," Josef answered breathlessly, "but he may still feel that his story may be borne out and the ransom found. As yet, Van Kemper has made no official statement of Benito's wrongdoing beyond breaking into his establishment, and that is not apparently enough of a cause of concern for Benito while the issue still stands unresolved. Sir," he continued before the captain could ask more questions, "with your permission, I would like to bring this matter directly to Governor Diedrik and give him full particulars. I have the distinct feeling that there is more going on than a simple ransom payment that went wrong. Benito is too earnest, and the amount that he claimed was stolen was ten thousand pesos. That spells political trouble if it is not handled smoothly."

"*Ten thousand?*" said the captain with understandable surprise. "What, is Van Kemper harboring a royal duke or King Philip's own prize-winning stallion?"

"Exactly sir," Josef said with relief. His captain was seeing the difficulties involved and was much less likely to think that Josef was attempting to play the situation for personal glory and end his military career with even higher distinction. "We have no idea who is being held at Van Kemper's, and you know that if we ask him, then all this will be handled in an official capacity. It may well be handled that way yet, but if the ransom was paid (whether or not it was received) and Van Kemper's charge is not released, that could be very troublesome for the governor, particularly if this hostage is worth the sum that Major Benito claimed. I think you'll agree that neither you nor I wish to accept the responsibility of mishandling such an apparently important issue."

"No indeed," said the captain emphatically. "Go at once, sergeant. See the governor as quickly as you can. I will keep Van Kemper occupied as long as I can, though he is officially free to go. I will try to put Benito at ease so that he does not feel compelled to invoke diplomatic privilege, but you must hurry."

"Yes sir," Josef said with relief. He saluted and began to hurry out the door.

"Oh, and sergeant?"

"Yes sir?"

"Please make it clear to the governor that you and I are in agreement on this issue and that I sent you with all expediency, would you?" Evidently the captain wished for his share of recognition as well.

* * *

It was approaching midday and the last of the supplies were being loaded aboard *The Constance*. The tide was in, and Roy hoped to set sail within half an hour. He had been nervous for the last two hours, ever since he had returned from the fort and had been told that a guard had inspected his ship for the missing ransom. Brian had handled it very well, and the chest from Benito's ship had already been disposed of, but now Roy kept an eye out for return visits from the authorities. He did his best to hide his unease, not only because it would not do for the locals to think he was in a hurry, but also because he had new crew to think about. No sailor relished the idea of joining a crew only to find that his first experience upon signing aboard involved a nervous captain. Experience showed him that this truth did not only apply to *new* crewmembers.

Not many had been signed aboard earlier that morning. There were four Englishmen who had decided against joining Sir Sebastian's venture, a Frenchman who had lately arrived aboard a ship from Martinique, and Jan. Jan was by far the greatest find among them, but they all seemed competent and disciplined, and all had demonstrated some small proficiency with a pistol and a blade—even Jan, though he doubtless would prove infinitely more useful with the tools of his trade. Roy had mixed feelings about the size of the crew. With the new recruits and the Dutchmen from Gilbertsen's ship, there were but two dozen aboard, if he included himself. It was true that his ship was small and that two dozen men were about all that it could house comfortably. However, privateer crews were often larger on such vessels anyway, and the discomfort was compensated by the added manpower and the possibility of larger targets. *I would give much for just ten more men.* He would need footmen for what he had in mind. With the crew he had, his best targets could be found on land, unless he happened upon another small or undermanned trading vessel like Gilbertsen's.

As he stood musing over his new crew, he saw a sight that he had been dreading. Three mounted soldiers stopped at the edge of the docks. Two of them dismounted and made their way straight for *The Constance*, leaving their reins in the hands of the third. "Captain Toppings?" one of them called up to him. He appeared to be a sergeant, nearly fifty years of age, and his expression was that of a man who was not prepared to waste his time or his words. Roy was sure he had seen the man giving orders at the fort earlier when he and Ajuban were taken there, but he had not yet spoken to the man.

"Yes?"

"Governor Diedrik requests your presence, sir."

"Begging your pardon," said Roy hoping to dodge the request, "but I need to weigh anchor before the tide goes out. Is this a matter of urgency?"

The soldier—whose expression said that such a distinction should not matter in regard to a request of the governor's—replied, "He said it should not take so long as that and you may find it to your advantage. You may take my mount, sir." He gestured to his companion who held the reins at the edge of the docks.

"Brian, take over for me here, would you?" said Roy.

"Aye sir," said Brian impassively. Roy clambered down and the two soldiers escorted him away.

Apparently the huffy sergeant would proceed back to the fort on foot while his two companions escorted Roy to the governor's mansion. He did not recognize either of them, but it was only when the three of them had arrived at the mansion that he realized they were the governor's own guards. It was just as well that he was not being accompanied by anyone who had interrogated him earlier, as far as he was concerned. He was quite tired of putting on a show for everyone who had some new question about the affair, and the governor would surely prove to be demanding enough.

The mansion was quite beautiful, in a simple and solid sort of way. It was also very well guarded and secure, Roy noticed, as he was led through the hallways by one of the soldiers. The other had taken the horses back to the stables and gone back to his post. Roy's nerves had settled somewhat upon realizing that he was not to be detained, though of course he still could be if he put a foot wrong. "You may find it to your advantage," the sergeant had said. *Maybe I will get that reward after all.* The hopeful hint he had given to his questioners earlier had really been for show, but a little extra bonus would not go amiss. In any case, Roy could not have refused very well and he was encouraged by the fact that only one guard escorted him, as would be the case with a guest.

The paintings he was led past indicated a taste for battle scenes and an eye for realism, though the relief carvings on the archways were mainly those of tropical birds and other exotic animals. Roy let himself enjoy the décor, especially as he had learned long ago that preparing and rehearsing for such important meetings was close to useless and appeared as nervousness to others. It was an unpleasant truth of leadership that a leader must at once appear decisive and well prepared. The more Roy's preparations were made in private, and the more his public actions seemed swift and resolute, the better his men liked it—as did anyone else he dealt with.

It was not long before they came to a door near the east end of the mansion, but no sooner was Roy's escort about to knock than the door was opened from the other side and a Spanish officer came storming out with a very black look on his face. They moved aside as the man strode past, and Roy felt sure that his visit with the governor was about Major Benito and that he had not been given good news. Roy's spirits rose slightly at this. The escort knocked on the still open door, though Roy stayed out of view out of respect for protocol. "Captain Toppings to see you sir," the man spoke in English. It seemed to Roy that quite a few of the soldiers in Curaçao spoke English in addition to their own tongue.

"Enter," replied a clear, low voice.

Roy was shown into a very pleasant room, well lit by the large east-facing windows, and decorated much as the rest of the mansion was with the addition of several fine works of metal and glass, including a fair arsenal of decorative but serviceable weaponry adorning the walls. Frans Diedrik sat behind a large, heavy-looking desk made of some red-stained hardwood. He himself looked rather like he could have been kin to either Willem van Kemper or that sergeant that had come to fetch him, in that he was balding, middle-aged, sharp-eyed, and carried himself well. Governor Diedrik was rather more impressive (and intimidating) in manner though. Something in his gaze spoke of intolerance for foolishness and deception, and Roy could see at once why Tiede had spoken of him much as Roy had spoken of Colonel D'Oyley of Port Royal. He did not get up as he shook Roy's hand, but motioned for him to be seated. "Well met, captain," he said as the guard left them and shut the door behind him.

"An honor, governor," replied Roy.

"Will you have wine?" asked the governor. "It is an excellent vintage from France."

He poured a goblet for each of them from a glass decanter. Roy noted a

Venetian maker's mark on it. "You have excellent taste in finery, sir," he remarked as he inspected the matching goblet. They exchanged pleasantries briefly as civilized men at leisure would—a practice which was clearly important to the governor. It seemed to Roy that here surely was one who had been a soldier. His manner was refined, but there was a gruffness to his otherwise musical voice that spoke of a life of barking orders and being obeyed rather than exchanging pleasantries with diplomats and tradesmen.

"Captain, you are no doubt wondering why I requested your presence." It was not a question, but clearly the governor wished not to waste time, however much he insisted on gentlemanly protocol being observed. Roy nodded, but the governor simply continued, "It may interest you to know that the man who so briskly retreated from this office prior to your arrival was the first mate of *La Fortuna*, the Spanish vessel berthed next to your own."

Again, this was not surprising news to Roy, and he wished not to waste time either. "Was his visit in regard to Major Benito and his plight?" he asked.

"It was," said the governor. "He asked that Major Benito be released, and that diplomatic privilege be respected."

"And you refused him?" asked Roy with some confusion. "At least I can think of no other immediate explanation for his obvious displeasure with his interview here."

"I did," replied the governor with a curious look. He leaned forward and his next question certainly captured Roy's interest. "Would you like to know why?"

"I must confess that I am all curiosity, sir."

"I told him that we could not release Major Benito because he is no longer in our custody." This was nothing like Roy had anticipated. *He's gone? Where is he then?* Then Roy realized that the odd expression plastered to the governor's face was at once grim and somewhat amused. "Furthermore," continued the governor, "I told him that no claim of diplomatic privilege applied because the major had not been charged with any crime."

"What?" Roy was completely confused. "Why not, sir?"

"Willem van Kemper seemed indisposed to ask that he be charged," said the governor, quite casually now.

"Then where can he be?" asked Roy, convinced that Governor Diedrik knew exactly where Benito was. "Obviously he has not returned to his ship."

The governor became more serious as he explained. "Fortunately, one of my soldiers saw fit to consult me on the matter of the…incident at Van Kemper's, as well as the circumstances surrounding it. Several things immediately became clear to me. While this affair seems rather muddled at its core, and there is still much that is unknown, it was clear at once that it would be best to retain Major Benito. It was also clear that it would be best that Van Kemper retain his hostage," the governor obviously was not interested in denying the realities of the situation (privately, at least), "and that I could do neither of these things in an official manner without taking some very unwise risks."

Roy was impressed not only with the governor's candor, but that he had apparently found some way to get precisely what he wanted by unofficial means—though Roy supposed that he must be well used to doing so. *The man governs a town of smugglers and with a thriving black market. He must think like this on a daily basis.* "How did you retain them, if I may ask, sir?" He hoped that he was not asking too much, but only a simpleton would fail to be interested at this point.

"It's quite simple." Governor Diedrik was certainly enjoying himself, whatever the risks. "I had my soldiers tell Benito that he was free to go and that no charges would be pressed. He was escorted to the gate. I had arranged for Van Kemper's men to be there waiting for him with a cart. You see, we officially let him go. If Van Kemper retains him, however, well I have no knowledge of such things and it's none of my affair."

It was so blindingly simple. However, it showed such a flagrant disregard for the spirit of the diplomatic and legal policies involved in the matter that Roy would not have thought of it. Not without being immersed in such a place as this for a few years first. Of course Governor Diedrik knew where Benito was, of course he was being detained, and of course it had been officially arranged. It felt intuitively like so much nonsense to pretend otherwise. But if a man were to question anyone about it or try to prove it, he would get nowhere. Roy was sure that Spanish officials had appealed to the governor for his intervention regarding previous hostages, and he had no doubt sung the official song that he and his men had no evidence that any local citizen kept any such prisoners. Roy was very glad at that moment that he merely had to fend for his crew and his ship rather than a whole town. "But why should Van Kemper keep him?" Roy asked.

"Because he is expecting his share of the ransom," said the governor.

"Do you mean that you are going to collect a ransom for Major Benito?" Roy asked a little incredulously. That degree of personal involvement seemed like quite a political risk for the governor.

"Certainly not!" said the governor, sounding just a little too shocked for sincerity. "*You* shall collect a ransom for Major Benito. You hoped for a reward, did you not?"

This was too much for Roy. Many impulses arose at this news, not least of which was fear. The Spaniards would be even more incensed by his request for ransom, considering Benito had been sent to deliver an exorbitant ransom for a hostage who had not been freed. The fact that the ransom had not been delivered and that Benito had broken into Van Kemper's tavern would not matter to them. They would very probably be out for Roy's blood before long. And Van Kemper would be in a difficult situation as well, having failed to deliver one valuable hostage already, yet now demanding another ransom. However, the reaction that eventually prevailed upon Roy was amusement. He laughed long and loudly, if a little nervously. The way he saw it, he would be receiving a bonus for stealing the Spanish ransom money.

The governor merely smiled, though he appeared as ever to be sizing Roy up. "Keep in mind," he said, "that they may decide not to pay this ransom. I would be very surprised though if we did not hear some kind of interesting offer or news because of this demand." Roy's mirth ebbed somewhat, though the possibility that such a ransom would be paid was still quite appealing. "When you do receive news, I expect you to keep me fully informed about what you hear." Governor Diedrik managed to look slightly accusatory as he said this, as if he knew that Roy was keeping something back. Which, of course, he was.

"I understand," he said seriously. "Thank you, sir."

"Van Kemper will have a ransom request delivered to the man who so lately left this office," said the governor. "A verbal request, of course. He has been instructed to wait until well after your ship has left the harbor, however—assuming that is as soon as possible." There was no mistaking the governor's meaning. He wanted *The Constance* gone before any more trouble arose.

"Of course, sir. My ship is ready to sail as soon as I return." He drained his goblet and rose to shake Governor Diedrik's hand.

"Captain," said the governor as Roy turned to go, "I bear you no ill will if you had anything to do with the theft of the ransom money that was in Major Benito's possession, but if that is the case, I advise you never to let it be known. Officially, of course," he added with a smile.

"That is a very, very sharp man," Roy said to his escort as they rode back toward the docks.

"Aye, that he is," said the soldier approvingly. Roy certainly had much to think about, but he was decidedly pleased with how things had turned out— and that he had been allowed to leave at all.

Chapter 9: Windfall

Coya was awakened by Brian's voice and gentle prodding just after ten o'clock. She felt like she had barely slept, but with luck she would have only light duty until they were underway. It appeared that Brian had awakened Ajuban as well, and he looked no better than she felt. "Come on, you two," said Brian, "we're weighing anchor and the captain will want to address the crew once we're underway." He led them on deck where there was the usual bustle of men pulling and securing bits of rope—Coya was pleased that she knew the names for most of those ropes and pins and other parts of the ship now—getting the ship ready to make way. There were some new crewmen, a few of which glanced curiously at Coya though she had seen most of them the previous evening. She *hoped* it was curiosity at least, but she did not try to discern their intentions just now. Tiede was on deck, along with the other three from Gilbertsen's ship. He nodded to her, but he was among the newer recruits and those were tasked with preparing the ship for departure, with the exception of Jan. There were a full two dozen aboard now, and it certainly didn't take that many to handle such a small ship unless the guns were needed, so the senior crewmembers (which appeared to mean those recruited in Port Royal or before) were mostly allowed to take it easy, apart from Albert and Brian—and the captain, of course.

She regretted having missed a last meal in Curaçao, but thought it was perhaps best under the circumstances. She would be content just to get back to sleep. Some of the new crew appeared to be muttering to themselves disapprovingly about something. "What do they say?" Coya asked in halting English as William came towards her.

William looked back at them. "They are wondering when the captain will tell us where we are going."

"Will he not tell us that when we are gathered on deck?" she said after hunting for the right words.

"Most likely," said William noncommittally. "Most captains recruit crew for a particular venture. But they all knew last night that the captain was not going to disclose his intentions until today. I expect they are simply nervous about their new situation and finding reasons to grumble now that they have work to do."

Coya noticed that none of the original crew acted like this, though most would have liked to spend more time in Curaçao spending their shares. "I suppose you are right."

In very short order, the mainsail was raised, the anchor was hauled aboard and secured (mostly by Albert and Martin, it seemed to Coya, though others participated), and the ship was sailing due south out of the harbor, unhampered by the southeasterly winds. Brian appeared pleased to be at sea again, but the captain kept looking back at the harbor as it grew ever smaller in the distance. He did not have the same wistful expression on his face as the crew did. *I wonder if he will tell the crew about the ransom money.* She felt too tired to think about such things before even hearing what the captain was going to say, so she pushed the thoughts out of her head for the time being and waited. The rest of the crew's curiosity about their destination was largely lost on her. She probably wouldn't know where the destination was any better once Roy had told her its name, unless he simply intended to sail in a particular direction looking for more fat, slow ships to plunder. Soon Brian began to steer them eastwards, and some of the crew began muttering to each other again in speculation, but Brian secured the rudder as he waited for the captain to speak.

Eventually the captain seemed somehow satisfied with how far they had distanced themselves from the port and he turned around. "All hands on deck," he said.

"All hands on deck!" Ajuban shouted louder, just after him. Of all naval customs, Coya found this one most peculiar, or at least she did when it was clear that everyone had heard the captain in the first place, though she had never asked why this repetition was practiced. She fell in line along with the rest of the crew, and was again conscious of her diminutive height, though she did not feel awkward about it at all.

"I know that many of you have been wondering where we are headed," said the captain once the crew was mustered. Those who spoke little English stood next to those who could translate and Coya was grateful for Jan's help, as her knowledge of English was far from complete. "I beg that you humor me just a little bit longer," the captain continued. "I have news of another kind to share with you first." It was then that the captain recounted what had been found out about Major Manuel Benito and the ransom. He went into great detail, though Coya noted that he neglected to disclose *how* these things were discovered. Some of the crew looked to be very interested in the details, while others seemed merely impressed with the depth of the captain's information. But at that moment, he called Ajuban and Coya to approach him. Coya was not used to being singled out so visibly among the crew, but she was sure at that moment that he was going to tell them about the burglary. Before she could decide whether that would be unwise or welcome or both, he was turning them both to face the rest of the crew and telling all about how the two of them had planned the exploit together, how she had incapacitated the guard and crept aboard *La Fortuna*, how she had broken into Benito's cabin, stolen the chest from right under his nose, crept out again, and (with Ajuban's help) had gotten the ransom back aboard and left a false trail through the town. Ajuban continued to translate for her since they had been called forward and she wondered if he was noticing how the crew was reacting.

One or two of the new crewmembers had at first attempted to look contemptuously at her, probably out of jealousy of this special attention. By the end of the captain's tale, they simply looked dumbfounded and quite a few were grinning and laughing. The captain simply let them, though doubtless it was a breach of discipline. "Now let me impress upon each of you," he continued after the mirth had died down, "that I did not sanction or know of this exploit until after the fact. Although I laud their efforts, I would strongly discourage any of my crew from such activity again. It was extremely dangerous and could have caused trouble for Governor Diedrik of Curaçao and our business partner

Willem van Kemper as well." Coya felt her face flush, and no one was laughing now. "However, as everything turned out well," Roy continued, "I would like to congratulate these two of our crew. Well done, Ajuban, Coya." The crew began to cheer, relieved that the captain saw the incident as they did, no doubt. But there was something else in their glances to each other. The Dutchmen from Gilbertsen's crew looked questioningly at each other and at Roy. The newest recruits did not seem particularly pleased although they too were impressed. She did not have to wait long to discover the cause of this.

"No doubt you are all curious how this treasure shall be divided," he said. It had not occurred to her before now that the issue of how to split that part of the treasure might prove difficult. She was not sure if it could be defined as anything the crew had plundered, rather than as an individual theft. The rest of the crew was no doubt having the same questions running through their minds, and Coya suddenly understood why the newest additions to the crew did not seem as pleased as the rest of them. "As this was done with the help of other members of the crew," Roy continued, "as well as the safe haven of this ship, I shall be treating this just as any other plunder. Any crewmember that was already signed aboard at the time will receive a share. I regret that I must inform those who signed on this morning that they will not receive a portion of this treasure, and I can only implore them to view the good fortune of their fellow crewmembers as a sign that they have signed aboard the right ship." Coya's heart began to sink, but the captain had not finished. "As to the matter of how much of a share each man shall receive, this shall be determined by the usual manner, except that in addition to the twenty percent that Colonel D'Oyley of Port Royal will receive, and the ten percent that I shall receive, Coya and Ajuban shall each receive ten percent in place of their usual shares before the remainder is divided amongst the rest of the crew, for the simple reason that no one would be receiving any of it if not for their daring and initiative. That's a thousand pesos for each of them, for those of you who have not the skills of a moneylender." No one appeared upset with this pronouncement, and the crew in general began cheering. The Dutchmen were particularly enthusiastic, and Tiede even swept off his new hat and offered them a bow.

Coya was much relieved to be receiving more than her ordinary share. For an instant she found herself resenting that the plunder would be divided amongst the rest of the crew at all. None of them had really done anything that Coya and Ajuban could not have done themselves. But when she asked herself what they contributed, the selfish thought was extinguished at once. She would gladly trade so much of the plunder for the comradeship, home, and acceptance that she had gained when she had signed aboard *The Constance*, and she was certain that the feeling would grow still greater now that the crew had good reason to be grateful to her. *The captain is indeed generous to award such bonuses at all.* And with that, the desire for a greater share of loot and recognition vanished for good. A thousand pesos was far more money than Coya had ever possessed all at once.

The captain let this sink in and waited for the talk to die down before he continued, "I will dole out each man's payment within the next few hours," he said. "However, there is another part of this business that will affect you all." Coya perked up her ears at this. She knew none of what had happened after she had arrived back on board except that Roy had asked her to recount details of her exploits when he had returned to the ship before the crew signing, then relieved her of watch duty to get some sleep. But as Roy resumed speaking, Ajuban whispered translations of Roy's account of the entire affair of the burglary at Van Kemper's tavern, and of Governor Diedrik's solution to Major Benito's presence in Curaçao. The entire crew, Coya could see, were intensely interested in this development. Many were amused, and a few looked worried, but all were pleased by the captain's next statement. "As we have not yet received any ransom money for Major Benito, those of you who are new members of my crew are not excluded from a share of any ransom we may collect. Should we receive payment, it will be divided normally with no bonuses paid out owing to the fact that this was arranged by Governor Diedrik and is made possible mainly by his guile rather than any of our own efforts."

This time the entire crew cheered at the prospect of such a bonus, and several of them seemed to appreciate the irony of the situation, though Coya could not understand more than a word of two of their jibes without translation. The Dutchmen once again appeared to be most enthusiastic, and Coya could hear the name "Diedrik" interspersed in what they were saying. Judging by their tone, Coya was sure that they were all echoing the admiration for their governor that Tiede had shown the day before.

The captain allowed this mirth to continue for a short time, but then called for attention once again, and Coya was pleased to see that everyone came to attention as quickly as any crew could. "Now that I have told you all about this most fortunate incident," he began, "I can finally reveal our destination. I only waited this long so that no one aboard *La Fortuna* could possibly know where to find us once they understand what has happened to Major Benito." Many of the crew grinned at this, but they remained at attention. "We sail for the port of La Guaira, near Caracas. Or more accurately, we shall land some distance from the port and make our way on foot to the outskirts of Caracas. I have heard rumor of attacks by natives in the area, and with luck the rumors are true and there are fewer soldiers to stop us from spiriting more than food and supplies from the town. We should make landfall within the next two days. Until then, see to your duties, enjoy your winnings, and look forward to the loot to be had in Caracas. That will be all."

The crew cheered again, and Coya broke off to go belowdecks and back to her hammock as she had no duties to attend to. The attempt was short-lived, however, as a good portion of the crew headed her off. Many of them wished to praise her, clap her on the back, shake her hand or otherwise show their appreciation. All four of the Dutchmen accosted her in this way, and Tiede's friend Jacob even danced a comical little jig, catching her up in it until she laughed. Eventually Ajuban chased them off with a bark (and a laugh) to attend to their duties, but between them, Justin, Martin, William, Albert, and even Jan and a couple of the other new crewmembers, it was half an hour before she was able to climb into her hammock again. As sleep stole over her, she felt more contented than she had since she had fled from her home so many years ago.

* * *

Coya discovered over the course of the next day that her popularity with the crew had grown still further since Roy had told the tale of her theft of the ransom. Ajuban received quite a bit of praise himself, but the crew seemed to think that Coya was due more of the credit for the deed. It became quite clear that she had made instant friends of all of the Dutchmen, each of whom had received more than three hundred and nineteen pesos for simply being part of Roy's crew and sleeping through the night while she risked her neck aboard *La Fortuna*. They had, as yet, not had to fight or risk their lives for Roy at all, and they already had good reason to be glad of their decision to abandon their commissions under Gilbertsen. They were all quite aware that they owed all of that to Coya and Ajuban.

Surprisingly, none of the men who had benefited from the situation appeared to show any more interest in her as a woman than usual. If anything, she caught *fewer* such looks from them, though none of these glances had ever been intent enough to faze her. Indeed, they had displayed no more interest in her womanhood than she had shown them. Now the men seemed friendlier than before, and they treated her more like an equal crewmember than they had previously. She stood by the rail pondering this the next afternoon when she spotted the one crewmember that still snuck lustful glances at her when he thought she wasn't looking. He was an Englishman—one of the new recruits—and he had approached her twice already. He was friendly, respectful and amicable, and reasonably attractive, but the times that Coya had caught him looking at her made her think that he might not be as friendly and respectful as he presented himself. She had tried to busy herself with other tasks to throw him off, which was difficult considering how little there was for her to do most of the time, but now she was clearly at her ease and unoccupied.

He made his way towards her, but as she resigned herself to having a polite conversation in her broken English with this man who gave her such a bad feeling, Jan appeared at her side and began speaking to her in Spanish. "You have an admirer, it seems," he said.

"You may call it that," she replied with relief, "but I don't think it is admiration I see in his eyes when he looks at me."

"Yes, I believe you're right about that. But then that is why I stepped in. I've noticed that you have successfully avoided conversations with him so far, but I thought you looked like you needed help this time."

"Thank you for that," she said, "but I am surprised you noticed those instances." She was honestly curious as to why he should have been paying so much attention to her interactions, though his attention was much more genuinely respectful than the Englishman's.

"Well," said Jan with a sigh, "one condition of my employment on this ship is that I shall not generally have any regular duties so that I may preserve my 'delicate surgeon's hands.' So there is precious little else to do on this tiny ship than to observe and talk to everyone else."

Coya nodded. She had wondered why Jan appeared to have so little work to do, even though no one had many duties on such a small ship in calm weather. "What is that man's name?" she asked. "I could ask him, but then I would have to speak with him myself, and I am sure that he already told me once anyway."

"That's Daniel. I don't know much about him, but I think you're probably right to shun his company."

"I suppose I can't avoid him forever when we're both on this ship. Sooner or later I will just have to tell him that I'm not interested, but he won't simply ask me so that I can say so; he just engages me in false speech, so I avoid him."

"Well, who knows?" said Jan with a shrug. "He may not stay with the crew past this mission, assuming he even survives. Maybe you won't have to avoid him for so long."

"I'll be hard pressed to avoid him even that long on this ship," she said. She hadn't really thought about crewmembers *leaving* the crew, though she knew that this sometimes happened. As at home as she felt aboard Roy's ship with actual comrades, it just didn't occur to her that others might not feel the same way. *Besides, no one left while we were in Curaçao.* That was a promising thought, though of course few aboard would likely have wanted to disembark in a Dutch town far from Port Royal. "If I had something to occupy myself with, I might just manage it, but most of what the others want to do is to gamble their pay with everyone else." Gambling looked fun, from what Coya could see of it, but the idea of simply *giving away* chunks of the largest sum of money she had ever earned for the sake of a game was something she was not yet ready to consider.

"Well, if you like, I can occupy some of that time teaching you English," offered Jan.

It was a curious offer, and if it were not for Daniel's leering (as well as her overhearing with disturbing regularity the manner in which many of the crew spoke of women) she probably would not have suspected any ulterior motive. Looking at Jan though, she picked up no trace of one. "William is already teaching me," she said, "though admittedly I would like to learn faster."

"It's all right, I have plenty of free time and I enjoy teaching. I've also offered to teach William more about navigation."

"All right," said Coya, feeling relieved.

"If you like, I can teach you how to gamble as well, and we don't have to actually exchange any money." He shared a knowing smile with her. Apparently he had divined her reasons for avoiding the pastime, though how he understood was beyond her. He looked over at Ajuban who had just come from the captain's cabin. "At the moment though," he added, "I have to see the captain about something. If you will excuse me?"

He turned and headed towards the captain's cabin, but before Coya could do more than wonder what he wanted to see the captain about, it occurred to her that perhaps she should find someone else to talk to before Daniel noticed she was unoccupied again. *I would give much for a jungle to disappear into right now.*

* * *

A map of the countryside and the coastline near Caracas was stretched over Roy's little desk, held in place by a pistol and a couple of gold coins. In order to avoid being spotted by passing Spanish ships or the port of La Guaira north of the city, he and Ajuban had agreed that they should sail away from the coast and around to the other side of a very small cape east of the port. Brian claimed there was a serviceable beach in the area, and there they could set out for Caracas on foot. The problem was that it would take the best part of a day at the very least to get to Caracas on foot from that far away, and they would need to leave enough people on board should the ship be discovered. On top of that, Roy was worried that he would not have enough men to carry much loot so far back to the ship, particularly if any men fell dead or wounded.

He and Ajuban had been discussing that very point for quite some time, and neither of them was happy with the situation. However, it had been decided in the end that they would have to leave enough men to handle the cannons as well as sail the ship, and *The Constance* would raise the Dutch flag should any ships pass by. From a distance, the flag should be far more visible than the ship's name, and anyone passing would probably conclude that it was a smuggler. Even the Spanish were generally friendlier to smugglers in this area due to their highly restrictive trade policies (which were greatly resented within most of the Spanish colonies). Brian was fluent in Dutch and could pull off such a front should they be inspected more closely, with the help of one or two other Dutch crewmen. All the same, Roy was very worried about the decision to leave more than a skeleton crew, and he felt like he had not truly resigned himself to the decision even though he had ruled on it already.

As he sat musing over this and poring over the map of the countryside, which promised many hours of climbing up hills and down into valleys, Jan knocked on his open door. "May I come in?" he asked.

"Certainly," said Roy turning to face him, "I had something I wanted to discuss with you anyway. But first, what can I do for you?"

Jan pulled two rolled parchments from a small case at his belt and handed them to Roy. "I wondered if you and Ajuban would perhaps sign these documents with one witness present," he said. It was an unusual request on a privateer ship, and Jan obviously knew it, but Roy took the document with interest. It read:

Contract for Service aboard The Constance, Capt. Roy Toppings
The Eleventh of May, 1660

To Whom It May Concern,

I, Captain Roy Toppings, wish it to be known that Jan Huisman will serve aboard The Constance as a surgeon, and as such is due the full three shares standard to each crewmember. In the event of his death, Jan Huisman's share, as well as any wages that have not yet been paid to him directly, shall be paid within thirty days to his daughter, Isobel, residing at 7 Kerk Straat, Curaçao (allowing for changes in surname or residence following the drafting of this document). Should this payment not be made within thirty days, an additional two percent shall be rendered for each month that lapses between Jan Huisman's death and the date of payment. Should I, as captain, be unable to fulfill this contract, it falls to First Mate Ajuban and my officers to fulfill or to arrange for a third party to do so.

We the undersigned recognize this contract as legally valid and binding:

The second document was identical to the first. "I didn't know you had a daughter, Jan," Roy said.

"Yes sir, she just turned fourteen in March," said Jan.

"I find it even more surprising that you wanted to take up this dangerous life with us in light of that fact." Roy's tone was not without concern, but Jan's reasons were his own. He was welcome to share them, but Roy would not question them as he would question the motives of other men. Discovering the reasons and temperament of his crew was one thing, but he was lucky to have a surgeon at all and could not easily risk passing up the opportunity just to satisfy his curiosity.

"I know sir, but you must at least understand why I would wish to ensure that my daughter is compensated should I fall injured or ill and die."

Roy noticed the evasiveness in Jan's reply and said no more, merely nodding his assent. "Very well, if you would fetch Ajuban and Tiede, I would be happy to sign these documents, if it will ease your mind. I would have done as much without a contract if I had known, but I agree that it is always best to have a contract when you can arrange it."

"Thank you sir," Jan said sounding relieved. He turned and left to fetch the other two men.

Roy read the document again and pondered what might be behind it. *"Fall injured or ill?" I suppose he's worried about malaria or something, but I would hope he could do something about it in either case.* Still, if Jan was injured, no one would be able to help him out much.

Jan returned followed by Ajuban and Tiede, and Roy explained about the documents. After he had finished reading them aloud, he addressed the others. "Ajuban, as first mate your signature would ensure that this document is binding if you're willing to give it. I've chosen Tiede as a witness because he is a resident of Curaçao and is in a better position to handle things locally should any difficulties arise."

"No problem, sir," said Ajuban.

"Of course, sir," said Tiede. Jan seemed relieved that no one asked further questions about the document, and soon they had all signed both copies. Ajuban's signature looked like that of child, but it was legible and far better than the "X" that had been his mark before Roy had begun teaching him his letters. Tiede's was little better.

"Thank you, sir," said Jan as he gave Roy one of the documents. The other he rolled up and put back in the case. "So, what was it you wished to discuss with me, captain?" he said once Ajuban and Tiede had left.

Roy told him of the plan to land to the east of Caracas and make their way inland. "The ship will most likely be far from where any fighting would take place," he said. "It's rather too late to buy extra provisions, but is there anything that you would recommend I prepare in the event that we have to haul wounded men over a far distance under your care?"

Jan thought for a moment and said, "You may want to build a few stretchers before a battle, but you can likely do so in the woods at any time unless we are caught by patrols. You will also need to order that plenty of bandages and clean linen be brought along for the wounded, and we will need to store extra water. Wounds don't stay clean long in the heat of the jungle."

Roy pondered this. He had considered the need for stretchers, but Jan was right that it would be best to build them later rather than carry them to Caracas. But his knowledge of medicine ended with the application of bandages and water. "Thank you," he said at length. "I will see what extra provisions we can spare room for, but we cannot afford to overburden ourselves either. You may go."

Jan nodded. "Sir," he said, and left. Roy's doubts redoubled once again as he considered Jan's words and the raid he was planning. It seemed he had hired more crew simply to have someone to leave on board, and he would be heading into the jungle with barely more than a dozen men carrying extra supplies. *And Coya, of course.* Now he would see if she was indeed as good as he thought she was. He had not exaggerated when he told her that she would make a fine military scout, but the Spaniards would have their own military scouts to contend with, and it would be hard to travel over rough terrain for a day or more bearing loot and wounded men with pursuers tracking them. But the plans were laid, and there was no turning back since he had announced his intentions to the crew—not without some newer and better reason to do so. He just hoped the loot would be worthwhile.

Chapter 10: Valley of the Dispossessed

It took two short trips in the longboat to bring the raiding party to shore. The boat was only big enough to comfortably carry about eight men, and the men took a week's worth of provisions with them as a precaution. Coya noted that the provisions did not appear to include much beyond the same unsavory biscuits they ate aboard the ship, water, a few oil canvases to keep out the rain, torches, some climbing tools, extra weapons and powder, medical supplies, and an awful lot of rope. It promised to be an uncomfortable and cheerless few days, and as she was tasked with finding a quick and clear path, she was determined to make the journey take as little time as possible.

It seemed odd to her that Roy favored this Dutch smuggling charade that left so many crewmen behind in light of his desire to have a larger crew. She was not sure how she felt about the deception, but she remembered her tactic of luring soldiers further into the woods with sling stones when she first met Roy. Roy's plan was a *social* deception and felt different somehow, but she supposed she just wasn't used to it.

The captain had picked his companions for this mission well. In addition to himself, Ajuban and Coya, he included Jan, Albert, Daniel, Justin, Tiede, Bert, and all five of the other new recruits whose names she had not yet learned. Brian, as ever, remained with the ship, and William and the other Dutchmen were left to help with Brian's task, while Martin was left in charge of the ship's guns in case of a confrontation.

"With any luck, you will see us in three or four days," Roy said to Brian as he hoisted his pack and the raiding party set out towards the forested hills before them. Coya took the lead with Ajuban following not far behind, and

Roy and the others trailed behind him in single file. The hills twisted and climbed towards a high ridge in the distance to the southwest, and as it was already mid-afternoon, Coya hoped to camp somewhere on the other side of it before day's end.

It took some time to find a suitable path through the undergrowth and around the steeper hills. She would normally have tracked any large game to paths that were large enough for them to use, but there was very little evidence of large game this close to the sea. According to the rough map the captain had shown her, they should reach several small streams on the other side of the first ridge, but it was essential to find a suitable path over the ridge or they could waste an entire day scrambling among dense underbrush and switchbacks. Eventually, however, she found tracks leading to a creek, and this led up into the hills in the direction they wished to go.

Coya found that her trepidation about the journey vanished sometime between entering the forest and leading the men up the narrow watercourse. It had been several years since she had set foot in the forests and jungles of the mainland, and though she had done much to escape them, she often missed them. Less than an hour under the canopy, she recognized a faint smell like a reminder of home. Perhaps it was her imagination, but it seemed to her that the very land had a different odor and feel to it than the islands of Jamaica and Curaçao that were her only experiences of life outside of this broad expanse of earth. She felt that she was in her element as completely as she had ever been, yet she was now a guide and huntress rather than a fugitive from the oppressive wilderness. "This way," she shouted to Ajuban as she led the way up what looked to be a solid, steady climb parallel to the stream, and she sprang from stone to stone with a lightness of heart and step that she had not known for many a long year.

They topped the ridge well before dusk, and she found a sheltered and comfortable campsite in the valley on the other side before another two hours had passed. And when it was her turn to watch in the dead of night, she sat and drank in all the sounds and smells of the forest in contented silence.

* * *

All the next day they traveled west to avoid the steeper, taller cliffs and mountains to the south, but still spent their time climbing down into gullies and up hills, now scrambling among the rocks, now cutting their way through undergrowth, crossing narrow streams just often enough to keep their boots wet as the waters from the early morning rain fell from the heights and joined up at the bottom of each valley. Ajuban felt in good spirits as he tramped along in Coya's wake, happy not to have to act as pathfinder for a change. He was a hunter in his youth, but his home in Africa was not this overgrown. He had never entered woods as deep as this, but Coya had spent years in the jungle learning simply how to survive there on her own, which he had never had to do. Nevertheless, it had been months since the series of simple raids on small settlements near the south coast of Cuba, and Ajuban enjoyed exploits that involved his abilities as a hunter far more than the prospect of outmaneuvering ships and firing cannon volleys at enemy hulls. He was glad to sense that Coya felt she was in her element and was more relaxed than usual.

His main concern was that they had not brought enough men to execute a successful raid or make off with anything very valuable, and if they did, they would have to carry it back through miles of rough terrain. With luck, they would not also have to worry about being chased the whole way back. "Dese natives we heard about might not like us passing t'rough deir lands," he said to Roy when they were stopped for a moment.

"Hopefully seeing a native guide at the head of the column will placate them long enough to talk to us," said Roy. "They could even be convinced to help us."

Ajuban hoped they were on the other side of the town as he thought this unlikely, but if they could be persuaded, Roy could potentially attack with two or three times his own force without having to worry about equal shares or finding space aboard the ship for so many crew.

Thinking of such possibilities was a skill that came more and more naturally to Ajuban since he had been promoted to first mate and had the opportunity to speak with the captain on tactical matters as an equal. He and Roy had learned much from each other's experiences with business matters as well. Though their backgrounds were radically different, they had worked through the details of what had turned out to be some rather successful operations. "I suppose dere's not much to be done until we scout de town and de port," said Ajuban, and Roy agreed. Ajuban focused on enjoying the trek through the wilderness and on keeping an eye out.

There was little talk amongst the men. Coya sometimes stopped to look for signs of a clearer way forward, but she generally made up her mind quickly and they would set off again. They seemed to be making good time, but there were sounds of thunder approaching steadily throughout the afternoon, and it began to rain again as they stopped to discuss which might prove the safest way over the next rise. They had been traveling generally westwards, but now Coya expressed doubt about maintaining that course. "We should turn further to the south than we have been traveling," she said. "The land is firmer southwest of us towards the higher part of the next ridge and there will be less chance of slipping in the mud, but the longer climb will delay us. We must begin to pass over these higher southward ridges, however, or we will simply find ourselves using the same western paths around them as the Spaniards."

"We have two high ridges to cross before we reach the outskirts of the town," said Roy as he followed her gaze to the southwestern heights, "and the map indicates that there is gentler terrain between them if we head westwards once we cross the one before us. I'd like to pass both of them before dusk. If this route you suggest will accomplish that, I don't mind traveling south on flatter ground on the other side after dark."

Coya nodded and led the way southwest into what turned out to be a narrow valley cradled in a long spur of a tall hill, and it was this spur that they intended to cross. They reached the foot of it after only an hour, by which time it had begun to rain heavily. The hill was fairly steep, but it was very rocky and proved easier to climb than they had anticipated. "It is just as well that we took this path," Coya said as they began to climb. "If we had gone the straighter way, it would have taken at least another hour to round the ridge, and we would have come to softer, tangled lowlands which would be much harder to manage in a downpour than this single ridge."

"What about de oder side of dis rise?" asked Ajuban. Roy had said the ground was gentler there, but perhaps the rain would change all that.

"The map is not detailed enough for me to guess how that climb will treat us," she said to Ajuban's dismay, "But with all the rope that we brought, it should be easier getting down from there in the mud than it would be to climb up in it."

"In any case," said Roy, "it will be better to make the climb *down* sooner than we would have been able to climb *up* if we had we gone the other way, before the rain has had a chance to soak into the ground."

At this, Coya shook her head and said, "If this rain keeps up, it could wash us clean off the other side of the slope, and that will be far more likely if it doesn't have time to soak into the ground." Fortunately they were speaking in Spanish and none of the men who were immediately behind them understood what Coya had said. It was not very comforting. *It's a good t'ing dat de captain brought so much rope.*

The rain did not slacken until after they had climbed down the other side, but that climb was much easier than they had feared. The far side of the slope was just as firm, but it was also gentler and more densely wooded with many roots and footholds. The raised valley was also wider and shallower here between the ridge and the southernmost line of tall mountains, making it easier to cross the swelling brook that cut across their path and ran to the northwest towards the very lowlands they had avoided. By the time they had crossed this deepest part of the valley, they had squelched through nearly a quarter mile of muddy ground, but the captain pushed them on for another three miles. The terrain was gentler here, though the ground sloped northwards away from the main line of worn peaks on their left. Over that high ridge lay the valley of Caracas, but the ridge itself paralleled their course to the west until it curved to the northwest where the heights became little more than hills. As they reached the point where the ridge turned to the northwest, the captain called for a halt to gather their strength for the final ridge crossing.

"What do you t'ink, captain?" asked Ajuban as the group huddled together under the thick canopy woven by two barely separated trees. "I don't t'ink dat any tracks will have survived dat storm to lead us to useable pat'ways over dat ridge, and it won't be easy to tell de main watercourses from de smaller ones for a while." The rain had settled down to a steady drizzle, and the heights were shrouded in mist, barely visible but for their outline. Finding a solid path up the slope would be very difficult unless they virtually stumbled upon it, and if the way they chose proved to have treacherous footing, it could delay them until after dark. There were no more than three hours left of daylight, and the twilight would be much darker in the haze that enveloped them.

"I think," said the captain after a few moments' thought, "that we should head west along this side of the ridge until we find a path over it with stable footing. We will have to head southeast from here once we cross, but the land is generally lower to the west and we will probably have more luck in that direction. What do you think?" he asked Coya.

She nodded. "I think you are right. In these conditions, that is the most sensible way. I cannot find a path in this by searching for any signs but the path itself. We may as well search westwards."

In the end, it was little more than an hour before they found a suitable path, and the rise was actually lower at that point as well. The way over led due south and was like a wide, flat spur of a low hill leading all the way to the top. It had less dense undergrowth and fell away on either side, rendering the falling rain a mere annoyance on the path itself. The slope was perhaps a mile long and still took them an hour to climb, but they were over it well before sundown. The shadows lengthened as they climbed down into the valley that led southeast to where Caracas lay, but the air was less misty on this side of the ridge and they could clearly see a way down, though they did use the ropes to help them down the upper reaches of the muddy slope. To the northwest on their right, the ridge sank into low hills where the road to the port lay. The taller hills on the other side of the road threw shadows over the low passes to the north. To the southeast, the land became more densely wooded behind an arm of the next hill and the rain was gathered into small creeks that ran down towards the Caracas valley. Far to the south, Ajuban could just see the large watercourse that emerged from the hills southwest of Caracas and made its way into the valley where it turned eastwards, cutting right through the southern part of the town. The westernmost reaches of Caracas stood twinkling with lamplight to the southeast of them, not five miles distant.

"Coya, see if you can find a way around that hill that isn't too visible from the town," said Roy pointing southeast. "We will probably end up making camp in those woods on the other side of it."

"Aye sir," she said, the phrase sounding strange in her accent, and off she went into the damp wilderness again.

She came back just as the sun was setting behind the hills on the other side of the road. "A short distance from here, the way is sheltered by rocks," she said. "I followed it for some time and it appears to run into a path that is overshadowed by dense thickets. We should be able to travel southeast unseen as long as there are no patrols in the area." The hill had three short spurs and she led them around the first of these for half a mile until they had reached the cover of the rocks where it was safe to light torches without fear of discovery. She carried none herself, as she had no need of one and would probably be the first to spot a patrol, but Ajuban and the captain followed not far behind with torches held aloft, both peering anxiously around in the misty dusk air for signs of trouble. They were a little bit too close to Caracas to be careless about hiding their presence, and Ajuban found the notion of Spanish patrols much likelier in light of the recent raids on the town. *At least in dis darkness, any real trouble will probably be carrying lights as well.* They had only traveled a mile and had barely entered the first large thicket of tall trees when he realized he was wrong. Behind a tree that stood not fifteen feet from him, Ajuban saw the glint of steel in the torchlight. It looked to be coming from the tip of a pikestaff. *Spanish!* He cursed and immediately drew a pistol, shouting to the others, "Soldiers in de trees!"

There was a flurry of activity behind him as the others drew weapons, and Coya came hurrying back with a knife in her hand, but Ajuban mostly kept his eyes on the figure he had spotted. Oddly, the figure made no sudden movements, but emerged from the shadows in a casual manner, peering directly at him. He could see that it was a man, dark-skinned just as he was, and appeared to be dressed in tattered and dirty breeches and an ill-fitting vest of similar quality. The man's hair was slightly matted, and he carried what did indeed look to be a Spanish pikestaff, but he was clearly no soldier. He appeared only to be interested in Ajuban, and that was the strangest thing about him, considering that he probably had half a dozen pistols pointed at him. "What was it that you said?" he asked.

What surprised Ajuban was that the man had asked the question in Igbo, Ajuban's native tongue. He thought back to what he had said, and realized that the curse he had uttered when he spotted the pike was in Igbo. "You are from Igboland?" Ajuban asked in return, using the same language.

The man nodded. "From the Niger Valley." Ajuban met other Africans often, but he rarely met one from the same region as he. The man looked around at the others, and then back to Ajuban with a curious expression on his face. "You are not a slave?" he asked.

"No," answered Ajuban. Clearly the man had taken in the fact that Ajuban was well armed and that the others were simply waiting to see how this exchange turned out rather than shouting orders or chiding Ajuban for not translating. "My name is Ajuban, and these are my friends and shipmates," he said, gesturing to the others behind him as well as to Coya, who lowered her knife but did not appear to relax any further than that.

"Who are they? Where are they from? What brings them here?" He did not offer his name and was clearly wondering whether or not they were a threat, but it had been a very brave (or foolish) gesture to walk out into the open with so many weapons pointed in his direction.

"If you would like answers, you should ask the captain," here he pointed to Roy. "I assume that you speak Spanish, and some of us do as well, including him. He will answer your questions as much as he may."

The man studied Roy for a moment and said in Spanish, "Very well. What can you tell me of yourselves and why you are here?"

Roy tucked his pistol away, signaling the others to follow suit (though Coya's hand idly remained on the hilt of her sheathed knife). "My name is Roy Toppings," he said with a slight bow. "I am an English captain from Port Royal, and these are my men." He introduced them all, making it clear that Ajuban was his first mate. "More than that, I cannot tell you until I know more about you and your business," he concluded.

The disheveled man looked interested and appeared less wary as he pondered this news. He looked at Coya and said to Ajuban in Spanish, "I had t'ought dat she was perhaps a friend of one of de natives here and had stepped forward to speak to her before I realized my mistake, or maybe you would not have seen me." He turned to the captain and asked, "So she is one of your crew and not simply your guide t'rough dis land?" Roy nodded, but gave no other information. He simply waited for an answer. "My name is Belonwu," the man said abruptly, "I and oders like me live in dese woods away from Spanish eyes. We do not concern ourselves in deir affairs more dan we need to, and we do not have any dispute wit' de English or any oder peoples, but we do not wish to be found."

"I understand," said Roy. "You are all Cimaroons?" he asked. It was the Spanish term for escaped slaves and outlaws living in the wild.

"Not all," said Belonwu, "but nearly all. What is it you wish to do in dis land? Where do you go?"

"We had heard that there have been several raids on the Spanish by natives of this area, so we decided to try our luck at a raid ourselves. We have no quarrel with any others we may meet here, be they Cimaroons or no." Roy apparently decided there was no harm in confiding in Belonwu. Ajuban suspected such would be the case from the beginning, but that decision was for the captain alone.

Belonwu laughed. "I do not know where you hear such tales, but dey are bot' more and less accurate dan dey could be." He appeared to ponder a decision for a few moments, then said, "Come wit' me, I will show you to our camp and you may speak wit' de oders. Be warned dat dere are many of us." This warning was no doubt intended to put to rest any thoughts of capturing them all and selling them as slaves. He gestured for them to follow him down the very path that Coya had been leading them along, and the captain ordered the men to march in single file. Now he set Coya as the rearguard, probably hoping that she would spot any sign of trickery in the darkness.

There was little speech as they followed Belonwu, but Ajuban walked with him and they spoke in Igbo. "I was taken three years ago," Belonwu said in response to a question from Ajuban. "Our village was raided at night by the Aros, and our sentries were killed before they could give warning. We had learned that there were slavers in the area, so we kept watch, but we did not expect the Aros coming from behind us."

Ajuban had only learned after the fact that some Igbo clans like the Aros would often raid the villages of other clans with help from the watchmen in that village, and would sell the captives to European slavers. In exchange for the help, they would bribe the watchmen with a few gold trinkets and some supplies that were quite rudimentary by European standards, such as battered old muskets and a little bit of coarse gunpowder without any primer. He chose to keep this to himself, as Belonwu seemed bitter enough without suspecting his own people. *None of it matters now anyway.* That world and that life were long gone, though the experience was doubtless still somewhat fresh for Belonwu. "I was taken many years ago," said Ajuban. "The crossing was terrible. Many died on the ship. I think I would have too, but there was a leak in the deck above me and the water would cool me, even though it stung."

Belonwu nodded and sighed. "After the Aros sold us to the Spaniards, we were loaded aboard a great ship. Only one of the children aboard our ship survived the first week," he said. "This made the captain angry, so he punished the crew. And then they would get angry and take it out on us, but they made sure to keep the other child alive. I think that they were ordered to feed him some of their own food as part of the punishment, so they took what they lost out of ours. It was a miserable time, but the winds were kinder than they could have been."

Ajuban mused over the fact that the crossing from Africa was invariably considered a chief event among slaves not born in the new world, and everyone had a different story to tell even though the accounts probably all seemed remarkably the same to a casual observer. The things they noticed when stuck in their own thoughts for weeks on end, as well as the parts that they reflected upon later, these were all like different stories of manhood rituals that the villagers would talk about around the fire at night. Except, of course, no one ever remembered *these* stories with fondness. "When did you escape from the Spaniards?" he asked, wanting to move the conversation in a more practical direction.

"Last fall," said Belonwu. "I was being whipped for having a little carved figure of an elephant. They thought that it had something to do with pagan religion or something like that, and also they were convinced that I must have carved it myself without being given permission to have use of a knife, so they whipped me and left me tied to a tree for the night. I think one of the barbs on the whip must have cut partway through a rope, because when I regained my strength, it was easy to break through the rope and escape into the woods." Ajuban looked more closely at Belonwu and noticed that there were the ends of a few scars visible on his back above the neck of his vest. "What about you?" asked Belonwu in his turn. "How did you come to be first mate of this captain's ship?" He sounded somewhat impressed.

Ajuban told his story. He had not been treated as cruelly as Belonwu since his arrival in the Caribbean, for which he was very lucky, and he used the opportunity to tell about the captain's generosity and fair-minded attitude. If these were the "natives" that they had hoped to find, but were actually Cimaroons for the most part, Ajuban's account of his own situation might curry enough favor with them for Roy to enlist their aid. Roy had told him once that many attacks against enemy settlements were only successful because of help from local guides and outlaws who knew the area. *Maybe dey can at least give us recent news and tell us how many soldiers dere are here.* Ajuban dared not hope for more, but Roy's plan had so far paid off.

* * *

They traveled for only another mile around the hill before they were in the heart of the woods they had seen earlier from the heights of the ridge. It was here that they began to glimpse dim firelight away in the trees to their left but still perhaps a quarter mile ahead. Belonwu gave a high-pitched call that sounded rather like a birdcall, but not one that Coya had ever heard. She suspected that it was some African bird that Belonwu (and maybe Ajuban) was familiar with, but Coya had no idea how far away Africa was or what was there besides other people like Ajuban and Belonwu. It had been somewhat pleasant to listen to their strange speech together, but her attention wandered before long as it often did when she listened to speech she had no hope of understanding.

"Dis way," said Belonwu after they heard what sounded like an answer to his call, and he led them through the trees in the direction of the light. Coya had little idea what to expect from this development, and she was very wary about the situation, but both Ajuban and the captain seemed in good spirits about it, and Ajuban would fall back from time to time to speak in a low voice with Roy. She could not hear what they said, but she gathered from this and from Roy's earlier comments to Belonwu that they had anticipated the possibility of such an encounter, and things appeared to be progressing as they wished.

Coya had noted the state of Belonwu's dress and appearance, and felt a peculiar surge of smugness. For once, *she* was part of a well-ordered group of people, her clothes reasonably clean, and she carried all the arms and money that she needed, while this outlaw lived in the jungle she had escaped and showed all the signs of hard living. She felt momentarily ashamed of herself for thinking these things, but she could not deny the fervent gratitude that welled up in her for the fact that she was not sharing this man's circumstances. He did, however, seem to know what he was doing, and the jungle appeared not to trouble him at all. She was mildly upset at not having spotted him, but she knew that she could not expect to see every hidden thing in the jungle at night, and no one else appeared to think critically of her for it.

As they neared the source of the light and Coya could actually see the campfires, she became more aware of how cold and wet she was. She hoped these Cimaroons were friendly to them, because she wanted nothing more than to sit by one of those fires and eat something hot before falling into a dead slumber, hopefully on a dry patch of land. The Cimaroon camp, however, looked like it was no less soaked than the surrounding woods. She did not see any sign of tarp, tent or other shelter, nor did anyone appear to have dry clothes or blankets. She had of course been used to such conditions, but her situation had improved in Port Royal where she seldom had to sleep with no shelter at all.

Several of the Cimaroons looked up as the captain's group approached. None appeared to be grabbing for weapons—evidently the signal Belonwu gave had not been a warning—but there was trepidation on many of the faces she saw. And all of those faces were as dark as Belonwu's. There were at least two dozen of them, and she did not see any sign of these "natives" she had heard were in the area, but Belonwu's words had not encouraged such hope in any case. She knew that she was far from her own home, and even other natives in the area would be unlikely to understand her speech, but she had held out some hope for the possibility in spite of all reason.

Some of the Cimaroons stood and joined those who had already been awaiting their arrival, expressions of mingled curiosity and wariness on their faces, but a surprising number remained around the fires shivering or resting without more than glancing at the newcomers. Coya thought they must be quite worn out to show so little interest. *Or ill.* Not all of those shivering looked like they were merely cold. Jan looked closely at them as well, and then spoke quietly to the captain, no doubt voicing his more learned observations.

One of the Cimaroons stepped forward and approached Roy. "I am Jorge," he said in Spanish, and his accent indicated that he may have grown up under Spanish rule rather than having been brought across from Africa. "Welcome to our camp."

Much to the surprise of the Cimaroons, Roy extended his hand to Jorge, who clasped it somewhat nervously. "I am Captain Roy Toppings," he said. "This is my first mate, Ajuban, and these others are also members of my crew." Several of the Cimaroons looked surprised by this revelation and stared at Ajuban as if waiting for him to show some sign that he was merely a slave as they had suspected. A few looked similarly at Coya, but Roy continued, "We have traveled all day in this foul weather. May we share your fires and your company for the evening?"

Jorge looked around at the others, but said to Roy, "If you mean no harm to our camp and will not reveal us to those who mean us harm, you may stay. We have too little food to share, but you may trade with us for it if you wish." It was quite clear that the camp was in need of supplies, but they must be desperate indeed to make such an offer. The Cimaroons, on the whole, did not look very well fed.

"There is no need," replied the captain, "but we may be able to make you other offers. We have come here on the rumor that the natives here have been raiding the Spanish. While it appears that these rumors are not quite accurate"—several Cimaroons chuckled at this—"we nevertheless wish to take advantage of the situation. Perhaps we could help each other."

Jorge pondered this, but the expression on his face was troubled. "Perhaps we could help you," he said at length, "but how could you help us? We take only supplies and food, and we don't kill anyone when we don't have to, but you are planning a different kind of raid, I think."

Roy appeared to ponder this question, but Coya did not think this was a new concern to him. Eventually he said, "Well, first we will have to assess the situation and see what sort of a raid is possible. But we have some amount of supplies aboard our ship, and more could be arranged in the future if you are able to help us a great deal." Several of the Cimaroons looked suspicious when he said this, and it occurred to Coya that Ajuban's presence and status might be quite a bit more valuable than she had originally thought. If the captain treated him as an equal and trusted him with such an important position as first mate, it must occur to the Cimaroons that he would be more likely to deal fairly with them. "Another service I can provide for you," continued Roy, "is the care of a skilled physician." Here Jan inclined his head to Jorge. "It appears that some of your number would benefit from this arrangement." Roy gestured to some of those who sat shaking by the fires, but his expression was more sympathetic than businesslike.

Just as with Ajuban's impact on this negotiation, Coya realized that Jan was also useful in that regard. This group of Cimaroons might well render a great deal of aid in exchange for the services of a doctor or a local medicine man. She remembered something about Jan packing extra medical supplies by the captain's orders, and thought perhaps it had to do with more than the expectation of combat wounds inflicted on crewmen.

Jorge considered this, and whispered with some of the others near him, but they appeared to favor the offer for the time being. "We can scout the area for you in exchange for some supplies and medicine for our men," he said, "if you have supplies to spare and useful aid to render."

"We will set up a makeshift shelter for them tonight," Roy said. "Doctor, what would you recommend?" he added turning to Jan.

"We should keep them dry to start with," said Jan. "Hopefully they will improve after they have had a good night's sleep and something hot to drink, but I will look at each of them in turn and help as I can. I have ample supplies on hand."

After some deliberation, Jorge nodded. He then gave some quiet instructions to Belonwu, who headed south away from the camp again. "I have sent him to inform our scouts of our arrangement. I will send one of them to scout the port and the other to scout the town in the earliest hours of morning. They will return after dawn and you can make whatever plans you wish with our help. They will tell you what they see and what the soldiers are doing. If there is anything else you wish them to find out you should tell me tonight, but first you may rest and eat with us."

Roy assented to this arrangement and before long Coya and the others were seated around the fires with the Cimaroons, eating and drinking what they had. Jan did not sit with them but went straightaway to tend the ill and bring them food and drink himself. Roy had brought a small quantity of tea with him, and he now brewed this and gave it to Jan to serve to the Cimaroons who seemed weak or ill. Coya was not sure if he had intended to use this treasure himself or if it had been meant for the crew to enjoy, but the Cimaroons were grateful for his generosity. Even if some of them clearly did not appreciate the taste, Roy simply told them that it made him feel better when he felt ill, and then they made sure to drink it all.

Before long, there was a rustling in the trees and Coya heard Belonwu's voice as he returned to the camp. Two other men accompanied him, but these were not Cimaroons—they were natives. Coya gazed briefly at these two, for they were much like her own people in appearance. They did not appear to notice her at first as they took in the sight of all the newcomers to their camp huddled around the fires, but Belonwu brought them to where Jorge sat with Roy and Ajuban. Perhaps they were the reason Belonwu had indicated that there was some truth to the rumors Roy had heard of natives raiding Caracas, or perhaps there were more of them that were not present, but clearly these were the scouts Jorge had referred to. Coya was not sure how she felt about Roy using these scouts instead of her. Perhaps he was trying to keep his crew out of danger, or perhaps he relied on their knowledge of the town and the surrounding area, but Coya still felt a desire to prove herself worthy of the post that the captain had chosen for her.

As the scouts and Belonwu sat with Jorge, Ajuban and Roy, and introductions were made, Coya discovered that she was close enough to hear their conversation. They were not trying to keep it quiet, so she did not attempt to ignore what they said. "What else would you have dem find out?" asked Belonwu at one point.

"At the port," answered Roy, "I merely wish to know what ships are there, Spanish or otherwise, and what strength of men and horsemen. As for the town, Coya will accompany your scout to find out what we need to know.

Won't you Coya?"

Aware that she was being addressed, and that the captain assumed she was listening even though he was not facing her, Coya felt no less pride that he had included her in the excursion as she immediately answered, "Yes, sir, of course."

The natives, who had finally noticed her presence in the group, scowled visibly. One of them began translating Roy's words for the other, who apparently did not speak Spanish. It was a moment before Coya realized that although the accent was quite different, they were speaking her own native language, Quechua. "He says that woman is to go with us," he finished. "That one who intrudes upon her betters and dresses like a man."

Neither of them looked pleased by the prospect, and their disdain was perhaps clearer to Coya because she could understand them, but she was not the only one who had noticed their reaction. Even as Coya felt the heat rise in her face, realizing for the first time how outlandish she must look to her own people, Roy addressed them, "If you two have some problem with that, you had better voice it in a way that I understand or I shall simply think that you are daunted by the task itself." There was a definite chill to his tone that no amount of tea could banish, and Coya's embarrassment was instantly replaced by anger at the two scouts. Words and thoughts began tripping over themselves in her mind, all wanting to be released. *No. I shall speak them this time, not just think them.*

"It's all right, captain," she said, "I will attend to it." She glared at the two natives, stood up and walked right up to both of them. Then she crouched down, sitting offensively close to the one who had spoken, and said in her own tongue, "I have survived in this jungle for many years, exactly as you see me." The two of them started at her use of Quechua, but their expressions darkened still further as she continued. "Not only have I survived, but I have prospered. You cannot say as much, and my leader relies on *me* for these tasks. I give *my* permission for you to help me, but do not overestimate *your* position in this arrangement, or the value of your services."

They looked quite offended, as was Coya's intent, but she had effectively just claimed leadership and authority over them, and for either of them to dispute it, they would have to appeal to a higher authority or refuse to cooperate. They were clearly contemplating both options, but Coya guessed that they could choose neither, and for the same reason: they needed the Cimaroons, and the Cimaroons needed Roy and his offer. Both of the scouts wore clothes and shoes that were clearly in good repair, were of European design, and had probably been stolen in the Cimaroon raids, as were the knives at their belts. The two of them could not expect to do as well by themselves as they could with the Cimaroons. The Cimaroons surely needed them as well, and indeed conversation had stopped as a number of them watched the progression of this unintelligible confrontation anxiously, but Coya and Roy had the upper hand in the bargain and the Cimaroons had no reason to refuse Roy's offer. Should the scouts take issue with the arrangement, they would be the only ones.

"What did you say?" whispered Roy. Ajuban, Jorge and Belonwu waited curiously for Coya's answer as the scouts consulted with each other a few yards away.

"With apologies to your camp," she said to Jorge and Belonwu, "I made it clear that they are the beggars in the woods and I am the official scout for our group, so if they want to complain about who makes the decisions, they can take it up with me, someone in charge, or the gods themselves."

Belonwu, Ajuban and Roy diplomatically stifled their amusement, but Jorge looked concerned. "I hope they will not refuse to help," he said. "We need them if we are to survive out here, so we try to keep them happy." At that, Belonwu's expression sobered a little.

"They need you just as much as you need them," said Coya, but Jorge looked skeptical. "You think they can survive in the wilderness without you, and you may be right, but to do so by yourself takes its toll. Maybe they remind you frequently how much you depend on them, but I can promise you that they are far less miserable with your help than they would be without it." She knew from her own experience that this was so, and Jorge seemed to perhaps guess as much, for a new light of understanding dawned on his face. It was no wonder that the others followed him, and as she watched his expression, Coya found herself wondering if the natives would continue to enjoy receiving the most food, the best gear and the newest clothes—as was clearly the case—for much longer.

Eventually the natives agreed to the arrangement and, to Coya's surprise, formally apologized to her for their rudeness. It was all she could do to accept their apology gracefully, as she realized with embarrassment that she should not have been so surprised. In the years since she had left the mainland and gone to what was now Port Royal, she had forgotten that her own people and most of the remnants of the empire of the Incas had been quite friendly to each other. Most Europeans never realized this, and likened all of the natives they encountered to the cannibals and savages they encountered on many of the Caribbean islands and in other parts of the lands they controlled on this side of the vast waters that separated them from Europe. Coya had not noticed until now that she had begun to share those same views, even of her own people. The thought depressed her, but she began to remember her interactions with others she had grown up with as well as the natives who lived in Cartagena or just outside of it, and suddenly she greatly appreciated the presence of these two strange scouts in this even stranger camp of outcasts. Indeed, once the initial unpleasantness between them had been resolved and they had finished talking with Jorge and the captain, they seemed interested in speaking with her. It was rare that they encountered anyone who spoke their language, and one of them—his name was Ispaca—had lived in the deep jungle most of his life and had never learned much Spanish at all.

"Our settlements lay many days to the south and west," said Challco, who had earlier translated for Ispaca, "but they were destroyed many years ago by Spaniards. I was fishing upstream when my village was attacked, but they had killed or captured everyone else. I could not get to them, so I traveled north towards the other villages we traded with."

"It was much the same in my village," said Ispaca, "but we had heard there were Spanish raiders in the area and we posted a watch. I was one of the lookouts and I spotted them when they approached. I signaled to the village so that they were prepared. Our soldiers and hunters killed many of them, but still they destroyed us. Some of us escaped, but afterwards most of us ventured south or west. We knew that if we went too far north, we would run into more Spanish settlements, but I wanted revenge on them."

"You did well to kill many of them," said Coya appreciatively, "their soldiers are well trained."

"We saw no soldiers," said Ispaca, "There were many men with guns, but none of them wore the garb or insignia of the Spanish tercios."

"But how did you know the difference?" Coya asked, feeling suddenly confused, "You had seen Spanish soldiers before?" She tried to think back to when her own home was attacked. *Were they simply violent men with guns?* She could not recall having seen any soldiers either, now that she thought about it.

"Yes," replied Ispaca, "we had scouted far to the north, almost as far as we are now, and we encountered their patrols on two occasions. We kept out of sight as much as we could. These other men were well trained also," he added. "If they had attacked our village before we surprised them, fewer of us would have escaped."

Coya sat quietly in thought for a while as she listened to Challco and Ispaca talk of their experiences and their homes. She had of course seen Spanish soldiers since her home had been invaded, but although she could tell the difference between a soldier's uniform and anyone else's garb, she had never reconsidered her initial perception that Spanish soldiers had destroyed her home. *I don't suppose it matters now.* Even so, she began to wonder who those men had been and what they had come for. *Probably the same thing any conquerors come for: the land.*

She did learn through their speech that she was right about how much better off they were with the Cimaroons. Their stories of living in the wild before they joined the Cimaroons were not much more hopeful than hers, if at all. But they seemed to regard the Cimaroons as barbarians in some way just as they did the Spanish, though it came across only in subtle ways. *Hopefully that will change once they are forced into an equal status in the camp.* She suspected that Jorge would see to that. Coya had not viewed the Spanish as barbarians, nor any of the people they had enslaved, but she imagined that one way in which Challco and Ispaca had adapted to their situation was to retain some measure of their own culture to give themselves purpose and drive, even if that meant viewing everyone else as outsiders. It was probably far easier for two together to preserve some aspects of a culture than it was for one alone.

They were curious about her experiences as well, and soon she found herself telling them her own story. They seemed greatly impressed with her account and asked many questions about life near Cartagena and in Port Royal. They especially enjoyed her tale of the Spanish defeat at the hands of the English, as she knew they would. "How did the English manage to stop them from retaking the island?" asked Challco.

"Fortunately there were many English ships in the area," Coya said, repeating information that she had overheard many times outside of taverns and in the marketplace, "and their ships were smaller and faster. The Spanish troops are very well trained, as we have agreed, but the English gunners are also well trained. They sank the Spanish ships before they could land many of their soldiers." Challco and Ispaca laughed long at the Spaniards' expense just as Coya had, though she found this fate less amusing now that she had some experience aboard ships. Even so, she felt no remorse for the Spanish as she told her tale. As much as she enjoyed being a part of Roy's crew and had enjoyed the greater general freedom in Port Royal since it had been captured and renamed by the English, there was something about sharing her experiences with her own people that was like rain at the end of a drought.

Conversation turned towards her experiences aboard Roy's ship and the overland trek she had led over the last two days, but soon she began to feel quite tired as the ground and her clothes felt less damp. As the rest of the camp began to nod off, Coya curled up on her blanket by the fire she shared with the scouts. "Whichever of us wakes first wakes the other?" she suggested to Ispaca, who agreed, as Challco would be setting out before them. "Sleep well." With that, she slowly drifted into a contented sleep, feeling more at home than she had for many years.

Chapter 11: A Fair Trade

Coya awoke to Ispaca's gentle prodding at her shoulder. It was quite dark, and she still felt tired from her long journey and from the cold, damp night, but now she was as dry as she was likely to be and was eager to find out what the Spanish were up to. She washed quickly and ate a small scrap of dried meat from her provisions before setting out. Ispaca indicated that Challco had already left for the port, but it was several miles over rough terrain and it was unlikely that he would return until after they did. It had been decided that Ispaca would accompany Coya to survey Caracas because there was less cover in that direction as the trees had been cleared for some distance east of the town, and Ispaca was a more experienced scout than Challco. And, if necessary, Coya could translate for Ispaca and understand anything they might overhear.

As they set out, Roy seemed to hear their footsteps. He rolled over and opened his eyes as they passed. "Wait," he said, "I nearly forgot." He leaned over and reached in his pack to pull out his telescope, which he then offered to her. "Take this; you will need it more than I will."

"Thank you, captain," Coya answered, taking the telescope and tying it to her own pack. "With luck, we will return by noon." Roy turned over again, and she continued on her way with Ispaca. As they left the Cimaroons' little clearing and approached the path to the north that Challco would have taken, she glanced briefly that way and wondered what he would discover. But her path was south and east, and there was much she wished to discover before the sun peeked over the eastern hills.

The two of them continued south through the forested valley that sheltered the campsite and soon topped the spur that formed the southeastern wall of it. Once they had left it behind, they made their way eastward for another mile until Ispaca steered her towards a quick path southward down the slope. It was not so much a path as the remains of a rock fall that one could travel along by stepping from stone to stone down the shallow incline that lay between them and the deeper valley where Caracas was beginning to awaken. *This must be how they evade the patrols.* Such a route left little possibility for tracks, no matter the weather. Coya could hear the occasional door slam in the distance as they approached the edge of the woods. No doubt the farmers were beginning to attend to their morning duties. There was a small stream at the foot of the slope, no more than a sling's throw away from their hiding place, and Ispaca warned her that townsfolk who lived nearby often came to fetch water there at this time. "It would be difficult for them to see us here," he said, "but they may hear us if we are careless."

They sat surveying the city for some time as they had arrived too early to be able to discover much. Coya retrieved the telescope from her pouch and carefully extended it towards the cottages in the distance. She had never looked through one of these before, even while on watch. She was amazed how near everything seemed to be. She could clearly see a farmer working in his yard, and she could count the sheep in a pen three fields away to the south. Focusing her attention on the town, she saw the beginnings of wakefulness. The small fort was manned by guards who looked alert despite the hour, just as Coya had expected. Only one soldier patrolled the walls above, and two sentries stood on towers at opposite corners of the fort. In Cartagena, a guard had stood on every tower at any hour of the day or night, and there were at least two gate sentries instead of the lonely guard she spied from the trees, but this fort was like a glorified guardhouse compared to those in Cartagena. Briefly she shifted her gaze to the governor's mansion which was on her side of the river overlooking the north bank, but there appeared to be no activity there as yet.

She handed the glass to Ispaca, who seemed similarly amazed by the clarity of what he saw. He even took the glass from his eyes several times just to see how much farther away everything looked without it. "This bargain with your captain," he said, "we must see if we can arrange for him to include a few of these devices in the supplies he is offering."

"Are there always so few guards at the fort at this hour?" asked Coya.

After panning his view to where the fort was, Ispaca answered, "This is their *usual* number of lookouts, but of late they have favored only one lookout on the northwest turret and more guards at the northern guardhouse over there," he handed the telescope back to her and pointed to a small, sturdy-looking structure that she had not noted before. If it was being used as a guardhouse, it must have recently been converted for such use, as it did not appear to have been constructed for the task. It had uneven bars on the windows and the door looked newer and heavier than seemed fitting for it. "Now they have just as many guards down there," Ispaca continued, "but they keep their full watch at the tower as well. Could your presence be known?" he asked.

"I don't think word would have traveled so fast unless our ship had been captured within hours of our leaving," she answered. "I feel sure that we would have heard gunfire if that were the case." *Unless they were completely outgunned from the start and couldn't escape.* That wasn't a pleasant thought.

"What is going on over there?" asked Ispaca, pointing towards the main plaza. She raised the telescope to where he had pointed.

There appeared to be a great deal of activity in the marketplace now. Of course vendors would be setting up their wares for the day, but Ispaca no doubt knew that as well. What had probably caught his attention was that the marketplace seemed to have spread right into the streets in some areas, and several residences had vendors opening up booths that seemed to have been temporarily erected right up against their walls. "It looks as if they are setting up for some sort of fair or festival," she said. She knew there was no holiday or religious observance scheduled, as she tended to keep track of those because of the increased chance that she would find some unattended coin. She watched for some time, as vendors seemingly prepared for heavy traffic. Indeed, some of the townsfolk were already meandering into the marketplace, though the sun had not yet passed above the eastern hills.

"Do you have dealings with anyone inside the town who could tell you what is going on?" she asked.

"No, we are completely cut off from them," said Ispaca. "It was decided not to attempt such dealings so that our location and our plans could not be compromised."

Coya watched the marketplace in silence for several minutes longer, turning to survey the fort and the guardhouses from time to time, but it was long before she had any clear ideas about what might be the occasion for the activity she was witnessing. It was when she started paying close attention to what kind of wares the vendors were selling that an idea struck her, but she said nothing until she had studied the scene a while longer. As it turned out, there were many tools and goods of worked metal and leather, as well as wines and bolts of cloth, finished garments, furniture and books. She also saw signs of entertainers practicing feats of agility and musicians tuning their instruments, evidently for the festivities that often accompanied marketplace fairs. "If your camp wants to conduct another raid soon," she said aloud as she put the telescope away, "you should wait several days until after we have gone and things have calmed down, or strike when they are distracted with coming after us if we are very successful, but you should do it soon."

"Why?" Ispaca asked curiously. "What did you see?"

"There appears to be a wealth of new supplies for sale at the marketplace today," she answered. She studied his expression to see if he understood the implications of what she had said. She was not disappointed.

"We had better head back," he said, "and see what Challco discovers at the port."

"Agreed," said Coya, and they turned back and disappeared into the trees once more. "I will need to know more about the surrounding terrain," she said after a few minutes of silent, stealthy travel through the brightening woods. "Particularly the terrain near the road to the port," she added with a grin.

"What would you like to know?" asked Ispaca.

* * *

Roy was perfectly content to sit in the Cimaroon camp and wait for the scouts to return, but he would have welcomed a hot meal made over a fire. Unfortunately it was a practice in the camp not to light fires during daylight hours. The light of small fires could not be seen from the town at night due to the distance and the cover of trees and hills, but the smoke from fires could be seen for miles in daylight unless extreme care and skill was taken not to let the fires smoke. That is what they had said to him when he had asked, and though he was sure he could build a fire that smoked little, he found it more politic (and safer, he admitted to himself) to subside on the issue under the circumstances. He pitied the Cimaroons who were ill though. They clearly would have appreciated a hot meal as well. They seemed to be in better spirits since Jan began tending to them and the crew had erected a few makeshift shelters for them. Some seemed all but cured, though many needed further care, but all were eager to hear what the scouts would have to say and to find out what Roy's men would do.

His men were just as eager, especially after the miserable day of traveling they had endured the day before. Some of them quietly discussed the difficulty of transporting any loot back through the jungle and the hills to the ship, or how they might stage two raids on different parts of the town, but Roy deliberately kept himself from making any plans until he heard what the scouts had to say. Instead he ordered his men to perform a variety of tasks, partially to prepare them for a raid but mostly to give them a focus for their excitement. He even sent Albert and Daniel to find firewood, though there was obviously no chance of a fire in the camp before sunset. "We may need it for a diversionary fire," said Roy when they seemed confused by the order, "and we may need it if we have to leave without conducting a raid, but if not, it will save us the trouble tonight." They looked quite interested by the prospect of a diversion, but Roy had no idea how such a tactic could be useful at present. *That will give them something to talk about, though.* It would also separate Albert and Tiede, who together had been excitedly speculating about all kinds of ridiculous possibilities. Meanwhile, Justin made sure the gunpowder was still dry, Tiede and Bert took down the tents and packed them, and the rest of the men cleaned and maintained the weapons, including those carried by the Cimaroons. They all finished far too quickly for Roy, but he had done what he could to keep them focused.

"De men seem excited," observed Ajuban in tones of dry understatement. Roy shook his head in the direction of Tiede who was already excitedly speculating again, but this time with Bert, as both of them stood drinking their fill of water upon finishing their tasks.

"I just hope the scouts return soon, before the men start feeling their nerves," he replied. He was grateful that Ajuban shared his view and temperament in these situations; it was part of why Ajuban was his first mate.

"I t'ink dat de one who went to de port should be back soon. Dey say it is not much furder dan de town if he went as directly as he could, and he left in plenty of time last night. He will probably be back before Coya, and she said she should be back by noon." Judging by the position of the sun in the sky, that was still a couple of hours away, but Ajuban seemed to think that Coya had probably given herself some extra time in case of difficulties.

In fact it was no more than ten minutes after Ajuban said this that she returned with Ispaca, followed by the lookout who had been watching for their approach, and everyone present gathered to hear their report.

"Captain, has Challco returned yet?" she asked, looking around for him.

"Not yet," Roy replied expectantly. "Why? What have you found?"

"I can't be sure without hearing Challco's report," she began, "but I think there is a trade fair going on in town."

It was not immediately clear to Roy what she meant by this. "A trade fair? Is that some kind of festival, or do you mean there is a trade ship in the port?"

"It is both," she answered. "In Cartagena, when a trade ship was in port from Spain, the city would hold a kind of festival. The marketplace was filled with vendors selling many supplies and valuable goods from Spain, and there was feasting and entertainment, music and dancing. Today there are many such goods being sold in the marketplace. The vendor booths are choking the plaza, and I saw entertainers setting up in places as well."

"Were there many soldiers?" Roy asked earnestly. Trade ships from Spain ran heavily armed and tended to carry a large complement of soldiers. If they were in town, he could forget about all thoughts of a raid.

But Coya seemed very excited by this question. "Usually there would be quite a few soldiers, and they would stay at the forts. But while Ispaca says there were more soldiers than is normal," here she nodded to her companion, "I did not see a great excess of them beyond what we expected."

Roy was puzzled. "What can it mean?" he muttered half to himself.

But Coya answered, "Captain, I think that what soldiers there are probably stayed at the port. Most may have remained in the fort that overlooks the harbor which Ispaca says is larger than the fort in Caracas. It may be that only a small number traveled to the town to escort the merchants and their wares. Also, on the last day of these festivals, the vendors pack up and load all of their remaining goods or those that they purchased onto mules or wagons to take them back aboard the ship—"

"Along with any profits and goods, and whatever gold or silver the Spanish government has extracted from local mines or from further inland," Roy finished, seeing the direction her suggestions were taking.

"Exactly."

"How long did these festivals last in Cartagena?" he asked her.

"Until the merchants had sold all they were likely to sell," she answered. "Usually two or three days."

"Do you know if this is the last day of their festival?"

"No sir, but Challco may be able to tell us if any merchants arrived at the port from the road. Some merchants pack up early because they have sold all they can, but they are unlikely to return to the ship or to load any goods aboard it until the day before the ship's departure. Or perhaps those living in the port of La Guaira are holding their own fair and he will be able to see if the merchants load their goods back onto the ship, but that may not affect when the merchants in Caracas depart for the port. Assuming there is actually a trade ship in the harbor," she added in the interest of keeping speculation separate from her observations.

"There is," replied Challco who came striding up, trailing the last lookout that had waited for him. They all waited expectantly for his report, and he dutifully continued though he was plainly weary from his long overnight trek and curious about what Coya and Ispaca had discovered that had gotten everyone so excited. "There was a large Spanish ship in the port—a galleon, I think. There were a great many soldiers, though I would not have seen so many if I had not waited for some time and then gotten closer."

Roy was surprised by the tale he began to unravel. Apparently he had decided that with such a large ship in the port, he should get close enough to find out more about it. He had therefore crept into the port itself and had seen many soldiers and workers busy at the docks and at the fort. Fortunately he reported that there were few horsemen, and it was unlikely that any of them were new additions from the galleon. He indicated that there were merchants selling wares from the ship, but from what Coya had reported, it sounded as if most of them had gone on to Caracas. "Were there any men in carriages or with loaded mules arriving there and loading goods into the fort or onto the ship?" he asked. It was an unlikely prospect at such an early hour, but it was worth a try.

Challco seemed surprised by the detailed nature of Roy's question. "I did not see any in the port, but I did spy two of these in the distance as I came back. They were traveling towards the port from the town, but I thought they were merely bringing supplies for the ship's next journey. There *were* men loading barrels of food aboard."

"Did you find out what kind of food?" Roy asked excitedly.

"I was close enough to hear something about loading salted beef," replied Challco, clearly thinking this was not very useful information.

But it was all Roy needed. "Excellent," he said, "that means today must be the last day of the fair. No captain loads his perishable goods more than a day before setting sail. Coya, how well-guarded were the merchant wagons when they returned to the ships in Cartagena?"

"Only well enough to discourage any thieves from making trouble, but the wagons merely had to cross from the marketplace to the docks. They did not have to cross miles of deserted road to get to the harbor."

"Since that is precisely what they have to do in this case, do you agree that it is likely they will escort most of the goods back to the port at the same time in order to guard them more efficiently against raids?"

"It would make the most sense, I agree," she said, "especially as the road to the port winds much and takes at least several hours to travel, according to Ispaca."

Roy smiled. "Then we must be ready to set up an ambush when they set out from the town. If we can catch them somewhere between the town and the port, we might flee with the goods before word reaches the forts in either location. Coya, after you've had a bit of a rest, I want you to scout along the road ahead of our group for a good place where many men could hide close to the road, unseen from either direction but particularly from the south."

"Yes sir," she said, though she looked at him questioningly, casting glances at the other two scouts.

"Jorge," said Roy, taking the hint, "we will need to discuss how this affects our bargain and how we can both profit from continued cooperation." He already had a plan in mind, and the two of them separated from the others for a moment, along with Ajuban and Challco. He did not have enough weapons for the Cimaroons to help in the ambush effectively, but they should help to solve the problem of how to transport any looted goods back to *The Constance* without allowing the Spanish soldiers to catch up with them. He may also have need of their help with carrying wounded men, which was a point he had been worried about ever since he had agreed to berth the ship so far away from Caracas.

Challco had nothing to add beyond suggesting that Ispaca help Coya with her scouting, and Jorge quickly agreed to the plan, though he was a shrewd negotiator and was aware of the potential value of what Roy was trying to spirit away from the Spaniards. "As we discussed," he began, once they reached the subject of compensation, "I would like continued medical care for any of those men that are ill but that accompany you to the ship with your doctor. In addition to this, I expect the appropriate medicines to be administered and given to us for continued care of all our ill men, along with written instructions for how to use them. On the subject of supplies," he continued, "I will list the supplies and amounts that you are to bring to us in exactly thirty days' time from the time we reach your ship. Be assured that this will require nearly all of the space in your hold, though you must provide as much of this as you can out of the goods you already have aboard your ship when we reach it."

Roy felt quite disinclined to haggle or balk at these suggestions, though he was surprised to find that Jorge could read and write. Apart from the bargain being quite reasonable, Roy would be getting the better of this deal and Jorge knew it. "These terms I accept," said Roy gratefully as they shook hands to seal the bargain, "provided that we manage to make off with enough goods to justify the expense. However, I suggest that you let Ajuban discuss the items on your supply list with you." Here he gestured to his first mate, who nodded approvingly. "He will be able to think of other goods you would find useful in the wilderness that you should add to the list. My surgeon should also revise this list once we reach the ship."

"That is a most generous suggestion, captain," said Jorge with a touch of surprise. Challco was appreciative as well. "I will welcome his assistance, thank you."

"You are welcome," replied Roy. "It is in my interest for both of us to benefit from this arrangement. It clears the way for future business arrangements between us, should any other profitable opportunities arise for the both of us." To Roy, it was certainly fitting that he get the better end of the deal since his men would be doing the fighting and Jorge's men would largely stay out of it, but Jorge and his Cimaroons would make very strategically placed allies should they remain at liberty for very long. He only hoped that he would not learn to regret obliging himself to come back in a month's time. Such obligations had a way of turning out to be burdensome when it came time to fulfill them. *And it won't exactly make any new crewmembers happy to* give away *goods rather than looting them.*

Jorge seemed quite satisfied with Roy's response, and Roy hoped it would go a long way towards maintaining a healthy level of trust once they all reached his ship with any hypothetical loot. "What would you like us to do in the meantime?" asked Jorge. "Do you have further instructions for the scouts?" Challco appeared curious about the same point, but he seemed much more amenable to helping than he had the previous night.

Roy directed a thoughtful gaze to the scout, remembering what the man had discovered. "Did you see if the soldiers from the ship wore the same uniforms and colors as those who are usually on duty in the port?" he asked.

"I could not tell," said Challco. Roy thought he almost seemed embarrassed about it. "I do not know the differences in their garb. Ispaca may know. He is more familiar with Spanish soldiers and their habit. One of them did say they were nearly behind schedule for the troop muster, so I would guess that he was a soldier from the ship, but I did not notice any difference."

"I don't like the sound of that," Roy muttered to Ajuban. *Troop muster?* Roy suddenly wished that he had not been forced to leave Curaçao before poking around for more information or questioning Major Benito. "Clearly the rumors we've heard are true, and major military action is imminent. I think it would be an enormous coincidence if it did not involve our new *associate* in Curaçao."

"Should we send someone to find out more information, captain?" asked Ajuban.

"No, there is no time and there is nothing more we can do about it until we return to inform Governor Diedrik. Perhaps we will find out more from the raid, if we survive, but we are indebted to Challco here for discovering so much." Challco bowed to acknowledge the compliment, but had no further information to share.

"Let us rejoin de oders den," suggested Ajuban. "Unless we have oder private matters to discuss?"

Roy agreed to this, and it was best to get his plans moving as quickly as possible. Most of the others were still milling about, waiting and talking in low voices. Coya had wasted no time and sat on the ground taking her rest as he had suggested, and Ispaca had followed suit.

After Roy briefly informed everyone of the arrangement he had reached with Jorge, he asked Coya the same question he had asked Challco, but neither she nor Ispaca appeared to have observed any differences between the soldiers. "Ispaca says he never paid any mind to the differences in the Spanish uniforms," said Coya, translating for Ispaca. "He says he thought them to be signs of different families they belonged to or different lords that they served." Apparently he had never had any reason to care about such trivialities when he could be sure that all Spanish soldiers would be hostile to him.

"So they often are," Roy affirmed. "However, sometimes they signify whether the soldier is with the navy or a local garrison, a footman or a horseman, or a number of other such things." If he knew how many soldiers in Caracas were actually from the ship, since most of them were likely to escort the merchants back to the port, he might be able to estimate how many soldiers he would have to deal with. "Very well," he said, "we will simply have to see what we're up against when the time comes." If there were too many soldiers, he might try to renegotiate his bargain with Jorge at the last minute and enlist their help in the fighting, however limited their arsenal was.

"Ajuban, have the men lash together five stretchers, just in case any men fall wounded," he said, recalling Jan's initial advice. He didn't like to give such an ominous order, and some of the men obviously felt the same way about it when they heard, but there was no sense waiting until they were all being pursued by soldiers or horsemen. *And we will certainly move faster than if we had to carry our wounded on our backs.*

Soon the stretchers were finished and everyone except for the most ill Cimaroons set out behind Coya and Ispaca to find a good place for an ambush along the road. Roy still needed more information, and he hoped Coya would succeed in her task, but it would take a lot to convince him not to make an attempt on the merchants and their goods. As Coya and Ispaca moved ahead and Roy contemplated how much loot he could spirit away, he forcibly banished the hope that any of his men who might become wounded would be of the weaker and more portable variety.

* * *

Although Coya was in her element again, running through the wilderness all day was beginning to lose its appeal. Even so, she had a focus for her energy and tasks to keep her mind from nervousness.

She felt a sense of accomplishment from her earlier scouting mission, but she was troubled by this issue of distinguishing between soldiers from the ship and soldiers stationed in the area, and she felt sure that a real military scout would know all about such differences. While she supposed that these were simply things she would grasp with further exposure and teaching, and overall she felt that she had overlooked very little else on her mission, she still felt strangely disturbed by that one detail.

Perhaps it was because only the previous night the subject of distinguishing Spanish soldiers from other Spaniards had been broached. She was not even sure yet that it made a difference to her if those responsible for the invasion of her village were soldiers or civilians, but the need to distinguish between one kind of soldier and another seemed to bring the issue to her mind again for some reason, and she did not want to be thinking about it at the moment.

As if to distract her from these thoughts, Challco came jogging up from the main group. "Some of the Cimaroons are having trouble keeping pace," he said, "and your doctor insists that they need to rest. The captain says we can wait for your report here." They had already come far from the camp, and Coya was grateful that they had followed in the first place rather than waiting all the way back at the camp.

After Challco had gone, Ispaca redirected her down a side path branching northwest of the one they were on. "This is the best way to the road if we don't want to be seen from the town," he said.

"Are there many streams or bridges along the road?" she asked, shaking off her reflective mood. She had not seen any bridges when they had descended from the hilltops the day before, but some views were obscured at the time.

"No," he answered, "but further north where the road turns east and then north again, there is a stream east of the road, and at that place the stream becomes wide and shallow. We cross it at that point."

"No soldiers have been posted at the crossing?" Coya asked, surprised.

Ispaca laughed. "I'm not sure they even know about it," he said. "Besides, they have not had any reason to guard it. We have only raided the northern reaches of the town, so defending the river crossing miles to the north would not stop us and pirates normally only raid the port. Their lumber harvesters are also much closer to the town on the north and west, far from the stream I speak of." He chuckled again. "They have not even cleared the forest around the crossing to make it visible from the road! Sometimes others use it though." Coya perked up her ears at this, but he continued, "They usually travel through in the early hours before sunrise with mules bearing loads as heavy as they can carry through the hills. They cross the river and travel down the road to the town. Jorge thinks they are smugglers and has told us to leave them alone."

"Do you know what path they take through the hills?" Coya asked. She found this all very interesting, and the possibility of a path most of all. She had found a practical and discreet way through the hills in rough weather, all in enemy territory, and she was suitably proud of this, but Roy and his men had been only lightly burdened and could travel at leisure. Any path that could take heavily burdened men (or even pack animals) back through the hills in less time would be of crucial importance if they were being pursued by soldiers. Of course, running into smugglers on that path could be a problem, though it could also make for another source of plunder.

"Yes, I know the path," said Ispaca. "I have only traveled far along it once or twice though, when game was scarce. It is a good path, but there are places that are treacherous in heavy rain. Especially for pack animals, I imagine," he added, having shrewdly guessed the direction of her questions.

"What is it that Jorge thinks they are smuggling?" she asked after some thought. It was idle curiosity, but she only asked when she realized that the captain might be interested in knowing as well.

"We don't know. Sometimes they have small barrels with them, sometimes large sacks, but we don't get close enough to find out. I examined their trail once after they had passed out of here again on the same path, and I found a few coffee beans, but that is not surprising if they bought goods here. We have little use for such items."

They soon turned due north to keep a good view of the road and to look for a place to hide many men. According to Ispaca, the route they were taking would only leave them with one stream to cross, and it was the one he had spoken of with the shallow crossing. They traveled in silence for another hour and the noon sun was blazing overhead before Coya saw the stream away to the west. They came down from the higher hills and it was lost from view once again as they made their way towards it.

When they reached it, she discovered that it was not very noisy, as the current was gentle and the watercourse was straight and unobstructed. They crossed quickly, and Coya was pleased to note that the water was only thigh deep even on her and there was sure footing all the way across. Just as Ispaca had indicated, the riverbanks on either side of this convenient ford were wooded and there was little chance of their crossing being seen from the road. The road itself was still half a mile distant in any case, and there were thickly wooded hills that extended still further towards the road north of the ford. They traveled towards the bend where the road came from the east and turned north, but they stayed just inside the woods so that they could see the road and anyone passing on it without being spotted themselves. There was a wagon traveling at a leisurely pace up the road north of them towards the port, and Coya could just make out another one over a mile to the west.

She turned her eyes north and found that as the road stretched northwards, it ran closer to the hills encroaching on the east. These hills marked the eastern edge of the low valley that led to the coast, and the road appeared to have been made to skirt them a short distance from where she stood. It was not far beyond that point that the road curved to the east again and ran onto the thin strip of lowlands and beaches separating the tumbled hills from the sea, and it was on that strip that La Guaira was located. However, every point along the road that was visible to Coya from her hiding spot was completely invisible to anyone in Caracas or La Guaira, and the hills along this short northern stretch not half a mile distant looked as if they would provide a raiding party with good cover until the merchants were virtually on top of them.

Coya climbed to the top of a low hill and found that she could see a guard post just beyond the point where the road turned towards the coastal strip. No one at that guard post would be able to see an ambush along the stretch that skirted the low hills, but they would doubtless hear any gunfire in the vicinity. If the guards were attentive, it would be nearly impossible to ambush anyone on the road without it being instantly known by the soldiers to the north. She frowned. "That guard post is a problem," she said simply, as Ispaca joined her on the hill.

"Yes, it is clearly visible from the port and close enough to catch wind of an attack here," he replied, fully understanding the difficulty. "We don't go near it, not even at night. It is not worth risking a stray moonbeam glancing off of a metal buckle or something like that and alerting the soldiers. They send messengers or scouts along the road sometimes as well, especially since we started raiding the outer reaches of the town. I don't know why they don't have more guard posts at this bend, or at the one to the west on the way to the town."

"Do they ever pass along the road at dusk or later?" Coya asked. It was likely that the comings and goings of messengers were unpredictable, but the bulk of the merchants would probably leave Caracas well before dusk and arrive at the port in total darkness, and she would feel much better about a raid at dusk if messengers or mounted soldiers were unlikely at that time.

"Sometimes, but from what we have seen it is a rare occurrence. If an important ship docks at that time, they might do so."

It was not the most comforting news, but it was really the best she could hope for. They climbed down the hill and made their way north once more. Coya made for the hills to the north that lay closer to the road, but they were outside the woods and she wanted to get a closer look at them to see if they provided any cover from the north and south. "Wait here," she said to Ispaca when they reached the edge of the woods, and she began to cover herself in dirt, leaves and branches for camouflage in case any patrols happened by while she was in the open. She then proceeded to move stealthily alongside the road, crouched low to keep out of view of anyone who might observe her presence. She moved quickly in this fashion until she was at the feet of the two exposed hills.

The larger of these two hills stood right against the road, but the smaller was just south of it and off the road a bit more. She realized that she could sit behind the larger hill and her view to the south was completely blocked by the smaller hill and she could easily see the road to the north. However, her view further north was screened by a spur of a larger hill behind her that ran northwest right up to the bend in the road as it ran east towards the guard tower and then on to La Guaira. Men could creep around both sides of this hill towards the road, and those on the road would have merely seconds to react. No one would see a thing from any of the forts or guard posts, though they would hear the commotion shortly after battle commenced. In any case, it was the best spot to stage an ambush that she was likely to find. She smiled to herself. She had found just what the captain wanted.

She peeked out from behind the hill to see if anything was on the road, and was glad she did so. There were two wagons approaching from the south, and they were close enough that it was only another moment or two before she heard them. One was clearly the one she had seen earlier, though it had obviously rounded the bend where Ispaca still waited for her. The other she had not spotted before and its faster pace had moved it close to the first so they approached her hiding place close together. She lay flat in the shadows behind the north end of the larger hill and waited for them to pass, then slowly she crept back to the trees where Ispaca waited and brushed the dirt and leaves off of her clothing. She would have to repeat the process later, but she wanted to travel comfortably.

"Is that as good a position as it appears from here?" Ispaca asked her, shading his eyes and examining the hills she had crawled back from. "It seemed to conceal you from those wagon drivers."

"It is a good position," she affirmed. "I could barely have designed a better one. I hope that fact is lost on the Spaniards, since they appear to have deliberately placed the road right next to these hills." She turned her gaze north. "How far would you say we are from the port?"

He followed her gaze, considering. "Barely five miles," he said. "Maybe less. Thankfully the fort is on the other side of the port. It may take some time for soldiers to make their way here from the far end of the port, but I would not count on it. They reserve most of their horsemen to deal with problems on the road, and their horses will not tire after only a few of miles at a gallop, if their riders handle them well."

"We must return," said Coya. "I think we have all the information we need, but we must find the quickest way from here to the river crossing. We can't afford to be delayed once we are being pursued and are bearing heavy burdens. On the way, you can tell me more about this smugglers' path you mentioned earlier. I think we shall need it before the day is done, or at least the traffic on the road would seem to indicate so."

"I can do more than that," Ispaca replied. "I can show you where it begins, if you don't mind a slight delay. No more than half an hour," he said, seeing the troubled look on her face.

"Very well," she said. After all, it was best that she know as much as she could as early as possible, and it would not take long to return to Challco and the others. *And I will have time to tell the others about it should anything happen to me during the raid.* The thought wasn't welcome, but her concern was simply practical, and she felt strangely light of heart. Her feet were sore and she was hungry, but she had done what she had been signed on for.

Chapter 12: Window of Opportunity

Major Manuel Benito had no idea how long he would have before a reply was received from his government, but even if they agreed to pay a ransom, he was doubtful that he would be released in the end. Someone had stolen the ransom money the last time, and though he now doubted that it was Willem van Kemper, he thought there was a fair chance that someone would do it again. Either way, he could not count on being ransomed. As far as escape was concerned though, he had very little to work with. Van Kemper's rooms were quite secure, and the furnishings were too sparse to use in many creative ways. Furthermore, most of them were nailed down. The furnishings that would be easiest to separate from the floor were the table and chair simply due to the leverage that could be applied against them, but they were made of pine rather than some harder, sturdier wood. While they were therefore even easier to separate from the floor, they weren't good for much else. If he tried to use a pine board to shift the steel bars on the door and window, he would probably only succeed in breaking the wood. The only implement he was allowed was a thick iron spoon at meal times, and they took that away after he was done eating. It was far too thick to use on the lock, or for any fine work, and next to useless for much else.

Nevertheless, he had a plan and had been working on it every day since he had been taken virtually from the very gates of the Curaçao fort by Van Kemper's brutes and imprisoned as a hostage in the upper floor of Van Kemper's tavern. At the rate he was going, his plan would take at least a few more days, and that could be more time than he had. And the more time it took, the more time his captors had to notice what he was up to, or at least that he finished his meals long before the end of the half hour he was given.

One of the biggest problems was that even if he did escape, the only way out was through the door, and it had to be open or at least unlocked at the time. This was not the main problem with using the door, however. The main problem with the door was that it led to the *inside* of Van Kemper's tavern, and he would still have to get out of the building then. The only way to do that, from what he had seen of the place before, was through the front or the back door downstairs. The latter was quite a bit more secure than was usual, especially since someone had tried to break into it a few days ago. Using the front door required passing through the common room and being seen or possibly stopped by those inside it. Sheer surprise might help him there, especially if he managed it during morning hours, and once he got to the street or to the next street over, he was reasonably sure he could escape.

He would of course prefer to free Baron Valdez as well, but at this point he was more worried about compromising his mission than freeing Valdez. He had not been questioned about his mission yet, let alone tortured, but once his ransom holder returned, Manuel had no idea what the man might do. He had virtually no acquaintance with Captain Toppings at all.

Van Kemper had not hesitated to tell him that his ransom holder was Captain Roy Toppings. In fact he had been quite free with all of the information that Manuel had asked for, which was the main reason that Manuel found it hard to believe that Van Kemper had any part in the fiasco with the ransom. To him, this new arrangement was just another business transaction, and it had apparently been forced on him. He was little happier about holding Manuel for ransom than he was about Valdez' ransom being stolen. Simply put, he now had the expense of keeping *two* hostages and had not received a peso for either of them. Now that the law was out of his business, he seemed disposed to regard Manuel as more of an ally in the matter than an enemy, though of course he was very professional in how he treated all of his hostages. Still, the most that Manuel was likely to gain from Van Kemper's attitude was that he would not be scrutinized more than any other hostage, in spite of the fact that he had broken into Van Kemper's tavern to fetch Valdez—a fact that Van Kemper seemed to regard as quite understandable, if unwelcome.

Van Kemper had told him Captain Toppings' story about how and why he had followed and apprehended Manuel. It sounded plausible, and that was presumably why the city guard let him go, but Manuel's instincts warned him that there was more going on than that. The fact that Toppings had been given charge of Manuel as ransomer was more than a simple reward for the civil service of apprehending a burglar, and the governor must have some reason to keep Manuel in town rather than let him claim diplomatic privilege and leave. In all probability, the governor had learned of the presence of Baron Valdez in Van Kemper's establishment and wanted to find out more. The Spanish government had long known that Governor Diedrik was no fool. He maintained and defended a large town with a thriving black market in an area that would be considered Spanish territory were it not for the irreconcilable fact that it was held by the Dutch. Curaçao and the neighboring islands of Bonaire and Aruba were surrounded by Spanish colonies to the east and west, immersed in Spanish shipping lanes, and thoroughly removed from all the other Dutch colonies in the New World. While Manuel was sure that it was no accident that Dutch smugglers thrived in an area heavy with Spanish trade (he had long argued against the restrictive Spanish trade policies with his friends and comrades), he certainly recognized that Diedrik had overcome some very formidable obstacles. The man knew what went on in his own town, and Manuel would not put it past him to have ordered the burglary of the ransom himself. If he wanted to find out more about what Manuel wanted with Valdez, he would probably succeed sooner or later, and it was now Manuel's foremost task to make sure that did not happen.

The huge brute that fed and checked on the hostages slid back the wood panel on the outside of the door and looked in through the bars, bringing Manuel out of his thoughts. He had finished his work only a minute or two before, as he had no accurate way of keeping time beyond counting the seconds in his head. He had learned that Van Kemper's staff did not always keep such good time and would check on him early at times. He heard keys rattle, and the brute came in to retrieve the spoon and the dishes that now only contained the little bit of potato that Manuel always left on his plate. Soon he was locked in his little room again, and the door panel was slid shut once more. He could do little but wait and think now for another six hours, feeling the clash between the long plodding hours and the sensation that he was quickly running out of time.

* * *

Ajuban sat with Jorge, discussing the list of items the Cimaroons wanted in exchange for their services. Challco had made some suggestions and then left them to talk about it themselves. There was very little that Jorge had overlooked, and Ajuban's mind was largely free to wander, but he did mention certain considerations from time to time. "You should ask for at least a couple dozen crossbows and a few hundred bolts for dem," he said to them. "Dey don't make de noise dat guns do and you can reload dem faster. Dey will be useful if your camp is attacked or if you are badly in need of wild game. You don't have to worry about keeping gunpowder dry eider."

"I don't think that anyone here has ever used one," said Jorge.

"It is easy to learn," said Ajuban. "I can teach you in a few minutes and you can teach de rest, but you should have more weapons dan you have now. I can tell you how to care for dem as well."

"The scouts know how to make arrows," said Jorge, "and bows, but we need arrowheads for that. Perhaps we should just put those on the list?"

"Crossbows are more accurate wit'out de years of training dat make a good bowman," said Ajuban shaking his head, "and you should have at least some bolts for use wit'out having to spend valuable time making dem. It will be useful dat you can make your own later, but you should have weapons dat are ready to use first. However, if you can make arrows, you should get de arrowheads and fletchings for making dem as well."

And so it went. From what Ajuban could read of the list, and the questions that Jorge asked from time to time, it almost sounded like they might move out of the immediate area and set up a sturdier encampment somewhere nearby. Ajuban tried to consider what gear might help with such an endeavor, but the Cimaroons were used to thinking of exactly what supplies they needed. They were quite interested in the ship's biscuits that had been fed to some of their wounded the previous night. This interest surprised Ajuban somewhat at first, but as tasteless and unsatisfying as they were, they would keep you on your feet. They were cheap, took years to spoil with proper storage, and Roy could fit an awful lot of them into his hold. Beyond these considerations, they had listed everything from rope, shovels, tents and garments, to bandages and two extra pairs of boots for each man in their camp. Fortunately Justin turned out to know how to size their feet.

Ajuban was relieved when the task was done, and it was clear that Jorge had been well aware of how much Roy's ship could carry when he had said that he could fill Roy's hold with these supplies. He had barely stood up and waved the captain over when Coya and Ispaca returned.

Roy diverted towards her and the others began to gather around them as well. "What have you discovered?" asked the captain immediately.

"Sir, I have found a good place to arrange an ambush," she said.

"Did you discover how many men it would conceal?" Roy asked excitedly.

"It could conceal all of us, sir," she answered. "However, we will be slightly in the open to any patrols passing on the road as we approach it, so we must creep through the shadows from the woods, and we must try to blend in as much as possible. Once we attack, we will still be concealed from the town and the port, but there is a guard post nearby that will almost certainly hear the gunfire. We should go soon. It is not far, but most of the merchants may have already left Caracas to get to the port before dusk, and we do not know how fast they can travel by wagon." Ajuban looked at the sky. There were only a few short hours of daylight left, and he guessed that if she was right, the merchants might be along any time now.

"Captain," continued Coya, "I must also report that there is an easier path back through the hills to the east and Ispaca has shown it to me. Apparently smugglers use it sometimes to reach a shallow river crossing that gives them access to the road. We must also use this river crossing." Ajuban's ears perked up at the mention of a smuggler trail. Those were often quite reliable.

"Do the Spanish know about this crossing?" the captain asked, looking at Ispaca.

"He said that they did not appear to know of it. It is not guarded and it is within the shelter of the woods. There aren't even guard posts at the bends in the road except for the last turn towards the port, out of view of this stretch of road."

"If it truly is a smuggler's pat'," chimed in Ajuban, "it is very likely dat de Spanish *do* know of it and deliberately leave it unguarded and unwatched." The others looked at him questioningly, except for Roy. Ajuban had seen

233

enough of Spanish trade to know how smugglers made their living. "Many Spanish towns benefit from smuggling as much as de smugglers do, and de trade laws imposed by Spain are not popular wit' most merchants and governors here. As long as de Spanish pretend ignorance of how de smugglers enter deir towns, dey can pretend not to know dat dere is any smuggling going on." He had seen very similar arrangements in Hispaniola and Cuba, and it seemed much more likely that the governor of Caracas knew exactly what that river crossing was used for, especially considering what Coya had said about the lack of guard posts near it.

The Cimaroons were somewhat amused by this news. Rather than worrying about the Spaniards being able to easily determine which route they were to take eastward, they obviously thought it amusing that Spanish greed provided them with an unguarded means of escape. Coya and Ispaca clearly saw the danger, but it sounded like the best (or only) way to cross the river safely.

They soon decided to set up near the road in the place that Coya had found, attack the main group of merchants and soldiers, spirit away their goods, and retreat hastily through the hills via the smugglers' path. "Captain," said Ajuban, "considering how much we may have to carry, and how easy the pat' east sounds, do you t'ink we should leave behind most of de supplies we won't need dat are on Jorge's list?"

"Good idea," said Roy, "see to it. Mind that we keep enough canvas to keep our powder dry and whatever rope we might need to secure our loot though." Much of the rope had been used to make the stretchers, but Ajuban quickly gathered half of the remaining rope and all but a six-foot square of canvas and left the goods with those of the Cimaroons who were too ill to make the journey eastwards but had accompanied them so far to help cover the group's tracks after the raid.

They traveled slowly out of caution rather than necessity as there could still be patrols nearby. The captain had ordered that there be no unnecessary speech, but excitement and nerves were clear on the faces of those present. Ajuban wondered if they realized how much the coming night would wear on them. If they succeeded, they would probably spend the entire night carrying sacks, crates, and probably wounded men over hills pursued by Spanish soldiers. If they failed, it would be worse.

He noticed Coya fiddling with something from her small pack. It looked like a flute or a pipe, but she was not likely to be using either anytime soon. Upon further inspection, it appeared that it was simply a hollow wooden tube and she was cleaning it. Ispaca looked at her curiously as well, and he looked as if he would say something, but then he looked at Ajuban and remembered to keep quiet. *I suppose it's some kind of blowpipe.* He had never seen her carry it before though, nor had he noticed her with any darts or poison. He couldn't imagine what kind of poison would be fast enough to keep a man from crying out, but he supposed she knew what she was doing. They would definitely be close enough for her to use it, and a man who thought he had been poisoned might possibly be more distracted than a wounded man, but he hoped she would not go charging into armed soldiers with just that thing. A moment later, he saw her check that her pistol was working properly and he thought no more of it.

"I think our prey is on the way," said Roy with his telescope pressed to his eye the next time they stopped in a high enough place. "I see soldiers heading north followed by laden mules." The shadows were long, but the air was clear and he apparently had little trouble seeing from his vantage point. He stood there for two full minutes, then shut his telescope and urged them on. "There are only fifteen soldiers—fewer than I had planned for, but still more than I'd like. Still, it's not bad, and there aren't any wagons with them."

The absence of wagons guaranteed that they would be more vulnerable and easier to stop on the road, though a panicking mule was harder to loot than a stationary wagon with well-trained horses tethered to it. Wagons provided more cover for the soldiers though, so the fewer of them there were, the quicker the raid could be completed. "The wagons must all have been hired out by the merchants who left early," observed Jan. "They're probably all at the port."

"Are any of de soldiers carrying horns?" asked Ajuban. There was little chance of stealth once they attacked the mule train, but it sounded certain that it would be mostly dark before the soldiers walked into the ambush. With a great deal of luck, the sound of gunfire would be blown away on the wind or lost in the hills, or perhaps the soldiers at the guard post would mistake the sound, but horns would make sure that everyone in the area knew something was wrong.

"I couldn't tell," said the captain, "I'll take another look once we get closer to our destination. At least we know they won't beat us there."

"We might use the mules on this smugglers' path Ispaca spoke of," said Jan, who was clearly interested in the raid itself beyond the grim work it would most likely provide for him.

"Perhaps," Roy said noncommittally, "though the weather might prove too hazardous, and mules will be easy to track should we need to leave the path in a hurry. And they might make a good diversion."

Eventually they reached the edge of the woods and could all see the hills that Coya had spoken of. She pointed up the slope that they were standing next to and said, "This hill has a good view of the road and the guard post. If you want to get a good look at the soldiers before dusk, this is the best time."

Roy nodded and beckoned to her and Ajuban. The three of them made their way up the slope, making sure to keep in the shadows as Coya had suggested, though it seemed unnecessary from here. At least it did until they reached the top. The mule train had traveled quickly over the gentle road, while Roy's group had had to make their way through the woods. It had been an easy journey, but it was no comparison to the road, and they were slowed by the ill Cimaroons. Ajuban hoped that none of them would fall behind or be captured once they were making their escape. It appeared that the soldiers were no more than an hour distant, and the captain's men had yet to camouflage themselves and sneak toward the back of the hill Coya had chosen down below them by the road. Roy peered out from behind a tree, surveying the mule train to the west and the guard post to the north. "There is a soldier with a horn in the front of the column, and another one at the back," he said. "Do you two think you can deal with them quietly?"

"Do you want us to position ourselves on opposite sides of de hill captain?" asked Ajuban. "Coya would still have to creep forward if we are to hit dem at de same time, but I can shoot far wit' dis." He patted his crossbow for emphasis. There was very little wind—perfect for shooting.

"Can I borrow that for a moment?" asked Coya, pointing to the telescope.

Roy handed it to her curiously, but she pointed it toward the large hill that was to be their cover. "There is a fold of land covered in deep grass on the north side of the hill," she said. "It is only yards from the road, but I believe I can lay hidden there."

"You want to *lie down* within a few yards of Spanish soldiers and try to attack one?" asked Roy incredulously, but Ajuban waited to hear what she had in mind.

She handed the telescope back and pulled the blowpipe from her pack. "I can shoot him with this," she said. "In the twilight, he will think it is only a mosquito or a fly, until the poison sets in."

"But Ajuban still won't know when to attack from his position," said Roy, "unless he can see all of this happening."

"I t'ink," said Ajuban, warming to the idea, "dat once de poison starts working, de people behind him will be distracted. If I shoot de rearguard when I see dat, dey may not notice for a few moments. I'll shoot him in de chest and see if he can find any breat' to blow into dat horn."

Roy looked from one to the other of them. "All right," he agreed, "but I'll keep my pistol trained on that guard of yours, Coya. If this doesn't work, I'll shoot him myself to signal the attack, and you'll need me to keep them from getting you once they realize you're right next to them." He turned to Ajuban, considering. "It makes sense for us to be at either end of the hill to lead the fight in both directions," he said. "The soldiers are only in the front and the rear of the column, so that's where we will concentrate. You stay back and keep shooting until I give the order to charge."

"Aye sir." If they managed to kill the two men with horns before anything else happened, there would be just as many of them as there were of Roy's men (discounting the Cimaroons), and hopefully they would be surprised or unaware of the situation until the rest of Roy's crew had all fired at least one shot each. Roy generally seemed to prefer to let Ajuban hang back and shoot from cover since he could fire his crossbow several times before a pistol or musket could be reloaded, but in this case it made sense to have an officer leading each of the two groups of men once the charge began. Ajuban wasn't terribly worried, but he was glad of the iron breastplate he wore into these little skirmishes. It hadn't done much for the Spaniard who had previously worn it, Ajuban reminded himself, but Roy's pistol hadn't been aimed at the man's chest.

They made their way back down the hill and Coya began helping to camouflage everyone while Roy explained the plan. Then they made their way slowly, quietly through the shadows to the back of the hill. No horn sounded and everything seemed to wait in suspense around them. All the plans were made and everything was ready. *All right,* now *I can worry.* Ajuban donned his breastplate and smeared dirt on it to dull the shine. Then he strung his crossbow and waited, listening.

* * *

"Remember," whispered Roy, "don't shoot the mules unless they bolt, and wait until we've done with the soldiers before worrying about that. There's no need to mistreat the beasts, and we might find a use for them." *And we can't afford to hit the goods.*

"Aye sir," replied Ajuban and passed the order along to the others.

The men were tense but excited, as far as Roy could tell. He and half his men were waiting just round the north end of the hill and it was difficult to see the faces of those on the south end in the failing light and with nearly two dozen Cimaroons between his group and theirs, but he could hear the excited muttering and whispering in the gray shadows. "Quiet down there, men," he said without sharpness, "there may be patrols in the area." He had not seen any, nor did he expect that there would be any, but it would be better for his men to exercise more discipline under the circumstances and to remember where they were and what they were trying to do. His reminder had the desired effect, and soon they were sitting silently in wait. With twigs and dirt and leaves littering their clothes and skin, they may as well have been some form of grasping, barbed undergrowth. Roy hoped they would be less visible at a distance as well, but once the fight commenced, he had no further need of stealth.

He peeked around the north side of the hill to where Coya lay hidden, and it was several moments before he could see her at all. She was no more than fifteen yards distant from the men, or ten from where he crouched now. Her blowpipe was held perfectly still near her face and looked like the shoot of some tiny sapling. It would take minimal movement for her to ready her shot, and the darkness was deep in the grass that concealed her. Roy ordered the men in his group to string out towards him where he sat as his position was still concealed from the road. *Better to already be in position than to move round this side of the hill when they might hear us.* Once the mules were close at hand, the signal would be passed from one man to another by a tap on the shoulder beginning at Ajuban's position, and the men on the north side were to creep the rest of the way toward Roy's position as far as they could under cover. Ajuban and his men would, however, be visible unless they remained hidden until the rear soldiers were nearly past his position, so he would have to wait until the last moment.

Some of the Cimaroons wanted to help in the fight as well, but Roy tried to discourage this by invoking the bargain he had made. "I have no qualms about receiving aid beyond the parameters of our bargain, but each of you that is injured is one less man to help us carry the goods, and that is my principle concern." Thankfully Jorge sided with him on the issue and reminded them that they would not be among any wounded who were to be carried along under Jan's care. They said no more, but Roy still occasionally noticed a Cimaroon pick up a stone or grip a knife at his belt. He was mostly relieved that they had quieted down as well, especially once the signal came. They had been sitting in the shadow of the hill for fully half an hour, and the men had begun feeling restless. As far as Roy was concerned, the signal could not have come too soon. He felt the tension ripple towards him from the others, and he steadied his pistol to cover Coya should anything go wrong. He felt rather than heard his men creep up towards his position, but he crouched stock-still and focused.

He could hear the slow *clop* of the mules' hooves and subdued conversation moving closer on the road. Coya clearly heard it too, as Roy saw her move the blowpipe, presumably to her lips though he could not see her face at all now. A few long minutes later, the soldiers came into his obscured view and he felt the tap on his shoulder that had been passed along from the southern end of the hill. He knew there were mere moments to pass before chaos erupted. Ajuban's men were probably creeping around the south side of the hill at that very moment. He aimed at the first soldier, who was carrying his musket in readiness like all the others. His horn bumped along at his side on its strap. Roy waited a moment and suddenly he saw the soldier's hand fly to his neck. *This is it.* If the man noticed what was going on, battle would commence. If he didn't, Roy's men might get a few more of them and thin the odds before the soldiers resisted.

The soldier seemed to brush something away, then looked at his hand. Roy saw his expression in the dim light of the merchant's torches, and he knew. The man looked straight from the blood on his hand to where Coya lay hidden and reached for his horn. Roy was just about to fire when he caught a sudden movement from Coya's position and a knife sprouted in the man's chest. *That's done it.*

As the soldiers began to look around and react, Roy aimed at the second one in line and shot him in the temple. Roy dropped his pistol and instantly drew a second from his belt. His men, ready for the signal, came rushing out and all fired into the forward line of soldiers. A few of the soldiers were hit and he saw two of them fall, but he hoped that Ajuban's men had done better as he heard shots ring out from the other end of the hill. He couldn't afford the time to find out.

The merchants began shouting and panicking, but the soldiers did their best to discover where their attackers were and to aim their muskets. A couple of the soldiers in the forward section actually had the presence of mind to get behind the mules and fire at their assailants. One of the newer recruits named Ben fell, but no one else was hit. Apparently the growing darkness was foiling the Spaniards, and many of their torches had been dropped in the chaos. It was all to the good in Roy's estimation, but he hoped that Ben was all right as he fired another shot.

This time, he shot one of the soldiers behind the mules—again in the head. He knew he was easily the best shot among them, and the best way to keep any more of his men from being wounded was to deal with the soldiers behind cover while his men dealt with the rest. After this second shot, and another from his men, Roy dropped that pistol as well and drew his blade. "Charge!" he yelled to his men and rushed toward the head of the line. He heard them following, and as he stepped out from the shadows, he saw the whole scene. There were still many soldiers standing at the rear of the column, and most of them were aiming muskets at Ajuban's men who came rushing out at his signal. These soldiers had obviously been too confused to fire when the others had, and now Ajuban and his men were running right into them as they fired.

Ajuban himself staggered briefly, but kept charging. With a pang of worry, Roy saw Justin fall, and a couple of Ajuban's men lagged as if they'd been hit, but the others held with Ajuban as the Spaniards swept out their swords. The rearguard lay still on the road, his horn and the broken end of a feathered shaft crushed under his chest. Roy saw all of this in a moment, and turned his attention back to the soldiers he was running towards. Coya sprang up from her hiding place, pistol in hand, and kicked the horn away from one of the more levelheaded merchants who had made a grab for it from the fallen soldier. She crossed to the other side of the road and fired at the other man who had been hiding behind the mules. *Excellent, now it's all bladework.* With that, Roy and his few men crashed into them like a hail of arrows.

Roy quickly dispatched the first of them almost before the man could ready his sword, and Albert and Daniel began fighting with two more right beside him. Coya drew a knife and hopped back from the mules that had been startled by her shot, and Roy caught another glimpse of the battle at the south end of the line. Ajuban had run one of the guards through, and Tiede managed to catch one of them in the leg, though he seemed to be limping himself as he did it. With dread, Roy noticed that two of the soldiers still had not fired their muskets. "Coya!" he shouted and gestured to them. Hopefully she would take one of them down. As for the other, Roy sprinted in his direction. Apparently the soldier had hit the ground as soon as he heard shots, and had just picked himself up again, gun in hand. *I can't reach him in time!* The realization was quickly rendered unimportant as, with his left hand, Ajuban drew and fired a spare pistol he had tucked in his belt and the man collapsed to the ground once more.

Roy continued his charge toward one of the merchants who had snatched up a dropped musket. It seemed to Roy that the Spaniards had clearly been bested, but these merchants were protecting their livelihoods, and some men were as desperate as others were bold. He had no time to convince this merchant that it was a lost cause—not while his men were still in danger—so he slashed the man's arm causing the musket to fall from his limp hand, and then punched him for good measure. A moment later, Roy heard a sickening crunch a few yards behind and turned to see that Albert, apparently unable to best his opponent with steel, had exploited an opening and landed a hard left hook to his face. The soldier's nose was clearly broken, and Roy supposed the man ought to consider himself lucky not to be dead, but it was difficult to apply the term "lucky" to anyone who had been hit by Albert.

The few remaining conscious soldiers surrendered quickly, having arrived at the same conclusion Roy had after surveying the scene, but Roy was aware of the sound of horns blowing dimly in the distance. *They know.* It would not be long before horsemen would arrive from the north, and Roy knew he had to act quickly. Jorge, who had been watching from the hill, signaled to his men and they came hurrying out to bind and gag the soldiers and merchants. "Blindfold them too," said Roy, "and get them out of earshot." He didn't want them to know where he went with their belongings. "Nice work, Coya," he said, turning to Coya as she came up to him. She looked puzzled, however. "For dealing with that soldier with the musket?" he clarified, but she looked embarrassed.

"I missed," she admitted. "But apparently Belonwu was watching and threw a stone. It hit the soldier's helmet, but it was a hard enough throw to knock him out."

Roy and Jorge looked at Belonwu, who grinned. "Well," he said, remembering Roy's earlier sentiments about the Cimaroons aiding in battle, "it seemed dat de fight was basically over, and his gun was not pointed in my direction."

Roy smiled as well, but he had no time for mirth. "We need to calm the mules," he said. Several of these had spooked at all the gunfire and violence, but Challco was already tending to them. Roy suspected he needed help. "We have to unload them and get going before any more soldiers arrive." The mules spooked too easily to be reliable if Roy and his men were being chased, and they were too easy to track. With only two men who needed to be carried, Roy judged that there were enough men to carry all the goods. He also had an idea, but he would need to speak to Challco once the mules were reined in. Most of the torches had gone out, and perhaps the Spaniards would not be able to see what was going on once they made their way from the guard post…

Justin and Ben were badly hurt, but they were still alive and conscious. Now that the fight was over, the men were torn between excitement at their victory and the prospect of loot, worry about the Spanish horsemen who were no doubt on their way, and anxiety over their two fallen comrades. Ben was new to the crew, but Justin was well liked and handy to have around as well. Jan did what he could to help those with wounds with a little help from a flask of brandy, but he had little time, and very shortly Roy ordered that Justin and Ben be put on stretchers and everyone busied themselves with the goods.

Challco got the mules under control with very little help, and as they were being unloaded he said, "Captain, I thought it might help you if I led these mules into the woods to the west of the road after they have been unloaded. It might throw off pursuit, or at least make the soldiers split their forces."

The two scouts were not among those designated to carry goods to Roy's ship, and it was the very same plan that Roy had been contemplating a moment before. "Can you do that by yourself?" he asked, plainly indicating that he was in favor of the idea as long as it didn't cost him any men.

"It is the sort of thing I used to do before the Spaniards came," said Challco.

Clearly there was a story behind that remark that Roy had not heard yet, but there was no time to ask. "Very well," he said, "but don't let them catch you. Once the mules are far enough into the woods, leave them and hide from the soldiers." Challco nodded and began to gather those of the mules that had already been unloaded.

"Captain," said Coya as she stooped and picked up one of the horns that the soldiers had carried, "If I were to enter those woods as well, I could blow this horn in the same manner that the Spaniards at the forts did. With luck, they would think that a patrol there had found us, or at least a separate group, and it might have the same effect."

"If they have any patrols in that area," Roy said. However, he considered her small frame and her abilities in the dark. She wasn't likely to be good for carrying much, and this might prove a far more useful task for her. "Agreed," he said after a moment, "but only if you then make your way straight back here. We need you to catch up with us before we have gone far on this path Ispaca spoke of. You will have to *run* from the woods on the west side of the road, because you will be in plain sight until you reach the woods to the east, and that must be half a mile."

She seemed a bit more daunted by the prospect, but she said, "I'll do it. I can travel fast, and they will not catch me."

"Go then. And hurry." Roy had a bad feeling about the idea, but he decided to trust to her instincts. She nodded and retrieved her gear, then headed off quickly to the west.

In short order, all the soldiers and the merchants were bound, gagged, and blindfolded. Roy had made sure that they did not hear a word of these conversations by having them be led off the road into the shadows, but he hoped they would not notice the sound of mules going one way and his men going the other, and that they had not been able to hear that the mules were to be unloaded. Either way, he could delay no longer. He could see through his telescope that horsemen were indeed approaching from the north. "All right men, let's get moving," he said. "Quickly now, we only have minutes to get to the trees before the pursuit begins."

The Cimaroons loaded up most of the goods, and Roy's men took up the two stretchers and the remainder of the goods. He was glad to see that he could keep one man other than himself free to fight without having to stop, but if their pursuers caught up to them, it would cause delays. He could not afford delays, and neither could Justin or Ben. Jan would not have time to do anything more for them until after they had crossed the river.

Not long after Roy and his men made it into the denser part of the woods on their way to the ford, the horsemen from the guard post made it to the spot where the soldiers had been attacked. He saw through his telescope that they had gone off the road to where the prisoners had been dragged. "Come," he said, closing his telescope again, "they will be after us very soon unless they are completely fooled by the ruse with the mules. We have to make it across the river before they catch up with us, or we will face another fight like that one." It was not necessarily true, as there were fewer soldiers and the Cimaroons would be obligated to help, but these soldiers would not be surprised and the Cimaroons were not well armed. But the men picked up their pace as if making it to the river was as far as they had to go, and Roy did not spare another look back. He would not until they were approaching the river, if he could see the soldiers at all. *Hopefully they can't ride those horses far into these woods.* He was not confident about that notion at all, though.

Roy chose Tiede to be the only other man who did not need to carry anything. The friendly Dutchman's limp had become more pronounced, in spite of the fact that the wound had been cleaned and bandaged. A musket shot was still lodged in the wound, but Jan dared not remove it without the time to do it properly. They had discarded the other three stretchers in a thicket of trees by the road, and now Roy was worried that he might need another one. If there were another battle, he would certainly need them. He did not intend to leave any of his men behind. To keep Tiede's mind off of his wound, Roy enlisted his help in reloading all of the pistols while they walked. But Tiede's concentration was not what it should be, and the second time Roy caught him forgetting to add the shot before ramming the wadding down the barrel, he took over the entire task by himself. "Can you make it to the river?" he asked.

"I think so sir," said Tiede, "but I don't know how much further than that I can make it on my own legs. I crossed those hills just like everyone else, and it was no picnic even without a wounded leg."

Roy considered for a moment and said, "Once I've done with the reloading, I'll take Albert's place and he will carry you. Jan won't like it if I make your wound any worse by making you walk."

Tiede managed a weak smile. "I wouldn't want him to be upset with you, sir."

Soon Roy was holding one end of Justin's stretcher and carrying a heavy pack, and Tiede was more at ease traveling clutched to Albert's back. Fortunately it was Tiede's calf that was wounded, so Albert could still hold onto his thighs as he carried him as gently and quickly as possible through the woods. Albert was quite strong, but he couldn't be expected to carry Tiede all the way back to the ship. Even Jan hadn't expected the wound to worsen so quickly. "I'd have kept one of the stretchers otherwise," said the surgeon.

By the time they reached the river, Roy was anxious to know if they were being pursued and, if so, how closely. Jan held Justin's stretcher by himself for a moment as Roy scanned behind them through his glass. He thought he saw torches in the distance, but his view was much obscured by trees, distance and darkness. Without waiting for further information, he put his telescope away and hoisted Justin's stretcher again. "All right men, we can't risk any further delays. Make sure all your powder is above water level and start the crossing. We will refill the water bottles after we cross, but we have to start climbing the first slope before we stop for a rest." He didn't want those horses reaching them. If the riders had to dismount to follow them, it would be so much for the better. It was possible that horses could travel along the smugglers' path as well as mules, but he hoped that they could not travel along it with any speed.

Suddenly Roy heard a sound in the distance that worried him. At least it did until he realized what it probably was. He heard horns sounding, but it seemed like it came from far away. "Don't worry, lads," he said, "that's probably Coya trying to make sure they stay confused." The men looked more at ease than Roy felt—less so when they heard the faint sound of gunfire and of a loud shot or explosion moments later—but they began crossing the river without further delay. The crossing was swift, and the men were well motivated to get out of this very open and untenable position. Roy felt as though a great weight of worry was lifted from his shoulders as soon as he set foot on the other side, as if they were sure to escape. He did not revel in the sensation, but rather kept them going just as he had said he would, until they reached the steeper hills of the ridge and stopped to rest.

Roy could clearly see the torches below on the other side of the river by then. They were being pursued, and by horsemen, but they were probably an hour behind him now. Those Cimaroons responsible for covering their trail had done a good job and had departed after crossing the river and making it to the woods, but the Spanish had decent trackers as well. Those men could pick up their trail with ease once they were across the river, as long as they scouted enough inside the borders of the encroaching woods. He needed to shake them off, and soon.

Tiede groaned as he was lowered to the ground. He was sweating. The river crossing had done him some good, and the water had soothed his leg as it dangled in the current below Albert's hip. Jan changed the bandage and

Roy helped him build a new stretcher, but it was slow work without Justin to help them. They rested as well as they could, even as they watched ten horsemen cross the river, but Roy knew they were in for a long night.

Chapter 13: Diverse Decoys

It was deeply dark and Ajuban was helping Albert carry Tiede's stretcher. They had begun to climb the first ridge along the smugglers' trail, though the path was much gentler than the one they had used on the way to Caracas. Thankfully Coya had told them about the smugglers' path in detail or it would have taken some time to find in the dark, if indeed they could have found it at all. The slope was gentle enough for a mule, but when he looked behind, he was pleased to see that the torches of the horsemen behind were now following only slowly. No soldier would ride a horse up the slope, though horses could be led. Now the head start they had made to elude the soldiers was beginning to pay off. And yet the captain's men and the Cimaroons moved more slowly still.

"Ajuban," said Albert from his end of the stretcher, "I have an idea for how we might deal with our pursuers once they get a little further up this slope."

"Go on," said Ajuban. Albert didn't often come up with ideas, but Ajuban was happy to entertain any suggestions at this point.

"I noticed a patch of level ground off of this trail lower down," he said. "If we could leave a false trail there, I think we could ambush them. There was a lot of cover down there."

"Sorry," said Ajuban, "de captain isn't likely to spare de men, and we don't want any more wounded men to carry."

"Just a minute," said the captain. He was close enough to hear them, and it was odd that Albert had brought the suggestion up to Ajuban in the first place when he could as easily have mentioned it to the captain, even though the captain had been busy speaking with someone else a moment before. "Do you mean just you and Ajuban?"

"Yes sir, begging your pardon," said Albert, "I should have made that clear."

"I'm listening," said the captain. "How would you set up such an ambush, just the two of you against half a dozen?" Some of the soldiers who had crossed the river had scouted both up and down stream, one on each side going either direction. Now there were only six men pursuing them, so perhaps the captain had changed his mind about fighting.

"Well sir," began Albert, "I brought several grenades with me in case they should prove useful." Everyone had been issued with one, but Albert had asked Ajuban for a few more. He was very good at throwing things with force and accuracy, as Ajuban remembered from his demonstration at the docks of Port Royal, so Ajuban had agreed. "As I said, there is a lot of cover in that area, and if we lobbed a few grenades at them as they inspected the clearing, well I think that would deter most folk from pursuing us further. Who knows?" he said with amusement. "They might have their own wounded to look after rather than bothering further with us."

Roy pondered the proposal for a moment. Ajuban thought it sounded plausible too, and there was little doubt that Ajuban and Albert could catch up with the rest of the burdened crew and Cimaroons later. "All right," said the captain, "but don't stick around to finish them off. Throw the grenades, and fire once if you have a clear shot. Otherwise make your way back to us as quickly and invisibly as you can. We will continue on at the best pace we can manage."

Ajuban knew that the captain begrudged the loss of both of them due to the need to carry gear and the wounded, but if it meant losing their pursuers, it seemed like a worthy exchange. "How far is dis clearing you spotted?" he asked.

"Only about half an hour behind," replied Albert.

"You had better get going to set up the false trail," suggested Roy. "We will rest here for a moment and redistribute the goods, then continue on. Good luck."

Ajuban set down his pack, grabbed his crossbow and motioned for Albert to follow. In the interest of stealth, neither carried any extra gear, but Albert had to make sure to keep the grenades from clanking as they made their way down to the clearing. Ajuban didn't expect any trouble on the way down to the clearing, but it was best to be cautious anyway. If the soldiers advanced more quickly than it seemed from above, and the ambushers ran straight into them, the two of them wouldn't stand much of a chance.

Nevertheless, they reached the clearing quickly and without incident. It seemed much closer than Albert had indicated, but they had an easier time getting down the slope rather than up it, and they were without burdens. Occasionally they had caught glimpses of torches below, and it seemed that they still had some time to make ready their ambush, but from the clearing they would not be able to see the soldiers approaching until they could see torches split off from the path towards it. They would probably hear the soldiers approach before they saw them, unless the soldiers were being very quiet.

Ajuban busied himself with obliterating the trails leading up the slope in the immediate area—what was left of the signs that Roy's men had gone that way, as well as Albert's and Ajuban's footprints leading back down the hill—and began making a false trail into the clearing, while Albert kept a lookout and fished around in his pack. Albert had wisely brought a torch stave and a couple of slow matches from the ship. These were normally used to fire cannons, but Ajuban supposed they would work just as well for lighting several grenades. Furthermore, the slow match could be lit before the soldiers were close enough to hear the sound, and the light could easily be shielded until they were ready to use it. Albert had helped Martin with the shipboard cannons, so perhaps that helped him think to plan this sort of thing before they had ever left the ship, but Ajuban was no less impressed. He would try to remember to mention all these details to the captain. *Assuming I make it back to tell him any-t'ing.*

It took some time to plant a trail that the soldiers could possibly believe had been made by many different men, but it gave Ajuban something to do rather than wait in the darkness under the trees surrounding the clearing. He wasn't sure he had time to scout for the soldiers' position after he was finished, so he retreated into the darkness with Albert. "What now?" he asked in a low voice.

"When we see them coming," whispered Albert, "I'll light the slow match and hand it to you. You hide the light, and I'll wait with a grenade in either hand. When they are in the clearing (and preferably looking the other way), you grab a grenade. Then we'll light all three, wait a few seconds, and toss them all into the clearing." Even if none of the soldiers were hurt by the grenades, the sound of three of them going off at once would probably frighten the life out of them.

Ajuban hoped that none of the grenades went off in their hands, or that the fuses didn't make too much noise. He had picked a path to the clearing that made it unlikely that the smell of the slow match would be carried to the soldiers by the east wind. "And den we shoot anyone in our way and make our escape?" he said.

"Exactly," said Albert. It wasn't a bad plan, though it was risky. At least they could be sure to make their escape more quickly than the soldiers since the two of them were already briefly acquainted with traveling the path ahead in the dark.

There wasn't much more to say about it, so they stood silently and waited. They were several yards from the clearing so that they would not be seen or heard, but they had a clear view for throwing. After less than ten minutes, Ajuban heard the sound of men climbing up the path. He motioned for Albert to light the slow match. He hoped as he took the torch stave that the soldiers found the trail into the clearing. Ajuban had not made it too hard to find, but he didn't want it to be too obvious either. Roy and the Cimaroons had made efforts to conceal their trail up the slope, so an obvious trail into the clearing might raise suspicion, but he was relieved to see them approach the clearing slowly as Albert readied the grenades.

Ajuban had left signs in the clearing to indicate that a group of men had rested there. There was a little bit of spilled gunpowder here, a bit of bandage there, there were a few passable indents in the earth where a crate or heavy sack might have been placed, and scattered crumbs of biscuits that Ajuban had sacrificed from his provisions (though it was unlikely he would miss them later). With any luck, it would fool the soldiers into stopping long enough to investigate and, subsequently, to be pelted with grenades. As a precaution, he had also led the trail out of the clearing again and through the trees for a few yards, though there the dummy trail ended.

The soldiers moved nearer, with two men in front scanning the ground. Ajuban could hear low muttering as the men commented to each other on what they were observing, but they were clearly trying to move quickly enough to catch up with Roy's men. If they stopped to scan the clearing, Ajuban knew it wasn't likely to be for very long. As soon as the two men in front crouched in the clearing and the other four stood scanning the trees and waiting for the two trackers to report, Ajuban signaled for Albert to light the grenades. He lit his own at the same time, but the soldiers did not appear to see the glow revealed from the uncovered slow match or to hear the fuses burning as they muttered to each other about their findings in the clearing.

Ajuban and Albert waited for three agonizing seconds, hoping they would not be noticed and that they would not blow themselves to pieces by waiting too long, but they didn't want to give the soldiers any time to react. The fuses were five second fuses, but if a fuse was wrapped incorrectly, it could go off a second or two early, and that would be the end of both of them. "Now!" whispered Albert, and they threw their grenades straight at the soldiers.

Two of the standing soldiers were facing roughly in their direction when this happened, and they reacted surprisingly quickly by shouting, "Down!" and diving aside. Of the two facing the other direction, one of them dove away as well, and the other simply dropped, but a grenade landed practically on top of him. The two trackers who had been crouched to the ground never had a chance as they were caught right in the middle of one of the blasts. They were torn to pieces and the clearing was plunged into darkness after the fiery glow of the blast, as the trackers had been the only ones carrying torches.

The timing was perfect, as was the placement of the grenades, and it was to the soldiers' credit that any of them survived the three nearly simultaneous blasts. One of them rolled behind cover and another actually managed to take a shot from where he fell, hitting a tree very close to Albert who had moved away from Ajuban after the throw. Ajuban quickly grabbed his crossbow and aimed a shot at the other man who was still recovering from the blast and from his fall. The soldier was fumbling with his musket and aiming roughly at Albert's position when the crossbow bolt took him in the side. His shot went wide as he gurgled in his throat, falling flat on the ground once more.

Ajuban whistled for Albert to retreat, and they both broke cover and ran towards the path by a different route than the soldiers had come. Another shot rang out, but they both kept running undeterred. "Nice plan," said Ajuban between breaths as they ran. "I don't t'ink dat de two of dem will come after us by demselves after dat mess we made back dere."

"That should give the captain some room to breathe," said Albert. "I would have liked to get them all so that no one could report back to those other scouts who went along the river, but I'll wager it will take them some time to muster any force that would be able to threaten us now."

Ajuban wasn't so sure. The fort at La Guaira might have sent many men to rendezvous with these forward scouts without waiting for a report. If what the Cimaroons were carrying was very valuable, it was fairly likely that they would do so. He was also anxious to get back to the ship quickly, in the event that they guessed Roy had a ship berthed along the coast eastward. Even though it would probably have to sail against the wind, that galleon in the port might be able to beat them to their destination and capture *The Constance*. The fewer men that were left to report back to any advance force, the better. Nevertheless, they had accomplished what they had meant to, and Albert was in good spirits about it. Ajuban was as well, but the captain had taught him to think about the next task rather than reveling in the completion of the previous one.

After only a few minutes running back up the path to catch up with Roy and the Cimaroons, Ajuban heard distant horns and gunfire in the valley behind them.

"Do you hear that?" asked Albert as they panted forward. "It sounds like it's coming from the road or thereabouts."

"I hope dat Coya makes it safely back," said Ajuban and wished that he hadn't. Albert's expression turned to one of worry. *Why does he t'ink dat it's his job to protect her all de time?* Albert had been acting that way ever since he understood that Coya was to join the crew, though it seemed to Ajuban that Coya had not realized it yet. When they were aboard ship around so many men, it was convenient that someone like Albert should be protective of her, but it could be unfortunate in situations like these where Coya had to go off by herself, risking life and limb for the good of the crew. Ajuban worried about her too, but he was second in command of Roy's ship and crew, and he could not afford the luxury of being sentimental until the work was done. "Don't worry," he said aloud, "if anyone can escape de Spanish soldiers, she can. She has done it before." They ran on into the shadowed heights.

* * *

Coya plunged into the woods west of the road, at a different place than Challco was leading the mules to. She had seen horsemen ride toward the scene of the ambush with alarming speed, and they were just beginning to converge on it moments after she entered the cover of the trees. She did not believe they had seen her, but Challco would be lucky indeed if they did not spot the mules, though that might help her little ruse. He was moving the beasts at a fair speed through the grass. Perhaps it helped that they had been frightened by the battle, but he had kept them mostly in line and heading where he wanted.

She plunged further into the woods. It was her intention to make as if she were a Spanish patrol that found men waiting in the woods for the mules. Even if there was no patrol in the western woods when she blew the horn, the Spaniards might think that scouts had gone there following a trail, so she wanted to be well to the west of Challco when he got all of the mules into the woods. Hopefully they would not quickly stray out again after he left them and snuck back to the Cimaroon camp, or the horsemen might see through the ruse and break off pursuit. So far no one had pursued her or the mules, but she aimed to encourage them to send men into these woods if their scouts were not already so inclined.

Coya was tired from her labors. She half wished that she could convince the Cimaroons to carry *her* right along with the loot when she returned. Even so, she was used to long hours and frantic activity. Her time on the outskirts of Cartagena and Port Royal had hardened her for these kinds of tasks. She ran on. Soon she stopped and turned to look in the direction Challco had been going. She couldn't see anything through the woods, but at the rate that Challco had been going, she guessed that he had entered the woods some minutes ago. It seemed like as good a time as any to try her diversion.

She looked around in silence, listening for any sign of soldiers, and then she began blowing the horn wildly. She realized too late that there was more to blowing into a horn than just, well, blowing into a horn. It made little awkward sounds at first, until she could figure out what her lips were supposed to be doing to make the horn sound as loudly as the soldiers at the forts had. Fortunately the sounds she was trying to imitate took little effort, but she hoped that no one who heard could tell that someone completely inexperienced was trying to sound a horn. "Maybe they will just think I'm a wounded scout," she muttered ruefully.

She ran south towards the road to the town for about fifty yards and blew again as if she were a scout running to meet up with patrols near the next bend in the road. Then she ran another fifty yards or so and did this again. She had barely stopped blowing when she heard shouts not far ahead of her. *Oh no.* The shouts continued as Coya heard noisy and hurried movement heading in her direction. She had not planned for what she would do if there *was* a patrol in the woods and she happened to run into it.

She could see them now, their torchlight passing into the open from behind dense undergrowth. They clearly had seen her. Without hesitation she let the horn fall, drew out a pistol and began to run away from them and to the east. It was small comfort to her that she could see well in the dark and they could not as shots whistled past her and wood splintered from the trees around her. She stopped and fired at one of them. He fell, but she ran on without waiting to see if he got up again. She heard a horn sound close behind her in exactly the note she had been imitating moments before, and she would have laughed were she not fleeing for her life. She tucked the pistol back in her belt and drew another one, thankful that she had had the foresight to load them both shortly after she had entered the woods. As she did so, her hand brushed against the grenade she carried in a pouch. She had only ever seen them used when the English troops had landed to attack what they later renamed Port Royal, and she only ever remembered she had one when she had to handle it or something bumped against it, but if ever there was a time to use it, it was now. Unfortunately lighting a match while running was not something she understood to be very effective.

Her pursuers were losing ground, but she was probably wearier than they, and scared. She turned and fired again when she could get a clear shot, but she didn't even wait to see if she hit anyone before tucking the pistol away and fumbling with her grenade and a match. Briefly she stopped, lit the fuse with shaking hands and tossed the grenade back the way she had come, then ran on as fast as she could. She had wisely watched the battle for Port Royal from a distance, so she was not prepared for the noise of the blast that followed seconds after she lobbed the grenade. For a moment she thought wildly that the Spaniards had brought a cannon into the woods before she realized that her grenade had gone off. She heard screams behind her, but the sound only made her run faster.

When her head cleared of panic, she realized that she could no longer hear the sounds of pursuit nearby, so she began to go more slowly and to zigzag through the undergrowth, making her way back to the edge of the woods nearest the road. She took just a moment to catch her breath and wipe the sweat from her face as she peered out from the trees. To her dismay, there were horsemen riding up and down the road at somewhat regular intervals, as well as a few scouts patrolling the ground to the north and south. She had no idea how much time had passed since she had fled from the Spanish patrol—perhaps half an hour, perhaps longer—but the soldiers had not been idle in their search. *How in the world am I going to cross* that?!

It was half a mile from where she stood to the woods on the other side of the road. Perhaps further. Of course it was dark out, but she would still be out in the open and there were horsemen everywhere. There seemed very little point to even trying to stay in the shadows or flit from cover to cover, so there would be nothing for it but to just run straight across. The truth of the captain's words sank in, and she felt sure that he had only agreed to let her go because she thought she could manage it. She observed the scouts for a few moments, gauging her chances. Even if they couldn't ride her down, they could still shoot at her as she ran right through the middle of their patrols. She knew her legs wouldn't be up to the task if she didn't rest for a few minutes, but she was worried about the patrol in the woods behind her catching up to her again as well.

In the end, Coya rested only until her pistols were reloaded and she saw what looked like a large enough hole in the Spanish patrols moving up and down the road. Then she immediately broke cover and ran straight towards the road. Not more than twenty seconds passed before there were shouts and horns blowing on either side, and her mind only let her focus on putting one foot in front of the other as fast as she could move them. She was committed to her action, and the only possible results were that she would escape or be killed or captured. She ran on, barely paying attention to what was happening to her left or right, just staring at the trees on the other side. She heard the sound of some sort of explosion echo through the valley from somewhere far ahead of her, but it barely registered as all her attention was focused on running. As she neared the road, shots rang on either side and the cries of soldiers sounded closer than ever. Still she ran on, not daring to second-guess herself, change her course, or even look around. *I will not be left behind!*

With a start, she realized she had crossed the road, but she did not let herself focus on any feelings of triumph. Horns were still sounding around her and the shouts and gunfire continued. The sound of hooves galloped on the turf behind her, getting nearer. She made it to the tree line and immediately turned and drew a pistol. This horseman needed to be dealt with, and the trees were still sparse enough to allow him to ride her down. She aimed and fired, hitting his arm, but her hopes surged as she saw him topple from his saddle. Horsemen were beginning to leave the road and come after her, so she turned and fled immediately. If she could only make it across the ford, she felt she would be safe. Even if she couldn't, she could still hide on this side of the river for a little while. *I'll swim for it if I have to.* She was not carrying any extra gear, and risking water getting into her powder horn might end up saving her from the soldiers. Nevertheless, she switched pistols, turned to the shadows southeast of the road and made all speed for the ford.

There was no one in sight at the ford, so she stepped into the river. The water was cool and she felt new strength as the heat and fatigue washed away from her. She held her powder horn above the water and ducked herself under just once, as it was all she had time for before she hurried across the river. Just as she reached the trees on the other side, a horseman broke through the trees on the far bank and fired a shot, but it was too late. She had taken cover and was on her way to find her companions. The horseman began sounding a horn, but she did not stay to shoot at him with her remaining pistol. She could not afford to take time yet to reload her guns, and scouts had probably gone after the captain and the Cimaroons. She might happen upon one at any moment, and then she would have more need of her last shot. Relieved to see that the horseman was not pursuing her on his own—Coya thought he probably knew she could load a gun and fire before he could get across even if he didn't assume the one in her hand was loaded—she turned to make her way towards the smugglers' path.

Letting relief flood through her with a shudder for a moment, she made her way to the foothills as quickly and quietly as she could. She had no light other than the stars, but she needed none. The moon would not rise for a few hours yet, and that only worked to her advantage for the moment. She traveled for several minutes before she was satisfied that the horseman had not changed his mind and crossed as soon as she had fled, then she stopped just long enough to reload and continued on. She allowed herself to think back to what had happened as she had run across the road and realized how lucky she was to be alive. Her pursuers had mostly fired at her from far off, and she had evidently picked the right moment to break cover.

Then she remembered the explosion she had heard in the woods ahead, and realized that if it had not involved her flight, it must have involved the captain's group. She guessed that it was even louder than the grenade she had thrown at her pursuers, and it had sounded like it may well have been near where the smugglers' path should lay. *The captain is in danger.* Her heart sank. How could patrols have caught up to them so quickly? Was there a patrol on this side of the river before the ambush? Had some of those horn blasts signaled to patrols in the area to cut off the Cimaroons? *In any case, they won't know I'm here.* Tired or no, she made up her mind to investigate. If she could find the place and help out in time or free any of her friends if they had been taken prisoner, she would do so, though it had been several minutes since she heard the noise. Hopefully such an act would prove more useful than her diversion in the west woods had.

Coya allowed herself a few minutes' rest and a few of her ship's biscuits to recover from her ordeal, but she was soon on her way again. She hoped that she would be able to sleep properly before daylight, but the captain had not planned on doing so, so she cut into her next day's ration to keep her strength up in anticipation of a much longer night. Once she arrived at the smugglers' path, she decided it would be better not to be seen on it in case a patrol had followed the captain, but she kept it on her left and made her way through the shadows of the trees. She did her best to be stealthy, but the brush and her fatigue made it difficult at times.

After perhaps half an hour, she heard the sound of low voices. She crouched to the ground, peering around in the starlight and listening for the source of the voices. They sounded as though they were speaking Spanish, but she could not hear much of what they were saying. Whatever they were saying, she could not hear more than two or three voices speaking. She crept very cautiously towards the sound and soon discovered that there was a clearing not far off the smuggler's trail, and in the clearing she could see signs that the captain's men had fought with several soldiers. Two soldiers were sitting on the ground discussing something, but they appeared to be facing back towards the path, away from her. Concerned, Coya looked at the remains of the bodies as well as she could from a distance, but they all appeared to be wearing the garb of the Spanish soldiers. Drawing a pistol quietly with either hand, she crept around the ring of trees until she was behind them and only about a dozen paces away, but she had to strain to hear what they said. If any of the captain's men had been taken prisoner, she hoped to find out about it, but otherwise it might be wise to dispatch these two men and catch up to her friends.

"They're going to want to know why we failed to follow the brigands," said one of them. "Captain Gutierrez is going to want that cargo back aboard his ship regardless of what happens to us." Coya was pleased to think what this might indicate about the value of the cargo they had stolen. She still had little idea what the mules had been carrying.

"I'm not risking my neck for the likes of him," said the other. "Not after what happened here. I don't think there were more than two of them that ambushed us, but according to the men we freed there were at least a dozen of them."

"What do we tell them then, lieutenant?" said the first man.

"We tell them more or less what happened," answered the lieutenant. "We were ambushed with grenades and guns, and we were the only survivors. Both the trackers are dead, so what can they expect us to do? Even if we assume that they took the smugglers' trail, one of us would have to report back while the other…would do what, exactly? Follow them? Alone? On a hunch, in the dark, and after having been ambushed once already? Besides, we're not even officially supposed to know about that path." Evidently these soldiers were well aware of what the trail was used for, just as Ajuban had suggested. More importantly to Coya, it sounded as if those of Roy's men who had ambushed these soldiers had escaped.

"So do we both report back then, sir? Or should one of us stay here with the bodies?" The junior soldier did not appear to relish the thought of staying with the bodies, but he seemed frightened by the idea of splitting up at all. Coya's smirk was lost in the darkness. *Coward.* Though some part of her admitted that the scene was a grisly one and could unnerve anyone. She simply tried not to look at it much.

"No, neither of us is staying out here alone," answered the lieutenant to the obvious relief of the other soldier. "We will report back to the scouts at the river and wait for further orders to arrive. If these thieves have vanished by the time any new orders come, well then we don't have to risk our necks over it out in the wild with those Cimaroons on the loose. As far as I can make out, the only people who lose are leaving with Captain Gutierrez." Evidently nothing that belonged to the town had been stolen, but Coya was still surprised by such apathy. In any case, she was not inclined to let these two report back at all.

She began to rise slowly and crept out into the clearing directly behind them as quietly as she could, but still they did not turn. She aimed a pistol at the back of each of their heads and cocked them. They froze. "Did you hear that lieutenant?" said the junior soldier. Coya fired. The backs of their heads ripped open and both of them fell limp, their hair drenched with blood and singed by the muzzle flashes. It felt a very cold thing to do, but Coya had long ago accepted that this was part of her duty, and it had not been her first time anyway. She was far past feeling sympathy for the Spanish soldiers.

She despoiled them quickly in case anyone nearby heard the shots. The lieutenant had a loaded pistol that smelled as though it had been recently fired—Coya hoped that he had not wounded any of her companions with it—and a small amount of coinage (both of which she took), but there was very little else to be found on the rest of the men. One of them had a horn, but it looked as if the grenades the lieutenant mentioned had rendered it useless. After briefly rummaging around to find any additional (and more palatable) provisions, she left them where they lay and made her way quickly up the path. From what she had heard, it sounded as if these men had been part of an advance scouting party and that she had little to fear on her way up the path to catch up with her friends. Though still wary, she felt a tremendous sense of relief that she had made it this far. She would be glad indeed to see the rest of the crew again. *And to find out what goods we have captured.* The notion that they had taken valuable cargo that would be sorely missed made her forget for a moment that she was as tired as she had ever been as she made her way quickly up the path, ignoring the protests of her muscles once again.

* * *

Roy was beginning to wish that he had not allowed three members of his crew to take their leave of the rest of the group, leaving their burdens behind, but he supposed they were trying to compensate for how slowly the group was moving rather than to slow it down even further. They had delayed their pursuers with false trails and by ensuring that no one was sure if they had split up, but once the soldiers were certain of the trail, they would follow swiftly. Nevertheless, he and his group were traveling more slowly than ever without the help of Albert, Ajuban and Coya. It was also quite difficult for the wounded men to remain silent, as every jolt was another reminder of their wounds. From what Roy could tell, the shot had missed any of Justin's vitals, but such wounds had a way of becoming fatal if they were not ministered to quickly and thoroughly—which of course included removing the shot skillfully. Jan practically begged to be allowed to perform the necessary surgeries, but Roy wished to wait until the others reported back, and he would like to get a few miles further away if possible.

Fortunately, both Justin and Ben were fairly lucid at this point, though still in great pain. "Once they become feverish," said Jan, "we will have little time left to tend to them properly."

"Surely we must wait for daylight if we can," argued Roy. "We will give you enough light to operate and to attract every Spaniard in the area if we must, but I would like to avoid that dilemma if possible." Jan said no more, but made great effort to keep the wounds clean and keep the men cool.

Sooner than he had expected, Roy heard an explosion from further down the slope and he instructed the lookouts at the rear of the group to watch for Albert and Ajuban. "Coya as well," he told them. "It would not do for us to shoot any of our friends out of panic, thinking them to be soldiers." The men were on edge due to the close pursuit, even though they had gained nearly an hour on their pursuers. They all knew that it was extremely unlikely that they would keep that lead, and many of them looked over their shoulders every few minutes or any time they heard a noise from the valley below. He endeavored to keep those with the steadiest nerves in the rear, but unfortunately three of those were probably racing to catch up to them and two more were being carried in stretchers. He took turns with those on rearguard duty, but everyone had a heavy pack on his back or was helping to carry a heavy crate, sack, case, or stretcher. No one, himself included, was in a very good position to deal with a threat sneaking up on the group from behind.

Some time later, perhaps half an hour, Bert came jogging up from the rear of the group. "Albert and Ajuban, sir," he said. He could not yet speak much more English, but his meaning was clear. Roy motioned for him to take hold of the end of Justin's stretcher and made his way toward the back of the line. *I hope neither of them is wounded, because we can't afford to carry anyone else without leaving something behind.* He ordered a halt as he made his way back, and he waited silently with the rearguard.

Albert and Ajuban came up hurriedly, panting and puffing but thankfully whole and healthy-looking. "Captain," began Ajuban, "it worked. Dere were six of dem. We caught dem off guard but two of dem lived. We ran for it as you ordered. I do not t'ink dey will follow."

This was the best news that Roy had heard since they crossed the river. "Excellent! Well done. But I only heard the one explosion and some gunfire. What happened?" he asked. He had expected to hear a few grenades go off, but it sounded like things went well enough without all that.

Briefly Ajuban explained about the slow match and throwing three grenades all at once. "Albert here came well prepared, it seems," he finished.

Albert was doing his best not to beam, and Ajuban clearly meant to single him out for praise. "I'm inclined to agree," said Roy. "Well done, Albert. That should throw off pursuit, at least for a while. Hopefully until morning when we can make better time than in this darkness." They had still not lit any torches and Roy was determined that they would not do so until the Spaniards showed signs that they were sure Roy had come this way. As long as the soldiers were unsure, he was determined to keep them that way. "Have you seen or heard any sign of Coya?" he asked.

Albert looked troubled, but Ajuban said, "No sir, dough I t'ink dat may have been what de shooting and horns we heard coming from de valley a little while ago were about. I can't t'ink what else dey would have been making all dat racket over. It seemed to go on for a while," he added encouragingly. "Do you want me to go back and check on t'ings?" he asked. He surely knew the answer before he asked, but he was doubtless concerned, and Albert looked hopeful at the suggestion.

"No," said Roy with resignation, as Albert looked troubled once more, "she will have to catch us up if she can. I hope that she is all right, but we can't delay our progress any further. She knew the danger, now we must hope that makes it back safely." Privately he hoped at the very least that she would not be captured. *If she is coerced into telling what she knows before we get further along, we're all as good as dead.*

Albert and Ajuban fell in with the rest. Ajuban led the way, as he was the best scout Roy had besides Coya. Meanwhile Albert stayed with the rearguard. He had steady nerves, and he was the least likely of any of them to panic and shoot Coya. He'd be more likely to shoot anyone who even looked like he might mistake Coya for the enemy. In any case, something about Albert's presence among the men made the rest of them seem more confident.

They made better time now that they had two more strong men doing their part of the lifting once more, and Ajuban at least had a better understanding of what Coya had explained of the path than Roy did. Of course that meant it would be longer before Coya could catch up with them, but they could not count on her doing so anyway. Roy did feel encouraged by what Ajuban had said about the gunfire and the horns continuing for some time, and he hoped for the best, but he had to continue on as fast as possible now that their closest pursuers had temporarily been shaken off.

As he was pondering all of this, he heard what sounded like another shot in the distance behind. It sounded closer than the others he had heard earlier, as if it came from further down the ridge itself rather than in the valley. "What do you make of dat, captain?" said Ajuban glancing back towards him and gesturing back down the slope.

"I think that Coya has at least made it to the ridge," replied Roy. He said it loudly for Albert's benefit, as well as the rest of the crew. Justin even managed a weak smile. Roy thought it was almost certainly true in any event. He could not think who else would be getting shot at down there, unless it was meant as a signal. "I hope that she did not run afoul of those two men you left alive," he said, and Albert looked quite like he'd been poleaxed for a moment. "But in the darkness and the woods, I'd put my money on Coya any day, especially after you blew the Spanish trackers to pieces." Mild laughter rippled through the group, and they continued on up the smugglers' path.

They were all very glad for the path itself. It was as easy to tread as any path through these hills could be, and less tiring. Roy was quite sure that none but an expert horseman could ride the trail, and even then at a pace not much greater than a walk unless he wished to risk laming his horse. The trail led nearly due east for the stretch that they were on, though once it passed over the first ridge it apparently turned northeastward for a short distance, then east until they would need to break off and head for the ship. In other words, it went straight through the terrain that Coya had said looked dangerous during the downpour they had weathered the day before. Thankfully the weather gave no sign of inclemency as far as Roy or Ajuban could tell, and the Cimaroons seemed hopeful as well. With luck, they might even shave half a day's journey off of the time it had taken to travel to Caracas, even with all of the goods they had plundered. *Which would be completely impossible without the Cimaroons.* Roy was very aware of the fact, and he intended to do everything he could to honor their bargain to the fullest. Nevertheless, he was anxious to find out what loot he'd stolen. Before he would take the time to find that out though, he had resolved that they should have traveled as far as they could and that they would already be stopping to camp.

Another two hours passed as they trudged up the path with their earnings and wounded in hand, and no one had seen or heard any sign of pursuit.

They topped the ridge just after midnight and began heading down the other side. Few looked back out of fear or pursuit any longer, and Roy felt that they had dealt with a significant obstacle when a low whistling was heard from behind their group. Men spun around, and Albert peered into the darkness expectantly, his hand on his pistol, but they all heard the voice that followed. "Captain," panted Coya trudging slowly up as they halted. "Is everyone else accounted for?" she asked.

Roy was pleased beyond words, especially as she seemed unscathed, but he answered quickly, "Yes, we are all here. What happened down there?" he asked.

She told her story quickly, though she was obviously not in a hurry to get moving again. It appeared that she was regretting her idea of luring soldiers into the west woods, but it couldn't be helped now. "I'm sorry for how that turned out, and half the soldiers in the area must have seen me running towards these woods even if they weren't the ones shooting at me," she said, "but it appears that you have a good lead ahead of any other pursuers. I overtook two men who had survived an ambush of yours, and they seemed to be the closest of the soldiers for miles. I dealt with them."

Ajuban and Albert began laughing at that, most likely because they now felt safe in enjoying their own success, but also because she had made their ambush even more complete. "And after running through the middle of all their patrols!" said Tiede from his stretcher with a laugh.

At that, Roy noticed a look of concern fall across Coya's face and she made her way towards Tiede. "What happened?" she asked. "Is it your leg? Has it worsened?"

Tiede nodded soberly. Jan was changing his bandage again and Coya remarked on the swelling. Roy's mind was brought back once again to the plight of the wounded men. "We need to find a good place to camp as soon as we can so Jan can operate on the wounded," he said. "Do you have strength left to go ahead and find us a good site?"

"Aye sir," she said, sounding as tired as she looked, "I will find one as quick as may be." Then with a very uncharacteristic display of warmth, she pressed her hand to Justin's and padded off down the hill. Judging by the look on her face she was as concerned as Jan was.

Chapter 14: Under the Gun, Under the Knife

Roy sat up as soon as he heard the distant rumble, and found that the lookouts were already coming to wake him. "Cannon fire," said Ajuban as he ran over to Roy. "It's hard to tell where from, but it sounds to me like it's coming from de nort'west towards de harbor rader dan from de town."

"But you're not sure?" asked Roy. He had not been sleeping when the first rumbles were heard, and he couldn't tell much except that it sounded like it came from the other side of the ridge that lay behind them.

"No sir."

"Belonwu agrees with Ajuban," put in Jorge. The Cimaroons were just as anxious about the sound as Roy's men were.

Roy, however, was not very worried at all. "Either way, it seems like it's probably worse for the Spaniards than for us," he said. "With luck, whatever is going on over there will draw off our pursuers, particularly if that racket is coming from the port." Coya had told them all how she had overheard the last two soldiers from Albert's grenade ambush talking and how they did not seem to care much about the goods stolen from the galleon or this Captain Gutierrez.

"And if dis battle means dat *De Constance* isn't dere when we turn up?" asked Ajuban.

"Then we hide out in the woods until they turn up. I hope and guess that we won't have to worry about that possibility—it would certainly be bad for our wounded—but Brian has the good sense to keep far away from anything like that and he can outrun any ship in these waters provided he sees them coming. All we can do for now is rest and then hurry on our way when we have our strength back, just as we have been doing."

"Aye sir," said Ajuban grinning, and they left Roy alone after that. They were all exhausted, and another march after only a brief rest would not be welcomed by any man in the camp.

Ever since they had stopped for the night (and probably a good part of the morning) and had taken a peek at what they had stolen, Roy's main concern had been that soldiers would catch up with them. He was so certain they would come after him until either they caught him or he escaped that he had been unable to sleep. Most of the value of what they had captured was tied up in gold and silver plate, which alone amounted to a small fortune. There was also a substantial amount of copper, which Jorge guessed had been dug from a mine southeast of Caracas. Those portions of the cargo had certainly been destined for Spain when the ship would eventually make its way back across the ocean as part of the Spanish treasure fleet later that autumn. Added to that were many other valuables including a substantial weight of gold doubloons, several thousand silver pesos, a healthy smattering of precious stones and jewelry that had evidently remained unsold, more than two hundred pearls, three full sets of fine silverware, and a variety of goods from the East Indies that had also remained unsold. These included four casks of spices, about four hundred pounds of tea, three bolts of silk, and ten pieces of jewelry carved from ivory. One of the mules had also been carrying two small barrels of wine that clearly displayed French markings, and these had amused Ajuban to no end. Assuming they had not been gifts to the governor of Caracas from some French diplomat, they were undoubtedly bought by the locals from smugglers in the area and then traded to the merchants from Gutierrez's galleon. "So much for Spanish trade laws," Ajuban had said.

It was an impressive haul and it would take some time to appraise and account for it all, if they ever made it back alive. However, that was not all they had recovered. In addition to all of the traditionally valuable items they had spirited away, there were several long leather cases and small wooden crates that had given Roy a bit more confidence in his ability to fend off pursuers since their contents had been explored. These cases contained a wide array of swords and pistols, as well as a few muskets. Should their camp be attacked by soldiers, the soldiers would find themselves on the wrong end of their own weapons, and several of the blades were of the finest Toledo steel and crafted by a local master.

As glad as he was for the larger arsenal, the weapons worried him. The swords were nearly all variations on the rapier design rather than the common cutlass or the more ceremonial smallsword, and many of the pistols were intricately decorated and clearly custom made after the fashion of dueling pistols: they had narrower, rifled barrels for smaller shot and greater accuracy. In short, most of these weapons were clearly intended for officers and were not merely for show. More worrying still, *every last one* of the firearms they had recovered was a flintlock. Someone clearly had recognized the superiority of the flintlock to the wheellock and matchlock, and what's more, they had done so in some sort of official capacity and for a military purpose. All of these goods had been taken off of one or two mules that appeared to have been burdened exclusively with items made in Caracas and placed in the care of the soldiers from the galleon.

If Roy had realized the significance of this at the time of the ambush, or had seen what was in the cases, he would at least have searched the soldiers for documents or perhaps taken one of them as a prisoner for questioning. *Not that I could have spared the men to look after a prisoner anyway.* He resigned himself to putting off his musings until later, but he had a bad feeling about it all. Perhaps those weapons were merely meant for officers who had ordered them for their own private use and the Spanish military was not about to switch to all flintlocks for their soldiers, but he could not imagine that several officers or soldiers would be receiving weapons of that quality and practicality all at once without some tangible reason for it. An imminent military excursion was the most likely, considering what other information had made its way into his possession since the rumors in Port Royal.

As the distant cannon fire continued, he lay back down to get some sleep. If anything would distract the local soldiers from their pursuit of him, a battle with someone else close at hand would do it. His focus must remain on treating the wounded and getting the men and cargo back to his ship. Justin and the other wounded men were sleeping, but their foreheads glistened with sweat. Jan insisted on operating as soon as there was enough daylight to do so, and Roy had agreed, come what may. Roy closed his eyes and at last relaxed enough to fall asleep with the echoes of cannon blasts rolling through the still pre-dawn air.

* * *

Dawn came with no further signs of pursuit. Jan examined all three of the wounded men and cleaned their wounds for surgery. They all looked more fearful than relieved, but he was used to that. "I'll need hot water," he said, "quickly, please." He'd had preparations made before it was fully light so he could set to work immediately.

The weather promised to be unbearably hot and that was very bad for anyone with such wounds. He laid a hand on each of their foreheads in turn, and sure enough, they were all warmer than they should be. Thankfully they were all conscious. "They have fever," he said. "We need to gather as much cold water as we can to keep them cool after I treat these wounds, and we should not move further for several hours after I have done so." He very much wished that he had been able to operate sooner. Now he would need all his skill to keep the wounds from festering further than they already had. He had bandaged the wounds as well as he could, but without removing the shot, bandages only delayed the inevitable.

"I will need to remove the shot as soon as possible," he said to the men, "but before I do, I want you to take these." He opened a small canister and held two of the little black pills up for them to see. "These will help with the pain." They all eagerly took two or three of these as he directed, and he began laying out his tools.

Once he was ready and water was brought over, he pulled the captain, Ajuban, and Coya aside. "Captain, in addition to removing the shot, I will need to cut infected tissue away from the wounds in order to save their lives. This heat will make doubly sure that the infection will spread further if I don't address it now, but it will be a painful process for them."

"What did you give them for the pain?" asked the captain.

"Laudanum," Jan answered simply. "It should dull the pain as much as possible, but they may make quite a bit of noise. If you are worried about pursuers—"

"You do what you have to," said the captain. "We will just have to risk the noise. I don't think they're after us anymore anyway."

"Then I could use an extra pair of hands during the surgery," said Jan. "Someone who I can count on not to be squeamish about it."

After a brief discussion, it was agreed that Coya would help in the surgery. "I have never seen a surgery," she had said, "but I have seen far worse things." Jan supposed she had at that, but surgery affected some people differently than violence. Ajuban had clearly stated that he would find it difficult to watch, and Coya seemed to be the best candidate, so they soon set to work.

None of the wounds had hit vital areas or organs, and they each handled the pain differently after the laudanum had done its work, though only Tiede let out a growling shout at one point. *Perhaps I should have given him a third pill as well.* Laudanum could be addictive and was not to be lightly prescribed, though in cases like these the patient wouldn't notice any pleasant effects of it in light of the overwhelming pain of surgery. Normally only two pills were used at a time by those who even knew of the virtues of laudanum, but Jan had found that three were more effective and not really more dangerous. Tiede's wound was a leg wound, however, and three had seemed excessive in his case. Soon all of the shot had been removed along with the rotten tissue, though the three men were all tense and dripping with sweat by then.

After cleaning the wounded areas, Jan bandaged them with Coya's help— she had proved competent and only had to look away once during the surgeries—and called the captain over once more as Coya was dismissed to get some rest. "These men need to be stripped, washed clean with a rag and cold water, and then wrapped in dry blankets. I can attend to that. After that, they must be kept dry and cool, and they will have to avoid sitting or standing for at least two days. We have to make sure that they get enough water and food, and I will change the bandages again before we leave this place."

"Very well," answered the Captain with relief. "Is there anything else? Do you think they will be all right?"

"I probably won't know about that until tomorrow," Jan replied, "but in the meantime I will check on the ill Cimaroons as soon as I've finished with these men. After that, I would greatly appreciate some sleep, but I leave that decision to you as it has little to do with medicine." Jan had been up most of the night tending the wounded and needed rest almost as much as they did.

The captain grinned, in spite of his obvious worry. "Very well, doctor, rest while you can. You've done well."

"By the way, sir," said Jan, "how did we do?" He had not yet heard much about what had been looted.

Roy smiled broadly, "We did well, Jan. We did quite well."

* * *

Coya awoke feeling much less ill from fatigue and the experience of helping Jan. Surgery itself had been very interesting, but she also found it deeply disturbing somehow. She was glad for the understanding of medicine that some men had, but she hoped she would never have to help perform that task again. She'd lied when she said she'd seen worse, but she was determined to help those men as much as she could. She no longer felt the need to prove herself to the captain or any other member of the crew, and she no longer felt out of place among them—that was not the issue. Rather she felt that they had all shown her their respect and admiration, or at the very least that they acknowledged her abilities. Many of them actually liked her and sought her friendship. They had become a family of sorts, and they had done well by each other. And then they had need of her. She would not have let them down.

And there was Justin. Justin who had scoffed at her openly as she stood in line to sign aboard *The Constance*, Justin who had made jokes at her expense in a language she had not understood the first time that they met, Justin whom she had defeated to the laughter of all minutes later. And yet…and yet he had accepted defeat gracefully, if not gladly. He had treated her fairly since that day, had cooperated with her no less than any other crewman, and had accosted her to shake her hand warmly and pat her on the back after Roy had explained to the crew about the stolen ransom money. She *liked* Justin, and there was no longer any trace of animosity on his part though it had been less than two weeks since she had sparred with him at the docks of Port Royal. Of course she respected his skills as well, from his ability to fix problems with the ship to his seemingly broad knowledge of needlework and many other things that involved working with his hands, but none of that was half as relevant as the realization that he was the closest thing she had to family, as were all the other members of Roy's crew. It mattered not at all that she had not known Ben's name until yesterday; he was every bit as much a member of Roy's crew, and every last one of them was due her utmost efforts if they were in trouble. *Well, maybe not Daniel.* That one still looked at her in a way that made her uncomfortable.

Jan had spoken much with her as he operated. "It helps me to focus," he had said, but she also thought he'd tried to give her something to think about other than what she was witnessing. He approached her again as they prepared to set out again. Here," he said, reaching into his bag, "chew these." He handed her a handful of small, oblong leaves.

She looked at them with a curious expression. "Coca leaves?" she said. "I remember the soldiers used to chew on these sometimes when they would go on long journeys."

"You are clearly still tired, and sleep after one's first surgery tends to be…troubled. These will help to keep you awake and on your feet," he said. She shrugged and began chewing on them two at a time. It was reassuring to know that he had once felt just as she did. Coya had been only a teenager when Spaniards had attacked her village, and had not been aware of the significance of coca leaves, so she was somewhat pleased at the information, feeling she had new insight into her own people.

As they trod the smugglers' path, now in bright sunshine, Jan walked with her for a while. "I studied all of the local medicinal practices," he said when she asked how he knew about coca leaves. Coya was feeling much better and found herself in the mood to listen more than speak, so Jan spoke much of his past. "I even worked briefly for the Spanish when I visited Puerto Cabello with a Dutch diplomatic mission there from Sint Maarten many years ago." He told her about how he had been hired on as the ship's surgeon, but just for the voyage, mainly because he had decided to move to Curaçao and start his practice there. "The mission stayed in Puerto Cabello longer than expected," he explained, "so I helped the local physicians in dealing with a fever that had broken out. The Spanish physicians, however, had no knowledge of the medicinal practices of the 'pagan savages' (as they called them), and I was forbidden to use their resources to treat the natives, so I secretly spoke with those natives who kept their own knowledge of remedies alive." He had treated many of the suffering natives in this way, but his stay eventually had come to an end and the ship had continued on to Curaçao where he disembarked. "That was over seventeen years ago now," he said, clearly feeling his age. Since then, he had met and married his wife, become a father, and begun a successful practice of his own, but that all seemed to bring him back to where he was now. He pulled himself out of his memories and focused on Coya and their situation once again.

"Did you know that your presence would help the captain win favor with the outlaws?" she asked, meaning the Cimaroons.

"I honestly hadn't thought about it," said Jan. "I didn't think that they would be involved at all, actually. I suppose I should have, though. From what I understand, the captain's business arrangement has precedents. The Spanish have made enemies of nearly everyone in the Caribbean with their rapid colonization and exploitation of the natives as a work force. Spain tries from time to time to make peace with the other nations, especially those under Catholic rule, but the sheer flood of wealth into King Philip's coffers from the colonies, coupled with the extent of Spanish military campaigns and colonization frightens the nations of Europe into wariness and conflict. Many of the privateers and pirates in the area partner with the outlaws and victims of Spain's military and religious oppression for mutual benefit, and a significant fraction of the wealth carried by the Spanish flotas gets diverted into foreign hands as a result."

"You know much more about all of this than I do," said Coya, feeling overwhelmed.

"Only for the last few days," said Jan with some embarrassment. "Since I have few duties on deck, I've been spending my time aboard *The Constance* reading a few books. One of them is about maritime practice. I'd hoped it would have more about naval tactics than it does."

Coya laughed. "I suppose it is a good way to learn about more than which rope tightens what sail," she said. "I would never have known that enlisting aid from outlaws was such a common practice, but if I had, I might have been less worried about encountering these raiding tribes we had heard about. But perhaps the Cimaroons are not aware of this practice either, or they would have been less wary?"

"Well, outlaws and natives haven't always rendered aid willingly," said Jan. "We are fortunate to be serving under a captain who is willing to make such arrangements rather than one of those who simply tortures and bullies those living in the wild for information."

"I'm still not sure the Cimaroons expect the captain to bring their supplies," said Coya. Jan merely nodded. It was after noon and soon he went to check on the wounded men.

Coya had an easy time navigating the smugglers' path—it was hard to mistake it in full daylight, and she had let Ajuban lead the way. "At dis pace," he said when he joined her, "we should get dere perhaps by midnight. Hopefully de ship is still dere."

Coya said nothing. She didn't like to think what would happen to the wounded if *The Constance* had been driven from the coast. They had all done what they could do, and pursuit was no longer a worry. Now all the men looked forward to was a sight of their own sails.

Chapter 15: Tales of the Three Brothers

Roy and his men reached the shore perhaps an hour before midnight. The sight of *The Constance* waiting for him offshore was all that Roy could have wished for after so much toil, and he was impatient to load the goods aboard. He saw Jan in the torchlight, and the man looked like he could do with a good night's sleep, but he wished to give final treatments to the Cimaroons. While he did this, Roy's men loaded their burdens aboard the ship by boat. As soon as those aboard *The Constance* had spotted them, Martin and William had rowed out to meet them at the shore, and after a brief reunion, almost everyone began loading goods into the boat. "Ajuban, give Jorge's list to Martin and instruct him as to what to bring back here when he returns with the boat," said Roy.

"Aye, sir," said Ajuban and busied himself with his task, occasionally barking orders at those doing the loading.

Men were hooting and hollering about the goods they had captured, joking about what they would do with their shares, but Roy looked out to the north, out to sea.

"I see no ships," said Coya at his elbow, divining his thoughts. She looked much better for the sleep she'd had, but Roy had no intention of putting her on watch for the entire night.

"You did very well on this venture, Coya," he said. He had not given much thought to how well everyone had done, but now that they appeared to be out of danger, he could let himself think of such things.

Coya only said, "Thank you, sir," but she was clearly pleased, and no doubt the rest of his crew would appreciate similar sentiments.

"Once you are done saying goodbye to the Cimaroons, you are free to return to the ship and take up your post, but I only want you on duty until two o'clock. You need more rest, and I would like you to be fresh and alert by the time we near the port of Caracas on our way back."

"Aye sir, thank you again," she said. "Are the wounded going to be all right, sir?" she asked.

"Jan says he won't know until tomorrow, but he seems optimistic at the moment. Time will tell."

She was obviously uneasy, but she nodded and made her way towards the other men on the beach. She seemed to understand that she was exempted from loading duties, so she joined in the conversations and celebratory mood that prevailed.

Roy went to join Jan, Jorge and Belonwu who were talking amongst the ill Cimaroons. These appeared to be in better spirits for Jan's treatments and advice, even though Roy suspected part of it was due simply to having a doctor in attendance at all. "Make sure that any cuts and scrapes are washed immediately. If they are deep, also treat them with the salve I have indicated. Salt water may help if you are near the shore and are out of supplies." Jan appeared to be giving everything from traditional medical advice to cooking tips, mostly along the lines of making sure that meat be thoroughly cooked and not left unattended or in the open for very long beforehand. He was also making sure that they understood what he was saying as he jotted notes at a furious speed, though only Jorge could read and write. If something were to happen to Jorge, it would not do to have Jan's notes become useless, so Jan encouraged them to talk about the information he was giving them and to ask any questions they thought of.

"Jorge," said Roy after Jan had finished, "some of the supplies you requested are being brought out of our hold. I will meet you back here in exactly thirty days from tomorrow to deliver the rest, if that is acceptable."

"Thank you, captain," said Jorge. "We might not stay in the Caracas valley after this night's work, but we will meet you here. It is good to meet a man of his word, and I trust we will have pleasant dealings with you in the future."

Roy knew that Jorge was at least a little bit worried that he might break their appointment and just make off with the goods once they were all loaded aboard, but he intended to keep his end of the bargain. "Good luck to you out here in the wild," he said. "I hope that you may evade the Spaniards as long as anyone in this part of the world can. Until next time, Jorge, Belonwu." He shook hands with them and turned back to his men.

He had let the men know that there was no need to hurry. Those with the raiding party were tired, and those aboard the ship welcomed the excuse to visit the shore, so it took two hours to load all the goods onto *The Constance* and bring back those supplies destined for the Cimaroons. The wounded men were taken last so that they might rest on the shore for as long as possible. They were brought one by one and hoisted aboard with great care, still on their makeshift stretchers, and eventually Roy and his men were back aboard and waving to the Cimaroons who waved back in very good spirits and turned back to their life in the wild. The men had expelled their jubilation on the shore and had exhausted themselves with the toil of loading and rowing, but many of them stayed awake for some time talking in low voices on deck.

Roy made his way to the stern where Brian stood at the helm. "Take us in a wide arc north of the port," he said, "but closer than before. I want to see what there is to see. Perhaps that galleon is heavily damaged or is no longer there. I'd like to know what that cannon fire was all about, but it's not worth risking our necks and our loot over, after all we went through to keep it off that galleon."

"Aye sir," said Brian, "I can get us within good telescope range, and anyone following us will be hard put to it to catch up if they try. We should be in position for a good view after dawn."

"Very good." Brian's estimates of how soon they would reach a particular point at sea were seldom wrong, though occasionally he would somehow manage to cut even more time off of their voyage if the wind offered the opportunity to do so. "Any trouble while we were away?" he asked the navigator.

"The men were a bit tense and bored, sir," answered Brian casually, "but nothing out of the ordinary. I've been teaching William about navigation in Jan's absence, and he is coming along well," he observed. "Jan also has quite the head for it, as well as a good deal of *patients*."

Roy groaned at the terrible joke. "Evidently you were bored as well," he said as Brian tittered unapologetically. "I confess that I'll be glad to get back to Curaçao and hear what there is to hear. I'd enjoy at least a few days in town without any further adventure. We should get quite a bundle for the goods in our hold now."

"When would you like me to inspect and catalogue the goods, sir?" asked Brian. In addition to the role of navigator, he also did the accounting.

"Tomorrow," said Roy. "There is quite a variety of goods to be appraised, and I think that Jan and William may both be able to help with that. Ajuban too, since we retrieved a quantity of fine-looking blades and pistols." Ajuban had a fair degree of knowledge about weaponry due to his time as a merchant's slave. His former master had an interest in such things, and Ajuban had picked up some of his knowledge and interest. Roy supposed it was one of the few times when Ajuban had been allowed to forget for a moment that he was a slave and his master owned him, as even the most heavy-handed master will sometimes forget his position when gripped by his own passions.

Brian nodded, "Aye sir. Anything else?"

"Yes, have William relieve Coya of watch duty at two o'clock. She needs the rest. Right, I'm going to my cabin. Wake me for anything important, or wake me at dawn."

Roy turned, but he first made his way to some of the crew that were still awake and off duty. "You lot should be getting some sleep," he said sternly but kindly. He raised his voice so everyone could hear, "You've all performed superbly, but we're not back in port yet and I mean to have a look at La Guaira—from a distance, of course," he said with a smile. "We will catalogue and appraise our loot tomorrow. In the meantime, I want you all to be as rested as possible should anyone try to keep us from spending it."

"Aye sir," said a few men, and soon they all made their way to their hammocks or places on deck.

Roy did not wait for them, however. He made his way down to the hold where Jan was checking on the wounded before getting some rest himself. "Are they having any trouble sleeping?" he asked in a whisper.

"No sir," said Jan in an equally low voice. "That is a hopeful sign, but I still won't know until morning.

"All right. Get some sleep when you've finished. We will want your help cataloguing the goods tomorrow. We have an interesting haul, and your knowledge may prove useful."

Jan looked curious. "Of course, sir," he whispered. "I'd be happy to help." Roy wasn't sure how far the surgeon's knowledge extended, but he may as well test it out. *I'll wager he knows as much about those spices we found as anyone would though.* He was sure that one of them was cinnamon, but he was neither herbalist nor cook.

"Good night then, Jan. You've done well, and in difficult circumstances, regardless of how things turn out for these men. If you need anything, tell Brian. Have him wake me if there is anything that needs my attention."

"Thank you, sir," said Jan. "Good night, captain."

With that, Roy took his leave and made his way straight to his cabin and his bed that he had missed these last several days. *What would I give for a bed in an inn somewhere?* It was an idle thought, but he realized there wasn't anywhere he would rather be just then than at sea with a hold full of valuable cargo on a ship that was about as uncatchable as any could be.

He awoke when he heard a knock at his door, but a quick glance out the window showed him that it was indeed dawn. "Thank you, Brian," he said.

"Nearly there, sir," said Brian outside the door.

Right on schedule. Roy splashed some water on his face and combed the tangles out of his hair before making his way out of his cabin to the helm.

"I decided that it would be easiest to approach from the east so the view from the port would be partly obscured by the sun," said Brian as Roy approached. "We are still far enough north to keep out of the way of any ships there though."

"Good, good," said Roy. He held his telescope aloft and extended it toward the port of La Guaira. The view was puzzling to him. He saw a ship in the distance, but it was definitely smaller than a galleon. It was also heading north along a course that would take it near them. There was no sign of any larger ship in the port. "Strange."

"Sir?" inquired Brian.

"What do you make of that ship?" asked Roy, handing the telescope to him and taking the helm.

Brian looked through the glass. "Looks like a fore and aft rigged vessel," said Brian, "moving at a fair clip. Can't be the galleon."

"Keep on course," said Roy taking the glass from Brian again. "I want to see their colors before I decide what to do."

"Aye sir."

Roy stood peering through the spyglass for a few more minutes in silence until he could make out the blue coloring on the ship's flag. "Not Spanish," he said, but Brian remained silent. Once they had set sail, Roy ordered that the English colors be flown, but sailing under false colors, however serious of an offense it was considered to be, was a common practice of smugglers, pirates, privateers, and even warships that were commissioned to hunt any of those. A few more moments and he could tell with certainty that they were flying the English colors. Then he saw the flag dip slightly and stay there. "She's hailing us," said Roy.

"Accept?" asked Brian.

"Agreed. Ajuban!"

"Aye sir?" said Ajuban poking his head out of the hatch to the hold wearily but attentively.

"Dip our colors, we're being hailed. And rouse the men."

"Aye sir. Men!" shouted Ajuban loudly. "On deck and dip de colors!"

"Aye!" said men from around the ship, and Ajuban made his way out of the hold followed by others who had been wakened.

Martin answered the hail and Roy saw the approaching vessel raise their flag once more in response. "Stay on course," said Roy, "but be prepared to maneuver north if they're faking. They're as heavy in the water as we are."

"Bigger than us?" asked Brian casually.

"Isn't everything?" said Roy with amusement, and Brian smirked. Roy pressed the telescope back to his eye. "It's a large sloop, so they probably outgun us, but they are heavy in the water indeed. I wonder if they need assistance."

"Shall I have men load de guns?" asked Ajuban as he approached.

"Not yet," said Roy, "but have them stand ready. If there's anything amiss, we might be better off running for it. She's slower than us. Tell Jan to check on the wounded," he added. "Then have him report to me."

"He's already on it, captain," Ajuban said.

"Very good." Jan apparently knew his first duty well enough not to need telling. *And I suppose it's his instinct to tend to them anyway.* A ship's doctor who cared about his charges was a valuable asset, but Roy's mind was more on his men. It was morning, and he wanted to know the worst at once.

When Jan approached, Roy put his glass down and gave his full attention. "Sir," began Jan, "it is still too early to be certain of the fate of the wounded men, but they all show definite signs of improvement. I think they will all recover. Tiede should be fit to return to light duties after another day, but none of them should lift anything heavier than a pistol for some time."

Roy was relieved, though he was still down three men until he made it to port. "Thank you, Jan, you may return to your duties."

"What duties do you t'ink we should put dem on when dey are up and about?" asked Ajuban in a low voice. "Dey won't even be able to load de guns, it sounds like."

"We can have them be the ones firing the guns, if need be," answered Roy. "A stave and slow match are not heavier than a pistol." With luck, they wouldn't run into trouble before reaching Curaçao, but Justin was quite handy with ship repairs. With him out of commission, they might have to see how one of the others would work out. *Maybe Jan can fill in, if he's as good with planks as he is with limbs.* Brian could help if need be, but not in the middle of a battle.

He ordered that the small arms be loaded just in case of trickery, but very soon it became clear that the ship he had been watching had been in a battle recently, though it appeared to have been patched up. It had a full complement of guns, with a few added as well, but it certainly looked as if it might have been on the receiving end of heavier guns not very long ago. There was no sign that they had readied the deck guns and there were men mustered on deck shouting to those aboard *The Constance* once they were in range.

"Stand down, men," said Roy, "They're English indeed." Ajuban repeated the orders to all, and they could all hear the shouts in English now. Roy's nerves relaxed to such an extent that he became aware of how worried he had been. He chided himself for speculating as much as he had, but with such valuable cargo aboard, he was determined that nothing should go wrong.

Both ships trimmed their sails, but Roy did not dare send a boat across until they were further from La Guaira, or until he knew who the captain of this ship was. They were obviously able to read the name of his ship as they were approaching his port side, but he could not see along their stern. As the ship drew alongside though, he could make out the name of the ship: It was *The Sea Dervish*—Captain Henry Morgan's ship. "Captain Toppings, Captain Morgan requests permission to come aboard," shouted a voice from their deck.

"Permission granted," shouted Roy gladly. He had met Captain Morgan before in Port Royal, and evidently Morgan remembered the name of Roy's ship. Both ships slowed as much as possible and a boat was lowered into the water from the deck of *The Sea Dervish*. Soon Henry Morgan was being rowed across to *The Constance* by a few of his men, and there was still no sign of any activity in the port. *No doubt he will be able to explain that.* Roy was sure now that the cannon fire they had heard two nights ago had something to do with Captain Morgan, but he was also sure that Morgan would be just as interested in his tale.

Captain Morgan was a stocky fellow with rosy cheeks and a boisterous manner. Roy knew him to be generally good-natured and merry of mood, but his mannerisms usually made his company seem wearying before long. He was one of the men who had helped the English take control of Port Royal four years ago, and he had since achieved a significant measure of fame as a successful privateer once he had become captain of a ship of his own. After his more successful ventures, he tended to set up in the middle of one of the busier streets in Port Royal with a barrel of rum and insist that the locals have a drink with him, and Colonel D'Oyley was quite content to indulge such displays considering the wealth that Morgan brought to Port Royal. Most of his exploits had been on land, but he had a skilled crew and evidently had caught the Spanish napping this time, from what Roy could tell. It seemed impossible that he had missed the galleon in the dark, and the only reason why it should be absent from the port now that Roy could think of was if Captain Morgan had sunk it.

"Welcome aboard *The Constance*," said Roy as he helped Captain Morgan aboard. He had mustered his crew on deck and they stood at attention in the presence of both captains. As Morgan's small retinue mustered on deck as well, Roy introduced his crew. "You remember my first mate, Ajuban," he said. "My navigator, Brian Thornton…." He worked his way down to the more recent additions to his crew, "Three of my recruits are wounded and resting below, but this is our new ship's surgeon, Jan Huisman."

"It's an honor to meet you in person, captain," said Jan. "Word of your exploits precedes you."

Captain Morgan, always happy to accept praise, simply smiled and bowed with a flourish. "At your service, Dr. Huisman."

"Coya," Roy continued knowing that she would be glad of the information, "Captain Morgan is one of the officers who helped the English win the battle for Port Royal." The words took a moment to register with Coya who still had problems with so much English, but she smiled at Roy and then at Captain Morgan, though seemed unsure whether or not she should speak. "Coya saw the battle from the island," Roy explained. "It was her first experience witnessing Spanish defeat, though it hasn't been her last." Captain Morgan laughed along with some of Roy's crew, but he was obviously unsure what to make of Coya aboard a privateer ship, so he simply smiled at her and they moved on down the rest of the line. Morgan introduced his own men briefly, though Roy was terrible at names when he had other things on his mind. Morgan's first mate had remained at the helm of *The Sea Dervish* and these men who accompanied the captain were merely an honor guard of a sort.

"Come, let us exchange news over a bottle of wine," said Roy. He had many things he wished to ask Captain Morgan, but he was anxious to get underway again as well.

"It would be a pleasure," agreed Morgan, following Roy to his cabin. Roy motioned for Ajuban to fall in as well, though Roy's cabin was cramped.

"What news from the east?" asked Captain Morgan when they were all seated holding pewter goblets and sipping a fine vintage that Roy had purchased in Port Royal.

"You may be surprised to hear," Roy began, "that our news is likely similar to that which you would share."

Roy grinned, but Captain Morgan looked only momentarily puzzled. Then he nodded and said with a laugh, "Then…that was *you* that the soldiers of La Guaira were after?"

"Indeed they followed us most closely at first," agreed Roy, only slightly crestfallen that Morgan had worked it out so quickly. "We ambushed a mule train carrying a large quantity of valuable goods from Caracas to the galleon in the port," he continued. "Perhaps you can tell us what became of the ship?"

"Of course," laughed Morgan loudly, "but all in good time, captain. I should like to hear this tale completed before I begin my own." He had already drained his goblet, and Roy refilled it with all but the dregs and told his tale, expanding on the parts that Coya, Ajuban and Albert had played. "We heard cannon fire before dawn as we camped for the first time after the raid, but I had no idea who the Spanish could be shooting at."

"Well the first of those shots came from us," said Captain Morgan as he began to share his own tale. "As we sailed into view of the port, we realized that the Spaniards were not keeping a proper lookout. They seemed to be distracted by something inland and did not see us approaching for several minutes after we came into view, even in the moonlight. When we were close enough, I could tell that at least two dozen horsemen followed by three or four score footmen had but lately set forth from the south gate of the fort, for they were well on their way along the road. I could see several civilians aboard the galleon arguing with the officers on deck, and there was no sign from the fort that they had spotted us. I had originally cursed our luck that a heavily armed galleon was in the port, but providence had seen fit to keep the devils ignorant of our approach, so I ordered us closer. We knew that if we had any chance of taking the ship or the port, it was then."

Captain Morgan was obviously enjoying the telling of his exploits, and Roy was as inclined towards amusement at the Spaniards' predicament as he was, but Ajuban interjected, "How did you manage to deal wit' de fort?" he asked. The fort overlooked the harbor and the Spaniards would never leave it completely unmanned unless it was on fire or if the town itself was besieged by overwhelming forces.

But Morgan said, "We managed to make our way with all speed into the port and along the north side of the galleon before they were aware of us. We fired a volley into her hull and raced around to the west. It was very risky: if the galleon's guns were loaded, they would finish us with one volley at that range. As it turned out, they had barely begun to make the ship ready and we caught them dead in the water. Before anyone could respond, we had put ourselves on the other side of the galleon from the fort, and the fort had to worry about hitting it instead of us. The only guns that the galleon was able to fire at us were swivel guns and one or two nine pounders they managed to maneuver into position, but our next volley put those out of commission as well. We took a few hits from the fort, but nothing below the waterline. We closed with the galleon and boarded immediately. They had barely gotten underway and had turned north to bring their port guns to bear, but we swarmed over the deck by then. They had only a skeleton crew aboard, and their captain was on his way to the town to argue with the governor. Once we had taken the ship, I dropped anchor again and had men load the starboard guns while others looted the hold and loaded the aft guns with grape shot to point at the docks in order to deal with any soldiers who returned. The fort continued to fire sporadically, but they were apparently reluctant to fire on the galleon and hit their own captured men. We opened the starboard gun ports and fired everything at the fort."

Ajuban laughed outright, and Roy shook his head incredulously. Captain Morgan had turned his abilities as a commander in the field towards the situation and defeated the Spanish not through naval warfare, but by turning the galleon into a fortress and holding it against the port until all resistance had crumbled.

"The fort finally began firing on the galleon," continued Morgan, "but many of its guns were damaged or blocked by rubble, and we cared not if they sank their own vessel, so long as we carried off the goods intact and took few losses. Before the soldiers could come at the docks in force enough to deal with my men on the galleon and aboard *The Sea Dervish*, we had spirited away all of their most valuable goods and beat a hasty retreat as the useless galleon sank into the harbor."

"But that was yesterday morning," said Roy puzzled. "Why are you only now leaving the area?" he asked.

"We made sure that there were no vessels left afloat that could come after us," he answered, "so we conducted repairs yesterday within sight of the port to monitor their activity. There were quite a few men gathered there, shaking their fists, repairing the fort, and impotently wheeling cannons to the dock, but we were well out of range of any attack. We kept a watch through the night and rested, then set sail at dawn. I imagine that the galleon only had a portion of its valuables aboard when we plundered it because of your own raid, but without that, we never would have been able to take advantage of the situation."

"So where do you go now?" asked Roy. "Port Royal and Colonel D'Oyley who is no doubt awaiting his share of the spoils?"

"No," said Captain Morgan looking troubled now, "First I must put in at Curaçao to see about a ransom that was to be paid for one of my charges."

Uh-oh. Roy had a sinking feeling that he knew who this "charge" might be. From the look on Ajuban's face, he was thinking the same thing. But Roy said, "You seem uneasy over the matter. I would not think that a paid ransom would be a source of disquiet for you or your crew."

Captain Morgan shifted in his seat, leaning forward. "Well," he said in urgent tones, "I questioned a few of the men we captured aboard the galleon and they had news for me that made me wonder about this prisoner of mine and whether it would not be better if he remained locked up."

Roy couldn't see how he could avoid the subject any longer with any honor—not to an esteemed colleague and ally such as Captain Morgan. "Is this prisoner named Colonel Javier Valdez, by any chance?"

"Ah, you have heard that tale?" Captain Morgan said, sounding a bit disappointed that he would not need to tell of it. Then he apparently caught their expressions. "Why, what has happened?"

Without further hesitation, Roy told the whole tale of Ajuban's stealthy eavesdropping at Van Kemper's tavern and their theft of the ransom money, though he hoped at least to put Captain Morgan's mind at ease about whatever disquieting information led him to believe that perhaps Colonel Valdez should not be released.

He had not expected Morgan's immediate reaction, though he realized when Captain Morgan began laughing uproariously that he probably should have. *His own crew can probably hear him from aboard his ship.* Roy and

Ajuban both grinned in spite of themselves. "Well fair's fair," said Captain Morgan, still laughing. "It was very well done, and even if you have cost me the immediate gains of a ransom, I have to appreciate the cheek of it! And now my mind can be clear about retaining Valdez, and that's a weight off, it is."

"Why, sir?" asked Ajuban, echoing Roy's thoughts as well. "What information did dese prisoners tell you dat made you worry about letting Valdez go?"

"Well, the galleon was to deliver a small contingent of soldiers to Coro, presumably for some kind of campaign. They said there was some argument about it between the galleon's captain and the governor of Caracas since Caracas was already undermanned. But the more I think about it, the more I wonder if Colonel Valdez is wanted to lead this expedition."

Roy had not given the matter much thought since leaving Curaçao, but this information about troops being mustered in Coro was disquieting. "We captured a document along with the ransom money," Roy said with a sinking feeling. "It said that Colonel Valdez was to be brought to the house of Captain Adán San Ramón in Coro. It was signed by Admiral Sergio Cadiz." Captain Morgan looked surprised, but not less worried. "I thought that Valdez must be wanted for some kind of campaign in the Caribbean, whatever Major Benito said," continued Roy, "but I didn't think that any actual force was mustering in Coro as well. I thought perhaps the muster was in Maracaibo or elsewhere, and that Valdez was to be taken to Coro because it is the Spanish port closest to Curaçao."

"Perhaps that is exactly why they are mustering troops there," said Morgan with sudden understanding, and Roy realized exactly what he meant before he continued. "Perhaps they intend to invade Curaçao."

It made perfect sense to Roy. The Dutch had taken Curaçao many years ago, and it had been a thorn in King Philip's side ever since. Curaçao was the center of illegal trade along the Spanish Main south of Port Royal from Panama to Cumana. Not only was it isolated from the other Dutch colonies; it was fairly isolated from any colonies at all except for those ruled by Spain. While it was true that this illegal trade benefited most of the Spanish colonies in the area, King Philip would not see it as beneficial due to the shipping duties that Spain would be cheated out of, and Curaçao was a haven for many pirates and privateers acting against Spain. "You may be right," he said. "Part of the cargo we captured from Caracas was a shipment of fine blades and flintlock pistols and rifles, most of which look custom made. I guessed they were destined for officers for some imminent military campaign, and Curaçao is the perfect target, if King Philip personally authorized it. That might explain why a Spanish officer with diplomatic status would dare to try breaking Valdez free when the ransom deal went wrong, and why they were anxious to avoid any haggling. Besides, if they successfully attacked Curaçao immediately after, they would certainly be repaid their ten thousand pesos. But…if they were already building up a force in Coro before now, wouldn't smugglers from Curaçao soon hear of it? I must confess that is why I assumed a location for the muster that was less visible and more secure, such as Maracaibo. If smugglers were to find such a gathering in Coro, Governor Diedrik would be on his guard whether the force was destined for Curaçao or not." To Roy it seemed as though the Spanish were anxious that Valdez be freed quickly and that they were willing to endanger diplomatic relations with Governor Diedrik to achieve that end. They could be anxious to move before the governor could act on any news.

"Not necessarily," answered Morgan. "Coro is not a very good market for smugglers since Captain Myngs burned the town last year. Smugglers have tried to undersell the Spanish trade ships sent to resupply the town, but there is tighter security and many of the merchants still have too little gold to deal with smugglers and Spanish trade vessels alike. It's just possible that smugglers would not notice what goes on in Coro for as long as it takes to muster a fleet. Most smuggling is done overland with transactions taking place outside of the town to the west, away from the port."

"Captain," Ajuban cut in addressing Roy, "do you t'ink dat dis 'amnesty' dat Captain Torres spoke of has any-t'ing to do wit' all dis military activity?"

Roy and Captain Morgan looked at each other, and Morgan was clearly pondering the possibility for the first time, just as Roy was. How did Ajuban connect that? "A map," said Roy, scrambling for papers in his desk. "What I need," he said as he shuffled through his collection of maps, "is a map of the area covered by the amnesty. Aha!" He pulled a map out of the pile and laid it out for them to see. "The amnesty was a peculiar one," he said, "covering the shipping lanes of several colonies rather than just one or two. Only the president of New Granada would normally offer amnesty for so much of the region, not the governor of Maracaibo. Torres said that the area covered by the amnesty was from the coast of New Granada to the fourteenth parallel, between La Guaira and Santa Marta."

He swept out the area with his fingers to demonstrate that it did indeed cover not only Spanish territory, but the waters around Curaçao as well. On the surface, it simply appeared that, as Torres had said, the governor of Maracaibo wished to cover his more important trade routes. However, the amnesty would also bar attacks against ships bringing troops to Coro and would make discovery less likely, if it were successful at keeping privateers away. "We still can't be certain," said Roy, "but I believe we have some questions to put to Major Benito when we return to Curaçao."

"Who is this Captain Torres?" asked Captain Morgan, with just a hint of suspicion. "How did you come to speak with him?"

"We slipped past patrols near the Maracaibo Lagoon by pretending to be a Spanish trade vessel," Roy said with a grin. Morgan laughed loudly once again and clapped him on the shoulder. *Dear God, is he like this all the time?* Henry Morgan was to be married soon, and Roy could not help but imagine his betrothed without thinking of either an equally boisterous woman with thick skin or a tough, mean-tempered hag who was very hard of hearing. In any case, Morgan seemed satisfied that Roy's discovery of this information was not due to an interest in signing the amnesty.

"Valdez wouldn't know about dis supposed campaign, would he?" asked Ajuban, turning to Captain Morgan. Roy was pleased that Ajuban was as direct with other captains as he was with Roy, and was not afraid of how they would react to being spoken to without the deference they would normally expect from a Negro.

Morgan, however, was always less jovial and more formal when he spoke to Ajuban. "I don't think so," he said. "It has been months since I captured him off the coast of Santo Domingo, and he was merely involved in some kind of patrol duty there. Valdez hasn't given any sign that he has urgent business elsewhere, but he *is* a man who knows how to master his emotions."

That was true enough, from what Roy had heard of him, though it amused him to hear Morgan say it with admiration, as if the feat was some kind of inexplicable magic trick. "I think we should sail to Curaçao together without further delay," said Roy. "If Curaçao can expect imminent attack, we might be able to persuade Benito to enlighten us. Governor Diedrik certainly should be told, if that's the case." The way Roy saw it, Diedrik had done him a favor by handling Benito as cleverly as he had, and in return he had asked to be informed if Roy discovered anything important that came of it. Roy felt he must share this news with the governor, and it helped no one but King Philip of Spain for Curaçao to be attacked. "Perhaps we can help in the defense, if it comes to it. For a price, of course," he added, and Morgan nodded his agreement. Whether or not it was in either captain's interest for Curaçao to be sacked, they were not about to risk all in defense of Curaçao without compensation.

"Depending on how Sir Sebastian's expedition turns out, we may not have to wait for Benito to tell us any-t'ing," observed Ajuban.

Roy had forgotten about McLaughlin's raid, but Morgan looked confused. "He was intending to attack Coro," Roy explained. "He was recruiting at Van Kemper's tavern when we were there." *I hope he is all right.* Roy did not know McLaughlin well, but if the Spanish were mustering in Coro, McLaughlin's chances of survival were rather slim.

Captain Morgan's expression was as dismal as Roy's thoughts. "Captain," he said, standing up, "I think I had best get back to my ship and we should do as you suggest. I'll meet you at the docks of Curaçao. Godspeed," he said, extending his hand. Roy shook it vigorously, as there was no other sort of handshake with Morgan.

Ajuban snapped a salute. "Captain," he said. Morgan returned the gesture, and they made their way back to the deck.

As Morgan saluted the crew and climbed back into his boat after his men, Roy sighed. *Why isn't anything ever simple?* "All speed for Curaçao," he ordered.

"All speed for Curaçao!" echoed Ajuban to the crew. To Roy he said quietly, "I suppose Jan should be glad he signed onto *De Constance* instead of McLaughlin's ship after all."

* * *

It was no later than two o'clock the next morning when Ajuban was awakened in his hammock by William. "Sir, Coya has sighted a sail."

"Right den," said Ajuban, hoisting himself out of his hammock and onto the floor of the hold. As an officer, he always had use of a hammock when off duty due to the greater need for him to stay sharp and focused. He still felt tired, but as he navigated between the bodies of sleeping sailors on deck who had been displaced from their hammocks by the three wounded men, he was grateful that he had probably slept better for it. Fortunately for everyone, Jan had pronounced by dusk that evening that all of the wounded would recover, apart from random aches or instances of stiffness. He wasn't worried about tales of a ship sighting since they were still sailing alongside *The Sea Dervish*, but he hurried up to the deck and wiped the sleep out of his eyes.

The captain had clearly just emerged from his cabin as well, but he was already peering through his telescope as he yawned. He quickly frowned and shut his telescope again. "I can't tell more than that it's a ship," he said. "It appears to be sailing on an intercept course, but it has been traveling due west since we spotted it and hasn't changed course. Perhaps she is making for Curaçao as well." The ship was north by northeast from *The Constance*, but was making good speed running with the strong east wind—better speed than they were. *She must be bigger dan us.* *The Constance* could outrun larger ships in a crosswind, or running at beam reach or broad beam reach as it was called, or even sailing into the eye of the wind, but square-rigged ships were very well suited to sailing with the wind. Some small ships, such as *The Sea Dervish*, were rigged to be faster in a direct wind than *The Constance,* but were slower in a crosswind. From what little Ajuban could see, and from the speed of the ship, he guessed it was probably a barque or a brig.

Roy's view through the telescope confirmed it moments later when he said, "She's a barque flying English colors. And she's hailing us. Signal our acceptance, Ajuban."

Ajuban gave the order, happy that his curiosity would be satisfied without much worry. A barque could outgun either of their ships, but Roy and Captain Morgan would sail rings around her if she intended any harm. Morgan's crew signaled their acceptance as well, apparently having observed the hail. The barque did not need to change course, but she did trim sails a bit so as not to outpace them.

Roy was clearly still debating whether or not to have men load the guns, but in the end he decided it was better to be safe than sorry, regardless of the waste of gunpowder if there was no danger. He ordered no other preparation, but it was highly doubtful that the crew of the barque could see them loading the guns. Neither Roy nor Coya could tell if those aboard the barque were doing the same. Soon Roy could read the name of the ship. It was *The Swordfish*, though Roy said he didn't recognize the name. Moments later, however, Captain Morgan shouted over to them, "Have you met Captain Rowling, Roy?" *His first mate must feel redundant.* Captain Morgan needed none to shout his orders for him in case they were not heard.

"I have not," Roy called back. "I take it that is his ship?"

"Aye, he's a shark in the sea lanes, that one."

But Ajuban and Roy had *heard* of Edmund Rowling. Where Captain Morgan was a good sea captain and an excellent tactician on land, Captain Rowling was virtually unrivalled at sea by any of the other privateers out of Port Royal. His expeditions on land had never yielded much wealth, but he had outmaneuvered, outfought and outfoxed no less than five warships that had been sent to hunt him—two of which he had captured. *If de captain is right about Coro, we could do no better dan to have Rowling wit' us as well.* With luck, Captain Rowling *was* going to Curaçao as his course suggested. If he did business there with regularity, he would certainly be interested in the suspicions they had to share.

Once again, the crews went through the exercise of aligning the ships and furling the sails, but this time Roy requested permission to board Captain Rowling's ship "if for no other reason than that his cabin will be the biggest one to meet in," Roy had said, and he asked Ajuban to accompany him. Soon Brian was left at the helm and the Captain and Ajuban rowed across to *The Swordfish* alone, while Captain Morgan and a few of his men did the same. Roy had brought no others of his crew, not only because he could not spare them, but also because he was more concerned that they be well rested than he was with putting on a show for anyone. Ajuban noted that Captain Morgan had no such concerns. *He can probably spare de men as well, I suppose.*

They secured their boat once they reached *The Swordfish,* then clambered up onto the deck. "Cap'n Toppings, I'm pleased to be meetin' you. I am Cap'n Edmund Rowling." Captain Rowling was an athletic looking man with dark, wavy hair dressed in practical clothes decorated by only a little scrollwork on the sleeves and neck.

"At your service," said Roy with a bow.

"This here's my first mate, Jombo," Rowling continued, indicating a Negro next to him who was slightly shorter and broader than Ajuban and dressed very similarly to Captain Rowling. *I like dis captain.* Ajuban smiled broadly, and Jombo noticed.

"You are Captain Toppings' first meete?" he said in an accent that Ajuban did not recognize.

"Indeed," said Roy, "this is First Mate Ajuban." There was just a moment when Roy and Captain Rowling seemed to size each other up, as if they had each just learned something important about the other and decided they approved. Ajuban glanced at them and realized that they were both dressed practically, seemed mild-mannered and apt to dispense with formalities, and they both bore themselves with confidence and directness. *Dese two are going to get along just fine, I t'ink.*

Moments later, Henry Morgan and his small retinue clambered aboard and introduced themselves, though Morgan greeted Captain Rowling with his usual warmth and hearty handshake. "Edmund! Good to see you, captain," he proclaimed. "We have much to discuss since we last met!"

Captain Rowling's crew was mustered on deck, and the usual formalities were observed. Ajuban knew Roy well enough to see that this was not necessarily a contradiction with a general disposition towards informality—where Roy's crew was concerned, Roy wished to afford them every bit of praise that they deserved, formally or otherwise. Edmund Rowling clearly had a similar view of things, and Ajuban was sure that his men stood up a bit straighter when he spoke of them. Ajuban did his best to remember names, but Captain Rowling's crew was quite a bit larger due to his fame and the simple fact that *The Swordfish* could hold many more men than either of the other captains' ships. He did note, however, that many of Rowling's crew were Dutch, and there were a fair number of Frenchmen aboard as well. *He must do a lot of business in Curaçao.* That certainly would help them in enlisting his aid, or at least piquing his interest in the possible situation with Coro.

Soon the five of them—Captain Morgan seemed to prefer to leave his first mate on *The Sea Dervish* most of the time—stepped into Captain Rowling's cabin and sat down, sipping an excellent Italian wine from fine Venetian crystal goblets. As Ajuban expected, Captain Morgan did most of the talking, but Rowling had his own news to interject into the long narrative. "I'm just returnin' to Curaçao from plunderin' ships out of Cumana an' Isla de San Margarita," he said, "an' men aboard those ships also mentioned that soldiers garrisoned at each of those ports had been reassigned to some other colony, but they didn't know where. I expect they've been shipped to Coro too."

"I wonder why thee are gathering men from all of these pleeces instead of simply sending a force from Speen," said Jombo. "It would be harder for anyone to find out about it, and it would teek less organizeetion."

"We heard in Curaçao that a Spanish fleet had been destroyed in a hurricane late last year," said Roy. "Perhaps King Philip *did* send a force, and now Admiral Sergio Cadiz is improvising with local troops." Ajuban remembered little enough about that topic at Van Kemper's tavern, but then he had been snooping around upstairs at the time.

"If that's true," said Captain Morgan, "then Spain has been planning this for probably the last year. Why then would they not have approached Colonel Valdez before I captured him?"

"Well," said Roy, "assuming that you are correct and they did not approach him, perhaps they simply wished to organize secretly and then enlist his help once the muster was complete."

Things continued in this vein for some time, and Ajuban's attention wavered periodically. His curiosity was satisfied for the moment, and he felt that there was not much else to be gained from more speculation. At least Captain Rowling was just as interested in helping them as Morgan was, and apart from the information he had added, that was all that Ajuban thought needed to be accomplished at this point. Finally he spoke up. "Gentlemen, we appear to have reached de point where we have all de facts before us but can't make much more of dem wit'out returning to Curaçao."

Roy stepped in at once before Captain Morgan could get another word in. "I agree, Ajuban. We need to find out more about this, and every hour that we delay our return to Curaçao is another hour that we remain in the dark. I suggest we return to Curaçao and see what we can find out about McLaughlin's expedition or any other news about Coro. If that yields nothing, and Benito won't crack, we can always sail by the port and take a look. Any fleet there would be hard pressed to catch us."

"No, but they might jus' follow us back to Curaçao an' attack immediately," said Rowling. "It sounds to me like they're nearly ready if the muster be as far along as it sounds, hence the hurry to acquire Valdez. No doubt they hoped the ransom would've been handled by now, an' any delay endangers the secr'cy of such a plan."

"In dat case," said Ajuban, "we may already have received a ransom offer for Benito from Coro. If dey t'ink dat Benito might reveal de plan, dey would certainly want him back as soon as possible, even if he is not personally necessary for de attack. Dey may even have made anoder offer for Valdez as well." The more he thought about it, the more Ajuban believed it extremely likely that they would discover a generous ransom offer awaiting them at Van Kemper's tavern, and the Spanish would be even more determined to recover the funds from the coffers of Curaçao.

"In any case, we should make haste to return to port," Captain Morgan suggested, as though it were his idea all along. "Captains, are we agreed that we will do what we can to find out the truth of the matter and bring it to the attention of Governor Diedrik?"

"Aye," said Roy and Edmund together. Ajuban smirked inwardly. *He really likes to be de center of attention, doesn't he?*

They drained their goblets—though Captain Morgan had long since drained his for the second time—and stood up to exit the cabin. "It was a pleasure to meet both of you," said Roy to Captain Rowling and Jombo as he made ready to climb down to the boat, "and your crew as well."

Ajuban nodded his agreement.

"An' you as well, Cap'n Toppings, Ajuban," Rowling replied with sincerity, shaking both of their hands. "Godspeed to you. I look forward to a drink an' a meal with you both in Curaçao—hopefully in better accommodations."

"I expect Van Kemper will oblige," said Roy.

They climbed down to their boat after making their farewells, Ajuban and Jombo saluting each other's captain. As Ajuban heard Captain Morgan making his farewells in much more grandiose fashion, he found himself more excited to return to Curaçao than anything else, regardless of what news they may hear. Danger or not, he could not help his eagerness to find out the truth of the matter and to plan for what was ahead. *And we have Captains Morgan and Rowling wit' us now.* Ajuban was not usually one to put any stock in divine providence, but meeting up with both captains was about as fortuitous as he could imagine should their suspicions prove to be true. "Captain?" he said, emerging from his thoughts for a moment.

"Yes?" Roy said, yawning a bit. Now that the night's excitement was over, he was obviously feeling the consequences of being roused in the middle of his rest.

"Do you t'ink we should let de crew know our suspicions yet? Some of dem have families in Curaçao." He was especially thinking of Jan who he knew to have a daughter.

Roy thought for a moment, but said, "I think we should tell Governor Diedrik first, and abide by his decision. They are still citizens of Curaçao, and he should have the chance to decide what and when to tell them. However," he added with a grin, "if he chooses not to mention it, well, men do let things slip sometimes when they have had enough ale in them..."

Once again, as they climbed back aboard *The Constance*, Ajuban was reminded that he was exactly where he wanted to be.

Chapter 16: Work for Idle Hands

Marius Gilbertsen was late. He was still hours away from Curaçao and he was sailing into the wind, which was no light breeze. Briefly he considered that if he still had his cargo fluyt, he could not sail into such a wind at all, but it did no good. *If I still had my ship, I would not be in this predicament in the first place.*

He was only just returning from being stranded with the remnant of his crew and one day's provisions. All he had to show for it now was a slightly better longboat than Captain Toppings had left him (as it had sails as well as oars), no crew, and several bags of coffee beans under an oiled canvas in the middle of the boat. He prayed that no one ever found out what he'd done to buy the coffee and make his way back towards Curaçao, but he had not had much choice. Once he made his way home, he would have the means to get a new ship and crew, but getting back had been the truly difficult task.

It was not difficult for him to keep his mind off of it though, as he had new, more uncomfortable things to think about. It was the middle of the night and having miles of ocean within arm's reach in the dark was something that gave him no comfort, but the shiver that stole over him had little enough to do with that. The only reason he was sailing into the wind was that he had diverted from his original plan to sail at high tide through the narrow, shallow channel of the Paraguaná straits. These lay between the coastal peninsula where Coro was located and the "island" north of it, but the two were connected by a sand flat during the hours of low tide. The sand levels seemed to rise year after year, and before long it was entirely possible that there would be no more channel there even at high tide. Marius did not usually use that route unless he was on a tight schedule and had a skilled crew that knew the waters, but he had thought it a better idea while all alone in his tiny boat with no chance of sleep until he reached home. It would probably have shaved half a day off of his journey, but once he had gotten a good look at the Coro harbor from afar, he prudently decided to turn back and take the long way, traveling around both peninsula and island.

What is such a fleet doing in Coro of all places? He had deep misgivings about any possible answers he could come up with, but he was at least sure that it was no treasure fleet that was berthed there. There was not much reason for treasure ships to stop in Coro unless they had been ordered to resupply the town. And by no stretch of the imagination did that require more than one ship, let alone seven of them—one of them a war galleon. He was only grateful that they either had not spotted his little longboat or had considered it not worth pursuing through the straits. He had documentation from his friend Ciro, a customs inspector in Gibraltar, but that would not help him very much if he had stumbled upon some large-scale naval operation that the Spanish wanted kept secret. Now that he had left Coro far behind, he certainly intended that Governor Diedrik should know exactly what devilry was going on less than a day out from his own waters. *Perhaps there will even be a reward for the information.* Marius did not consider himself to be particularly greedy (though it reached his ears that others thought so), but he had suffered heavy financial losses and every ducat that came his way was welcome.

With luck, the weather would remain clement until he reached Curaçao—his boat could not take any kind of rough weather in the open sea—and he would live to tell the tale. And if he did... A new scheme to rebuild his fortunes began to coalesce in his mind, and his worry over the Spanish fleet planted the seeds of new business endeavors where moments before there had grown doubt and bitter frustration.

* * *

The crew was excited to return to Curaçao, and Coya was no exception. She felt like she was returning to a comfortable second home and her mind was at ease.

The arrival of three English privateer ships at once had appeared to put the port authorities on edge until they were sure that there was no attack intended. Men had been mustered aboard the old Spanish warship in the harbor that acted as the town's main line of defense in the water, supporting the fort's cannons. But as they stood down, the customs officials flooded the docks. *They are probably eager for the hefty bribes they can expect us to pay.* Roy had explained how customs officials would no doubt drive a hard bargain out of suspicion that the three ships had conducted some organized raid and returned with a significant amount of trade goods. The captains had little room to negotiate, as their ships were obviously low in the water. They could either pay the steep bribes or pay the still higher taxes and fees that any legal trader must pay.

"Brian, William, Tiede," said the captain loudly, "you take charge of the sale of goods. Enlist whomever you need to from the crew, but remember not to carry anything yourself or to walk very far, Tiede." Tiede had been encouraged to get up and exercise his leg on occasion, but he had been ordered not to strain himself at all. Coya was very relieved that all of the wounded men were supposedly going to recover quickly. She felt sympathy for Tiede for having to limp around and deal with the goods, but the captain had been unable to spare Jan for the task—he was still busy attending to Justin and Ben, and would be moving them to his practice in town. "Albert, Bert, Luuk, you three guard the ship," Roy continued. "Daniel and Martin will relieve you once the goods have been offloaded, assuming that happens in the next few hours. Everyone else make sure to report back here at dusk."

They secured the ship as a customs official approached. "Good day, captain," he said. "Toppings, isn't it? You weren't gone long, but it appears your business went well." He was overtly eyeing the ship's waterline. "Papers, please," he said.

"I think you'll find everything in order," said Roy as he handed over a rolled parchment. Coya could not see how much money the captain had handed him, but there was a distinct *clink* as the scroll was handed over. After some fumbling with it (presumably so that he could unobtrusively pocket the coins), the official opened and read the parchment. Coya knew that it was the very same document that William had forged from the original that they had obtained from Marius Gilbertsen. Doubtless it did not fool the customs official, especially when presented with a bribe, but apparently Roy wished to keep up appearances with so many onlookers eyeing the three ships.

"Right then, standard docking fee of one ducat please," said the official. Evidently he did not consider that the bribe covered that fee, but Roy handed over another coin and smiled. "Thank you, sir," said the man, "Enjoy your stay in Curaçao."

Whatever Roy thought of the transaction, he kept it to himself as he turned to the others. "Right, Ajuban and I have some business to attend to at Van Kemper's tavern if you need to find us," he said. Coya felt sure that he meant the issue of Major Benito and his ransom. "Anyone who is off duty can join us if he wants to. Or if *she* wants to," he added with a wink at Coya. She was glad of the invitation. She had just begun to realize that she had no idea what she would do if she could not tag along, as she spoke no Dutch and was still considered an outcast when not in the company of crewmen, however much she felt she belonged here. It was a lonely thought, but she banished it at once. *Things are certainly better than they were before, at least.* And with that she joined Roy and Ajuban. To her dismay, Daniel joined them as well, but she could not tell if it was because she had or for his own reasons. They had, after all, recruited him at Van Kemper's tavern in the first place. In any case, she was not concerned about his consistent attempts at personal interaction as long as Roy and Ajuban were around. *I will have to meet some new people just to keep myself busy when they go off to deal with Van Kemper though.*

Meeting new people didn't seem as though it would be difficult. The crews of The Swordfish and The Sea Dervish were also disembarking, and many of the men seemed inclined to intermingle after seeing the same faces for days on end at sea. Some of them joined Roy's group, and Coya saw several of his crew head into town with men from Captain Morgan's and Captain Rowling's crews. She had come to understand that sailors loved news and any new stories that promised to be interesting. Surely some of them had been told about Captain Toppings' raid on Caracas, and they would probably want to hear the tale told in full so that they could retell it and embellish on it after several pints of ale. Coya made up her mind to get to know those men who had joined their group, provided that they didn't look at her the way

Daniel did. Perhaps if she made new friends, she would be able to join them from time to time and wouldn't be dependent on Roy and Ajuban and the others for companionship.

Although she had made up her mind to make an effort, the prospect unsettled her. She still was not accustomed to socializing, especially the kind that sailors seemed to enjoy, and she was unlikely to be accepted as readily among others as she was among Roy's crew. She half wished that she could tell the tale of the ransom theft, but Roy didn't want that tale to get about too soon in Curaçao.

As they made their way from the docks, she realized that Roy was motioning for Captains Morgan and Rowling to join them. She sighed inwardly. She had no idea how to behave around other ship captains without standing at attention. Just meeting Henry Morgan had been stressful, especially as Roy had singled her out a little. It seemed like it had a positive effect on Captain Morgan, but she had never been comfortable when she was singled out for anything, even if she was pleased with the reason.

Both captains joined Roy and his group, along with a few other men. Roy made introductions, and Coya was surprised to learn that the Negro accompanying Captain Rowling was his first mate, Jombo. He grinned at her, and she felt just as comfortable as she had when she had first met Roy and Ajuban. *Perhaps being one of these 'Brethren of the Coast' puts me on more of an equal footing than I thought.* "Pleased to meet you," she said, but otherwise kept quiet for the moment as they continued on their way to Van Kemper's tavern.

"Did you see the small Spanish sloop, *El Picaflor,* berthed in the harbor?" asked Captain Rowling.

"No," said Roy, looking troubled, "I was preoccupied. I wonder if she's here about the ransom."

"I would be surprised if she weren't," said Captain Morgan. "We shall find out soon enough, I'll warrant."

"She was farther down the docks," said Rowling, "but she was flagged as a diplomatic vessel."

"Just like Benito's ship, *La Fortuna,*" said Roy. The others nodded, though Coya had no idea whether or not that was normal. "I thought at the time that it was odd that an issue of ransom should warrant diplomatic license, but perhaps he had other business with Governor Diedrik that the governor did not disclose to me."

"I reckon you were right that the Spanish wished to ensure that Benito couldn't be seized or prosecuted should he run into any trouble," said Captain Rowling, clearly referring to some conversation they had held previously.

"I think that is most likely," said Captain Morgan. He sounded very sure, but Roy and Captain Rowling said no more.

Coya was confused by all of this, but she had not been privy to anything the captains had discussed when they met each other at sea. Nevertheless, since she was supposedly off duty and free to be herself, she asked, "But why would they expect him to run into trouble handling a ransom? Or why should they take such a precaution if they did expect it?"

"Ah, we will have some things to explain, I suppose," said Roy in a low voice. "For now, just let me say that we are concerned that the Spanish are mustering troops in Coro and that they might attack Curaçao. It's possible that they wanted Valdez to help them, and that's why Benito was sent with such an exorbitant amount to ransom him. We're going to try to persuade Benito to tell us what the situation is. To answer your question, if the Spaniards were desperate enough to break Valdez out of Van Kemper's tavern in the event that the ransom failed, they might have given Benito diplomatic status so that he could not be held if he were caught. They would not want him to be questioned, if they were planning an attack. You should keep all of this to yourself for now though."

Coya was pleased that she felt she had understood all of what the captain had said, though she had some pieces of it before now, but she would have given a great deal to have been present when all of them had discussed these things previously. *I wonder if I'll ever be included in those discussions.* It seemed clear that only the captains and their officers had discussed these matters, and Roy was open enough with her to fill her in on the basic facts, but she wished for still more. "How are you going to persuade Benito to tell you anything?" she asked quietly. She did not think that Benito was likely to tell them anything willingly. The expression that came over Roy's face though, as well as the looks he shared with the others, made her wonder for the first time if he would actually force the information from Benito. She had no real reason to think that he wouldn't, but it was hard to imagine such things from him.

"We will just have to find a way," said Roy, "but I may be forced to compel him to tell us." She wondered if he would go so far as to do so himself, but her recollection of Ajuban's story about Roy's feelings over his dead sister and her memory of his ferocious attack on the two Spaniards in Port Royal left her with few illusions that he was above it. She was not sure how she felt about that. Although she had no love for the Spaniards, torture was against her experience and instincts. She found herself thinking once again how Ispaca and Challco had been refreshing reminders of what her own people believed in and how they behaved, and she told herself that she must not forget it again.

"I seem to recall," interjected Captain Morgan, "that Van Kemper has a man in his employ who is somewhat experienced in such methods of questioning captives. Perhaps Van Kemper might lend us his services."

"For a price, no doubt," said Captain Rowling, "if I know Van Kemper at all."

"I think he will be reluctant to damage a hostage," said Jombo, "for fear that it might negeete any ransom deal, or at least lower the value of the hostage."

"I suppose we can only ask," said Roy, pragmatic as usual, "and see what Van Kemper says. We will soon find out for ourselves, it seems." He gestured ahead, and there they saw Van Kemper's tavern down the street. "Remember," he said to Coya, Ajuban and Jombo, "you should not reveal our suspicions in public. We want to bring this to Governor Diedrik before any tales are spun. We don't want to cause a panic." Coya was unlikely to be asked to tell of any news or tales anyway, but she had not considered that point. She was unused to thinking about the effect that her actions or words would have on local society because she was so often left out of society, but Jombo looked a little crestfallen that he would be robbed of a good piece of gossip to share over a pint of ale.

In short order, they filed into the tavern and found a table large enough to accommodate them all. They were quickly served by a young woman that Coya recognized from her previous daytime visit to the tavern a week before, and soon they were enjoying what once again seemed to be a fine feast. She listened to what the others discussed, particularly as an excuse to ignore Daniel when he tried to engage her in conversation. When some of the other crew from Rowling's and Morgan's ships left the table and made their way closer to the bar, she excused herself and joined them. They appeared surprised, but not annoyed, so she did her best to engage in conversation after listening to them share gossip with others in the place. To her delight, she found that a couple of the crew had heard of her already. She quickly realized, however, that the reason for this was something perhaps best left undiscussed in Van Kemper's tavern—or in Curaçao at all.

"She's the one who made off with a pretty penny what was goin' to be paid in ransom by the Spaniards," said one of them to some local friend of his. "Cap'n Morgan told us we should be gettin' our share o' the ransom soon, but 'e didn't reckon with 'er stealin' it first."

She didn't know if she should try to stop them talking about it or not, but she was too near the bar and Van Kemper's staff might hear. She felt pleased in spite of herself, but before she could say anything, one of the others said, "How did he take it when he found out?"

"Oh, 'e said 'e thought it was a gran' joke on 'im," said the first man, "an' a load off 'is min' (though 'e didn't explain what 'e meant by it), but that it was a wonderful blow to the Spaniards. Besides, 'e's still got the man locked up an' won't let 'im go without the ransom." Coya was pleased to see that they had the presence of mind to lower their voices whenever the bartender was near, but she felt it was only a matter of time before they let something slip. *I'd better make sure I can get out of here and back to the ship in a hurry if Van Kemper's men come after me.* She was more worried about them than the soldiers, since Roy had made it sound as if Governor Diedrik suspected him and his crew of stealing the ransom anyway, but she would watch out for the town guard as well.

"Well, we thought that it was fair game until it was paid," she said with a smile. "Besides, we didn't know which captain the ransom was to be paid to."

The others laughed and one of them called over a few friends who had just entered. "Oi! Bill! Ronald! Come and meet some friends of ours." *Oh no.* Coya resigned herself to being the center of attention for the present, but she was determined to move such talk away from the bar if at all possible. *Why here? Why now?* At any other time and place she would have welcomed the camaraderie in spite of the amount of attention she was receiving, but it seemed that it was just her lot to have *some* reason to feel awkward and uncomfortable whenever she spoke to new people. She noticed Roy and Morgan getting up to speak quietly to the bartender. She could not hear what Roy said, but she did not doubt that it was something like, "I need to speak to the landlord about a mutual associate." Sure enough, soon afterwards she saw Van Kemper emerge from the back and lead the two captains through a door into a back room somewhere. Daniel immediately turned his gaze towards her, but she turned back to the men she was speaking with and he kept his distance, making his way to another table. *At least they're keeping him away.* But she was worried that by the time Roy came back, the tale of the ransom theft would be all over the common room. "So has anyone heard how Sir Sebastian's venture turned out?" she asked, trying to change the subject.

"No," said one with a worried look, "he has not returned yet."

"Relax," said another man, "he's probably taken over the town and is still celebrating before he leaves. He took a fair number of men with him, and Coro has few defenses."

"I thought he was only interested in plundering it," said another. "Coro has few comforts as well—little enough to make it more appealing a place to celebrate than here."

"Well, here he would have to pay for lodgings, food and drink…" And so the discussion went on. As more men gathered around, Coya successfully led them to a table further from the bar and did her best to remember names and participate in the merrymaking, but her presence seemed to encourage the retelling of the ransom theft and she was asked no less than three times to tell it herself.

"I don't know what the landlord would think of that tale being told here," she had said. "He was supposed to receive the ransom, and I don't want to sour our business relations with him." That had not stopped others from telling it, however, and telling a much more grandiose and unbelievable tale than was actually the truth of the matter. *No doubt they are hoping I will jump in and correct them by telling it myself.* She supposed that was how some gossip was started, but she eventually made an excuse and made her way back to the bar alone.

She felt good about her attempts to get to know the other sailors, but she was glad to be on her own once more. She watched as Roy and Captain Morgan came into the common room, but they did not stay. They waved Captain Rowling and Ajuban over discreetly and then made their way to a door that Coya knew led to stairs up to the second storey. Ajuban had discovered that hostages were kept in rooms up there, and no doubt they were going to speak to Benito. A large man that Coya had seen speaking with Van Kemper from time to time led the way. She sat alone for a few minutes watching that door every so often as it was close to where she sat. Then she turned and saw Daniel heading her way, and her relief turned to frustration once again. *Why can't he leave me alone?* She resisted the urge to fondle the knife at her hip, but at that moment she heard a door slam very close to her by the bar—the same door that the three captains had gone through only a couple of minutes earlier—and all eyes turned to the sound. Relieved that she was saved from Daniel's attentions once again, she turned towards the sound as well and found that perhaps Daniel's attentions might have been a better situation to deal with…

* * *

"I'm sorry to say," Willem van Kemper began in frustrated tones, hoping that this would convey both the appropriate sympathy and outrage at the crime, "that the ransom that was to be paid for your prisoner, Captain Morgan, was stolen off of the Spanish ship delivering it."

"It's all right," said Captain Morgan, "Roy here told me his tale already, and I am at least relieved that Colonel Valdez is still in custody after the incident." Captain Toppings said nothing, but looked slightly embarrassed at this. *And well that he should, after trying to wheedle a reward out of the situation.* Willem still felt somewhat bitter about the entire affair of Benito's ransom and being forced to answer questions at the fort, and Captain Toppings made a convenient object for his irritation, though he realized that the captain was not really at fault. "In the meantime," continued Morgan, "I ask that you retain Colonel Valdez until another offer of ransom is made, if you would be so kind."

"Well then, captain, I think you're in for a treat," Willem replied. "A new ransom offer came in just this morning, along with one for Major Benito," he said briefly turning to address Captain Toppings as politely as he could. "Captain Arroyo of *El Picaflor* paid me a visit as soon as his ship arrived. Eight thousand pesos has been put forward as the final offer for Valdez, and in light of the recent theft, I strongly advise you to take it, Captain Morgan."

"And what for Benito?" asked Toppings, and Captain Morgan looked on in interest.

"Five thousand pesos, captain," said Willem, "though there is a special condition in his case." Willem still did not know the ultimate goal of the condition that had been specified, but the intention to keep Benito from being tortured was quite clear. *What are they worried he will reveal?* He supposed it was something to do with some military campaign that Valdez would be needed for, but no one in Curaçao was likely to care except to sell the information to someone who *would* care. "The condition is that Major Benito shows no sign of ill treatment."

Captain Toppings did not react with quite the amount of surprise Willem had expected. "I see," he said. "Five thousand pesos is a lot to offer, but clearly they have some purpose for him and don't want him talking about it to anyone."

"That was my read on it as well, sir," said Willem. "Nevertheless, I trust it won't be an issue. The ship is still in the port awaiting an answer on both ransom offers. I would like to agree, but I wouldn't want to overstep my authority." He would be glad when this business was all over. He would receive less of a commission on Valdez than if the ten thousand had been paid, but what he would make from Benito would more than compensate for the loss and trouble.

"I'm afraid I cannot make an answer regarding this offer until I have spoken to Benito," said Captain Toppings, and all hope of the matter being resolved quickly and easily fled from Willem's thoughts.

They know something. It was clear now that these English captains had some information or some worry and wanted answers from the captives, but Willem was running out of patience. "Sir," he said diplomatically, "I strongly advise that you accept this offer. Benito is not likely to divulge anything willingly, and from what I've seen of him, I'm doubtful he will divulge anything under compulsion either."

"Nevertheless, I mean to try," said Toppings. "For that purpose, I wondered if I might purchase the services of your interrogator. Captain Morgan tells me that the man knows his business."

Oh he'd like my help rendering Benito worthless to me, eh? Willem was livid, but he kept his voice cool and collected. "Of course I can hire him out to you, captain," he said with forced courtesy, "for one thousand pesos."

"*What?*" said Captain Morgan indignantly, but Captain Toppings checked his own reaction.

"May I ask the reason for such a sum?" asked Toppings after briefly composing himself. There was no trace of anger in his voice.

"Simply put, captain," Willem began, as he abandoned any attempt at tact, "you are asking me to offer my help in rendering Benito valueless as a prisoner, and thus to give up my share of his ransom. If you want to ignore the condition stipulated by the Spaniards, then that is up to you. However, if you do so, you must take him off my hands or compensate me yourself. If you want my *help* in compelling information from Benito, you must pay me my share of the ransom, which is one thousand pesos under the current offer. Take it or leave it."

"Very well," said Captain Toppings, "I shall pay you one thousand pesos for the services of your interrogator. After we are done, we will take Benito into custody...provided that is acceptable to the benefactor of this arrangement."

Willem was quite surprised that Toppings had accepted his offer, though it put him in no better frame of mind. By "the benefactor of this arrangement," Toppings had clearly been referring to Governor Diedrik. Diedrik presumably had his own reasons for wanting Benito under lock and key, and he might very well turn down Toppings' request to take charge of him. In that case, Willem would be stuck with him for an indeterminate amount of time, even though he could expect no more profit to come of it. "I would advise you not to bring any further prisoners for me to take charge of in the future, captain," he said, though he accepted the gold that Captain

Toppings handed over.

"Agreed," said Toppings, and Willem could tell from the note creeping into Toppings' tone and the expression on his face that he was no more likely to seek out Willem's business in such matters than Willem was to accept it.

He stormed off and fetched his interrogator, returning in short order. Both captains broke off some discussion they were having as he entered again, and he found he resented being kept in the dark when his own interests were at stake as well. "And you, Captain Morgan," he said, ignoring Captain Toppings for the moment, "do you accept the offer of ransom for Colonel Valdez?"

"I very probably will," Morgan said reassuringly, "but I must see what comes of this interrogation first, and then speak with the governor. At that point, I shall return and give my answer. If the governor agrees, we may also tell you the reasons for these actions at that time." Willem felt a bit more at ease at these words. *So, they are keeping silent at the governor's wishes, or out of respect for his position.* Willem respected Governor Diedrik, and that made it easier to accept his current situation, and he also valued Captain Morgan's business, so he simply nodded and turned back to Captain Toppings.

"This is Wouter," he said, gesturing to the hulking interrogator at his side. "He speaks no English, but if you want him to handle the prisoner, just gesture to him like this." Willem gestured from Wouter to an empty chair as if a prisoner were sitting there. Wouter made no acknowledgement of the gesture, as he knew that Willem was simply explaining his methods. "Each time you do so, he will increase the level of compulsion he employs, up to a point. You may not know ahead of time how he will escalate things each time, but that makes him more effective as long as the prisoner is *aware* that you don't know what Wouter will do next. The rest is up to you." With that, he turned around and walked rudely from his office, though he heard one of them mutter something about fetching Captain Rowling and some other person. He had dealt with the two of them as much as he was inclined to at the moment, and he had instructed Wouter to take them up to Benito's room. He felt frustrated and disgusted with the turn of events, but with luck, he would not have to be bothered with either Valdez or Benito for much longer.

* * *

Manuel Benito felt excited that freedom was at last within his grasp. After nearly a week of feverish work during his mealtimes and constant waiting the rest of the time, he had finally completed the task he had set himself. The bit of potato he had left on his breakfast plate that morning would probably be the last, though he still thought it best to wait for the next morning to make his escape. His daily routine had not changed, and it still seemed that he heard the fewest sounds of activity during his morning meal than at any of his other mealtimes. He heard activity from the streets, of course, but he was not worried about being captured once he made it out of the building, and no single person he might run into was likely to be a match for him if they tried to stop him. *I'll at least have that big fellow Van Kemper has bringing my meals.* The man had clearly been chosen for his size and strength, but he was doubtless the biggest obstacle that Manuel would have to face in escaping as long as he did so at breakfast.

He was so fed up with his comfortable little prison cell that he had half a mind to escape the next time the door opened, but he had forced himself to be patient for one more day. It only made patience more difficult when he heard at breakfast that a ransom had been offered that morning, and that it was forthcoming on condition that he show no signs of ill treatment. *Couldn't the admiral have come up with something a bit less transparent?* But Manuel supposed that there were few ways to specify such a condition without giving anything away. The mission was becoming more compromised with each passing day, and the sooner he got out of his prison and back to Coro, the better their chances of success would be.

As he stood staring out between the bars on his window, he was pulled away from his plans by the sound of the slide cover being pulled back on his door. It was the big fellow, Wouter, and he was peering in to make sure Manuel was away from the door as he always did before entering. It was not a meal time, and Manuel wondered what this visit was about, but as the key was turned in the lock and the door opened, he saw that Wouter was followed by four men, all of them armed. The tall Negro was the one who had rendered him unconscious after he had broken into Van Kemper's tavern, but one of the others looked familiar as well. Manuel did not have to wonder who it was for very long. After the door was shut once again—though Manuel noted that it was not locked—the man spoke. "Major Benito," he said stepping forward beside Wouter, "we have not been formally introduced, but I am Captain Roy Toppings." So this was the man who was ultimately responsible for his incarceration. Manuel had only seen him briefly when they were brought to the fort after his failed attempt to rescue Valdez from Van Kemper's tavern. Captain Toppings gestured to the others as he introduced them, "This is Captain Henry Morgan, Captain Edmund Rowling, and my first mate, Ajuban."

Manuel had heard of Edmund Rowling, and of course Henry Morgan who had captured Colonel Valdez. They were two of the most notorious privateers in the Caribbean, and he had a sinking feeling that their purpose in visiting him was not to tell him that the offer for his ransom would be accepted. "And what do you want of me?" he asked politely. Whatever his situation, he prided himself that he was rarely one to initiate any breech of protocol or manners, and then only in the line of duty.

"We have questions to put to you concerning certain military activities in Coro," said Captain Toppings. "You will answer these questions as truthfully as possible. Wouter here is present to make sure that you comply, though I would prefer that his presence here remain unnecessary."

They know. Manuel was sure they had somehow found out about the forces gathering in Coro. The possibility of that discovery had not in itself been of primary concern when the plan was conceived, but the moment that he had been captured, keeping that information secret had become vitally important. Now he was in exactly the position he had worried about. It was for that reason that he had suggested Valdez not be told about the mission until his services had been secured, even before Valdez had ever been captured. Now they were going to try to torture answers out of him, and while he was determined that this should not succeed, he would do better to avoid the situation entirely. *So much for waiting until breakfast.* "What is it that you'd like to know?" he said as he sat down in his chair with a resigned sigh.

Wouter came closer so that he stood across the narrow table, close enough to strike Manuel should he be directed to do so. The others moved closer as well, and Roy began speaking, but Manuel was ready. He had gripped the table leg next to him in his right hand after he sat down, and now he ripped it clean off, sprang from his chair and struck Wouter hard across the face with the pine table leg, rendering him senseless. Before the others could react, he flipped the table up, knocking Captains Toppings and Morgan to the floor and sending Ajuban reeling backwards.

For many days, Manuel had been planning this, but his plan had been to deal with Wouter alone and make his escape down the stairs and out of the building. He had initially pulled the table legs nearest the chair away from the wooden floor at the bottom, pressing the timbers back into place as much as he could. If anyone were to bump the table, it would remain in place, but with two of the legs detached, he could easily flip the light table over. After that, at every mealtime, he had eaten as fast as he could and used the thick iron spoon to file through the top of the table leg just to the right of his chair. It took days, and the process left a larger and larger indent in the wood of the table leg. He found, however, that the potatoes he was fed each day (and for almost every meal) were roughly the same color as the pine leg, so he had patched the leg with some of them and renewed the patch each time he was given fresh potatoes, leaving the old ones on his plate to be taken away. The wood shavings were easy enough to conceal in the room, and he was thankful that no one had closely inspected any of the furniture since he had begun working on his escape plan. He was sure it all would have worked very well, but he was only just too late to take full advantage of the situation. Now he had five men to deal with instead of one, and he was quite sure that he had only felled the least dangerous of them with his makeshift weapon.

Manuel made to dash around the fallen table, but Captain Rowling drew his blade and began to fence with him. Manuel was good with a blade, and the table leg was about the right balance and weight in his hand, but it was shorter and less resilient—not to mention blunt. It was all he could do to fend off Captain Rowling's attacks, and in the meantime the others were recovering from his initial assault. Out of desperation, he grabbed for Captain Rowling's wrist and shoved him with all his might backwards. It wasn't much of a delay, but it got Rowling out of the way. Now the only thing that stood between him and the door was Ajuban, and he had a debt to repay to Ajuban for capturing him in the first place. Ajuban was fumbling for a pistol, and the only thing that Manuel could think to do was to charge at him with the table leg held out like a spear. It caught Ajuban dead center in the chest, and Manuel found himself briefly wishing that the leg were a bit more pointed as Ajuban fell and he made it to the door.

He could hear the sound of pursuit close behind him as he opened the door and ran down the stairs three at a time, jumping the last several steps. He knew the door at the bottom opened outwards, but to buy himself another second or two, he turned and threw his improvised club at his closest pursuer. Captain Rowling shielded himself with his arms, but the attack delayed him long enough for Manuel to kick open the door and run through. He could see the front door leading to the street, and all of the patrons in the common room looked surprised. He doubted that any of them would have the presence of mind to stop him before he made it out, even if they had any inkling that they should try to. *Almost there, just a few more yards...* And then he felt a sharp pain in his right leg as something sliced into it and he fell to the floor. He looked down at his leg and there was the hilt of a small knife sticking out of it. The pain was excruciating, and he was glad that his pursuers did not trip over him. He looked around for his assailant, and it appeared that a small native woman sitting at the bar had drawn and thrown a knife at him with barely any hesitation. She was *still* sitting at the bar!

At that point, Manuel found that he was surrounded, and he gave up thinking about anything but his maimed leg. The rest of the patrons looked on in alarm, and he supposed that none of them knew what to make of the situation, even if they guessed that he was a prisoner, but he didn't care. *So much for escaping.* Captain Rowling and Captain Toppings hoisted him up, and he winced as the knife shifted in his leg. "Coya, go and get Jan," said Captain Toppings.

"I'm not sure where he is," said the native woman, who was now standing behind Captain Toppings as they hoisted him back towards the door and the stairs.

"Never mind, I'll fetch Van Kemper and he can send someone. He'd probably prefer that anyway."

Manuel was hoisted back up the stairs and the sounds of frantic activity and gossip over this latest incident faded into the distance. "Van Kemper is definitely not going to like this," said Captain Morgan.

"I don't care what he likes," said Toppings. "He's been paid, and his man didn't help us at all so far." They set Manuel down on his bed, and Captain Toppings stood in front of him now. "You're still going to tell us what we want to know," he said to Manuel. "We're sending for a doctor to treat your leg, but there will be no more opportunities to escape." Manuel said nothing as they withdrew. They took Wouter and Ajuban with them and locked the door, leaving him alone again. If they really meant to torture him, the wound in his leg would probably be the least of his problems. They had left the knife in, probably to keep from aggravating the wound more, but he knew that they would make sure he wasn't about to wield it against them when they came back. There wasn't much he could hope to do now but to sit and wait. With any luck, the admiral would get things moving without further delay after receiving his answer about the ransom offers. Perhaps since he was injured, and the payment would not therefore be made for him, the admiral would do just that. Nevertheless, his leg throbbed along with his pulse. *I wish that doctor would hurry up.*

* * *

Roy was relieved to find that Ajuban, while badly bruised, had not suffered much more than a few fractures. He wanted to throttle Benito, but he still had questions that he wanted answered. He was glad to have Jan at hand to treat both Ajuban and Major Benito, but he had instructed Jan not to tend to Wouter without payment. "This would have happened without our presence there, from what I understand," he had said, "and I don't think tending to the man for free after paying a thousand pesos for his help is a very fair deal." Jan accepted this line of reasoning, and Van Kemper was obliged to pay for Wouter's treatment after much argument. Roy's initial business relations with Van Kemper had gone smoothly, but he was becoming less and less fond of the man. *He reminds me of that snake, Gilbertsen.*

Jan had tended Benito's wound with skill, and Benito had been as stoic about it as could be expected with such a vicious wound. Jan was now tending to Ajuban's bandages while Roy spoke with the other captains by Ajuban's bedside. "I think we should speak with Guv'nor Diedrik," said Captain Rowling. "This latest incident means that the ransom will not be paid, an' it may mean that the Spanish will fear they have been compromised as well. If they decide to take some sort of action, Guv'nor Diedrik should be warned about the possibility."

"I don't know," said Captain Morgan, "I would hate to bother him with speculation when we could get what we want out of Benito and *then* go to the governor with solid information."

"If Benito will give it to us at all," said Roy. He had seen men like Major Benito before, and he recognized a dedicated soldier when he saw one. On top of that, Benito was stoic, resourceful and intelligent. Men such as he were not easily swayed, and although he was not against trying, he felt it might simply be a waste of time.

"All the more reason to try now," said Morgan. "He is still recovering from his wound and is at his weakest. If he is going to crack at all, it will be while he is weak." *The man knows far too much about compulsion and intimidation for my liking.* Roy had the feeling that Captain Morgan resorted to such techniques rather earlier than was strictly necessary in these situations.

"Eider way," interjected Ajuban from his bed, "won't de governor want to know how de deal he arranged is going?"

Morgan looked annoyed, but it was Jan who spoke up. "From what I know of how Governor Diedrik operates, he will most certainly want to hear any information you have as soon as possible, if it is likely to be of any concern to him." Jan had only just become aware of what their concerns were, but he appeared to be keeping a cool head about it in spite of the potential danger to Curaçao. It was not strictly proper for him to be participating in the discussion without being invited, but only Captain Morgan seemed to mind.

"Besides," said Roy, "the governor specifically asked me to keep him apprised of any news that might concern him. I think he sensed that Benito was up to something in the first place."

"Well, you'd better have someone keep an eye on the major in the meantime," said Captain Morgan.

"He's locked up in his room now," Roy said. "I told Van Kemper not to send up any meals or open the door for any reason without my instructions or presence there." Roy didn't want to risk Benito trying some new escape plan, and Van Kemper had obviously not been very thorough about checking on him previously, or he would have noticed what Benito had been doing. Now the broken furniture had been removed from Benito's room, but Roy wouldn't count on him resigning himself to waiting around until they came back to question him, however wounded he was.

After a bit more discussion, it was decided that they should all speak to the governor and Captain Toppings made his way downstairs again followed by the others. Ajuban was left on his own in the bed that they had rented from Van Kemper, but Coya was still waiting in the common room along with a great many others who were curious to find out what had been going on upstairs in Van Kemper's tavern. Roy motioned for her to fall in and follow them out the door. He didn't want everyone listening in on their conversation, and she still looked as though she was worried that she had done something wrong. "Don't worry," he said once they had gone some distance from the tavern, "you did very well to stop Benito from escaping. I was merely going to ask you to check back at the ship and see if there is any news about how the sale of goods is coming along."

Coya looked relieved. "Of course, sir," she said.

"Jan, you should return to any duties you have for the time being, but I intend to come back to Van Kemper's tavern after the three of us pay our visit to Governor Diedrik."

"Aye sir," said Jan, though he seemed regretful that he was not going with them to speak with the governor. *I wonder if Diedrik knows that one of his surgeons has turned privateer aboard an English ship.* It had not previously occurred to Roy that the governor would probably know when a local surgeon became unavailable, but he supposed that it was unlikely anyone in authority knew exactly *why* Jan was unavailable.

Roy began to seek for a coach to bring the three of them up to the governor's mansion, but Coya put a hand on his arm. "Captain," she said, "is Ajuban going to be all right?" Roy and Jan had neglected to let her know the extent of his injuries.

"Yes, he will be all right," said Roy, "but he took quite a blow to the chest with that table leg." She looked at him curiously, as she had not heard the story of what had happened yet. "Long story," he said, "but Benito's wound has also been treated and he is being kept under lock and key, so if you see him up and about somehow, don't hesitate to hobble him again."

Captain Rowling laughed at that, and Coya smiled and made as if to depart, but hesitated once again. "Captain," she said in a low voice, "I heard that McLaughlin's expedition has not yet returned. I thought you would wish to know."

"Thank you, Coya," said Roy and dismissed her. She made a salute to all of them and made her way back to *The Constance*. "Well *that's* not a good sign," he said to the others.

"Come, let's continue on," said Rowling. "The day's growin' shorter."

They hired a coach and bounced along the bumpy road up the hill to the governor's house. Morning was already passing into afternoon, and Roy had not yet had a proper rest or refreshment beyond dabbing on some cologne, but he wanted time to figure out what should be done before that Spanish vessel in the harbor departed for Coro, and for that he needed more information.

They rode in silence until they reached the governor's house, as they did not wish the driver to overhear any of their conversation. They saw another coach waiting outside as they neared the house, and when they arrived and stepped down from their own coach, they instructed that their driver wait as well. "I shouldn't think this will take long," said Morgan.

They approached the footman at the door, but they were told first by him and then by the butler that the governor was busy with another guest. "Please inform him that Captains Toppings, Morgan and Rowling wish to see him about an urgent matter," said Roy. "We are content to wait here, if that is his wish."

"Very well sirs, this way," said the butler. He led them to a sitting room and left to inform his master of their presence. Not even a minute passed before he came back, however. "Please follow me," he said, "the governor will see you now."

Roy had seen no one leave and he half wondered if he could expect to see the captain of the Spanish vessel in the harbor come storming out just as he had experienced on his previous visit a week before. However, when they approached Diedrik's office and the butler announced them, the door opened onto a very unwelcome sight. Marius Gilbertsen stood there with a look of triumph on his face. *Uh-oh.* Roy knew that he would be lucky not to be hauled off to the fort and imprisoned immediately after his interview. Diedrik motioned for his butler to close the door. "Well gentlemen, we have much to discuss, it seems," he said.

Chapter 17: Needs Must

"That's him, governor," said Marius Gilbertsen pointing directly at Roy, "he's the one who attacked my ship!" *How did he get back here so fast?* It had barely been a week since Roy left Gilbertsen in a longboat with the remnant of his crew in the Maracaibo Lagoon, and here he was again, apparently none the worse for the experience.

"So I gathered," said the governor with a hint of boredom, though Roy wished that he could read the man's mind. "Would you care to explain yourself, captain?"

Roy saw no sense in denying his actions, but nothing he could say would likely make his situation any better. "Sir, I saw a ship flying Dutch colors in the Maracaibo Lagoon. Whether it was flying false colors or not, I had to assume that it was a smuggler ship." Smugglers were generally considered fair game for privateers and pirates, but Curaçao depended on smugglers heavily, and even in more lawful colonies, attacking any but pirate or enemy ships was ill-considered. Governor Diedrik was unlikely to be sympathetic to Roy's argument, though hopefully Diedrik had as little love for Captain Gilbertsen as everyone else seemed to.

Gilbertsen looked as if he would protest, but the governor cut him off. "Captain Gilbertsen was unable to show legal documentation?" he asked.

"He showed documentation with official Spanish markings," said Roy, "but none bearing any Dutch seal of approval." That was perfectly true. Whether or not Gilbertsen had found some legal (or at least discreet) way of trading with Spanish colonies, he had obviously neglected to go through legal Dutch channels. In Curaçao it wouldn't be necessary anyway, and would be far more expensive than paying the bribes to customs officials, but Roy hoped that the oversight meant Governor Diedrik was under no obligation to protect Gilbertsen's interests. *At which point, I still have to give him reason not to do so anyway.* Depending on the importance of the information he was there to impart, Roy might just get off with a stern lecture or a fine. He glanced over at his companions, but they stood as impassively as possible, waiting for some kind of resolution to this unexpected development. Rowling's lips quivered briefly as he glanced over at Roy, but he maintained his composure. *At least* someone's *enjoying this.*

Gilbertsen looked uncomfortable now, in his turn. Of course he had been smuggling goods and no one in Curaçao was likely to mind, but even so, no trader would want it declared openly that he was a smuggler in front of the authorities. "Well, we will leave that matter for later," said Diedrik, looking from Gilbertsen to Toppings and seeming a bit pleased with himself. "Does the news that you three bring involve the activities and situation of Major Benito? He has not been heard from for many days." Rowling and Morgan looked confused for a moment, but Roy had realized quickly that the governor was still maintaining the pretense that he had no knowledge of what happened to Major Benito after he had been "released" from the fort. Whether this was for Gilbertsen's benefit or was due to the presence of so many witnesses was unclear, but Roy was willing to play along.

"We have come to believe," Roy said before his companions could put indiscreet words to their confusion, "that he has been trying to enlist the aid of Colonel Javier Valdez for a military campaign, and that Spain is worried about the mission being compromised in Major Benito's absence." Rowling and Morgan appeared to have understood his discretion, so he continued. "We know that there has been a military build-up in Coro of late, and we are concerned about the possibility that this force may be aimed at Curaçao."

"You can confirm this military activity, Captain Gilbertsen?" asked the governor, turning to the still flushed Dutchman.

"Yes sir," he said, eyeing Roy with even greater dislike. *No doubt he wanted to be solely responsible for bringing this news.* Nevertheless, Roy was surprised by what Gilbertsen said next. "There were seven large ships in the harbor, and many soldiers moving about the docks."

"What sort of ships?" asked Captain Rowling.

"Four barques, two galleons and a war galleon," said Gilbertsen matter-of-factly, though apparently too annoyed to look at Captain Rowling.

"Was there any sign of recent battle?" asked Roy, thinking of Sir Sebastian's expedition.

"None that I saw," replied Gilbertsen in even greater tones of annoyance.

"What makes you think that this force is destined for Curaçao?" asked the governor, turning back to Roy and his companions.

"The amnesty," answered Captain Morgan. "The area covered by it includes the entire area around Curaçao and ships carrying troops to Coro would cause much less comment. People might simply think that they were patrolling or enforcing the terms of the amnesty. However, now that we have heard of this latest information about ships gathering in Coro, I would also point out that they must be *sailing* these troops somewhere rather than marching them, and any target other than Curaçao that they could have chosen would be much closer to others of their ports than to Coro. They would surely have chosen to muster at one of those rather than risk ill weather or discovery by taking a longer journey to their destination."

"Unless a fleet would be more easily noticed at these other locations," said the governor. Roy found that highly unlikely, but Diedrik added, "Nevertheless, I admit that what you say makes the most sense."

Gilbertsen looked alarmed, but Roy was surprised when he addressed the governor, "Sir, if you have no further questions or need of my presence, I have matters that I must tend to. I've no doubt that these fine gentlemen"—he glared at Roy—"have more experience with such matters than I."

Roy observed him closely. Gilbertsen apparently wanted to leave without even suggesting that Roy be hauled away in irons for attacking his ship, and that seemed suspicious in the extreme. *He wants to tell someone what he has heard.* If it was true, Gilbertsen could cause a panic. Rumor left far more room for fear than a formal announcement would.

"You may withdraw," said the governor, "but I command you not to speak of this matter to anyone, nor to disclose what you have seen of Coro. I will address the issue as I see fit." Clearly Governor Diedrik had arrived at the same conclusion as Roy.

But Gilbertsen agreed at once and bid his farewells to those present, with the exception of Roy (for which not even Roy blamed him). "He's up to no good," Roy muttered after the door had closed again.

"Very probably," said Diedrik, "but that is not your concern. You are lucky that I am not ordering your arrest here and now." The governor's tone was heavy and displeased, but Roy felt a great deal of tension leave him. If the governor was not threatening imprisonment already, he was unlikely to impose any significant punitive measures at all. Roy knew it would be wise to remain as helpful as possible though. "What I have to worry about now," continued the governor, "is what to make of this situation. Do you have more detailed information for me? You may all be frank now that Captain Gilbertsen is no longer present."

They told him all they could about what the Spanish soldiers had said, about the terms of the amnesty according to the conversation Roy had had with Captain Torres, and the weapons that Roy's crew had captured from the mule train. They even gave an account of Benito's escape attempt, but no one gave any hint that Roy and his crew had stolen the ransom money. "I understand from Major Benito," said Roy, "that Colonel Valdez was to be taken to Coro as well."

The governor looked at him shrewdly, but he felt that the information was important enough to share, even if he could not be honest about how he had obtained it. In any case, Governor Diedrik had already guessed that Roy might have been involved in the ransom theft and had simply cautioned him not to let it become public knowledge. "Do you know who is in command of the fleet in Coro?" asked the governor looking straight at him this time.

"I believe that Admiral Sergio Cadiz commands it," he said, remembering the document that had accompanied the ransom—the document he had since burned.

Diedrik sat for several moments with his hands steepled together, thinking and looking at no one in particular. Presently he focused on them again. "I thank you for bringing this to my attention," he said. "Now I must ask if any of you are willing to help rid me of this threat." He looked pointedly at Roy, and Roy suddenly felt sure that he would be thrown into a cell if he refused.

Nevertheless, he looked to his companions, and Captain Rowling raised the issue that they had previously agreed should be addressed. "We may be willin' to put our services at your disposal," he said, "but we must agree to terms."

The governor looked as if he had expected no less. "As for you, Captain Toppings, part of your reward should you agree to aid the town will be my refusal to incarcerate you or fine you for your attack on Captain Gilbertsen's ship. However, any of you that render tangible military aid against this threat shall plunder what you like from your enemies according to the terms of your existing contracts with the acting governor of Jamaica or anyone else that you are indebted to, and you shall be welcome in Curaçao—so long as you do not attack any of our ships."

Roy smiled faintly at that, but he had little choice in the matter. He had either to help Governor Diedrik or leave his house in irons. *Seven warships!* It was quite a challenge, and his ship was far too small for him to feel secure about tangling with any warships. Any one of them would outgun him at least twice over, no matter how well Brian steered the ship. However, the governor's offer was a fair one and the other two captains were inclined to agree to it. Should they be successful, there would exist neither threat nor plunder as far as Diedrik was concerned, and he need have no inconvenient official ties to the matter. In the end they all agreed to the proposal, but when the governor brought up the issue of defense of the town, Captain Rowling interrupted. "Guv'nor, with your permission, I'd like to discuss with my companions how we might best help your cause. It may be the case that defendin' the town be not the most effective means of combatin' the Spaniards, as they'll already be in these waters by then."

Governor Diedrik seemed as dubious as Roy felt about that statement. "Surely you're not thinking of attacking Coro," he said. "Here at least you would have our fort and warships to help shift the battle, whereas they would have their own fort and defenses in Coro."

"I don't think we shall attack Coro," said Rowling, "but I wish to keep our options open. We will of course inform you of any plan we're seriously considerin' before the day is done."

"Very well," said the governor, "but Captain Toppings may not leave the town until I give the word. I had my man send word to the docks after he admitted you into this office." *Well that clinches it.* Roy was not pleased with the turn of events, but at least he was to have help. He hoped that his crew didn't desert him once they heard what he was planning.

They made their farewells and were escorted back to the carriage waiting for them outside. The other one, presumably the one Gilbertsen had arrived in, was gone. "I'm glad you got one in on that rat Gilbertsen at sea, whatever the consequences," said Captain Rowling, as the carriage trundled down towards the town.

"Do you know him?" Roy asked in surprise.

"I attacked his ship once as well, though I treated him better'n he deserved. Several of my crew had grievances against him."

"Why didn't he set the governor on you as well?" Roy asked, feeling just a little bit wronged.

"Because Gilbertsen had been flyin' French colors," said Rowling with a smile. "He wouldn't want *that* bein' dragged out in front of the guv'nor."

"Why did you attack a French ship?" Roy asked. As far as he knew, most of the captains out of Port Royal were on good terms with the French.

"Because my crew recognized his ship anyway."

Captain Morgan roared with laughter, and Roy couldn't help but join in. "It must have been more than he could stomach not to be able to say a word against you in there," said Roy.

"He didn't dare treat me with any less respect than the guv'nor did," said Rowling. "He probably expected I'd mention the encounter at any moment."

"I almost wish you had and that we were both thrown in the stockade," said Roy in a low voice, his laughter dying down somewhat. "Now we have seven Spanish warships to deal with, and if that old crate that Diedrik calls a warship is going to be of any help, I'll take on that war galleon myself. I'd almost rather wait it out in a cell."

"Not to worry," said Morgan in an equally low voice to avoid being heard by the driver, "we'll be there too. We just have to think of a good plan. Perhaps they would abort the mission if we let on that we knew about it?"

"Strictly speaking, we don't *know* anything, but our suspicions seem much more reasonable since Gilbertsen's news," said Roy. "That was a good point you made about these forces being shipped somewhere, and probably somewhere close."

"Anyway," said Rowling, "they'd just deny it an' postpone the mission for another time. It would be better for everyone if that fleet were dealt with now rather than bein' allowed to scatter or grow."

"Well I certainly don't mind the reprieve," said Roy, "and the chance to discuss this further. I was surprised that you took issue with defending the town." That had been perplexing, and Roy completely agreed with the governor's point. If they were to take the battle to the fleet, they would be on their own.

"It will probably prove to be the best way," admitted Captain Rowling, "but there will be far less plunder if we only take on the ships an' soldiers, an' we'd probably be forced to sink most of the ships rather than loot them if we end up havin' any chance against them at all. There's also the possibility of sneakin' into the town an' settin' fire to the ships while they're in the harbor. But mainly I said what I did so you'd have some freedom, an' because we still have to see if we can get any details out of Major Benito."

Roy had forgotten about questioning Benito. Being threatened with imprisonment had driven it from his mind entirely. "Good thinking," he said. "I'd like to see how my crew is getting on as well, but whatever happens next, I'd not mind a hot bath."

They continued down the road from the governor's house, and Roy went through a mental list of things he needed to attend to before the day was out. It seemed like it just got longer and longer, but at the very least he was determined to make sure that all of his men received their payment for the previous venture. He was tempted to withhold it simply to force them to stay on, but he wanted to take none but volunteers with him if he was to fight a fleet of Spanish warships. *Who knows? With Curaçao itself in danger, recruiting might be easy for a change.* Or it might be once the governor made some kind of announcement. The thought reminded him of how Gilbertsen had left in such a hurry. *I wonder what he's up to.*

* * *

Marius Gilbertsen had been twirling this plan in his mind since the previous night, but now he knew the governor was not planning on making any sort of immediate announcement. However, he could do so at any moment, and Marius needed to act quickly before that happened. He had told the coachman to drive straight to Van Kemper's tavern, and if he found Van Kemper was in, they could act possibly even before those English captains had a chance to resupply.

Marius had partnered with Van Kemper on a number of business ventures in the past, from ensuring that Andries van Friedrich could not find another stable and affordable source of regular coffee shipments, to putting a rival brewer out of business and buying up his goods and property after the fact. Van Kemper was as shrewd as Marius himself when it came to business dealings, and each of them benefitted from the other's unique sources of information. In this case, Marius had valuable advice and Van Kemper had resources and business contacts that would enable them to act quickly. *Hopefully he has the funds to make it work.* Marius' own funds were less than they should be due to Captain Toppings' attack on his ship, but if his plan succeeded he might recoup the loss in a single day.

The coach stopped and Marius stepped out, happy to see the familiar bustle outside Van Kemper's tavern. It appeared busier than usual, but that simply meant that Van Kemper was more likely to have spare funds to back the venture he had in mind. Entering the tavern, he noted that it was even busier than it had appeared from outside. All of those little nooks and corners favored by the more discreet segment of the trading community were full, and large groups of men sat around tables talking animatedly about some recent happenings. At any other time he would have stopped to listen, but he was in a great hurry as he made his way to the bar. "I need to speak with Van Kemper," he said to the man there. The bartender was quite busy, but he recognized Marius and called to one of the servants to fetch the landlord.

Minutes passed before Van Kemper was led out of his offices in the back, and Marius was quite annoyed by the delay. "What can I do for you, Marius?" asked Van Kemper in a hurried sort of way. Clearly he had more going on than simply an overload of customers.

"I need to speak with you in private," said Marius earnestly, "and quickly. I have a sound business venture in mind, and it is extremely time sensitive."

"Very well," said Van Kemper tiredly. His eyes narrowed somewhat at the mention of a sound business venture, and he knew that Marius would not exaggerate about such things, but he appeared to have endured an eventful morning. He led Marius into the back where his offices were located and locked the door of his office behind them. "Make it quick," he said, "I've had the most unpleasant morning I can remember having for some time, and I could use a little bit of good news."

"I can't give you too many details," Marius cautioned, "but I have just met with the governor. He has ordered me not to reveal my knowledge on this subject to anyone yet, but I *can* say that I have very good reason to believe that there will shortly be a great need for arms of all kinds in Curaçao."

Van Kemper was immediately interested, Marius was glad to see. "You can act on this information without arousing suspicion?" asked Van Kemper.

"I am not sure, but certainly *you* would be able to do so," said Marius. "I do not have the means that I once had, but if we were to pool our resources and buy up as many weapons as we can, and as quickly as possible, we should be able to turn quite a profit once demand rises—and it will rise sharply, I believe."

"What has happened to render you short on resources?" Van Kemper asked. No doubt he suspected that Marius simply wished him to take all the risk while he himself would reap some reward for the tip off whether it paid off or not.

"I was attacked in the Maracaibo Lagoon by an English ship under Captain Roy Toppings," he said. "He took all of my goods, personal possessions and money, and he sank my ship."

Van Kemper shook his head in disgust. "I know the man," he said. "He sold some goods to me about a week ago, and he currently has a prisoner in my care, though I should be shot of him soon. Most of the trouble I've had this morning can be laid at Captain Toppings' door," he added.

Marius was furious. *He sold my goods to exactly the person I was going to sell them to!* He wondered if the crewmembers who had deserted him had suggested the deal to Toppings. "With luck, Diedrik will have him locked up," he said. "The weasel actually went to visit the governor while I was there and I told the governor what he had done. I'm not sure Diedrik will take action, but I would not recommend entering into any business dealings with

Captain Toppings."

Van Kemper sat in thought for a few moments. "I think I can guess what information you are not allowed to reveal," he said at last. "It would explain many of the facts that have come to my attention. Captain Toppings was here not long ago, and he must have gone straight to the governor after he left here. But let us not speak of that further," he added, coming out of his thoughts for a moment. "I will help you in this venture, as long as you have enough resources to contribute in a meaningful way as well. I don't wish to risk my own money without some indication that you believe in the venture as much as you claim."

"Of course," said Marius. He had enough money saved that he could contribute perhaps two thousand ducats comfortably, and he had yet to sell the coffee he had returned with. "I will get the money to you as quickly as I can fetch it. In the meantime, I also have a quantity of coffee to sell, if that might count towards part of the finances for this transaction."

"It will, but it is not likely to be worth as much as it would have been had you arrived on schedule," said Van Kemper. "Van Friedrich tells me that he has secured a contract and that he only requires a small amount of coffee to supplement what he has already purchased. We will have to find other buyers from now on, it seems." This was a sore blow to Marius. He had made a tidy profit from Van Friedrich for the better part of a year by keeping his shipments sporadic and unpredictable. Now he would have to take quite a financial risk in order to invest in the plan he was putting forth to a great enough extent that his losses would be mostly recovered.

"How much will you give for eight hundred pounds of coffee?" he asked with trepidation.

"I cannot offer more than twelve ducats," said Van Kemper apologetically.

Marius' heart sank. He could tell that Van Kemper was being as fair as he could, but he might have sold it for twice that to Van Friedrich, were it not for this contract. He did not have time to verify that news of this contract was valid, but Van Kemper was not likely to deal sharply with him under the circumstances. "Very well," he said, "I will return with as much of my savings as I can spare, but you should start buying immediately." He turned towards the door and Van Kemper stood up to unlock it. "Start with your contacts at the docks," he added, "they will be the first merchants that those English captains will turn to if they need guns." Marius knew the position that Governor Diedrik was in, and he suspected that the English crews *would* need all the guns and powder they could get their hands on.

"Good idea," said Van Kemper, "I'll get started immediately. Before dusk, if anyone wants pistol, musket, shot, powder, blade, cannon or blunderbuss, they will have to come here to get it."

Marius climbed back into his carriage moments later, and as it rumbled away towards his home, he wondered whether it would be more satisfying to see Captain Toppings locked in a cell or to see him come into Van Kemper's tavern to buy guns at inflated prices and fill Marius' pockets once again.

* * *

Marquis Jean-Baptiste Augustin was beginning to tire of his time in Curaçao, and he had much business to take care of in Tortuga, but he found that there was something new to be learned in Curaçao every day. Yesterday he had learned that Sir Sebastian McLaughlin's expedition had not yet returned, and that this was unexpected according to local sailors and merchants who had allegedly spoken with him before he left. The day before that, he had learned that Major Manuel Benito was being held for ransom at Van Kemper's tavern, in addition to Colonel Valdez. If today was to fit the trend, he expected to hear something as interesting as it was disquieting, and he did not want to leave without finding out more about this series of recent developments involving Spain and Spanish interests.

Governor Diedrik was no fool, as Jean-Baptiste's many visits to him had proven, and Diedrik must naturally suspect that he was gathering valuable information in addition to the business deals he had been arranging with the governor and other wealthy and influential locals. However, his dealings with the governor had gone well, and Diedrik seemed inclined to trust that he would not do anything to endanger their relations. It was just as well, for if anyone kept an eye on him, they might wonder who it was that came and went from his ship so often, and why it appeared to be a different person almost every time. It was difficult to keep up the pretense that Damien (or "Benoit Fiennes," as he was otherwise known) was still in the hold of his ship, especially as Damien was not usually present aboard the ship, although no one had come by to verify his presence since they had made sure he had nothing to do with the ransom theft a week ago. Damien was due back any time now, and Jean-Baptiste waited patiently in his room at an inn near the docks to hear what news of interest he had to report today.

Only a few more minutes passed before he heard a knock at the door. "Enter," he said, turning towards the door. Damien entered and locked the door behind him as usual. It was impossible to make out the remnants of his bruises under the paint and plaster that held his affected features in place, but Damien no longer winced each day as he put on a new set of features or removed them after he was back aboard ship.

Jean-Baptiste gestured to a sturdy chair at the single table adorning the simple room and Damien took a seat. Jean-Baptiste had chosen an inn by the docks not only to keep an eye on which ships entered the harbor and who came and went from the docks, but also because many of Damien's more useful disguises would pass casual inspection without comment in such a place. He poured some wine for his trusted retainer, and Damien drank gladly before beginning his report. "Sir, it appears that Captains Toppings, Rowling and Morgan have information on Spanish military movements," he said. "There was an incident at Van Kemper's tavern: Major Benito emerged at a full run from one of the upstairs rooms with all three of them close behind him, and Coya, that native woman from Toppings' crew, she put a knife in his leg from five paces without even getting up from her seat as he ran through the common room."

"Go on," said Jean-Baptiste. Captain Toppings' crew clearly sported some unusual talent that would bear remembering, from what Damien had discovered. First one of them had sold a Diego Velasquez painting to Van Friedrich for a good price, then the captain's African first mate had felled Benito during the burglary at Van Kemper's tavern, and now this unusual native woman did the same during an apparent escape attempt.

"Well, it seems that they had been questioning Benito," continued Damien, "and he somehow surprised them and managed to escape the room in which he was held. After the incident, there was quite a commotion in the common room and I was able to slip away and listen to the conversation that followed. They are concerned about a military build-up in Coro and suspect that the force that is gathering there is bound for Curaçao."

As far as news that was both interesting and disquieting, today's reached new heights. "Did anyone spot you?" asked Jean-Baptiste earnestly.

"I don't believe so, sir," said Damien. "They had sent for a doctor, and he showed up soon after the incident, but I heard him coming just in time."

"Anything else?"

"Yes sir. Coya, the woman I mentioned, is the one who stole the ransom from *La Fortuna*."

"*What?*"

"Crewmembers from Toppings', Rowling's and Morgan's ships all seemed to know about it," said Damien. "I even managed to insinuate myself into the conversation and while she tried to keep it quiet, she did not deny what the others were saying."

Jean-Baptiste laughed. "I hope for her sake that this tale does not reach Monsieur Van Kemper's ears very soon," he said. "It sounds like Captain Morgan is taking it well though." He knew that it was Morgan who had captured Valdez in the first place.

"Indeed sir," continued Damien, "the three captains left to go and see Governor Diedrik about their suspicions after the doctor treated one of their men and Major Benito's wound. I found out what I could from other members of their crews before I made my way back here, but there is not much else to report aside from the fact that Toppings and Morgan appear to have conducted successful raids on Caracas and its port."

Jean-Baptiste paced for a few moments deep in thought. If Spain was indeed planning to invade Curaçao, many of the deals that he had arranged with the governor would be ruined, as well as the business deals he had arranged with Andries van Friedrich and others. Many of the French colonies in Hispaniola were on good terms with Spain, and official relations between the two countries were cordial for the moment, but King Louis had expressed his desire to undermine Spanish monopolies and power in the Caribbean, and the policies of Cardinal Mazarin (who still basically ruled France due to Louis' youth) did not specifically conflict with that goal for the most part. Curaçao was ideally situated to carry out such an agenda, and it was vital to international trade in a climate of highly restrictive trade laws. English trade policies had caused much friction with Holland, and Spanish trade laws kept international trade at a standstill among King Philip's colonies, barring the illegal smuggling that flourished along the Spanish Main. Curaçao was the only colony within sight of New Granada where French, Dutch and English interests (as well as those of many Spanish merchants) held sway, and Jean-Baptiste was determined to see that it remained so. "Return to Van Kemper's tavern and summon these captains to me," he said. "Tell them I wish to aid them in whatever way I can. I don't know if the governor will enlist their aid, but I could mediate some sort of mutually beneficial deal for all concerned in order to keep the defense of Curaçao strong."

"What shall I tell them if they think we are simply trying to find out what they are up to?" asked Damien. He was very good at his job, and Jean-Baptiste was glad that these concerns occurred to Damien just as they did to him.

"Tell them what you know if you have to, just get them here." If there was any way to find out all the details he could and to keep Curaçao out of Spanish hands, he wanted to be part of it. "Do try not to let anyone from the Spanish ship *El Picaflor* know about it though."

"Yes, my lord," said Damien. He rose and left the room once again without delay.

Jean-Baptiste had hoped he could see to other matters once he had heard Damien's report, but this was much more urgent. Even so, it was well past time for lunch and he made his way downstairs. Most of the other patrons ignored him, and so he was left alone with his thoughts. Several plans formed in his mind and were discarded for one reason or another. He was not quite sure how he could help, but Damien at least had made several contacts in the town already, and perhaps those would prove useful. If nothing else, and if there was time, he might be able to contact some of the French privateers in the waters of Hispaniola and they could organize some sort of unofficial raid on Coro. That, at least, seemed safer than waiting around in Curaçao for Spanish troops to invade the island. Either way, he hoped the governor would publicly address the issue soon. Jean-Baptiste greatly desired to consult with him, but he did not relish explaining how the matter had come to his attention. Then again, as he was not in a position to render any official aid, perhaps it would be better to keep well clear of the topic with the governor. After all, Jean-Baptiste's loyalties were to King Louis alone, and while Louis encouraged other governments to *perceive* alliances with France, the reality of his position was very different.

* * *

Manuel Benito felt physically much more at ease since his leg had been tended, but he knew it was only a matter of time before those three captains returned, and they would not be in a patient mood. There was little he could do about it, so he alternated between thinking about which things might be safe to reveal under certain circumstances, and praying and preparing himself mentally for the possibility of torture. His father had been a trade envoy to China and other eastern countries and had taught Manuel some of the eastern techniques for calming the mind, but he had been most moved by the centering prayers and prayers of quiet of the Catholic faith. The upper rooms of Van Kemper's tavern were quite insulated against sound, which helped him to focus, but all too soon he heard the sound of the wooden slat being drawn back on the door and voices as someone unlocked the door. He sat up and saw Toppings, Morgan and Rowling enter. Van Kemper closed the door behind them with an uncomfortable glance at him, but Manuel knew that all Van Kemper really cared about was a clean, sensible, and above all *profitable* transaction. His business with Toppings had proven to be none of these, as far as Manuel could tell.

"As I said," began Captain Toppings, "you have yet to answer the questions that we have a mind to ask. Your escape attempt was bold, I'll grant you that, but the wound you inflicted on my first mate has not endeared you to me and I am disinclined to waste my time."

"Ah, but that is precisely what you are doing," said Manuel. "I will not tell you anything useful. And while we are about it, this wound in my leg has not endeared you to me either." Gone were his attempts to be cordial, courteous, or even formal. If he was to be left defenseless, he at least could use words as his weapons.

"That is up to you," replied Toppings, "but we know more now than you might think we do. We know troops have been mustering in Coro from many Spanish colonies, we know there is a fleet there consisting of four barques, two galleons and a war galleon, we know it is commanded by Admiral Sergio Cadiz, we know this force is headed to Curaçao, and we know you wanted Colonel Valdez to assist in the assault."

Manuel couldn't believe his ears, but he mastered his reactions easily. *How on earth did they find out?* No doubt some smuggler friend of theirs had discovered the truth, as Manuel had warned might happen. "Well, it sounds like you hardly need to talk to me at all," he scoffed. "I hope you didn't pay very much for that information."

"Nothing, in fact," answered Toppings. "I only tell you all of this so that you can better judge the value of what it is you are withholding." He signaled to Morgan and Rowling who then advanced to the bed and hauled Manuel over to the chair that still stood in the middle of the room. They held his arms firmly to the arms of the chair and splayed his hands against the wood. Captain Toppings drew a knife. Manuel's heart began to race, but he made an effort to slow his breathing and calm his mind. "Think quickly," continued Toppings as he put his knife to the joint connecting Manuel's little finger to his right hand, "you can tell us the little that we wish to know, or you can pay the price of your secrecy one finger at a time." Manuel breathed as evenly as possible and said nothing, but it was clear that Captain Toppings was on the point of asking his question. "How many soldiers have been mustered in Coro?" he asked.

Manuel did not dare laugh, but he felt a slight sense of relief. It was entirely possible that these brigands would mutilate his hand whether he told the truth or not, but considering how little use the knowledge would be to them, Manuel hesitated very little in answering. He was as well disciplined as any soldier of King Philip's army, but some things simply were not worth being tortured over. "Five hundred men, in addition to the usual complement aboard the vessels you described," he said.

Captain Toppings stared at him unblinking, presumably watching for any sign of deception, but Manuel could tell that he was not very practiced at this sort of compulsion. "One more question," the captain said, "when was the invasion supposed to take place?"

Again, Manuel had no problem answering the question. "Once we had Valdez or had ascertained that we could not acquire him," he said. "Much good may that do you, since I have no idea what will be decided in my absence. As for the soldiers, the three of you are not likely to deter such a force without a great deal more help. You would do far better to leave this place and save your skins." Manuel was sure that three captains, no matter how renowned any of them might be, would make little difference in the outcome of the battle without much larger ships than they had. Even if Captain Rowling himself took command of the stolen and antiquated Spanish warship in the harbor, they could not hope to stop the force arrayed against them. The hardest part would be invading the town itself, but Curaçao did not have enough fighting men to stop the fleet, and most of them would probably surrender if they were offered quarter, once the troops landed. Nevertheless, part of the purpose of his remark was to gauge their resolve or discover any hint as to whether or not they had more help. He was satisfied to see a look of worry cross Morgan's face. Rowling looked displeased, but Manuel could not tell much from that.

Toppings, on the other hand, seemed somewhat pleased, and that confused Manuel more than it worried him. *At least he isn't going to mutilate my hand.* Toppings had removed the knife and the others let go of his arms. "Excellent," said Toppings, and the other two looked askance at him as well. "I will return later to check on you. Gentlemen?" he said to the other captains, gesturing for them to follow him out. As the door was shut and locked, leaving Manuel alone once again, he wondered whether he had inadvertently let on more than he had thought, but Morgan and Rowling appeared to react just as he had expected. *I suppose it's out of my hands now.* He felt momentarily guilty for divulging the little he had, but the feeling quickly passed. He was responsible for the muster and training of many of the men involved in the operation, and he had done everything he could to prepare them for this mission. If the information he had given was enough to thwart the invasion, then it would likely have failed anyway. He had considered lying about the number of soldiers involved, but he knew by reputation that Captain Morgan had more experience with torturing captives, and he didn't know what would be gained by such a lie anyway. With luck, those three captains were already discussing what to do next and would soon reach the conclusion that Manuel had been absolutely right that they would be better off leaving Curaçao altogether.

* * *

Coya felt that running errands was becoming a trend for her, though it was easier to feel as though the errands were important when she was all alone in the jungle doing something to help the rest of the crew stay alive. Running around in town checking on things for the captain while the rest of the crew enjoyed themselves was not quite as fulfilling. *Well, they aren't* all *enjoying themselves.* She was certain that Ajuban was not enjoying himself after his run-in with Benito, and the men guarding the ship surely wouldn't mind a little fun. And of course Brian, William and Tiede had gone off with some of the men to sell the goods, and Jan was tending to the injured… It began to dawn on Coya that very few crewmembers were without duties to perform. Roy trusted certain people to take care of things, and she supposed she should be glad to be among them, but so far it seemed that the crew in general spent precious little time enjoying their earnings. The only time she had been afforded to socialize had been interrupted by Benito bursting into the common room. Considering how her attempts to get to know the other sailors had gone, that was probably for the best. *I'll be lucky if Van Kemper doesn't already know about the ransom by now.*

Having heard little news from Albert about the sale of goods when she returned to *The Constance*, she had taken directions in halting English from Bert (in the end, he had drawn her a rough map) and paid a visit to Jan's practice to see how Justin and Ben were coming along. Jan was not there, but Justin had actually been well enough to hobble out of bed and let her in. He'd said that he and Ben had only just been told that they could get up and walk around, and Coya had been dubious about the truth of that statement, but Justin seemed disinclined to take advantage of Jan's pronouncement. She marveled at how much better he and Ben appeared to be faring.

For now, she was returning to *The Constance* again to see if there was any fresh news, as the captain had specifically asked her to find out what she could about Brian's and William's progress with the goods. With luck, she could bring good news back to Van Kemper's tavern and enjoy a meal and a drink. It was getting late in the day, and she was quite ready to be done with her duties and to receive whatever her share of the haul would amount to. She already had more money than she knew what to do with because of the bonus from the ransom theft, but she would enjoy seeing how much more would be added to that by the loot from Caracas. She spotted Albert standing on deck as she approached the dock where *The Constance* was berthed and she called over to him, "Still on watch duty?"

"Not for much longer, God willing," he answered with a bored look. However, it was clear he was feigning boredom when a smile crept across his face. "The goods are all sold," he said excitedly, "or all the ones that the captain wanted to sell, and the last of them are going to be unloaded onto the next wagon."

"Do we know what the total is yet?" Coya asked with equal excitement.

"Brian is working on that now, but it's a lot. Enough for me to claim this as part of my share," he added, displaying the sword at his belt. It was one of the fencing blades they had captured, and it was intricately worked around the hilt and guard.

Albert was clearly pleased with it and wanting to share his excitement. "It suits you," said Coya, much to Albert's satisfaction. It was a longer blade than Coya had usually seen on fencing weapons during her admittedly brief exposure, but Albert had been improving in his lessons with Roy and she had observed that he used the reach of his arms quite well—no doubt due to the peculiar fighting style he had learned in Tortuga. She had no doubt that he would be just as deadly with his new prize as he was with his fists, though Coya still found it amazing that the blades did not break constantly. Coya had bought a pair of dueling pistols out of the plunder without waiting to see what her share would be. She already had more than enough silver to pay for them, and she would get a full share on top of that, but now she would feel better prepared for the next time she was to be chased through the woods by Spaniards.

She looked around the deck and saw that William and Brian were at a small table erected by the helm. William spotted her and came over to them. "Brian is just figuring out each of our shares," he said. "From how much loot

THE WRATH OF BROTHERHOOD

there was, we can all expect a fun time in town."

Coya wasn't sure how much her share would be, but she enjoyed imagining what she could do with it. *I could probably buy my own ship now, if I wanted to.* She wouldn't dream of wasting her money on something like that—it wasn't as if she would ever have her own crew even if she knew how to captain a vessel—but the thought never would have occurred to her when she was haunting the streets of Port Royal.

"If you wait for a little bit," William continued, "Brian will bring the totals to the captain at Van Kemper's tavern once he is done with his calculations. Then perhaps we can all get paid and have a bite to eat—or at least those not on guard duty," he added, glancing at Albert with a laugh.

"The captain said I'd be off of guard duty once the goods are off the ship and we're all paid," said Albert. "Trust me, I've been counting the minutes while you and Brian worked out your sums."

"Brian will be done before that sluggard Tiede gets back with the wagon," retorted William.

"Is Tiede being slowed down by his leg?" asked Coya. If he had been busy trading all day, she could well believe it.

William looked at her as if she had misunderstood. "No. Er...maybe," he said. "I just meant that Albert here isn't going anywhere until we unload the rest of the goods. Tiede is fine, I'm sure. He says it mostly hurts when he walks, so we let him ride in the wagon most of the way."

Coya felt sure that she had spoiled some sort of joke or amusement, but William's sense of humor was often more subtle than she was used to. *Maybe I just shouldn't take things so seriously.* It was a hard habit to break. At that moment she saw Brian stand up with a paper in his hand. "All right you lot," he said still looking at the paper, "Coya, you come with me. William, you stay here and help guard the ship." Now it was Albert's turn to look amused, and William's expression turned slightly sour. "We don't want anyone spiriting away our gold before it gets paid out, and we still have goods to unload," continued Brian, folding the paper and putting it in his pocket. "We will be back shortly, assuming the captain is at Van Kemper's tavern when we get there."

Coya looked back at William and grinned at his sour face as she followed

Brian from the dock into town. She stuck her tongue out for good measure, and Albert laughed. "So are you actually going to take a meal in town this time?" said Coya jokingly as she walked next to the navigator.

"I'm looking forward to it," said Brian with a smile. Coya noticed suddenly that Brian did not smell like he had been at sea for days on end like the others did and realized that he'd probably had a bath before entering into business negotiations. She briefly felt self-conscious about her own condition, but if anyone were comfortable with it, it would be Brian.

"Do you think that the sum you're going to report to the captain will be more than he expected?" she asked curiously. She had not had a lengthy conversation with Brian for some time, and she was looking forward to seeing how he interacted with a group of people in a tavern rather than on the deck of a ship.

"I think it will," he said, "though I know he was mightily impressed with the goods once we had a proper look at them. And that saffron that Jan noticed fetched us quite a price." From what Coya knew, that had been Jan's largest contribution while helping to identify the spices and other goods from Caracas. With his odd knowledge of herbs and spices, Coya sometimes found herself wondering whether he could cook as well as he could heal.

"Have you ever been to Curaçao before?" she asked. "In town, I mean. Not just sitting on the ship."

"Aye, a few times. I expect that's why the captain chose me to help sell the goods this time. I've never done that here before, but I speak the language well enough."

The conversation continued that way with Coya asking questions and Brian simply answering them until they reached Van Kemper's tavern. She was a bit crestfallen, but she remembered well enough that Brian was not really in his element when talking to people, save on rare occasions. When they arrived, she saw Jan speaking to the bartender. "Jan," she called to him, "are you going up to see the captain?"

"In a manner of speaking," he said. "I'm here to take a look at Ajuban, but I hear that the captain is with him as well. Have you tallied the shares?" he asked in a low voice looking at each of them.

"I have," said Brian. "I'm just going to make my report to the captain and

Ajuban, so you two may as well come and hear the good news as well."

They made their way up the stairs to the room where Ajuban was temporarily housed and found not only Roy, but Captains Morgan and Rowling as well. "Have you the tally?" Roy asked, interrupting the conversation he was having with Ajuban and the other captains.

"You sold your goods already?" asked Morgan incredulously.

"I thought I'd have it done right away before you two flooded the market with your plunder," said Roy.

Brian withdrew the folded paper from his pocket and unfolded it. "Eleven thousand, four hundred eight ducats," he said. "After expenses, supplies, and the cost of the items we have contracted to carry to the Cimaroons, a standard crewman's share amounts to three hundred and eight ducats."

"And you and Ajuban?" asked Roy.

"Officers will receive five hundred thirteen ducats," answered Brian.

"Well done," said Rowling with raised eyebrows.

"The one virtue of having a small crew," said Roy with a shrug, but Coya could tell that he was impressed as well. "You're sure that your calculations will cover the cost of supplies for the Cimaroons?" he asked Brian.

"It should be more than enough," said Brian.

"I still think you should wait until we've dealt with the Spaniards before you pay your men," said Captain Morgan to Roy.

Coya did not like the sound of that, and neither did Brian from his expression. She felt sure that he was about to say something about it to Morgan, but instead he ignored the remark and turned to Roy. "In light of this good news," he said holding the paper for emphasis, "may I just take this opportunity to tell you once again how glad I am to be a member of *your* crew, sir?" The emphasis was slight, but Captain Morgan had definitely noticed it.

"Thank you, Brian," said Roy. Captain Rowling appeared to have a little bit of a coughing fit, but Jan did not appear concerned about it as he smiled and went to tend to Ajuban. "Brian, would you stay for a moment?" Roy asked as Brian turned to leave.

"Of course sir, what can I do for you?"

"We have a bit of a problem facing us, and I would like your input on the matter." Captain Morgan seemed even less pleased with this statement, but at that moment there was a knock on the door. "Yes?" answered Roy.

It was Van Kemper. "Captains, excuse me, but I have a man here who says he would like to speak with the three of you. He says that his name is Damien, but he won't tell me much more than that." Van Kemper clearly did not care whether they refused, agreed, or threw the man out the window. Come to that, the way he looked at them, Coya was sure that Van Kemper wouldn't care if they *all* threw each other out of the window. *He's probably still upset about that incident in the common room.* Coya shifted her feet a bit under his gaze.

"Show him in, please," said Captain Rowling after consulting with the others quietly.

Van Kemper did so with a shrug, and the man he ushered in looked like a grizzled sailor who muttered in a rough English accent and had a bit of a lurk to his gait. He did not say anything of import until Van Kemper had left and closed the door. "What did you want with us?" asked Captain Rowling at that point.

"Beggin' yer pardon sirs," began the man, looking around at the others in the room, "but I'd not mind a word with yeh three a bit more private-like, if yeh don't mind."

Morgan looked as if he was about to usher everyone else out, but Roy said, "Anything that you have to say is safe with all present. In any case, I would not interrupt our business for yours until we knew a bit more about what that might be."

"Or about who you are," put in Rowling.

"Very well sirs," said the man, but then he pressed his ear to the door and motioned for quiet rather than telling them more. When he appeared satisfied that no one was listening, he stepped further into the room and spoke in a low voice that was very different from the voice he had previously used. "My name is Damien Levasseur," he said. "I am here on behalf of the Marquis Jean-Baptiste Augustin. He wishes to speak with the three of you about the recent information you have uncovered concerning Spanish military activity." He again looked around at the others in the room.

Everyone was surprised by this statement, and were clearly wondering how this Damien Levasseur found out that the three captains knew about it. *He must be wondering just how many of us have heard the news.* Clearly he was sure that the captains were aware of what he spoke of, but he looked most at Coya and Brian, presumably to see if they knew as well. "An' what news is it that you speak of?" asked Captain Rowling, letting nothing slip.

"The news that you three were discussing in here before you went to see the governor, of course," said the man. "I heard you speaking of it, on general orders from my master of course," he added, noting that Captain Morgan had gripped his sword hilt briefly, "and reported what I heard to him at once. Your concerns are equally troubling to him and he would like to assist with the matter."

"And of course he would in turn find out all he wishes to know, and without having his lackey listen furtively at doors," stated Captain Morgan contemptuously.

"My lord already knows all he needs to know to be worried about the situation," Damien replied calmly, "but I suspect you have nothing to lose by accepting the marquis' services."

"And what exactly can he do to help us?" asked Roy. "He isn't likely to sail into a battle with that ship of his, and unless he expects to send for other ships in the area somehow, I don't see how his services would be needed." From what Coya understood, Roy had a good point, but Damien was noncommittal.

"That is not for me to say, monsieur," said Damien, who seemed as though he was beginning to worry that his summons would be ineffective, "but he is a fair political strategist and his opinions may prove useful to you."

"I don't see how any kin' of political strategizin' be likely to help us," said Rowling to the others, "but I don't reckon we have much to lose, just as this man says."

"But how do we know that he has the knowledge that he claims?" asked Morgan. "What is it you think you know, exactly?" he arched an eyebrow at Damien, who had clearly expected some development of this nature.

"In as few words as possible," he began, "I know that you are worried about the military forces mustering in Coro and that they may be planning to attack Curaçao, I know that you have Major Manuel Benito and Colonel

Javier Valdez locked away in this establishment, and that this woman here"—
he pointed straight at Coya—"is the one who stole the ransom money for
Valdez off of Major Benito's ship." Coya tried not to blush and shift her gaze
at this pronouncement. Everyone there knew the truth, but it was still
uncomfortable to have it proclaimed by an outsider, especially inside Van
Kemper's tavern. "Nicely done, by the way, mademoiselle."

Coya looked up, and found that Damien was addressing her and smiling.
"Thank you," was all that she found to say, but she was mildly pleased.

She looked around at the others, and they were all shocked at the extent of
what he had learned. She hoped that she would hear it all in greater detail
soon, but she was quite sure that the things Damien had heard were not
things that the captains or the governor would want spread about in the
streets. Indeed, no one else seemed to have a clear idea about whether to feel
worried, angry or merely foolish for having been compromised by this
Damien fellow. "I suppose we had better be more careful what we say and
where we say it," said Ajuban with a laugh and a grimace as his ribs reacted to
his laughter.

"I don't think that these things are generally known," said Damien,
"except for this young lady's part in the ransom theft. I'm afraid that several
members of your crews were rather less than discreet about it in the common
room." *I wish he had not pointed that out.* Coya was worried how this would
be taken, but she was grateful that Damien had not mentioned anything
about her discussing the matter with others. If he had noticed her speaking
about it at all, he would only have witnessed her attempts to encourage
discretion anyway.

As it turned out, no one seemed to treat the issue as if it were her fault. "It
was bound to come out, but perhaps it might be best if we left here soon,"
said Roy, and Brian and Ajuban agreed. "Is Ajuban all right to walk?" he
asked Jan.

"Yes, he should be fine, but he shouldn't strain himself tonight if it can be
avoided."

"Then I suggest we all go and pay the marquis a visit, after the crew of *The
Constance* has been paid for their labors," said Roy.

"Very good, sir," said Brian approvingly.

"But the marquis has only summoned the three of you," objected Damien. "It would not be fitting for the whole group of you to turn up."

"These are some of my best people," said Roy before Captain Morgan could voice his agreement, "and I value their opinions on the matter at least as highly as those of some marquis I have never met, so I will assume that if he really wishes to aid us, he will not send away anyone who is capable of helping due to a sense of misplaced propriety." Coya felt much complimented hearing these words, and Brian stood a bit straighter as well. Sometimes, as Brian had said earlier, it was good to be reminded of how glad she was to be part of Roy's crew.

Damien did not take offense, however. Rather, he appeared to consider this and said with a ring of sincerity, "I believe you are correct that this is exactly how the marquis will view the situation, monsieur. Very well, but make sure not to spread any of this talk outside of this room yet. The marquis would not wish his role in this to be generally known, especially with that Spanish sloop in the harbor."

"Where shall we find the marquis once we have finished our business?" asked Roy.

"He is staying at the Lonely Shrew. I will meet you there." Damien opened the door and checked that no one stood outside, but the hall was empty. Then he bowed to the captains and made his way down the hall in the same manner in which he had entered, muttering to himself once again with a different accent and carrying himself differently, with rather less grace than Coya guessed he was capable of.

"The *Lonely Shrew?*" asked Captain Morgan. "Why would a French diplomat bother staying at such a place?"

"More to the point," said Roy, "why would anyone give such a name to an inn?"

"The place started as merely a tavern," said Jan, "and was named so because it was a popular place for sailors and dock workers to spend their free hours rather than going home to their families. The landlord rented space to those individuals whose wives turned them out of their homes—probably for exactly that sort of behavior."

"I do hope you aren't speakin' from personal experience," said Captain

Rowling with a grin.

"No indeed," laughed Jan, "but I have paid visits to several of the patrons there to treat everything from injuries obtained at sea to lumps on the head administered by some of those very wives."

"I think it is very ill-advised to take this marquis completely into our confidence without at least informing the governor," said Captain Morgan bringing the topic back to their impending meeting. "We don't know where matters stand between them on matters of state or military concerns."

"Normally I would agree," said Roy, "but I feel that we are running out of time and we may need to give an answer to Van Kemper regarding the ransoms before the day is out so as not to rouse any suspicion from the Spaniards in port. Beyond sending a message to the governor's house regarding our intentions, I feel we should postpone any consultation with him until we have made better use of our time." The others assented to this and returned to their own ships to check in with the watch that each had posted. Captain Rowling had agreed to have a letter sent up to the governor, and Coya couldn't help feeling a little disappointed at the situation. She had been looking forward to a leisurely stay in Curaçao and a nice fat payout, but with all this talk of battles and military movements and spying, she felt that her time in Curaçao was likely to be short. She was at least glad to be going to this meeting Damien had spoken of, and to hear in greater detail what was going on. She didn't know what to think of the offer of aid that the marquis was supposedly extending, but she felt sure that anyone who could discover as many things as he did that others wished to keep secret was likely to have some ability to help whomever he wanted to.

Roy and Brian supported Ajuban as they walked down the pier to *The Constance*, and as Coya followed closely behind Jan, it occurred to her that all of them seemed worried—especially Jan. *I suppose I wouldn't have had a pleasant stay here for long anyway.* If what the others were saying was true, the Spaniards would come soon and interrupt everyone's party.

Coya immersed herself in her own thoughts as the crew—most of which had stopped by periodically to find out when they would be paid and had gathered at *The Constance* since hearing the sales and tally had been completed—received their shares of the loot, cheered the captain, and made their separate ways again. The experience felt somehow hollow as she looked to Jan and considered the other Dutch crewmen who had not been privy to the information that she had only recently heard. Now that all had been paid, anyone who wanted to could leave the crew and Roy and his ship could depart for other shores. The captain had ordered that everyone returning should do so before the morning tide, and this confused and dismayed many of them. Jan and the others with family here, they had a heavy burden thrust on them whether they knew it or not. *Hopefully the captain will clear this up in the morning.* For the moment, Coya was looking forward, with a sense of mixed curiosity and dread, to what the next few hours would reveal.

Chapter 18: The Best Defense

Jan was not entirely sure why Captain Toppings had insisted that he, Ajuban and Coya be allowed to attend this meeting with Marquis Augustin, but he was greatly concerned about the plot that had been uncovered. If it was true, his daughter Isobel was in danger right along with the rest of the town, so the more he could find out about it, the better. The four of them had joined up with Morgan and Rowling again and entered the Lonely Shrew. Much of the place was newer than the old tavern, having been added on when the landlord had a mind to turn the place into an inn, but it had always been a popular place for sailors and dock workers to hear the latest news. Jan suspected that was why the marquis chose the place, especially as it was clear that he had no qualms about employing spies to find out whatever he wanted to know. Roy and Brian helped Ajuban up the stairs, so Jan kept an eye out behind them to make sure that the marquis had not arranged any surprises. *I'm becoming as suspicious as this lot.* He found no comfort in the thought, but since he had learned of this plot to attack Curaçao, it was hard to relax or to take anything for granted. One thing was certain: he was very glad that he had not chosen to sign aboard with Sir Sebastian's crew. No one had heard from them since they set sail for Coro, and now Jan had a pretty clear notion why.

They had no trouble as they approached the room where the marquis was supposedly staying. Roy knocked and they heard a youngish, clear voice answer, "Enter."

Damien stood by the door as they filed into the room, and a thin young man with blond hair and a moustache and beard that matched his long face stood to greet them. Jan and the rest of Roy's crew had of course already seen him playing cards at Van Kemper's tavern before their journey to Caracas, and his expression seemed just as unreadable as it was then. "The Marquis Jean-Baptiste Augustin," said Damien to all of them. Then he introduced them one by one to the marquis, and Jan was mildly surprised to find that he knew all of their names.

"Please be seated where you may," said the marquis in a clear, pleasant voice. Jan looked around and discovered that there were only four chairs and one table in the room, but the marquis did not seem at all perturbed when Coya chose to sit on the bed, so he did the same. "I am afraid that my quarters were not designed for such gatherings, but one simply has to adapt to the situation." Captains Rowling and Morgan each took a seat, but Roy offered the remaining chair to Ajuban, saving Jan the trouble of insisting on Ajuban's behalf. Damien remained standing near the door. On the table were two trays with ten goblets between them, as well as a pitcher of wine and a bottle of rum. "Please help yourselves," said the marquis, and Captain Morgan wasted no time in reaching for the bottle and a goblet for himself. As the marquis sat down, he said, "I shall not waste your time with pleasantries under the circumstances, but I must first ask if any of you are currently engaged in hostilities with France in any way, whether it be against her soldiers, her colonies, her navy, or even her smugglers."

"No, my lord, we are not," answered Captain Toppings, and the other captains made similar answers.

"Then let us get down to business," said the marquis, and his usually amused expression became more serious. "You have discovered a plot to invade Curaçao, yes?"

"Aye, we have," answered Rowling.

"How certain are you of your information?"

"As certain as one could be," answered Roy. "We tricked Major Benito into revealing it himself." That had been a clever approach, in Jan's estimation. It probably had only worked because of the amount of other information that they *had* been certain about.

"And how did you manage to do that?" said the marquis skeptically.

"We knew so much already," said Roy, "that we slipped in our speculation about where the invasion force was headed amongst the facts that we had revealed we knew already, and the Major confirmed it by the way he answered our other questions." It wasn't quite certainty, but by tricking Benito into failing to deny the invasion of Curaçao when Roy asked *when* the invasion of Curaçao would take place, the captain had come as close to gaining an admission as he was likely to get out of Major Benito.

The marquis shook his head. "Well, it's as much as we could hope for, though he might have been playing along I suppose."

"What exactly be your interest in this matter?" asked Captain Rowling. "An' what were you hopin' to fin' out when you sent your man there to spy for you?" Jan's eye inadvertently followed Rowling's gesture towards Damien who was paying close attention, but keeping quiet. Then Damien shifted position slightly and Jan noticed a slight discoloration on his cheek. *I know where I've seen him before.*

"To answer your first question, monsieur," said the marquis, "it is in the interest of none but Spain for Curaçao to be invaded and seized by Spanish troops. It would damage trade with France, England and obviously Holland if Curaçao's thriving market were threatened, and several of the deals we have brokered here—official and private alike—would be rendered void. As to your second question," here the marquis' expression of amusement returned, "who *wouldn't* want to find out why three English privateer captains were visiting Van Kemper's tavern together, or what their conversations might reveal?"

This explanation pleased no one, though Ajuban laughed as he usually did, but Jan's thoughts had gone along a different path since he had recognized Damien and he chose that moment to speak up. "Oh come now, my lord," he said casually, "do you really expect us to believe that you had Damien here pose as a criminal and try to break into Van Kemper's tavern a week ago and you *didn't* already have an interest in what he and Major Benito were up to?" *Mercy, but that was satisfying.* His question had wiped the smirk right off of the marquis' face. Damien stared at him a bit wide-eyed, and Rowling and Morgan quickly contained their surprise and turned their gazes on the young diplomat. Ajuban laughed harder still and even Brian had a smirk on his face. "Careful Ajuban," said Jan with a grin, "you'll hurt yourself." Roy and Coya thankfully contained any surprise they may have felt as they waited for the marquis to answer, but Jan had revealed what he had overheard the night he followed the marquis and his servant back to their ship with "their prisoner" Damien in tow, and they were probably remembering that conversation.

"You seem remarkably well-informed, monsieur," said the marquis. "I am surprised you recognized Damien."

"I am a doctor," said Jan, "and I had a good look at his face after that incident. It has not yet healed."

"Indeed not," said Damien with a chagrined chuckle. *He and Ajuban would get on well.* The young French spy seemed able to find amusement in any situation, as did his employer.

The marquis looked from one to the other of his guests and answered, "Damien knew that Major Benito must be visiting Monsieur Van Kemper about a hostage, but we didn't know who it was at first. There was some rumor that it might be Colonel Valdez. I had hoped to perhaps ask you, Captain Toppings, as I had noticed your man Ajuban there slip through the door that led upstairs, but the events that followed would have made that difficult."

"If we could return to the matter at hand," cut in Morgan, "I think we are wasting more time than we ought on showing our hands for a game long over."

"Well said, monsieur," said the marquis. "Gentlemen, I infer from your visit to the governor that he knows the current situation as well?"

"He does," said Captain Rowling, who had already sent one of his men with a written update to the governor.

"And has he requested your aid?"

The captains looked at each other as if deciding whether or not to answer this question. "He has," said Roy.

"Then I would like, as I said, to offer my aid as well," said the marquis. "I cannot aid directly with ships or soldiers without it being seen as an act of war. Even doing so in defense of the town would likely result in suspension of my diplomatic privileges in the eyes of Spain, should I be captured. However, I can perhaps assist with planning the defense of the town or attempting to contact any other privateers in the area, assuming that there is time to do so. Do you know when the Spaniards are planning to attack?"

"I'm not sure you fully understan' the situation," said Captain Rowling.

"If all that you know was what Damien overheard us discussin' prior to visitin' the guv'nor, then you've not heard of the strength of the fleet arrayed against us. As to when they'll attack, we're still unsure of this."

They all spent several minutes discussing the particulars of the information they had obtained and discussing what Major Benito's comments might indicate. It appeared that no one was particularly concerned with the governor's instruction that they not spread the news to others, as the crews obviously needed to know in order to prepare and the marquis had already found out about the likelihood of an attack anyway. One thing that became ever clearer as they talked was that in order to have any sort of advance warning of an attack, they would need to patrol the waters west of Curaçao more or less constantly. Better yet, if they had a patrol within sight of Coro, they could harry the fleet all the way to Curaçao, but the fleet was unlikely to sail then. "Or if they do sail," said Rowling, "they still have four warships that are just as maneuverable an' deadly as my own ship. They could protect the larger ships until they were in position to lan' troops."

"And that's assuming that the sloop in Curaçao's port right now is not taking part in the invasion," said Brian, speaking up for the first time. "She's armed as heavily as any privateer sloop and could negate the advantage in maneuverability that our smaller ships have."

"What about sending men overland to sneak into Coro and set fire to de ships?" asked Ajuban. It sounded like a good idea to Jan.

"If we leave Curaçao before *El Picaflor* does," said Rowling, "they may follow us or simply beat us back to Coro an' warn the fleet while our men toil overlan' to the port. If they sail before we do an' suspect that Major Benito has compromised their plans, they may warn the fleet anyway an' watch for just such an eventuality."

"Den why don't we tell Van Kemper dat we accept de ransom proposals? Den dey won't t'ink dat dey have been compromised and won't warn anyone."

"I think it too likely that they will want to see Benito to make sure that he has not been mistreated," said Roy. "Even if we could hide the wound in his leg, we would have to find a way of keeping him from communicating the reality of his situation."

Jan felt somewhat crestfallen, but Captain Toppings' point was quite valid. As far as Jan could see, rendering the ships useless before they had a chance to fight was the best option. "What we really need is a fire ship…"

Jan had muttered this to himself and his thoughts continued along those lines for a moment in silence, but Coya looked at him oddly and asked, "What is a fire ship?" Everyone had more or less quieted down a moment before, and now they stopped and listened to Jan and Coya's conversation.

"A fire ship is a ship that is set on fire and sailed into enemy ships or ports," explained Jan. "The danger of fire keeps the enemy preoccupied and limits their maneuverability allowing your own force to continue the attack or carry out your own agenda." Brian nodded approvingly at this summation.

"Would that help enough in a sea battle against seven warships?" she asked.

"It would help only a little bit," said Jan, "but it would help far more if we could sail one into the Coro harbor before the ships ever left port. Unfortunately, I don't see any way that we could do so without any warning."

"If we could find a suitable ship to set fire to in the first place," said Captain Morgan.

"And of course all of us would have to be ready to attack immediately after sending the fire ship at them," said Roy.

Jan had not meant to speak his initial thought aloud, as it was more of a wish than an idea, so he felt a little bit annoyed that everyone appeared to be finding reasons that it wouldn't work. Then he looked at the marquis and saw that the man was smiling. "There is one ship that would make an ideal fire ship," said the marquis at that moment. "What about *El Picaflor,* the Spanish sloop in the harbor right now?"

"We can't capture her in the port without provokin' a diplomatic incident," said Rowling, "an' she may prove hard to catch once it's set sail."

But the marquis was directing a meaningful expression at Damien, who appeared to understand what the marquis was thinking of. "If we could hide one of the crew aboard their ship, however," said Damien, "he could set a fuse to the powder magazine and explode the ship as it sailed into the harbor." At that suggestion, a palpable silence penetrated the conversation as everyone realized the merits of such an idea. The marquis nodded his satisfaction at

Damien, and Jan was delighted to find that his idly spoken wish had generated a promising notion.

"That would be very, very dangerous for whoever stowed away," said Roy, "but if we could accomplish it, the effect could well even the odds."

"Especially if the explosion disabled any of their larger ships," said Rowling. "If those galleons have any time to fire their cannons or get a clear shot at us, that might well be the end of it for us."

"And there's still the fort to contend with," said Morgan. "Not to mention the probability that as soon as our ships are sighted, soldiers and crew will be ferried out to the fleet and they will be underway."

"That could help you as well as hinder you," said the marquis. "The more soldiers are on any ships that are disabled, the more of them you can dispatch at your leisure. Anyone abandoning ship will be caught in the midst of a battle, and if things go well enough, you could kill them with grape shot before they reach the shore."

"Even so," said Coya, after having remained mostly silent throughout the tactical discussions, "we would have to know when the ship was going to sail for Coro and be ready to follow it immediately."

"In dat case," said Ajuban, "we should do what I said after all and tell Van Kemper dat we accept de ransom offer for Valdez."

"And if we refuse the offer for Benito," said Jan as a new thought struck him, "we almost *guarantee* that the Spaniards leave at the next opportunity because they will want to warn the fleet that their plans may have been compromised. They will probably find out about the incident at Van Kemper's soon anyway, if they haven't already. This way we can force the issue."

"Excellent!" chirped Roy, and Jan was very pleased to see that everyone seemed to approve of his plan. Brian even clapped him on the back. Coya, however, seemed just a touch out of sorts. *She almost looks...sad.* She was smiling, but Jan was sure that he was right in his assessment.

"This really could work, provided we open fire on the fort as soon as the diversion begins," said Rowling.

Even Captain Morgan was complimentary, and seemed to forget entirely that he did not regard Jan, Brian, Ajuban and Coya as equals for a moment.

"It would be a stroke of genius to get the Spanish to load up their ships with soldiers only to have them catch fire before the battle has really begun."

"And Damien has made quite a few connections in town," said the marquis. "He could easily smuggle someone aboard among the provisions for the ship's voyage." The conversation wound to a rather uncomfortable hush as the implications of this were fully realized. *Someone is still going to have to risk all and stow away aboard that ship.* Jan was sure that the same thought had entered everyone else's mind, and he felt that he suddenly understood why Coya seemed sad.

"Gentlemen," said Coya, seeming awkward and out of place in her use of the term, "may I suggest that I be the one to perform this task?" Captains Morgan and Rowling were obviously surprised by the suggestion, as was the marquis. Damien was the only man that had no prior acquaintance with Coya who appeared to take it in stride.

"Coya," said Roy, "you don't—"

"I can do it, captain," she interrupted. "You know that I am no stranger to stowing away aboard Spanish ships, and I can pack myself neatly into a barrel if need be." She smiled at that, as did Roy, but Jan would have to ask about that story later, if he had the chance. "I am the obvious choice."

"From what I have seen and heard recently," said Damien before anyone else cut in, "Mademoiselle Coya is quite right. Anyone who could creep aboard a ship and past Major Benito to steal his ransom money from his own cabin is someone I would put my faith in to carry out the task we speak of." Coya looked very pleased and nodded her appreciation to Damien. "I can smuggle her into the provisions when they are prepared for loading, and I can provide what she will need."

"I see why it is that you wanted your companions to attend this meeting, captain," said the marquis to Roy.

"Bear in min', Coya," said Captain Rowling, "that men will be sent down to the hold where you're hidin' in order to fetch powder an' shot when they're preparin' to fight us. You may fin' it difficult to remain concealed, or to escape once you've prepared the fuse."

"Leave it to me, captain," she said, though her expression showed her gratitude for the warning.

"You may not be able to see when the ship is in the best position for you to light the fuse," said Captain Morgan. "You may have to rely completely on your ability to hear what is going on outside of the ship, and you will have to act on that information at a moment's notice."

"Don't worry about us," said Ajuban to her, "we will keep far enough away from de ship so dat we don't catch any of de blast ourselves, but you may have to swim to de shore if we are not close enough to fetch you or if we are under fire. If we fail, you can still escape."

They continued to shower Coya with advice and warnings, and she took all of it in, but Jan could not help but feel sorry for her. It was the most dangerous task he could imagine under the circumstances, and the likeliest consequences seemed to involve either getting captured or blowing herself up right along with the Spaniards. Eventually Damien spoke up again and said, "Sirs, if we are to implement this plan, we should send word to Van Kemper immediately regarding the two ransoms. Am I correct in assuming that we wish to set things in motion so as to ensure that *El Picaflor* sets sail on the morning tide?"

"If we don't, we risk the Spaniards departing tomorrow anyway, but without Coya on board," said Morgan.

"Very well," said Coya, "I am prepared." Jan doubted this, at least in the sense that she had probably expected to be enjoying no less than a day or two in Curaçao without risking her life and engaging in a naval battle, but he was sure that she was as mentally prepared for the task ahead as she was likely to be.

"In that case," said Damien, turning to address Roy and Captain Morgan, "I suggest that you each go separately to Monsieur Van Kemper about the separate ransoms, or send separate people. Even if Van Kemper guesses that the two answers relate to the same decision, it should not be obvious to any of the Spaniards should they happen to be observing your interactions."

"Agreed," said Roy and Morgan together.

"I should leave here at the same time with Mademoiselle Coya so that our movements are not observed after your decision reaches Spanish ears," continued Damien. "They will be very wary if they think their plans have been compromised, and we're about to give them every reason to think that is the case."

Jan turned to Roy. "Captain," he said, "I would like to accompany them. I can advise Coya about how to keep from cramping or otherwise damaging herself while she's hidden away. I would hate for her to succeed in her objective only to find that she can't swim away because of the inevitable toll of being folded into crates or barrels for most of the day. Besides," he added, "I might be able to help if Damien's contacts fail to achieve our ends."

"Very well," said Roy with a knowing look on his face. Clearly he guessed the real reason Jan wanted to go. *I just don't want this to be the last conversation I have with the girl.* Even so, what Jan had said was true. "I'm sure we can plan our end of things from here, but thank you for all that you have contributed, Jan. Be at the docks by four o'clock. We sail early."

With that, Jan and Coya left with Damien—or rather a minute behind Damien, until they were all a few streets away—and made their way towards a little tavern on the other side of the docks. They arranged to sit at different tables, and Damien was seated near a window with a convenient view of the docks and Melanie Rutger's outfitting warehouse. He kept watch, apparently waiting for the Spaniards to make a move, and Jan sat with Coya awaiting his signal. "Now we wait," said Jan.

* * *

An hour had passed since Coya had begun the dreadful wait for Damien's signal that would mean she would commit herself to this dangerous task. Initially she had thought she wanted to be alone while she prepared herself, but she quickly decided that Jan's company was much more soothing than the endless thinking and worrying that she would have been engaging in on her own. *I will have time enough for all that while I'm folded up in the hold.* Of course she wouldn't be able to pick up any other useful supplies she might think of at that time, so she would just have to trust that she and Damien were aware of what was needed. She knew very little about Damien except that he was obviously very good with disguises and was some sort of spy for the marquis. She had never even suspected him of being the same man that had attempted to break into Van Kemper's tavern and had been led away by the marquis and that Negro servant of his as she and Jan followed them. *I hope his plan to smuggle me aboard* El Picaflor *works better than his attempt to break into Van Kemper's tavern did.* It was, however, clear to her that he and the marquis truly wished to help them—for whatever reasons of their own.

"So that's what you meant about hiding yourself in a barrel at need," said Jan laughing. Coya had been telling him about Roy's idea to play at being Spanish traders to get into the Maracaibo Lagoon.

"I was all ready with a story too," she continued, "until William handed me those flags. Any story I could have come up with to explain why I stowed away would be useless as long as I was sitting on the flags of every nation at odds with Spain, as well as the English privateer flag."

"It may not have mattered with those border patrols, in light of what we now know about the troop muster in Coro."

"Probably not," admitted Coya, "but while a stowaway might have made the Spaniards suspicious of everyone else, the flags would have turned that suspicion to certainty. It would simply have seemed that everything Captain Toppings wanted to hide was sitting in that barrel. Which, I suppose, it was."

"So what will you do if you're captured this time?" asked Jan.

Coya smiled. She was surprised that no one had yet asked this. "Hopefully I would still be able to shoot the powder magazine," she said, "since I cannot expect a better end from the Spaniards. But I would not like to waste the opportunity to use the ship to our advantage by sinking it before it gets to the port."

"So this mission is of the 'do or die' variety to you then?" asked Jan seriously. "Why not simply retire from privateering with your current earnings? They may not be enough on their own, but they're useless if you're dead."

"I thought of that myself," said Coya. "But while my earnings are substantial, they are not enough to keep me from living in the wild for long." It was this realization that had prompted Coya to volunteer as quickly as she had. "You see, Albert or William can take their earnings and save them, invest them, buy land with them, or do any number of things. Roy could perhaps buy a bigger ship, and Daniel could buy a woman who wasn't repulsed by him." Jan laughed at both of these prospects. *Perhaps I'm beginning to understand their humor.* "I, on the other hand, have to be wealthy enough to be treated as a free citizen or an equal. I cannot simply invest my earnings and expect to not be cheated. I cannot purchase land without expecting that it be stolen. Until I am wealthy enough to have servants and guards, plantations and fences, I cannot live any other life but the one I am living, unless I return to the wild." It made her sad to say these things out loud, but she had given much thought to the matter since the raid on Caracas. She had heard others speak of their plans, and she had realized that beyond food, drink, and entertainment, she could not make the same sort of plans that they made nor live the same sort of lives that they dreamed of. Not yet, and not without help.

"So you volunteered not just to protect your friends or profits or Curaçao," said Jan, "you volunteered to protect your way of life."

"Exactly. I could abandon my friends and companions, but I cannot sign aboard with other crews and other captains. These are the friends and companions I have, and I am not likely to find others that will allow me the privilege of this life. Once they are gone, this way of life is gone for me as well, and I've grown very attached to it. Besides, it's not as if I have had so many friends in my life that I can afford to abandon them."

"I suppose that explains why you have learned so much English so quickly," said Jan. It was an odd comment, since they were speaking in Spanish as they usually did, but Jan did not wait to be asked for an explanation. "They say that the best way to learn a language is to fall in love with someone who speaks it. You are in love with this way of life and, to you, the language of this life is English."

He can be very eloquent at times. "That is a very clever way to describe it," she said, "at least in comparison with the life I have known." Jan appeared to understand exactly what she was saying, but that was part of why she had told him in the first place. *Now for the other reason.* "As long as we are speaking of why I have made this choice though, I am very curious about why you live this way at all. Why do you not simply go back to your daughter and your town, to be with them and help them should the Spanish arrive? Surely you would be of more use to them here, would you not?" She felt a twinge of guilt about using her confidences as leverage to get him to share his own, and he was clearly uncomfortable about the topic, but if he had wanted to spend time speaking with her before she risked her life—for so far he had not offered any medical advice—she thought that he ought to be prepared to really talk to her.

Jan did not disappoint. "I don't want to go into all the details," he said at last, "but let me just say that I feel the need to provide my daughter with a great deal of money in a short amount of time. She will have need of it soon. Don't misunderstand me," he added, no doubt seeing the suspicious look on Coya's face, "we are not in trouble nor do we owe anyone money, but I know that she will have need of whatever savings I can provide her with, and that is an amount that I have deemed to be inadequate so far."

"You have squandered your savings?" asked Coya rather more bluntly than she had intended.

"No, nothing like that," said Jan. "I invested some of it—unwisely, as it turns out. I bought some land here and elsewhere, I built my practice, but I have not saved a great deal of actual money."

"And you did not foresee the need?" asked Coya.

Jan seemed saddened by his own thoughts as he answered, "No. At least I did not foresee the urgency of it." He clearly was not willing to divulge more without great encouragement, and as Coya did not feel it was her place to prod him, she asked no more. *Perhaps some issue of inheritance fell through or he lost all that he had invested.* These were among the concerns others had that she didn't understand, and she could not help but wonder, but she tucked her thoughts away as he resumed speaking. "In any case, I will only receive my share if I am with Roy's crew and participating in whatever venture he has planned. As much as I might prefer to be with my daughter and to help in the town if the Spanish do get through the defenses, I have to look out for my family's interests first."

"Well, I am sure that she appreciates what you are doing for her and will understand that you are doing what is best, should things go wrong for us."

Jan looked even more uncomfortable now. *I wish I knew how to talk to people better than this.* Coya's flash of guilt was over as soon as it began, however. "She doesn't know why I am doing this," said Jan.

"I see," said Coya. "Is she upset with you because of it then?"

"She is distressed, to say the least."

Coya thought for a moment, remembering what it was like to have family. "You should tell her," she said. "We are going into a very dangerous battle, and should the worst happen, she should at least understand why you are allowing it to happen to you." She did not often give personal advice, but she was certain that she was right. Dealing with death was hard enough without the added trouble of having to wonder about the things that could have been resolved sooner.

"You're right, of course," said Jan. "I had been thinking along those lines already, but it helps to have someone else put words to them as well. I will attend to it after I see you safely tucked into the Spanish provisions."

They had not long to wait, however. No more than ten minutes had passed, and Jan was telling a funny story about an odd Englishman whose damaged eye he had had to remove when Coya saw Damien give the signal. He motioned discreetly for them to wait a moment, then went into a back room carrying a bundle that he had brought from the Lonely Shrew. Coya wondered what he was doing, as she had thought they were originally meant to follow him outside. He soon returned, however, and dressed in a manner that suited him much more than his previous disguises. *That must have been what was in his bundle.* He still carried the bundle, but she had no doubt that it now contained his previous garments. His face looked normal and was made up only slightly in the foppish manner that so many of the middle class merchants seemed to prefer. *No doubt that helps to hide his bruises.* She looked to Jan, and he grinned but continued to pretend not to pay attention to Damien.

Damien, however, winked at the startled bartender (who had not marked his exit and reentrance, but must obviously be intrigued by the table's apparent change of occupant) and tossed him a coin that glinted gold in the lantern light. Then he went back to watching the window and ignoring Coya and Jan as he had done throughout their time at the tavern. The two of them forced some light conversation, but they were both paying close attention to Damien now. Any moment now, she would have to stuff herself into a crate or barrel and stay there for the rest of the night. *I hope that Jan really does have some advice about that.*

Soon enough, Damien signaled that they should follow in five minutes and left the tavern. When they emerged after a count of three hundred, they found that he was having a conversation with Melanie Rutger, the same woman that Roy had sold many of Gilbertsen's goods to the first time Coya had been to Curaçao. It certainly didn't feel like it had barely been a week since then.

They waited until Damien motioned to them before they made their way over. "Hello, Mrs. Rutger," said Jan, before Damien could introduce everyone.

"Hello there, doctor," said Mrs. Rutger, "and hello again young lady," she said turning to Coya. "You were in here not a week ago, weren't you? Part of Captain Toppings' crew?"

Coya appreciated being remembered, and was pleased that Mrs. Rutger was smiling at her. She had thought the woman was pleasant from the first time they met. "Yes ma'am," said Coya.

"I have apprised Madame Rutger of our situation," said Damien as they entered her warehouse and closed the door, "and she has agreed to keep the knowledge to herself until the governor makes his announcement."

"Indeed," interjected Mrs. Rutger, "and it does explain why Van Kemper was in here earlier today. He bought up all of the spare powder, shot and firearms I had. I even acquired a couple of cannons recently, but he bought those as well. Obviously he knows or guesses what is going on." Coya wasn't sure why she sounded angry, until she said, "He will probably turn around and sell them at a ridiculously inflated price once the governor *does* make an announcement. I knew Van Kemper was up to something, but I thought that I may as well sell what I could." Van Kemper apparently had a very busy day.

Damien looked perturbed. "Did the Spaniards place an order for extra powder before Monsieur Van Kemper bought everything?"

"No, though they did try to order some along with the provisions they ordered for the morning tide, just before you came by," she said curiously. "I was glad to refuse them, but I see what you're getting at."

"I told Madame Rutger what we're trying to do," Damien explained briefly to Coya and Jan before turning back to Mrs. Rutger. "Once we're gone, I'll have a few barrels sent over from my master's ship. When it arrives, go and tell the Spaniards that you were lucky enough to acquire some from

Captain Rowling. Hopefully they will take that to mean either that their mission is still a secret or that we *may* know about it but that Rowling at least isn't preparing to fight them. Perhaps they will think that Captain Rowling doesn't know about it, even if the others do."

"Very clever," complimented Jan. The more powder that was aboard the Spanish ship when the magazine exploded, the more it was likely to damage the rest of the fleet in the Coro harbor. Coya thought that she would be suitably impressed as well, were she not preparing to lodge in a crate all day.

"Think of it as a donation to the war effort," said Damien. "The Spaniards apparently took the bait and are sailing on the morning tide, so for the moment, we must get to work on this food shipment of theirs."

The task as Damien began to explain it was to rig the crate with a fairly large false bottom for Coya to hide in, but with enough room above it so that the Spaniards could take their one or two daily meals during the short journey to Coro without noticing the false bottom. On top of that, Coya would need to get in and out without making too much noise or spilling food everywhere. Fortunately, as the food consisted entirely of ship's biscuits, it would not make much more of a mess than a pile of wood chips. "Which is basically what it tastes like anyway," said Jan. "As hard as this stuff is," he joked, picking up a biscuit, "perhaps it *would* make a lot of noise falling all over the hold."

"It would probably sound like someone had spilled grape shot," said Coya with a grin.

The Spanish were probably overordering in the event of a storm or to last them into the next voyage, but in any event, the crate was large enough that Coya wasn't completely daunted by the prospect of sitting in it all day. Damien instructed that she would probably be better off waiting until after the midday meal before climbing out of it, but privately she wasn't so sure about that advice. *I will just have to wait and see if I think it's more dangerous to cramp up in there or to risk hiding in the hold.* She had stayed hidden in a cargo hold for far longer, but that was on a much larger ship with three decks. Now she would be hiding on a small sloop, no larger than *The Constance*, and anyone entering the hold had a chance to notice her if she was out of her crate.

As it turned out, Jan and Damien managed to make the false bottom without much trouble. There were plenty of supplies and tools in Mrs. Rutger's warehouse with which to make the alterations, and Coya practiced getting in and out of it a few times after it was finished. They agreed that she should stay there until it was necessary to fit her into the crate, and Jan did give her some advice then about staying limber and focusing her mind in order not to cramp too much. "Get out and stretch when no one is around if you need to," he said, "rather than staying in there until you have to get out at a bad time."

Damien disagreed about some of his suggestions, especially that one, but in the end it was time for them to go. Coya was touched by Jan's concern for her, and she was struck by an idea. "Jan," she said as she pulled out a couple of very full coin purses, "why don't you put these with your savings here in town? That way I don't have to risk losing them. And if the worst should happen, well, I don't suppose anyone needs to know what became of my savings."

Jan was clearly moved by the gesture, and found little to say except "thank you," but that was enough for Coya. He kissed her dirty hand in farewell, as did Damien (if a bit awkwardly), and the two of them left Mrs. Rutger's shop.

Coya made sure that she had her knives and her new pistols secured on her belt, and she stretched her limbs from time to time in preparation for her stay in the crate. "Well, my dear," said Mrs. Rutger, "I don't mind telling you that I wouldn't like to be in your shoes right now."

But Coya felt strangely light of heart. "Actually," she said to the smiling woman, "speaking of shoes, could you look after those for me?" *It's not as if they'll be of much use anyway.*

Mrs. Rutger laughed as Coya took off her boots. "Of course."

* * *

Jan sincerely hoped that he would not be able to keep Coya's share and that she would make it back alive, but he had to concentrate on other things now. He and Damien parted ways before reaching the Lonely Shrew; he to see his daughter and Damien to have the gunpowder delivered to Mrs. Rutger and to inform the marquis and the captains about how their end of the plan had gone so far. "Tell Captain Toppings that I shall be at home if he needs to send for me," said Jan, "after a short visit to my infirmary to see how our injured crewmen are faring."

"Of course, doctor. Good luck tomorrow."

"Good night," said Jan, and Damien nodded as he continued on. Jan wound his way through the streets to where his practice stood and found that Justin and Ben were sleeping soundly. Their bandages remained clean, and he determined not to wake them until morning to see whether or not they would be fit for light duties aboard ship. *They would do well to stay here.* In all likelihood they would balk at missing a chance for more plunder, though Jan couldn't see how they would be of much use or why they should need to take such a risk for a bit more plunder. Jan had brought their shares with him and now he tucked the purses under their covers next to their hands. After leaving a quick note for each of them by their bedsides on the off chance that they failed to notice the surprise, he left them again and made his way home.

How am I going to tell her? Isobel had been quite upset when he had announced his plan to join a privateer crew, and he had foolishly failed to think of a plausible explanation, so she was simply kept in the dark beyond his admission that he needed to raise a great deal of money. He had visited her earlier in the day for a brief time, but she was more insistent than ever that he tell her what was going on. She was strong-willed and intelligent, and that only made him feel more certain of his decision. *She should have the resources to use her talents to their fullest extent.* The risk to his own person that went along with privateering was of no consequence compared to that need, but he could no longer keep his company from her without being honest about what was going on. It was better to have time to adjust rather than having to worry every time he went abroad with the captain. However, he simply could not think of how to broach the subject. *How does a man tell his daughter that he is dying?*

The headaches and tremors had not returned for some time, but he knew they almost certainly would. His colleagues in the medical profession were not quite sure what was wrong with him, but he agreed with their supposition that it had something to do with the growth that had been discovered at the base of his skull—the growth that had reappeared twice already after having been removed. The surgeon had only cut as far into the tissue as he dared, but Jan did not doubt that there was still some part of it attached to his spine, and there was no reason to think that it had simply ceased to grow. Like a weed, it would most likely keep growing back each time it was pruned, and the roots would delve ever deeper unless the whole of it was uprooted. He did his best to eat well and stay fit, and the incisions had been mercilessly sterilized each time, but it was impossible to know how useful these measures were in the end.

His daughter, of course, knew only that he had been ill a couple of times. On the most recent occasion, he had arranged for her to tour some of the property he had purchased on Aruba with the intention of using it for salt mining so that she would be gone during the procedure and the days immediately following it. With some effort, he had kept on his feet in the usual manner after her return, though he had claimed to spend a great deal of time with patients at the infirmary when he had actually had very few patients to care for and had taken long periods of rest in between seeing them. He and his colleagues all agreed that his condition was most likely terminal, but they could only guess at how long he had left. Perhaps a year. Perhaps less, or perhaps as long as two. None would wager on his chances of surviving longer.

Jan had kept his secret from the captain and the rest of the crew not only because he wished to be treated normally, but because his condition was a potential liability to them and he could well find his contract terminated if Roy became aware of it. He sincerely hoped that the tremors did not return in the midst of a surgery, or that he would not be incapacitated by the next recurrence, but his primary concern was maintaining his contract and his subsequent wage. Isobel deserved the largest inheritance he could give her, and his savings was nowhere near enough to keep her in any sort of life beyond the means of any average common woman. Sooner or later, his ability to continue in his profession would be restricted as well, and he would be even less able to provide for her future. *And God forbid that any of my earnings should contribute to my own medical care.* The last thing that he would wish was that his failing medical treatments should take precedence over his daughter's security and future.

Jan felt the scar tissue under his collar, and hoped yet again that the rigidity of the tissue did not force the growth further inwards where it could not be removed. He had only found out through trial and error that removing it helped at all, but he knew that its presence was doing him no good, and this outlook had been rewarded in the end. *I suppose I should just start by telling her about when the illness started and let her know what it really means.* There weren't many ways to dress up the truth in more palatable terms, and perhaps it was fruitless to focus on trying to do so rather than on comforting Isobel.

As he reached his darkened house and unlocked the door, he felt strangely at peace about the upcoming battle. *At least the choice I have made to pursue this life has put me in a position to really help Curaçao and my daughter as well.* If he died tomorrow, at least he would die a hero's death in defense of his home and his nation. Even so, he dearly hoped that he would have more time with Isobel. He stepped over the threshold and a lamp was lit somewhere upstairs. His heart sank and he took a deep breath. *Well, here I go.*

Chapter 19: Fire Ship

Roy yawned as *The Constance* sailed east into the rising sun and lamented to himself once again that he had not slept at all during his stay in Curaçao. *At least I have a proper cabin and bed.* The rest of the crew wasn't so lucky, and he was quite sure that Jan had not slept either. And then there was poor Coya who even now was stowed in a crate, probably being loaded aboard *El Picaflor* and most certainly wide awake. Damien had returned when the night was quite old, after Roy and Captain Morgan had both returned from informing Van Kemper about their separate responses to the ransom offers. Damien told them what he had arranged with Jan, Coya and Mrs. Rutger. After that, the three captains had stayed with the marquis in his room at the Lonely Shrew with Damien and Ajuban discussing what they would do next. Ajuban had drifted off to sleep a couple of times, and Roy had ordered Brian to go and get some sleep after they had agreed on the basic framework of the plan. "Use my cabin, if you like," he had told his navigator, handing him the key. "I shan't be using it tonight, and you will need all the rest you can get."

Brian had been the one to suggest using the wind with their three different types of ships and rigging in order to fool the Spaniards. Captain Rowling had set sail earliest, immediately following their meeting with Damien. They hoped this would not arouse suspicion, but it was common for smugglers and privateers to leave the port of Curaçao at such an hour, and shallow draft ships had little trouble with low tide in the harbor. Captain Morgan had set sail barely half an hour later, and after paying a brief visit to the governor to apprise him of the plan and get his approval, then waiting another hour, Roy was now sailing east. The other two ships, both of which were larger than *The*

Constance and were rigged to take some small advantage of direct wind, had sailed out of the port and southeast, far enough not to be visible to Curaçao. Of course, they could not see the port either from their respective positions, and Captain Rowling was furthest away. However, Roy was making for a point east of Curaçao that would be within sight of both the port and the other two ships, yet still far enough away that the Spaniards should not worry about being pursued. After all, *The Constance* was nearly identical to the Spanish sloop, and the Spaniards had no reason to believe that it would catch them up using the same wind and sailing in the same direction: southwest along the route to Coro.

Of course, Captains Rowling and Morgan also had little reason to believe that *The Constance* could double back in time to catch up with the Spaniards, but Roy knew that Brian could milk every ounce of available speed out of any wind, and he was more or less counting on Brian to get them close enough behind *El Picaflor* by the time Coya set it ablaze to begin the fight in the port of Coro. The other two ships should at least catch up with *The Constance* due to their ability to run with the east wind and they would not have as far south to travel. "If all else fails," Roy had said, "*The Swordfish* and *The Sea Dervish* should be able to catch up to them if we are not in place yet." It could be a gamble, as the two larger ships would be on an intercept course rather than following the same course as *El Picaflor,* and there was thus a possibility that the Spaniards would change course for fear of being cut off. If that happened, the privateers would not have their diversion of a fire ship before they were spotted by the rest of the fleet at Coro. In the end, however, they all agreed on the plan, and the larger ships would simply do their best not to make Captain Arroyo think he would be cut off so that he would maintain course toward the harbor. Then, at the least, Coya should be able to cause considerable damage to the port and fleet, and that alone might force the Spaniards to reconsider their invasion even if the English captains had to abandon their own plans of attack. "In which case," Roy had told Governor Diedrik, "we will fall back and defend the waterways leading to Curaçao."

The governor had agreed to the plan and could suggest no alterations, which was just as well since Rowling and Morgan had already sailed. Roy, however, was more obligated to the governor than they were, and they had all

told the governor that they would inform him of their plan. None of them had thought it would be prudent for all of them to be seen visiting Diedrik once Captain Arroyo of *El Picaflor* had been given reason to suspect their interference. After his visit to the governor, Roy had fetched Major Benito to his ship as he had promised Van Kemper, and he was sure that Captain Arroyo's men marked that. Roy, however, had made sure to have a large enough escort for Benito to ensure that no one would impede them.

Roy had explained the danger to the crew when they turned up at the dock and allowed any of them that wanted to leave or send a message to friends or family in town. He was pleased that no one had stayed behind. Once they had set sail, he told them the details of the plan, though he left out the part that the marquis and his assistant had played, and the whole crew was nervous and excited. He made sure that Benito heard it as well to judge his reaction, and the major's face paled as he realized how much damage such an explosion could do to the fleet. Roy made sure that he was guarded at all times and kept him tied up in the hold for good measure. He was pleased to see that many of the crew were genuinely concerned about Coya. Albert, however, was furious with Roy. He forced himself to speak with civility as a disciplined sailor should, but he could not keep from making it clear what he thought of sending a lone girl (as he obviously considered her, despite her age), however resourceful, on what had every possibility of turning out to be a suicide mission—whether she had volunteered for it or not. Roy sympathized, and he realized that he should have predicted it, but he felt deeply disappointed at this reaction. Albert had barely looked at him since the plan had been revealed. *Hopefully he will get past it before we get to Coro.* At the moment, there was nothing that could be done but to get on with the plan.

He looked around the deck and saw Ajuban leaning against a rail, peering at the port through a spyglass. Ajuban was still in bandages, though he had donned his Spanish breastplate already. Roy was glad that Ajuban had not even considered staying behind. Indeed, no one had, and Roy was proud of the lot of them. Even Justin and Ben had been unwilling to stay in Curaçao to heal, though they were ordered to rest in their hammocks until battle was imminent. At that point, their only duties would be to fire the guns, as that would only involve holding torch staves with slow fuses. Jan had approved this as a duty that was within their abilities, and they were content. *I don't have enough men to refuse any willing help.* Roy sighed. None of the captains had done any recruiting as that would draw attention from the Spaniards, but he would have given much for just half a dozen more men.

"Captain," Ajuban called from his position at the stern, "de Spaniards are leaving de harbor."

"Let me know when they change course," Roy called back to him. "I want to be ready as soon as they set course westward."

"Aye, sir." Ajuban continued intently gazing westward towards the port.

Roy lifted his own spyglass and gazed southeastward. He slowly panned his view southwards until he spotted *The Sea Dervish* and, farther away, *The Swordfish*. They had sailed south a short distance after reaching their positions, presumably to achieve their best points of sail as the east wind had not varied all morning. *They will catch up quickly.* With luck, the Spanish captain would believe he had time to get to Coro and let the larger warships deal with his pursuers rather than feeling in danger of being captured before reaching port. Roy and the others would chase him right towards the other ships, and hopefully Coya would do her part at that moment.

"She's out of de harbor and into open waters, sir," called Ajuban.

"Give the first signal," Roy called to Martin, who dipped the flag twice, though not too conspicuously. Morgan and Rowling would be watching that flag, but so much the better if the Spanish didn't notice. Roy peered out at the English ships and saw them signal their acknowledgement.

The air was tense with anticipation for perhaps ten minutes as they waited for Ajuban to speak. Finally, he called, "She's headed sout'west, captain."

"Give the second signal!" shouted Roy, "Change course to pursue, full speed!"

"Aye sir," shouted Martin as he dipped the flag one final time to indicate "west." "Signal away, sir."

"Aye sir," called Brian as men hurried to raise every scrap of canvas, "changing course."

Roy peered again at the ships of his two colleagues in this venture and saw their return signals. He watched as they changed course under full sails and then turned his attention southwestward. *Now we begin the hunt.*

Coya felt more cramped and uncomfortable than she had expected after perhaps two hours in her crate. *I must be getting old.* She had only just been loaded aboard the Spanish ship, or so she assumed from the noises, from the jostling as the crate was moved, and from the familiar tossing sensation she currently felt. Fortunately the Spaniards had few other provisions to load, and the customs official had not opened any of the goods during his inspection. Damien had said that he would make sure that there would be no detailed inspection, especially as narrow slits had been carved between the boards of the crate so that she could breathe, and he didn't want anyone to notice them. Coya could only assume he had succeeded. *Now if the false bottom is more obvious than we thought, no one will know until we're at sea and I can't escape. Terrific.* She waited and employed some of Jan's suggestions to fight off cramps, but did not dare to move much until it was more or less quiet outside.

She guessed it was perhaps another half hour before she heard shouts from above and felt as if the ship were no longer simply bobbing in place at the dock, but she knew she had longer to wait before even considering vacating her hiding place. Soon after the ship was underway and on course for Coro, the Spaniards would likely take their daymeal, as many would not have had time to breakfast before setting sail. Some would have done so simply so that they could trade away their tasteless biscuit for favors or goods from those who had not had the foresight, or else save them to have more to eat later in the day. She knew that she must wait until after the daymeal, even though it meant she might be caught inside the crate if they spotted the false bottom. The risk of that was less likely than that of being spotted in the hold as men came down to open the crate, but she felt no better about the idea of being caught while folded up helplessly in a box.

As the minutes flowed by, she became more acutely aware of her own anxiety about her situation in anticipation of the crate being opened, but she calmed her nerves as much as possible using more of the methods that Jan had taught her and counted out her breaths as she waited. She almost didn't notice the sounds of boots on the ladder to the hold, but she heard two men talking in Spanish as they came toward her hiding place. She felt and heard someone lift the lid off of the crate. "Biscuits again," someone said. "Why couldn't the captain have laid in better provisions?"

"Right," said the other man, "it's not as if better food would have time to spoil over the course of a day's journey." They continued grumbling to each other as they retrieved several biscuits from the crate. Now was the real test. They would be most likely to notice the false bottom while removing biscuits from the top of the crate. She breathed as shallowly as she could, with her mouth wide open to reduce the sound. She heard them replace the lid and make their way back up the ladder, dragging the hatch back into place as they reached the deck. *Excellent.* She let out a long sigh of relief, but continued to wait and listen for any sign that they were returning for more food. They did not return, and she began to consider leaving her hiding place as she became aware of the cramps once again.

She was just thinking that she would risk a venture into the hold to stretch when she heard raised voices above. She could not hear what they were saying, but she could guess. *They know they're being pursued by now.* If that was the case, men would probably come down to the hold to fetch more canvas and other provisions that they might need to increase their speed or load their guns. She decided to stay put for the time being, but her neck and her legs ached fiercely. *It won't be long before the pains sharpen.* Soon, however, men did come back down to the hold to retrieve supplies. From what she could hear, it did not sound like they were bringing up powder and shot, but *The Constance* likely wasn't close enough to threaten them, and it was probably too early for the other two ships to be visible. Soon the hold was quiet once again, but Coya had an unpleasant realization when she thought about leaving her hiding place. *I never practiced packing myself in here!* Someone else had always helped her put the top of the crate back on. She couldn't believe they had all made that oversight, especially her and Damien. Being stuck in the hold of a Spanish ship that was being pursued was not the time or place to practice either. Grudgingly, she made up her mind to stay in her crate as long as she could, no matter how much it hurt. *I hope this trip isn't as long as everyone said it would be.*

* * *

Captain Arroyo gazed northeastwards as the sun climbed higher in the morning sky. *El Picaflor* was making good time, but they were obviously being followed by the English ship they had seen set out from Curaçao an hour before them. He wasn't very worried about them yet, as the ship was more or less the same as his and was further away. They could catch up, but probably not before *El Picaflor* reached Coro. And if they did catch up, it would probably only be due to having fewer men or arms aboard, which wouldn't be good for them in a fight. *Let them come.* If they were fool enough to follow *El Picaflor* all the way to Coro, they would receive a welcome that wasn't much to their liking. He had ordered all possible speed, as it would be better to discourage his pursuers rather than have them spot the fleet at Coro, and he must continue on as the information he had was better delivered to the admiral without delay.

The captain paid close attention to the following ship for quite some time. There was little else to occupy him. The weather was fair and the wind steady, but somehow the little sloop was slowly catching him up. Every so often he would think that they were changing course and breaking off pursuit, but they always came out of their course correction with even more speed. *That navigator must be able to hear the wind's every fancy.* Well, once *El Picaflor* rounded the coast east of Coro, it could exploit the steady east wind and could quickly make its way south into the port to warn the fleet before the English ship could catch up. By then the fleet would be visible and Captain Toppings might turn back at the sight, though he would be almost on top of the warships. No matter what Captain Toppings thought he knew, he could not possibly be hoping to do anything against such a fleet. *Major Benito must have kept back all that he could.* It seemed the only explanation, unless he had been able to lie to them instead. It would have been difficult indeed to withhold much information in light of what captains such as Henry Morgan tended to do to prisoners who were uncooperative, but few understood the importance of this mission as much as Major Benito did.

Something about the situation seemed out of place though. Since Arroyo's ransom offer for Major Benito had been refused, the English (or Van Kemper himself) must have attempted to get information, but he could not understand why they accepted the offer for Valdez. Surely they were only curious why Valdez was needed so badly, or else why mistreat Benito at all? Perhaps they had not questioned Benito, but considered that the wound Benito suffered during the escape attempt would rank as mistreatment. If so, perhaps they did not want it to be discovered, but Arroyo had kept a watch on Van Kemper's tavern for much of the previous day and had known about it at once. *But if they did not attempt to coerce information from the major, why are they following us?* He could think of no sensible answers.

He panned his gaze eastward and then further south as the sun had climbed higher in the sky and the haze of morning light was lifted, and he thought he saw other shapes on the horizon. He lifted his spyglass. *Damn.* There were two other ships closing on a course that might take them to Coro as well, and Arroyo had little doubt that these were *The Swordfish* and *The Sea Dervish.* As soon as he spotted this, the lookout called out, "Sail ho! Two ships south-southeast of us headed west-southwest, captain."

"I see them," said Arroyo. "Maintain course."

"Aye sir," said the navigator just behind him at the helm.

There wasn't much chance that they would catch him up either, but with all three ships chasing him, he knew that there was more going on than he had originally thought. *Perhaps they* do *know what's going on.* But even three of these ships, and with captains as notorious as Rowling and Morgan, could not hope to significantly disrupt a fleet such as the one awaiting them at Coro. *If they're just trying to keep me from reporting back to the fleet, they underestimate the speed of* El Picaflor. Captain Arroyo smiled.

"Shall we load the guns, sir?" said his first mate.

"No," he said. "Leave the powder and shot in the hold for now. We will go faster if we keep the extra weight in the center of the ship." He had picked up some tricks from Adán San Ramón in Coro from the man's privateering days. Captain Ramón was a competent engineer as well, and he knew exactly how much of a strain he could put on any ship he sailed. "We have no hope of fighting all three of them alone, so we may as well try to outrun them until we have to fight."

"Aye, sir."

Captain Arroyo resumed his musings about what the English captains hoped to achieve by following him, but at the very least he was sure that the fleet would make short work of them. *We might have to deal with them before invading Curaçao just to keep them from interfering, and now is just as good a time as any.* He watched and waited, and as the minutes passed into hours, *El Picaflor* continued the race toward Coro. The English ships were closer than he would have liked, but he was still beating them and now it was simply a matter of time before the fleet became aware of the situation. Then the English captains would pay a heavy price for interfering in Spanish affairs. *We will send them to their friend, Captain McLaughlin.*

* * *

Coya had made sure not to drink much before she had stowed away in her crate so that she would be comfortable for longer, but she had been cooped up inside for quite a few hours and resolved to leave her hiding place now that the midday meal was finished. Tentatively she pushed at the false bottom and felt it shift. She pushed steadily until she felt it lift up and away only to encounter the lid of the crate. The biscuits crunched slightly as she continued pushing upwards, but they weren't even likely to show signs of the strain she was putting on them. She felt the top of the crate lift free, and resisted the urge to raise it high in the air to stretch out her arms. Instead, she tilted her head back to peer out and into the hold. She found that the ladder was within her view to her left and ahead of her. *I must be on the starboard side of the hold.* If the interior of the ship was as similar to that of *The Constance* as the exterior was, she could be sure of her position. Quickly and quietly she lifted the lid off and set the whole pile on top of some barrels to her right. A few biscuits slid out from between the lid and false bottom and onto the floor of the hold but made little sound. Slowly she stretched her body upwards out of the crate, her muscles aching after her long interment.

She stepped from the crate and looked back at the lid and the biscuits. She thought for a moment, then placed the biscuits back in the crate and hid the false bottom underneath it. There would be no more meals for the crew before she lit the powder magazine, and she would rather be able to hide quickly back in the crate without dealing with anything other than the outer lid. The crew had not sounded busy enough for any man to have missed a meal, and the voyage was not long enough for evening shifts to be kept, so she decided that the risk of her ruse being discovered was minimal. Coya placed the lid back on the crate and made her way to a dark corner near the front of the hold. There she stood stretching her legs, her arms, her neck and her aching back. *I wish I didn't have to get back in that thing again.* Either way, the worst of the hiding was over. She was not sure what time it was, but she thought it must have been at least eight hours she had spent in that crate.

After she had relieved herself in the bilge and taken refreshment from a water barrel, she began to look around for the supplies she would need. She had brought a tinder box with her, as well as three fuses that Damien had given her: each for a different amount of time, from ten to twenty seconds. Beyond that, she had nothing but her knives, pistols, powder and shot, and a small water bottle in case she had to make it to shore without being picked up by *The Constance*. It was dark in the hold, though not as dark as the crate had been, and the sun rode high in the sky, shining through the grate above the hold providing enough light for her eyes to see by. She did not dare risk any real light for fear that someone entering the hold would see it or smell the sulphur and smoke, but she had little difficulty seeing into the corners to find what she needed. The powder magazine was aft of the ladder behind a wet felt curtain, just as it was aboard *The Constance*. The ship was designed in such a way as to drain water towards the curtain and thence to the bilges so that no labor need be expended to keep the curtain wet as a precaution against fires. In Coya's case, the curtain provided concealment as well, but there was nowhere to hide should anyone pull it aside. The shot was stored in crates on the other side of the ladder, lining the way down the center of the ship and away from the magazine.

Coya stood considering the powder barrels which were held in place by cargo netting secured to the hull and deck by iron hooks. *I wonder if I can squeeze enough shot into place on either side of the powder.* It occurred to her that even if the other ships in the harbor failed to catch fire, a few of them might take quite a bit of hull damage from round shot and chain shot if she arranged it well. As the powder was below the water line, she would have to raise the crates of shot up on top of other crates or barrels or the shot would simply be propelled downwards through the hull and into the water. She had spoken to the others about the possibilities of using shot to maximize the damage, but she wasn't sure that she could move the heavy crates noiselessly or without being seen through the grate above the ladder. However, Coya had plenty of time to think of how to arrange everything. For the moment, she simply needed to see the layout of the hold and think about which fuse to use.

She made her way forward up the length of the hold, keeping to the shadows and walking silently. She found a quantity of lantern oil, and the beginnings of a plan began to form in her mind. However, after her muscles felt more relaxed and she had discovered where everything was, she crept back inside the crate and replaced the lid. Sooner or later the captain was bound to order men to fetch powder and shot to the deck as they entered port with the English ships close behind, and she could hear neither a sign of heightened activity above nor any sound of nearby ships or harbor.

Nearly two hours later, as she was beginning to consider leaving her hiding place again to take a look around, she heard men opening the grate and heading down the ladder to the hold. She had just put her hand against the lid of the now roomier crate as she held a knife in her other hand, but she stopped short before opening the lid. *That was lucky.* She sat crouched and still, keeping her breathing low and quiet as she listened. Men were heading for the aft area of the hold and there were also men close by her hiding place opening crates and handing things up the ladder to waiting hands. *This is it.* They were clearly fetching powder and shot, and Coya could hear more orders being shouted but could guess what was going on: *El Picaflor* was preparing for battle. Now she had only to hope that they left no one below to fetch goods or repair damage as need dictated like Roy sometimes did.

After a few breathless minutes, Coya heard the grate being replaced and the sounds of activity died down a few minutes later, presumably as the crew finished loading the guns on deck. *Now is my chance.* She raised the lid of her hiding place gently to peer around the hold. Discovering that it was empty, she quickly rose and stepped out, replacing the lid and creeping towards the remaining shot, shedding biscuit crumbs as she moved. Having had long to make her plans, she quickly checked to see which crates were still full of shot, then made her way to the spare bolt of cloth. It was felt, just like the curtain shielding the powder magazine from view. She cut a piece large enough to fit one of the crates onto, then made her way to where the oil was kept. Oil and cloth in hand, she oiled a wide path to the powder magazine and on both sides of the barrels before returning to where the shot lay. Then she laid the cloth on the oil and with all her might she lifted one crate onto the cloth. *Now I can move it quietly.*

She pushed and pulled the crate back towards the magazine and to one side of the barrels, making sure to keep it from slipping off the felt cloth, then repeated the whole process with another crate. She winced as the oil and the cloth began to wear thin and the crates made occasional scraping noises when she pushed them towards the aft end of the hold, but there was plenty of shouting on the deck above now to mask the sounds. Quickly she took barrels from the magazine and placed them upright on either side of the rest, then summoned up the strength to lift each crate of shot up onto them. *There.* She looked upon her work with satisfaction and felt fortunate to have been left alone long enough to arrange everything as carefully as she had. She retrieved smaller casks of chain and grape shot to place atop her sculptures on either side of the magazine and carved a hole large enough for fuse and air in the side of one of the barrels in the middle of the netting. She poked the fifteen second fuse through it, burying it in the powder. If she had to remove the grate and fire a couple of shots to escape, the fuse should give her enough time.

It was not long before she heard shouts above, and then shouts on either side of the ship. *We've reached the fleet!* Without delay, she lit the fuse with her tinder box, drew a pistol, and made her way quickly towards the ladder. Just at that moment, a man heaved the grate aside and began to scurry down the ladder. He clearly meant to fetch something from the hold as he did not seem to notice her at first. In desperation, desiring not to be noticed until she was up the ladder, she drew a knife and stabbed him in the chest as he turned around. Fortunately he did not scream, but she did not take the time to retrieve her knife before climbing the ladder, carrying her pistol in her left hand. She heaved herself over the last few rungs and onto the deck so that those on deck would not have time to catch her on the ladder.

Without time to take in her surroundings, she had the impression of a large mass to the starboard on her left and a few ships closing on *El Picaflor* from behind. All of her concentration, however, was on escaping. She scampered to the starboard rail as men began to shout and draw weapons, and the captain barked orders. She recalled hearing him shout "hard to port" before she had emerged from the hold, and with one final motion, she aimed her pistol at the helmsman and fired. She was sure she had hit him, but time was running out. *It's now or never.* She leapt over the side in a graceful but frantic dive and took a deep breath as shots rang out above her. Down, down she plunged, swimming as far out and as deep as she could, doing her best to get away from the blast and behind the ship where hopefully none of the shot she had placed by the magazine would hit her. *Now the fight begins.* She had done her part, and done it well, but Roy and the others still had worse to come.

* * *

Crewman Peña leapt aside as the small woman fired her pistol, but he did not have time to think or react before she was over the side and Captain Arroyo was shouting orders at him. "Peña! Get down to the powder magazine and check that it is secure!"

Peña had a bad feeling that the captain's grasp of the situation was as accurate as it usually was, and he practically jumped down the ladder to obey. Sure enough, he spotted a flickering light coming from behind the curtain to the powder magazine and made all speed to put it out. He shoved the curtain aside and saw the fuse alight and with only a few seconds left to burn before it reached the powder. Another two steps and he would be there. However, there was a slippery substance underneath his feet, and he slipped and fell prone as he ran. *Oil.* Panicked, he jumped up and leapt at the fuse. The sparks flared suddenly, and the light of them was the last thing he ever saw.

Chapter 20: The Battle of the Harbor

Roy had been pleased to find that *The Constance* had gained steadily on its Spanish prey all day, though he still found it amazing that Brian had managed to dog them so consistently. Morgan and Rowling had made good progress westward as well, but when they turned further south to follow *El Picaflor* towards Coro, they had begun to lag. Roy had ordered Brian to keep his course, but privately he had been very disappointed, thinking that they would have to alter their plans. Soon, however, the wind had begun to shift more to the northeast, and the larger ships once again had begun to catch them up. The next couple of hours had been nerve-wracking. Brian was squeezing every ounce of speed out of the wind that he could, but Roy had paid special attention to the deck of *El Picaflor* to watch for signs that they had captured Coya or that they were keeping men out of the hold, thus allowing her to accomplish her task.

Once they rounded the part of the coast that screened the harbor and the Spanish fleet from their view, Morgan had moved his ship to Roy's port quarter as it was his part to begin firing on the fort as soon as he could. Rowling moved to the starboard and made his way directly towards the war galleon, *El Huracán*. *He's certainly got guts.* Even so, *The Constance* was out in front, and although it was more maneuverable than the other two ships, Roy knew that one solid volley from any of the ships could finish him. He was mostly counting on Coya to accomplish her mission in time to distract the enemy ships while he fired broadsides at the war galleon and at one of the barques closer to the docks. However, most of the soldiers had been loaded aboard the larger ships and they were running out their guns even now. The two galleons were fortunately oriented north-south, one behind the other and away from the docks, minimizing how many guns they could bring to bear in the first few moments of the attack. His course would take him right between the two galleons and the war galleon if he stayed on it, which he had no intention of doing, but he had managed to harry *El Picaflor* into sailing past the war galleon and towards the opposite side of the two merchant galleons and nearer the docked barques which *could* fire on him almost as soon as he was within range. The Spanish sloop was cutting its course awfully fine, as if to take full advantage of the first merchant galleon's bulk so that Roy would have to fire at the larger ship instead. *Hurry up Coya.* He could not wait any longer. "Hard to port, Brian!" he shouted. "Prepare to fire the starboard guns!"

No sooner had Brian said "Aye, captain" than Roy saw Coya jump up onto the deck. He watched with rapt attention as she made her way to the rail and fired a shot. The helmsman slumped over and no one replaced him in the confusion, but Roy's eyes were fixed on Coya as she dived into the water and Captain Arroyo finally jerked the tiller over to give the galleon a wider berth. *This is it!* "Coya's jumped over the side!" he shouted to his crew (who he knew would worry otherwise) as he removed the glass from his eye.

He was only just in time to see the greater scene before him as the explosion tore the little sloop to pieces. Shrapnel blew straight out to both sides and into the first galleon on the starboard side and one of the barques to the former sloop's port side. Fires raged through the rigging and the decking on both ships and several crewmen were blown clear off the deck of the barque. The explosion destroyed a huge section of the galleon's starboard hull and the ship began to list heavily and take on water as cannons and men fell into the sea. Many of the longboats still in the water were shredded or capsized and dozens of men who had not been blown off the decks of the larger ships were beginning to jump overboard. Even if the captain of the galleon had failed to give the order to abandon ship—if he was still alive— men were wise enough not to wait. Flaming wreckage rained down on the second merchant galleon and two of the other barques, as well as the war galleon which had taken damage to its poop deck. With luck, the rudder had been disabled, but Roy could not afford the time to find out. *Well done, Coya!*

Many of his crew cheered, and Roy could hear the same aboard Rowling's and Morgan's ships, but the crew of *The Constance* also made ready for Roy to order the first volley.

Morgan was not yet in position to fire on the fort, as the foremost barque—*La Fortuna*, as it turned out—was already underway and sailed across the path of *The Sea Dervish*. Morgan, however, exploited their failure to fire at him during the distraction provided by the explosion, and maneuvered around them to fire his own broadside at the ship's waterline. *The Constance* had quickly turned to port and Roy seized his opportunity. "Starboard guns, fire!" The volley blasted holes in the already damaged hull of the war galleon as they continued trying to get their fires under control. "Man the port guns!" *If only I had enough men.* Bert and Daniel were reloading the starboard guns, but they were doing the work of eight men by themselves as the others rushed to man the guns on the port side. The war galleon fired a belated volley back at *The Constance,* but only a couple of shots hit. Thankfully they hit above the waterline, as the larger shot from the war galleon's cannon could sink Roy's little sloop in a heartbeat. *Hopefully Jan is okay.* The surgeon was currently in the hold keeping an eye on Benito and waiting to treat any injured men. No doubt Luuk was busy repairing the planking already. He had been assigned carpenter's duties as Justin was not yet fit enough to carry out that task.

A moment later, *La Fortuna* was alongside Roy's port side after Morgan's volley. "Port guns, fire!" Roy shouted, and *La Fortuna* took several blasts to its aft quarter as it turned to bring its own cannons to bear on Roy's and Morgan's ships. *They won't miss any more opportunities to fire.* Roy was sure that the distraction of the fire ship had played its part, but while many ships were still dealing with the aftermath, no captain would fail to keep his mind on the battle now that shots were being fired. Roy was shaken from his thoughts by a roaring explosion directly starboard. The galleon that had been alongside *El Picaflor* when it exploded had just exploded as well. Men and longboats were still being lowered into the water when the galleon's own magazine caught fire, and this second, larger explosion caused even more damage to the fleet and created yet more chaos. The loss of life was tremendous, and though the second merchant galleon had steered clear of its sister ship before the explosion, many soldiers on deck were thrown into the water or fell with shrapnel wounds and did not get up again.

Some of the wreckage even landed on the deck of *The Constance.* "Clear away that burning spar!" Roy shouted, and Ajuban pulled men from the port guns to put out the fire immediately. Fortunately none of the rigging had caught fire. *We got in a bit close, it seems.* "Reload the starboard guns!" Men ran from one side of the ship to the other to help Bert and Daniel finish reloading. Two of the barques had been berthed towards the south end of the docks behind the galleons, and they were still largely undamaged. So far they had been kept out of the fight due to their distance and the obstruction that the rest of the fleet created, but any moment they would maneuver into better positions, and they still had enough guns to sink all three English ships between them without help from the rest of the fleet.

Captain Morgan began firing on the fort, even as the barque that had been closest to the first explosion, *El Sabueso,* began firing at *The Sea Dervish.* The shots were ill aimed, and a barrage of small arms fire from Morgan's men felled several men on the deck of the barque, but Morgan did not change course. *What on earth is Captain Rowling doing?* Roy had not noticed any volleys from *The Swordfish,* though Rowling's gunners were renowned in Port Royal. Roy gazed back at Rowling's ship and noted that the man had passed up a chance to get in a perfectly good broadside on *La Fortuna.* Then he saw *The Swordfish* line up off the starboard flank of the war galleon, and her guns began to fire one at a time into the damaged aft hull below the water line. Four shots, five and the war galleon began firing back as it turned, but Rowling took little notice. Six shots.

On the seventh there was another explosion. Rowling had been targeting the powder magazine, which was always kept below the water line in the aft section. Even if he had failed to hit it, the ship would take on water and probably flood the whole aft section, powder, rudder and all. *I can't believe he did it.* But the wreckage of *El Huracán* spread wide over the waves in evidence of the miraculous turn of events, though it was too far away from the other ships now to cause further significant damage to them. *I wonder if the admiral was aboard that thing. El Huracán* certainly made a suitable flagship, and if Admiral Sergio Cadiz had boarded before the battle commenced, he was surely dead by now. There had not been enough warning for men to abandon ship, and Roy did not believe that anyone could have survived.

Morgan and Roy each fired another volley at *La Fortuna* as *The Constance* turned a complete loop to pursue the other more heavily damaged *El Sabueso* between them. "Reload port guns!" he shouted as Morgan continued firing at the fort. Chunks of masonry fell from the high walls of the fort, but many of its guns were as yet undamaged and it began firing back. Morgan's longboat exploded into fragments as a direct hit blasted into it from the hillside, and another shot took his bowsprit clean off, sail and all. *The Constance* took a direct hit to her midsection from the barque *El Sabueso* in spite of the quarrels and pistol shot that Ajuban and his men fired into the soldiers. It was much more difficult to interfere with the functioning of enemy gun crews on a barque by using small arms fire, as they were sheltered by the gun deck. Roy's cannons were all on the main deck and exposed to the elements, but so far he had not suffered losses unless those belowdecks had been hit. *Hopefully they hit Benito first.*

La Fortuna was sinking fast, but Roy was focused on his new prey, *El Sabueso*. Her rigging was heavily damaged and Roy was confident that she could not maneuver into position for another volley before he could put her out of commission. They passed close to the aft of the barque and Roy saw the captain there shouting orders to his crew. "It's Captain Torres," he said to Brian. It seemed like ages since Torres had stopped them as they entered the Maracaibo Lagoon disguised as Spaniards. But Brian had one hand on the whipstaff to steer and was already pulling a pistol out of his belt with the other. He fired at Captain Torres and Roy saw Torres fall as Brian shoved the pistol back into his belt. *I really do have the best navigator in the Caribbean.* Roy barked a short laugh before ordering his crew to fire yet again.

"Captain," shouted Albert, "I see Coya in the water!"

"We don't have time to pick her up yet," shouted Roy. "But prepare to throw her a line once we finish off this ship." He figured that the next volley should do it, but he needed to catch up with the other two barques that were closing on Captain Rowling. Rowling was moving across the path of the last galleon, and the barques were closing in to disrupt him.

"Aye sir," Albert shouted back. He sounded greatly relieved, so Roy guessed that Coya was swimming rather than floating lifelessly in the water.

"Fire!" Roy shouted. The volley from his port guns tore the enemy rudder to shreds and the ship was taking on water through a large portion of its aft section. "Reload!" Men began to abandon the enemy ship, or else Roy would not have risked sailing right by their starboard guns. He needed to reach Rowling's position as quickly as possible if he was to help against the remaining three ships, and Morgan began heading towards the southern docks after one last fruitful volley at the fort. Now that most of the targets in their vicinity were neutralized, Morgan and Toppings could expect more frequent volleys from the fort unless they sailed in closer to the last remnant of the Spanish fleet and forced the men at the fort to worry about hitting their own ships. *Caught between a rock and a hard place.* Morgan had damaged the fort and some of its guns appeared to be obstructed by rubble, but the massive thirty-two pounders it boasted were even deadlier than those aboard a galleon and Morgan's ship was in a bad state as it limped toward the docks under fire. Once on land, Morgan's men would be more dangerous than aboard his sinking ship.

"Throw Coya a line as we pass by, Albert," Roy shouted. He could use the extra pair of hands aboard for the task ahead, and she would no doubt prefer to get out of the water as well.

"With pleasure, sir," called Albert. As they began hauling Coya aboard without even slowing down, Roy thanked the heavens for all the rigging damage that the enemy fleet had suffered from the explosions. It was largely due to the fires and damaged rigging that Roy and Morgan had been able to outmaneuver the enemy barques, as the position of the port made sure that the enemy could make better use of the wind than if they were on the open sea. Sailing into the wind would have meant sailing slowly towards the shore and the docks, whereas the enemy barques had already been closer to the shore than the English ships and would have been able to sail into the fight at full speed had they suffered no damage beforehand. Now it was up to Roy to deal with the remaining barques and to allow Rowling to tackle the galleon, *El Camello del Mar,* if he could.

But Rowling was no fool and had made sure that the smaller ships could not approach unmolested. The nearest of the barques, *El Loro,* bore the scars of fire damage to her rigging, though her crew had managed to put out the fires. Rowling had apparently loaded chain shot into a few of his aft port cannons, for when he shouted "fire," the shots whistled through the air and tore away several lines and spars, and damaged the mainsail. *The Swordfish* continued on course to intercept the galleon, which had begun to turn her starboard guns on Rowling's ship. Morgan fired a last, deadly volley at the now less maneuverable barque Rowling had just damaged and Roy made up his mind to chase the other one. It was more or less undamaged and was closing fast in the northeasterly wind. Whatever happened next, the Spaniards would not be invading Curaçao, but for the three captains, the battle was now a fight for survival.

* * *

Manuel Benito felt very lucky not to have been killed by the shots that ripped through the hold of *The Constance*. One of them had gone right over his head, missing both him and Jan by perhaps a foot, though both of them had been hit by splinters of the hull. So far the shots had not hit below the waterline, but the hold was still taking on water with every wave and Jan was helping a Dutchman named Luuk to patch the hull. *Now for it.* As long as Jan was distracted, Manuel had a chance to escape. The powder magazine was only a short dash from where he was, and he had little doubt that he could find a way to detonate it. Of course, a short dash would seem much more achievable if his leg were up to the task, and the knife wound had been deep enough to impede him for at least several days. Nevertheless, he meant to try. It was a desperate measure, and he would not survive to see his wife Sofia again, but he would take at least one of the English ships out of the fight. Benito had frequently asked how the battle was going when he could not hear for himself, and the crew was surprisingly forthcoming with their answers. *I suppose they don't think I can do anything about it.*

So far, the battle had gone far worse for the Spanish fleet than he had anticipated, and not only had the admiral been slow to deploy the ships, but he had foolishly made a priority of loading as many soldiers aboard them as possible. One of the key reasons that the English won so many engagements at sea was that they treated their vessels as platforms to carry cannons, whereas the Spaniards had a habit of viewing them as troop transports. Manuel had trained the marines in his home of Santa Marta to adopt the English view where appropriate, and had helped design strategies for the fleet to reach Curaçao safely—at which point Valdez was to have commanded the land invasion—but obviously the admiral had reverted to traditional Spanish tactics when forced to improvise a defense. With soldiers crammed onto the warships, and the warships still too close to the harbor and to each other, the fire ship had done its job far too well. Manuel sincerely hoped that the seemingly insignificant pieces of information he had provided had not contributed to this tragic loss of life at the hands of the English captains. *If I can get to the powder magazine, I shall be redeemed in any case.*

Water had splashed on him frequently since the hull had been damaged, and he looked down at the ropes that bound him. Jan had tied them very well, and in a very curious and complicated fashion, but now they were wet and Manuel thought perhaps he could wriggle free of them. Every so often Jan looked back at him, but for the most part he was preoccupied with the repairs. Manuel twisted his arms and rolled his shoulders around backwards as far as he could, but soon found there was more to Jan's complicated web of cords than he had at first thought. Each time he tried to free one of his arms, the cords pulled harder on the other one somehow. Perhaps the tiny bit of slack generated by the wetness of the rope would allow him to free an arm without him doing any real damage to himself, but clearly it would have been impossible to escape without that slight advantage.

He kept an eye on Jan and waited for the best opportunity. When Jan was once again busy with the repairs, Manuel gave it one more effort. He turned and twisted, and pulled his hand further and further away from the cords. The pressure on his other arm was excruciating, but his hand was almost free. Then suddenly, he felt a searing pain in his shoulder and stifled a cry. He relaxed his hand at once, but the pain did not go away. Jan directed a piercing gaze at him. Apparently he had heard Manuel's stifled grunt. "You've dislocated your shoulder, haven't you?" he asked with a knowing smirk.

Manuel felt as if the blood were draining from his face from both the pain and from his efforts being discovered. "What did you do?" he asked in a strained voice.

"Major, I am a doctor," said Jan in satisfied tones, "and I flatter myself that I am a *very* good one. You won't be getting out of those cords without rendering your limbs useless to the point where you may as well have remained bound. Furthermore, I won't be treating your shoulder until you have given your word as an officer and a gentleman to cease your escape attempts—and not until after the battle, in any case."

"You would make an excellent torturer," Benito spat.

"Perhaps," said Jan, and if he took offense it did not show, "though I learned enough about torturers from listening to your inquisitors that I would not presume to claim such competency."

Manuel said nothing, but the pain in his shoulder flared with every breath. There was little he could do but sit and wait. It was still likely enough that the remaining Spanish ships would sink *The Constance* anyway, but he would prefer to die with honor if die he must. That, at least, would console him somewhat for the thought of never returning home again.

* * *

Ajuban's chest felt more bruised than ever as he pulled the lever back on his crossbow to reload once again, but the thrill of battle was in him and things were going well. A critical volley could sink *The Constance* at any moment, but the fact that they were still afloat and able to maneuver was remarkable in itself. *If only we had more men.* No doubt the captain was thinking the same thing, but Ajuban was more concerned with the Spanish soldiers than with their ships. Roy meant to board the last barque, *La Mongosta,* before the limping *El Loro* caught up to them, and had ordered two of the port guns to be loaded with grape shot and moved to the bow of the ship, but Ajuban was doubtful that so few men could take the ship even then. The small caliber cannon aboard *The Constance* could not fire enough shot to clear away many soldiers, and Ajuban's small squad of men was not likely to reduce their number much further. He turned to Coya who, though rather waterlogged, had joined his group since being pulled out of the water. "Bring some grenades up from de weapons locker," he said.

"Yes, sir." She smiled and vaulted down the ladder to the hold. If they could control the enemy deck with explosions and swordplay, in addition to Ajuban's cover fire, perhaps the captain stood a chance. Roy would be leading the charge in any case, and Ajuban meant to see that the first man to aim a shot at him died with a quarrel in his chest.

Ajuban only had Coya, William, Bert and Daniel at his disposal, and the latter three were to join the boarding party. Ben and Justin were ordered to join Ajuban and Coya to provide cover fire once the boarding party charged over the side, but they had a cannon volley to fire at the barque's gun deck first. "Prepare to fire!" shouted Roy as both ships prepared for a broadside, but the Spaniards got there first. The barque's eight starboard guns fired into *The Constance* as the crew ducked. Two of the Englishmen manning the rear port gun disappeared in a spray of blood as the gun itself was torn from its carriage. Ajuban could hear the hull splinter below and the sound of water rushing into the hold. Part of the bow was blasted apart, and the rail on which the port swivel gun was mounted was torn off and caught Tiede's friend Jacob in the face and chest with a sickening crunch, sending him overboard. Ajuban was not sure that he had ever spoken with Jacob for more than a few seconds at a time since he joined the crew with Tiede, Bert and Luuk, but he would miss the man's jolly manner and exuberance each time he received his share of the plunder.

He banished such thoughts and poked his head above the rail to survey the barque. "Fire!" shouted Roy, and their own volley answered back. Three of the gun ports were blown wider, and Ajuban could hear the cries from across the water as men fell with terrible injuries.

"Fire!" Ajuban shouted to his own men, and they fired shots onto the deck of the enemy ship just as another cannon shot sounded from the rear of *The Constance*. Justin had apparently discovered that the rear cannon, while now unmanned and unhoused, was still vaguely pointing at the Spanish vessel, and he had made his way over to it and fired. The blast caught several men coming up the stairs from the barque's gun deck, and the volley from Ajuban's men felled three more Spanish soldiers near the mainmast.

"Grapnels at the ready," shouted Roy, "prepare to board!"

Coya returned from the hold with an armload of grenades and snatched the slow fuse formerly carried by the two dead gunners off the deck as men took up their new positions. "Captain," she called, "Luuk is dead, and Jan has his hands full with the hull damage and with keeping an eye on Benito. He needs help with the planking."

Luuk as well? Ajuban saw Tiede and Bert both choke down their reactions and prepare to board *La Mongosta*. Tiede wasn't going to let his slight limp keep him from the action, and Roy had relented. Tiede looked even more ready for battle now.

"Send me below, captain," said Justin suddenly. "If I fall, at least the doctor will be there."

"Go," said Roy, not taking time to argue. Justin hurried down the ladder, wincing the entire way. "Brian, move us in."

As they waited for the last few seconds before boarding, Ajuban glanced around and saw Rowling's ship fire point blank into the lower gun deck of the galleon. Rowling too was preparing to board, and at this range, the cannon on the galleon's upper gun deck could not be aimed below the waterline of *The Swordfish*. He saw Rowling's men rush up the stairs just before the galleon's volley blew through his own gun deck, and Rowling was rapidly giving orders to his gunnery sergeant as he drew blade and pistol. *That's odd.* In the thick of battle, captains generally shouted orders, but Rowling was leaning in close when he spoke. Figuring Rowling was up to something clever, Ajuban turned his attention back to *La Mongosta* in front of him as Roy shouted, "Grapnels away!"

"Fire!" shouted Ajuban, and his small force of marksmen fired into the waiting soldiers to keep them from repelling or severing the lines being tossed over. The cannons loaded with grape shot fired as well, and soldiers fell screaming as the blasts ripped through them. Coya fired a pistol as she held a lit grenade, then hurled the grenade towards where men were still trying to get up the stairs from below. The enemy soldiers fired shortly afterwards, and Ajuban saw two of the newer recruits fall as Roy led them to the rail, but Ajuban focused on reloading his crossbow.

"Charge!" shouted the captain as he leapt over the side followed by Albert, Martin, and nearly all of the able-bodied crewmen from *The Constance*. Ajuban had already reloaded his crossbow and he fired it as one of the Spanish officers aimed a pistol at Roy. The man fell, pierced between the ribs, and Roy landed on his feet after firing his own pistol. Then he began to dance. At least it looked like a dance to Ajuban, just as it always did when he had a moment to watch. One man fell slashed across the throat by Roy's blade, and another was disarmed by a slash across the wrist and finished with a thrust to the heart before Ajuban had even finished cranking the lever on his crossbow. The soldiers could not get past him, and Roy's men boarded more or less safely behind him, beginning their advance towards the stern. Ajuban kept firing, and Coya continued to lob grenades at the stairs, driving men down to the lower decks or forward into Roy's boarding party.

Jan hauled Major Benito up onto the deck, still bound shoulder to ankle with cords. "Keep an eye on him," he said, "I have to get back down there and help with the repairs, unless someone up here needs my attentions." Benito looked white as a sheet, and his visage was not improved by his sight of the battle aboard the Spanish barque.

"No-t'ing you can do up here," said Ajuban as he fired another quarrel, "go on and help Justin, but make sure dat Luuk's body isn't lost at sea, if you can."

"I'm afraid there isn't much left of it," said Jan sadly as he leapt back down into the hold.

Four more men had fallen to the captain's sword, and Albert advanced side by side with him now wielding his new blade and a belaying pin in his other hand as they cut a swath towards the mainmast and the Spanish captain. Soldiers rushed up to form a line in front of their captain and Ajuban fired into them. Many times, Ajuban thanked the Heavens that Roy had armed his crew with so many flintlocks and had captured the ones the soldiers in Caracas would have sent here to Coro. Whenever he saw an enemy soldier aboard *La Mongosta* armed with a flintlock rather than the bulky wheellocks or matchlocks, he made sure to target them if he had no more urgent targets to shoot at. The sooner that Roy could reach the enemy captain, the sooner he could get them to surrender, assuming that Roy could best him. Coya was out of grenades, and *The Constance* had sailed further away from the barque anyway as all the lines had gone slack or snapped. The area behind the stairs on *La Mongosta* had caught fire, but men began to come up from below. "Keep firing at de men on de stairs!" Ajuban said to Coya and Ben. Meanwhile, he continued to concentrate on those advancing to help the enemy captain. He peered over at *El Camello del Mar* briefly and noticed that

Rowling's men were climbing aboard it or swinging over from the rigging, while the gunners aboard *The Swordfish* frantically reloaded the extra guns on Rowling's main deck as the ship sailed by the enemy's starboard quarter.

Captain Toppings soon engaged the Spanish captain, and Ajuban didn't dare fire into their duel, but his worries were soon banished when Roy sent the captain's blade flying from his hand. The captain called for his men to surrender, and soon Roy's small boarding party had disarmed them and claimed the ship. Ajuban turned his attention to the Spanish galleon. Those of Rowling's men who had not been killed by Spanish musket fire as they boarded were cutting through the soldiers and making straight for the stairs, but they left dozens of soldiers in their wake who quickly followed behind them.

"The fools!" said Benito incredulously, but with a note of satisfaction as he followed Ajuban's gaze. "They'll be caught between the gun crews and the soldiers."

"I wouldn't be so sure of dat, major," said Ajuban. He had noticed that *The Swordfish* had trimmed her sails after sailing far enough to have a better firing angle up onto the galleon's deck and the gunners had finished reloading, and now they appeared to be waiting for something. Perhaps fifty soldiers followed hard on the heels of Rowling's men as they ran down the stairs belowdecks. However, as soon as the last of Rowling's men disappeared from sight, the gunners aboard *The Swordfish* fired. Their close volley of grape shot, aimed at the dozens of soldiers crowding near the stairs, had a devastating effect. Perhaps two thirds of them fell, and at that moment, Rowling's gunners sprang up with muskets and fired into the remnant of the soldiers on deck, dropping many more of them. Now Rowling would only have to deal with the soldiers and gunners below, and the gunners would be ill prepared for them. Those on the lower gun deck had likely suffered heavily from Rowling's last volley of round shot before boarding, and were unlikely to render significant aid to those on the upper gun deck. *He's done dis before.* Ajuban would have wagered his share on it. He glanced over at Benito. The major's expression had turned rather somber.

"Get below and help repair de hull," Ajuban said to Coya. "Tell Jan dat we may be receiving wounded shortly, but he should keep working on de repairs until he's called for."

"Yes, sir," said Coya, and she headed down to the hold.

El Loro was low in the water and had turned back toward the harbor to stop Captain Morgan's men from taking full possession of the port. Morgan had deliberately beached his ship to keep it from sinking and was fighting off soldiers near the docks, but sporadic fire came from the fort as soon as English colors flew above *El Camello del Mar* and *La Mongosta*. *El Loro* was too damaged and slow to beat Roy and Rowling to the docks, and her captain surrendered once his ship was overtaken. The English captains were in a good position to land troops to deal with the remaining soldiers in the town, and Ajuban wanted to keep the men active until then. "Reload de port guns!" he shouted. *Dat fort could still sink us wit' one good shot.*

Ajuban had Ben secure the cannons and get the deck cleared of debris and any hazards like dropped slow fuses or loose powder, while he kept watch on Benito. Curaçao was safe. Now it was time to exact their reward from Coro itself.

Chapter 21: Rest and Restitution

Coya was glad to be on dry land once again, though she felt anything but dry and she knew the fight was not yet over. Several hundred Spanish soldiers must surely have perished in the battle, in addition to those killed in the initial blast of *El Picaflor's* powder magazine, but there were still soldiers at the fort and more had defended the south end of the harbor as the English ships approached. A barrage of grape shot from Rowling's new galleon had killed many of those Morgan had been fighting and scattered the rest, and under cover of the ships' guns, Roy and Rowling had begun to put men ashore.

Spanish soldiers continued to harry them from behind warehouses and shops as the privateers pushed them further into town in a forced retreat, but the captains had agreed to send a force of men directly towards the fort with the intention of setting a fire at the entrance and shooting any that emerged until the commander there issued an order of surrender. "Make sure the soldiers don't outflank you on the way there," said Morgan to his first mate. "Keep formation with swordsmen guarding musketeers and reload under cover as often as you can."

"Aye sir," said the first mate and set off towards the fort with thirty men.

Captain Morgan and his dozen or so remaining crew went with Rowling and Toppings as they divided their forces to sweep through the town. Roy had very few men left to lead ashore. At least one of them was under Jan's care back aboard *The Constance,* and he had left a few other men aboard both of his ships to stand guard and repair the damage. Roy now had less than ten of his crew accompanying him into the town. With most of Morgan's crew gone to the fort and so few crewmen remaining under Roy's command, the bulk of their raiding party consisted of Rowling's men who had not been assigned to guard the ships or man the guns (which still fired on the fort), and those totaled little more than those under Roy and Morgan combined. *There are more soldiers than that lurking behind those buildings.*

The soldiers still had a strong position in the town, but they generally had only a musket each, mostly matchlocks from what Coya had seen so far, and some were armed with swords. Roy, however, had made sure that each member of his crew carried at least three flintlock pistols and a blade, and the men under Rowling and Morgan were similarly armed. Coya could not understand why the Spaniards did not anticipate such tactics by providing their own soldiers with comparable armaments, especially as Roy had indicated these were somewhat typical tactics used by raiders of any nation, but she was not about to question her luck with shots still ringing out around her from behind buildings and trees.

"Jombo, take fifteen men into town an' search the house an' grounds of Captain Adán San Ramón for anythin' of value or interest," said Rowling. "He was almost certainly involved in the plan to invade Curaçao."

"Coya, Ajuban, William, Daniel, you go with them," said Roy. "All right, Albert, you too," he added as Albert cleared his throat.

"Yes sir," said Coya. *I wish Daniel hadn't been chosen.* However, Albert eyed Daniel darkly behind his back and Coya decided not to worry about him further.

"The rest of us should make our way to the governor's house," said Morgan.

"I agree," said Rowling, "but we should keep an eye out for anyone attemptin' to flee with their valuables on the way…"

The captains continued their hurried conference as Jombo and Ajuban led the way into town in search of San Ramón's house. The town was southwest down the road from the port and there were large houses on the east side, on the edge of the woods. They made it to the town unmolested as the land was flat and provided no cover for ambushes by soldiers. When they reached the town, almost no one could be seen on the streets, but they managed to find out which house belonged to San Ramón by asking a terrified cobbler who had been too slow to bar his door. The man was much relieved when they exited, leaving him and his business in peace. As it turned out, the house was almost directly south from where they now stood, and Jombo led them east for a short distance before turning down the narrower secondary streets towards it. Coya felt that any number of the houses and shops they passed could have soldiers behind them waiting to ambush them, but at least there was more available cover than if they traveled along the main road southwest or through the gardens that lay along the more direct southward path to the house.

They had passed what looked to be a major thoroughfare on their right that came up from the southwest and went on north through the center of town, splitting off from the main road again to travel north towards a tower Brian had mentioned overlooking the tidal flats. Coya had begun to wonder where the soldiers had gone when she heard musket fire from the right side. Apparently soldiers had been lying in wait for them to make their way along the main road and were hastily regrouping to block the path Jombo had chosen. "Teeke cover and advance!" shouted Jombo to his men, and Ajuban motioned that she should do the same, ushering the rest of his men forward as he brought up the rear. They moved from house to house, firing at any soldiers they spotted. Some of the Spaniards were surprised as Jombo and his men rushed forward before they could take up new positions. Ajuban fired a quarrel at a soldier who was reloading his musket behind a bush, and Coya saw the musket fall to the ground. In short order, the bulk of the soldiers were finished by a charge of Jombo's men wielding cutlasses and the rest scattered northward in the wake of English pistol fire.

After a few smaller skirmishes, they arrived at the grounds of San Ramón's house where they found only a few armed men who looked more like house guards standing ready while servants hurriedly loaded a wagon. At the sight of the raiders, the guards hid behind the wagon and fired. A couple of Rowling's men fell at the front of the line but the rest quickly rushed the wagon and the guards soon surrendered. "What have we here?" asked Jombo as he approached the wagon.

Ajuban stepped forward to inspect the cargo. He flipped up the lid of a chest on the back of the wagon and his eyebrows shot up. "Daniel, Albert, guard dis wagon and make sure dat no one takes any-t'ing from it," he said.

Jombo told a few of his men to stand guard and tend to his wounded men as well while the rest followed him towards the house. "William, Coya, wit' me," said Ajuban following close behind Jombo. There were two servants by the door who did their best to look non-threatening, and Ajuban stopped to ask them in Spanish, "Where can I find your master, Adán San Ramón?"

"Sir, he is not here," said the butler. "He was at the governor's mansion when the attack began and he has not returned."

"Den why were dose men loading a wagon?" he asked impatiently.

"Master San Ramón sent word of certain items we should pack and send after him to Puerto Cabello, sir." *He's probably already left Coro.* Coya thought it very unlikely that they would catch up to San Ramón if it were true.

"Were dere any more items you were to load?" asked Ajuban.

"Only what you see here in the hall," said the butler. There was only a small pile remaining and the wagon was almost full already. Coya supposed it was fortunate that they would not have to rummage through the house to find all of the valuables, but she could not believe they wouldn't have hidden anything once they'd been forewarned.

"Ajuban," said William, "perhaps we should look at the list of items they were given."

"It was a verbal list," interrupted the butler. "I assure you there is nothing on it that you do not see here." Coya could feel the implication that they couldn't expect him to say otherwise whether it was true or not.

"Very well," said Ajuban, "but we shall never-de-less search de house ourselves."

"As you wish, sir."

As it turned out, they did not find much of value beyond what the servants had already indicated. There were many fine furnishings, as well as a couple of paintings that William inspected, but most of the valuables had been collected already. "What of the paintings?" Coya had asked.

"I believe they are French," said William, "and quite well done, but I don't recognize the brushwork and they are not signed. As such, and considering that they are of landscapes, we aren't likely to sell them for very much. That painting we relieved Gilbertsen of was much more valuable both because of the artist and the subject." Coya did not fully understand, but William evidently knew what he was talking about and had been instrumental in fetching a high price for Gilbertsen's painting.

"Where would he acquire French paintings anyway?" she asked.

"According to de captain," said Ajuban as he approached from the hall, "Captain San Ramón was a Spanish privateer before he retired. He probably took dem from a French ship."

"Why would he take them if they weren't very valuable?" asked Coya. Normally privateers didn't take valueless objects.

"Maybe he just thought they were pretty," suggested William. "After all, he obviously didn't sell them."

"Well, wheder he stole dem, bought dem, or was given dem by someone else, we don't need dem," said Ajuban. "Come on, we're ready to go. Jombo sees little reason to t'ink dat any-t'ing is still hidden considering what is loaded aboard de wagon, and as you two didn't find much else, I agree."

As they made their way back towards the hall, Coya asked what she was dying to know. "What *is* in that chest on the wagon?"

"Enough gold to pay several hundred soldiers and supply several warships for a long time," said Ajuban. "Dere are oder documents in dere as well, and I t'ink dat we may as well just trundle dis wagon back to de ship before we go t'rough it to see what else we have. It promises to be a good day's work, in any case."

Jombo had posted some of his men at windows around the house, especially on the upper floor to watch for incoming soldiers, and he recalled them as men gathered around the wagon, preparing to depart. They made their way warily back towards the docks, but the sounds of fighting were far away on the north end of the town. As it became clear that there were no soldiers remaining to the south, William asked if he could take a look at the documents in the chest. "By all means," said Ajuban with a glance at Jombo, who nodded. Coya knew that neither of them, nor she for that matter, could likely read as well as William.

Coya was driving the wagon with Albert at her side, so she could not look over William's shoulder as he went through the documents, but after a minute or so, he spoke up. "Ajuban, I think we might want to send men to the local warehouses."

"Why is dat?" asked Ajuban, as he and Jombo made their way to the rear of the wagon to talk to William.

"Well," he began, "in addition to several hundred Spanish uniforms that might come in handy the next time we decide to play at being Spaniards on our newly acquired Spanish barque, there are logs here of what goods the galleons were carrying when they offloaded their cargo here."

"Cargo?" asked Jombo. "These ships ceeme here with wares to sell?"

"Apparently they were merchant ships that were commandeered by Admiral Sergio Cadiz," said William, "and the goods they were carrying were offloaded into warehouses by the docks. Some of the goods were to ship overland to other settlements, it seems."

"Somehow I don't t'ink dat dey will ever get dere," said Ajuban.

"Is anything else of interest in there?" asked Jombo.

"There are some shipping schedules," said William, "plans to attack Curaçao, a list of all the soldiers and what garrisons they were pulled from, a few invoices for ship supplies, and general logistical information relating to the attack. It appears that much of the operation was run from San Ramón's house, and that the Admiral himself was a guest there."

"It seems like we have de proof dat dey were going to attack, if Governor Diedrik needs any," said Ajuban.

"You mean he wasn't sure?" asked Coya. She had thought that the entire matter had been a certainty.

"Benito foolishly admitted it under questioning," said Ajuban, "or at least he implied it, but we didn't have any documented proof until now. We may as well turn it over to Diedrik since we don't have much use for it."

They continued on their way to the docks, but once there, Ajuban and Jombo organized raiding parties and quickly seized the warehouses. It turned out that there were few goods beyond what the galleons had stored there, but that still made for quite a prize. There was coffee and cacao, vanilla, dozens of bolts of silk, medicines, silver and porcelain dishes, a large quantity of sugar, fine wine, rum, tea, and many tons of Indian spices. Along with valuable goods that the town itself had stored, there were more than three hundred tons of cargo to haul back to Curaçao. Until their ships were in better repair and they were ready to leave, they decided to move all the goods to one warehouse and guard it. "It's a good thing that you lot *did* capture that galleon," William said to Jombo, "or I doubt we could transport it all." Such a cargo would have filled the holds of all three of their original ships and they still would have had to leave much of it behind.

"You did well capturing that barque too," said Jombo. "I don't know how you did it with so few men."

"We had help from our woman," said Ajuban as he clapped Coya on the back, "but we would have lost more men if we had had more to lose. It's harder for cannon fire to hit men dat aren't dere."

Coya could not help but think of Luuk, Jacob and the others. Even so, she was happy to be alive and Luuk at least had died to protect his family in Curaçao. *I hope that he left his earnings there.* More to the point, she hoped that the captain would afford Luuk's family a share of the spoils from Coro. "Ajuban, may I have leave to see how Jan is getting on?"

"Very well, but be quick about it. We don't know yet how de captain is doing, and he may need us at a moment's notice. And find out how de repairs are coming," he added as she made her way up the dock.

"Yes sir." Thinking of Luuk and his family had made her think of Jan. Whatever happened, Jan should be safe and he no longer had to worry about his daughter in Curaçao. *He will be delighted to hear about the cargo in the warehouses.* She sped up the dock in a thrill of excitement as the success they had all achieved filtered through the haze of the day's battles in her mind, though it was still second nature to keep an eye out for trouble as she made her way through the deserted streets. There was a fire raging up at the fort indicating that Morgan's men had done what they had intended, but Coya was anxious to share the news with Jan and then to find out how Roy was faring at the governor's mansion. There had been gunfire coming from that direction, but the relative quiet that had swallowed the last half hour was eerie, and she had not yet heard any of the typical sounds of privateers celebrating a victory.

* * *

Roy returned from the governor's mansion disappointed that the governor had escaped along with his household and some of the officers responsible for the plan to attack Curaçao. Roy had quickly discovered that the governor had taken most of his valuables with him as well. *He must have had his servants packing before the battle was even decided.* However, he had found something he thought could be very interesting. *I wonder if I should tell Major Benito that I have his diary before or after the next time I question him.* It was an amusing thought, especially as he had no intention of letting Benito go until he was sure the man would be of no further use.

He had not taken the time to read any of it yet. Roy and the other captains took what they could and made their way to the fort. Apparently Morgan's men had arrived there just in time to catch a troop of soldiers leaving the fort and heading towards the tower overlooking the tidal flats. "Captain," said one of Morgan's officers when summoned to report on the situation, "the prisoners say they were told to lie low at the north tower and return with the rest of the small garrison there to retake the town at night, since it appeared the town would fall after they saw us ambush the company of soldiers that fled from the southern district."

Morgan merely nodded. The fire Morgan had ordered at the fort's gate was raging and his men were camped outside under cover as Rowling's gunners continued firing on the fort from the galleon. No more soldiers could leave the fort in safety, and soon the garrison surrendered. Morgan ordered the fire doused and the men freed and armed several prisoners from what had been McLaughlin's crew, but McLaughlin himself was dead. He had been killed along with most of the crew trying to turn and flee from the Spanish barques that had been forewarned of McLaughlin's approach by lookouts on the tower. "The ships were waitin' for us on the other side o' the bluff shelterin' the harbor from view," said one of McLaughlin's men. "They caught us right quick, afore we could retreat." The remnant of the crew was ecstatic at their rescue, but they would not be among those left behind to guard the Spanish prisoners for fear that they might take their revenge. A dozen of Morgan's men guarded the prisoners, who were bound and locked in the fort. Any soldiers still free might try to rescue them, but Morgan continued the work the Spanish soldiers had begun to defend the fort from land attack by making sure many of the cannons there were loaded with grape shot and aimed at the road or surrounding grounds.

Roy knew that the men sent to San Ramón's house had fended off the soldiers in the area, but he could not be sure all of his crew had survived until he returned to the docks. Several of the townsfolk were skittish as they passed through town from the fort. Roy and Morgan had split their men off from Rowling's earlier as they headed towards the governor's mansion in order to plunder wealthy businesses and homes on their way through the town, and it was their force that had ambushed the soldiers fleeing from the south to outflank Rowling's troops. Not only had the townsfolk in the center of town been looted by Roy and Captain Morgan, but they had found themselves in the middle of a skirmish. "Keep an eye on those windows," said Roy, "some of the soldiers might have slipped inside those buildings during the fight, and we don't know that they all surrendered."

The captains agreed they would have to stay in Coro for the night, and that it was best to force the local carpenters to help them repair their ships, as they didn't have the men to guard both the loot and prisoners all night and render their ships seaworthy before morning. *Not that there has been much loot so far.* As they returned to the docks, Roy was pleased to see all of those he had sent to San Ramón's house still alive, though Jombo reported that some of Rowling's men had been killed or wounded. Jan had also spotted him from *The Constance* and joined the others, presumably to report on the wounded. Too many of his crew had been killed rather than wounded, and Jan had only two patients to tend to while Roy had several dead men to lament. "William meede some interesting discoveries," said Jombo as Captain Rowling followed behind Roy and Morgan.

Roy and the others were delighted with the news that William shared. "I find it odd that the admiral based this operation out of San Ramón's house," said Roy.

"Adán San Ramón used to be a privateer in these waters," said Rowling. "He was quite a terror to Dutch trade vessels. The French settlements in Hispaniola have grievances against him as well, but he's quite used to fightin' the Dutch an' he knows Curaçao well. Merchants in Curaçao don't generally care where a cargo comes from before they agree to buy it, though they soon learned not to deal with him as his name became more feared among the Dutch captains." Roy couldn't help but think how similar this was to his own behavior in regard to Marius Gilbertsen, but the thought simply amused him.

"Well if he used to attack the French as well," said William, "that might explain why he had several French paintings in his house."

"Worth anything?" asked Roy.

"I don't know," said William. "They are by a man named Gaspard Maillet, but I recognize the name only vaguely. I don't really know anything more about him, but there were seven of them stored away in crates. They were very well protected, and we only discovered them once we unloaded the captured wagon and went through the goods. We left two others in the house as they were unsigned and we didn't know about these yet, but I can fetch them if you think it's important."

"No," said Roy. "I don't think it's worth risking the trek back there with soldiers still around just for a couple of paintings, especially if San Ramón chose to leave them behind."

They discussed at length the goods that had been plundered and Roy was quite pleased about the seized military funds, as well as the logistical information. However, he did not yet inspect it for himself, for at that moment a small group of well-dressed men and women who appeared to be civilians approached the docks. Many of the privateers stood with muskets and pistols at the ready, but Roy expected this was to be some sort of parley. Jan and William stood whispering together for a moment as they both perused the confiscated military documents, but they quieted down as the Spanish townsfolk approached. "Gentlemen," said one of them as Roy, Morgan, and Rowling stood forth, "please let us introduce ourselves. I am señor Castro Almagro, and these are my colleagues, señora Marcela Arroyo, señor Mareno Rivera, and señorita Silvia Astoria. We are what remains of the town's council in the governor's absence." Roy looked on señora Arroyo with discomfort. She had donned a black gown over her clothes and her eyes were very red and puffy, but Roy guessed that she must now be the widow of the captain of *El Picaflor,* and she might even have watched as the explosion had scattered the ship all over the harbor. It was one thing to know that the men that Roy fought had families, but it was another thing to stand face to face with them. *Arroyo must have been on the council.* He thought it likely that Arroyo's wife had been given the honor of speaking for him in his absence.

Captain Rowling introduced them, "This is Cap'n Roy Toppings, Cap'n Henry Morgan, an' I am Cap'n Edmund Rowling. What can we do for you?"

"We have come to negotiate an official surrender," said Almagro, doing his best to keep resignation and distaste out of his voice.

"And what terms would you suggest?" asked Captain Morgan.

"We beg that you loot no more of the town than you have done and that you take no prisoners with you when you leave, either soldiers or civilians. In exchange, we will make sure that none of the townsfolk or the soldiers still at liberty organize resistance against you, provided you leave Coro as soon as possible." Roy had to admire the man's cheek, but then he supposed that discussing surrender with a load of armed men from a position of weakness required a good supply of nerve to begin with.

"Captain Toppings," said William before anyone could answer Almagro's proposition, "I suggest that we at least amend this to include taking a handful of prisoners from amongst the soldiers and officers."

"And who are you, sir?" Almagro inquired, his tone clearly implying that no matter who William was, he wasn't important enough to be interrupting the proceedings.

"William Ward of Devonshire, at your service," said William with a bow. Almagro did not appear to be impressed.

"Why do you suggest we take prisoners?" Roy asked him.

"Jan here has an idea that would almost certainly benefit from the taking of prisoners, but I don't think it should be discussed openly," answered William.

"However," said Jan, "we need not take any prisoners who are local to Coro. Soldiers from other colonies would be sufficient."

"I must protest to this amendment," said Almagro huffily.

"Calm yourself," said Rowling.

But Roy was in no mood to placate the Spaniards. "Señor Almagro, I don't believe that you have much leverage in this situation to protest anything, but kindly wait until we have made a counter proposal." Almagro subsided, but his face was red with anger.

"What would you propose, gentlemen?" asked Rivera.

"Cap'ns, I suggest that we agree to the bulk of their terms," said Rowling, "but would amend that we may take whatever prisoners Jan suggests—"

"Two from each colony represented, with the exception of Coro should be sufficient," said Jan.

"—an' that in addition to ensurin' us of no organized or armed resistance, they arrange to have men aid us in repairin' our ships. Then we will be able to leave sooner, and that would suit everyone." They had already decided to force the issue of help with the repairs if necessary, but this was a far easier solution.

"Provided, of course," added Morgan, "that none of their men be granted access to weapons, powder, or any means of making fire."

"And also," said Roy, "the prisoners we have already taken and bound shall remain so until we leave, and we shall retain possession of the fort until that time."

The four council members conferred with each other, but in the end it was Almagro who spoke again. "Gentlemen, it is not our lot to ensure the safety of any of the soldiers except those of Coro, and those you have spared from these conditions. We agree to your terms as stated, and we will send our carpenters and shipwrights to aid you in your repairs as soon as they can be gathered."

After each of the captains—as well as Jan—had nodded their consent, Rowling said, "Very well, we agree to these terms an' will respect them until all conditions have been filled or any have been broken."

Formalities were terse and strained as the council members departed. Once they were gone, Roy turned to William and Jan. "So what is this idea you were speaking of?" He had learned by now to pay close attention to Jan's ideas.

"Well sir," began Jan, "these documents that William found tell us how many soldiers each colony contributed to the fleet and the mission to attack Curaçao. That means that all of those colonies are short of soldiers, at least for the time being. Furthermore, it will take time for word of the battle to reach them—"

"—An' in the meantime we'll have free reign to attack the colonies an' exploit their shortages of soldiers?" said Rowling. "Brilliant!"

"I thought we might need prisoners to give us information about the defenses and layouts of their own colonies," said Jan.

"And I t'ink dere are many in Curaçao who would sign aboard once we give dem an idea what our next venture will entail," laughed Ajuban.

* * *

Coya was pleased that she truly could relax, even though she was forced to sleep in a Spanish town for the night. When she thought of it though, she realized that this fact contributed to her good mood rather than interfered with it. No matter the loot involved, being part of a force that was holding an entire Spanish town at its mercy was perhaps the single finest experience of her life. Her part in it was loudly praised by all three English crews, and Roy had assured her in front of everyone that she would be receiving another bonus, but she felt as if it were impossible for her to feel any more elated than she did for having exacted her revenge on the Spanish.

In the end, the town council had been true to their word and had sent skilled craftsmen to help with the ship repairs. Many soldiers were rounded up and their weapons were handed over to the English guards at the fort. Once the townsfolk understood the situation, many of them unbarred their doors and continued with whatever necessary business they had to attend to before dark. One enterprising tavern keeper, knowing full well that any drink they had looted from the town would not be made available until plunder had been divided between the three crews, opened his doors to the off-duty privateers to take advantage of the lack of competition from the other taverns in the town. Coya herself, in spite of enjoying the situation of the Spanish, preferred to stay near the docks in her off hours, as did most of the rest of Roy's crew.

At the moment, she was having a drink with William and Ajuban under a palm tree near the beach. Ajuban was singing some song from his home, though the language was strange to Coya and William. William was scribbling furiously in a book of empty pages that he had bought in the town, and Coya was simply enjoying the breeze off the harbor and rubbing her bare feet, wishing that she could get her boots back from Mrs. Rutger. She heard someone walking over the sand and turned to see Roy striding towards them. "Coya," he said in Spanish, "I have some news that you might be interested in."

He jerked his head to the side indicating that they should discuss it privately, but she felt a comfortable warmth from the drink and a deeper sense of camaraderie with her friends than she could remember feeling since she signed on. "It's all right, captain," she replied. "Whatever it is, I would not hide it from my friends. Not on this day of all days."

Roy looked uncertain, but shrugged and sat down with them. "I found this document among those from San Ramón's house, and I thought you ought to know that it concerns the shipment of the items taken from your home, from Ch'umpi Jallp'a." He struggled with the pronunciation, but she appreciated the effort. "They are to be shipped to Cartagena soon, and there are details here about the force assigned as escort, the time of delivery, and what is included."

He read off the items, but she sadly shook her head. "It is very kind of you to inform me, captain," she said, "but unless you wanted to lead men deep into Spanish lands in the heart of the jungle or to attack Cartagena and dare the walls of San Felipe, there is nothing that you or I can do about it."

"Are these items from the temple as you thought?" Roy asked gingerly.

"Yes, but let us think no more on it," she said. "My family is dead, even if others were enslaved and are part of that very caravan. I must shut the door on that part of my life as long as matters are out of my hands." Roy's revelation had not shaken her mood. Indeed, she felt a sort of balance, as if this news was a simple reminder of what she had today been avenged for.

"Very well then," said the captain as he carefully folded the document. "When you and William come back on duty, I want you to begin selecting which of the soldiers are to be made prisoner. We will want one officer and one enlisted man from each colony except Coro, if such can be found."

"Aye sir," said William, looking up from his scribblings.

"What on earth are you writing at such a frantic pace?" asked Roy.

"I want to write down what happened during the battle while it is still fresh in my mind," he said. "It will make quite a tale, and I often make sketches based on my notes of interesting things."

"So are you going to be a writer now instead of a privateer?" asked Ajuban.

"No," said William simply, "So far I'm enjoying this life, and it is taking me where I want to go."

"And where is that?" asked Roy sounding amused.

"Well, wealth is a great start when one wants to make a name for oneself, is it not?" suggested William.

"But you've already made a name for yourself, and in a very literal fashion," said Roy. "'William Ward *of Devonshire*,' as you seem to want to be known."

"Indeed," said William brightly and left it at that.

"All right," said Coya, "I must know. *Why* do you introduce yourself as 'William Ward of Devonshire?'" she asked.

William sighed. "I have six brothers and four sisters," he said. "Four of my brothers are older than me, as are two of my sisters. That makes me tremendously unimportant in terms of any sort of inheritance or hopes that my parents might have for me. Half of the time even my mother couldn't remember my name when she looked at me."

Coya was not satisfied. "But why 'William Ward *of Devonshire?*'" she insisted.

"Did you have trouble remembering my name after you heard it for the first time?" asked William.

Men at the docks turned and looked at the four of them as Ajuban's laughter sounded along the beach and, very probably, out to sea. Roy was laughing as well, and Coya, though less familiar with the significance of how Europeans named themselves, could not help but laugh as well.

The night was clear, with a bright moon as she stared up through the leaves of the palm tree. As she laughed, she remembered a dream she'd had on her last night in Port Royal. In this dream, she had found herself staring up at the sky through the undergrowth and canopy of the jungle as it closed in around her. Now the dream held no more terror for her. She dug her feet into the earth and watched with anticipation as men repaired *The Constance* for the journey home—the journey back out to sea.

Epilogue

Roy glanced at the paper he held, and a grim smile fixed itself on his face, as though it was loosely holding his thoughts in place.

"You called for me sir?" said Ajuban as he entered the cabin. Roy had returned to *The Constance* when it had been repaired and men were now repairing the barque he had captured. Now he was glad of the isolation his cabin afforded, but he needed Ajuban to perform one last task before he attempted to sleep—though Roy doubted that he would get to sleep for some time.

"Yes, Ajuban," said Roy. "Are Coya and William still at the fort?"

"Aye, sir."

"Go to them. When they select the prisoners we are to take aboard, make sure that Lieutenant Pablo Francisco of Santa Marta is among them, if he survived the battle."

Ajuban had a nervous look on his face, but did not question the order. He knew why Roy was asking. "Aye, sir," he said.

"That is all."

Ajuban left the cabin, and Roy shut himself away with his thoughts once again. He set down the list of Spanish officers and soldiers and began to pace. *I've finally found him.* As he felt the urge to do anything other than sleep, he sat down and began to sharpen his blades.

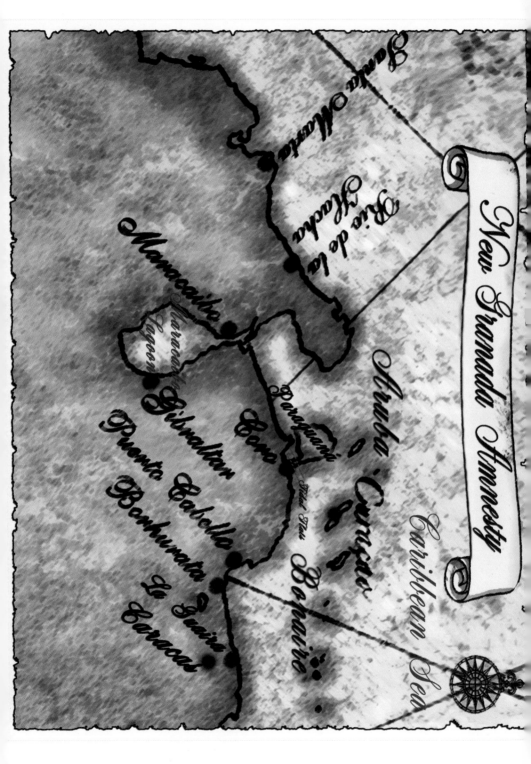